HOW HARD CAN IT BE?

Allison Pearson was born in South Wales. She is a columnist and feature writer for the *Daily Telegraph*. Allison's first novel, *I Don't Know How She Does It*, was an international bestseller; translated into 32 languages it was made into a movie of the same name. Oprah Winfrey called the book 'A Bible for the working mother'. Allison lives in Cambridge with her family and two poodles.

You can find her on Twitter @allisonpearson

Praise for *How Hard Can It Be?*:

'Once again, countless women will recognise themselves . . . Pearson has a gift'
The Times

'Revolutionary . . . Both funny and unflinching'
ELIZABETH DAY, *Daily Telegraph*

'As sharp and witty as ever . . . hugely enjoyable'   *Daily Mail*

'Made me laugh, wince, shudder and shed a tear!'   SOPHIE KINSELLA

'*How Hard Can It Be?* is that rare thing: a sequel that matches and even surpasses the original'   *Daily Telegraph*

'Brilliantly well observed'   INDIA KNIGHT

'Filled with smart insights into ageing parents, female friendships, tricky family dynamics and failed marriages . . . Kate makes good company'
New York Times

'Sparkling, funny and poignant, this is a triumphant return for Pearson and hopefully not the last we will hear of Kate'   *Daily Express*

'Funny, heart-breaking, wise and delightful'   SOPHIE HANNAH

Also by Allison Pearson

I Don't Know How She Does It
I Think I Love You

HOW HARD CAN IT BE?

ALLISON PEARSON

THE BOROUGH PRESS

The Borough Press
An imprint of HarperCollins*Publishers*
1 London Bridge Street
London SE1 9GF

www.harpercollins.co.uk

This paperback edition 2018
9

First published in Great Britain by
HarperCollins*Publishers* 2017

A catalogue record for this book
is available from the British Library

ISBN: 978-0-00-815055-6

Set in Minion by Palimpsest Book Production Limited,
Falkirk, Stirlingshire

Printed and bound in Great Britain by
CPI Group (UK) Ltd, Croydon, CR0 4YY

MIX
Paper from
responsible sources
FSC™ C007454

For Awen and Evie,
my mother and my daughter

Conceal me what I am, and by my aid
For such disguise as haply shall become
The form of my intent.

William Shakespeare, *Twelfth Night*

Nobody tells you about the balding pudenda.

Whoopi Goldberg

PROLOGUE

Countdown to Invisibility: T minus six months and two days

Funny thing is I never worried about getting older. Youth had not been so kind to me that I minded the loss of it. I thought women who lied about their age were shallow and deluded, but I was not without vanity. I could see the dermatologists were right when they said that a cheap aqueous cream was just as good as those youth elixirs in their fancy packaging, but I bought the expensive moisturiser anyway. Call it insurance. I was a competent woman of substance and I simply wanted to look good for my age, that's all – what that age was didn't really matter. At least that's what I told myself. And then I got older.

Look, I've studied the financial markets half my life. That's my job. I know the deal: my sexual currency was going down and facing total collapse unless I did something to shore it up. The once-proud and not unattractive Kate Reddy Inc was fighting a hostile takeover of her mojo. To make matters worse, this fact was rubbed in my face every day by the emerging market in the messiest room in the house. My teenage daughter's womanly stock was rising while mine was declining. This was exactly as Mother Nature intended, and I took pride in my gorgeous girl, I really did. But sometimes that loss could be painful – excruciatingly so. Like the morning I locked eyes on the Circle Line with some guy with luxuriant, tousled Roger Federer hair (is there any better kind?) and I swear there was a flicker of something between us, a sizzle of static, a frisson of flirtation right before he offered me his seat. Not his number, his *seat*.

'Totes humil', as Emily would say. The fact he didn't even consider me worthy of interest stung like a slapped cheek. Unfortunately, the impassioned young woman who lives on inside me, who actually thought Roger was flirting with her, still doesn't get it. She sees her former self in the mirror of her mind's eye as she looks out at the world and assumes that's what the world sees when it looks back. She is quite insanely and irrationally hopeful that she might be attractive to Roger (likely age: thirty-one) because she doesn't realise that she/we now have a thickening waist, thinning vaginal walls (who knew?) and are starting to think about spring bulbs and comfortable footwear with considerably more enthusiasm than, say, the latest scratchy thongs from Agent Provocateur. Roger's erotic radar could probably detect the presence of those practical, flesh-coloured pants of mine.

Look, I was doing OK. Really, I was. I got through the oil-spill-on-the-road that is turning forty. Lost a little control, but I drove into the skid just like the driving instructors tell you to and afterwards things were fine again; no, they were better than fine. The holy trinity of midlife – good husband, nice home, great kids – was mine.

Then, in no particular order, my husband lost his job and tuned into his inner Dalai Lama. He would not be earning anything for two years, as he retrained as a counsellor (oh, joy!). The kids entered the twister of adolescence at exactly the same time as their grandparents were taking what might charitably be called a second pass at their own childhood. My mother-in-law bought a chainsaw with a stolen credit card (not as funny as it sounds). After recovering from a heart attack, my own mum lost her footing and broke her hip. I worried I was losing my mind; but it was probably just hiding in the same place as the car keys and the reading glasses and the earring. And those concert tickets.

In March it's my fiftieth. No, I will not be celebrating with a party and yes, I probably am scared to admit I am scared, or apprehensive (I'm not quite sure what I am, but I definitely don't like it.) To be perfectly honest, I'd rather not think about my age at all, but significant birthdays – the kind they helpfully put in huge, embossed numbers on the front of cards to signpost The Road to Death – have a way of forcing the issue. They say that fifty is the new forty, but to the world of work, my kind of work anyway, fifty may as well be sixty or seventy or eighty. As a matter of urgency, I need to get younger, not older. It's a question of survival: to get a job, to hold onto my position in the world, to remain marketable and within my sell-by date. To keep the ship afloat, the show on the road. To meet the needs of those who seem to need me more than ever, I must reverse time, or at least get the bitch to stand still.

With this goal in mind, the build-up to my half-century will be quiet and totally uneventful. I will not show any outward sign of the panic I feel. I will glide towards it serenely, no more sudden swerves or bumps in the road.

Well, that was the plan. Then Emily woke me up.

3

1

Bats in the Belfie

Monday, 1.37 am: Such a weird dream. Emily is crying, she's really upset. Something about a belfry. A boy wants to come round to our house because of her belfry. She keeps saying she's sorry, it was a mistake, she didn't mean to do it. Strange. Most of my nightmares lately feature me on my unmentionable birthday having become totally invisible and talking to people who can't hear me or see me.

'But we haven't got a belfry,' I say, and the moment I speak the words aloud I know that I'm awake.

Emily is by my side of the bed, bent over as if in prayer or protecting a wound. 'Please don't tell Daddy,' she pleads. 'You can't tell him, Mummy.'

'What? Tell him what?'

I fumble blindly on the bedside table and my baffled hand finds reading glasses, distance glasses, a pot of moisturiser and three foil sheets of pills before I locate my phone. Its small window of milky, metallic light reveals that my daughter is dressed in the Victoria's Secret candy-pink shorty shorts and camisole I foolishly agreed to buy her after one of our horrible rows.

'What is it, Em? Don't tell Daddy what?'

No need to look over to check that Richard's still asleep. I can hear that he's asleep. With every year of our marriage, my husband's snoring has got louder. What began as piglet snufflings twenty years ago is now a nightly Hog Symphony, complete with wind section. Sometimes, at the snore's crescendo, it gets so loud that Rich wakes himself up with a start, rolls over and starts the symphony's first movement again. Otherwise, he is harder to wake than a saint on a tomb.

Richard had the same talent for Selective Nocturnal Deafness when Emily was a baby, so it was me who got up two or three times in the night to respond to her cries, locate her blankie, change her nappy, soothe and settle her, only for that penitential playlet to begin all over again. Maternal sonar doesn't come with an off-switch, worse luck.

'Mum,' Emily pleads, clutching my wrist.

I feel drugged. I am drugged. I took an antihistamine before bed because I've been waking up most nights between two and three, bathed in sweat, and it helps me sleep through. The pill did its work all too well, and now a thought, any thought at all, struggles to break the surface of dense, clotted sleep. No part of me wants to move. I feel like my limbs are being pressed down on the bed by weights.

'Muuuu-uuuumm, please.'

God, I am too old for this.

'Sorry, give me a minute, love. Just coming.'

I get out of bed onto stiff, protesting feet and put one hand around my daughter's slender frame. With the other, I check her forehead. No temperature, but her face is damp with tears. So many tears that they have dripped onto her camisole. I feel its humid wetness – a mix of warm skin and sadness – through my cotton nightie and I flinch. In the darkness, I plant a kiss on Em's forehead and get her nose instead. Emily is taller than me now. Each time I see her it takes a few seconds to adjust to this incredible fact. I want her to be taller than me, because in the world of woman, tall is good, leggy is good, but I also want her to be four years old and really small so I can pick her up and make a safe world for her in my arms.

'Is it your period, darling?'

She shakes her head and I smell my conditioner on her hair, the expensive one I specifically told her not to use.

'No, I did something really ba-aa-aa-aad. He says he's coming here.' Emily starts crying again.

'Don't worry, sweetheart. It's OK,' I say, manoeuvring us both awkwardly towards the door, guided by the chink of light from the landing. 'Whatever it is, we can fix it, I promise. It'll be fine.'

And, you know, I really thought it would be fine, because what could be so bad in the life of a teenage girl that her mother couldn't make it better?

2.11 am: 'You sent. A picture. Of your naked bottom. To a boy. Or boys. You've never met?'

Emily nods miserably. She sits in her place at the kitchen table, clutching her phone in one hand and a *Simpsons* D'oh mug of hot milk in the other, while I inhale green tea and wish it were Scotch. Or cyanide. *Think, Kate, THINK.*

The problem is I don't even understand what it is I don't understand. Emily may as well be talking in a foreign language. I mean, I'm on Facebook, I'm in a family group on WhatsApp

7

that the kids set up for us and I've tweeted all of eight times (once, embarrassingly, about Pasha on *Strictly Come Dancing* after a couple of glasses of wine), but the rest of social media has passed me by. Until now, my ignorance has been funny – a family joke, something the kids could tease me about. 'Are you from the past?' That was the punchline Emily and Ben would chorus in a sing-song Irish lilt; they had learned it from a favourite sitcom. 'Are you from the past, Mum?'

They simply could not believe it when, for years, I remained stubbornly loyal to my first mobile: a small, greyish-green object that shuddered in my pocket like a baby gerbil. It could barely send a text message – not that I ever imagined I would be sending those on an hourly basis – and you had to hold down a number to get a letter to appear. Three letters allocated to each number. It took twenty minutes to type 'Hello'. The screen was the size of a thumbnail and you only needed to charge it once a week. Mum's Flintstone Phone, that's what the kids called it. I was happy to collude with their mockery; it made me feel momentarily light-hearted, like the relaxed, laid-back parent I knew I never really could be. I suppose I was proud that these beings I had given life to, recently so small and help-less, had become so enviably proficient, such experts in this new tongue that was Mandarin to me. I probably thought it was a harmless way for Emily and Ben to feel superior to their control-freak(ish) mother, who was still boss when it came to all the important things like safety and decency, right?

Wrong. Boy, did I get that wrong. In the half hour we have been sitting at the kitchen table, Emily, through hiccups of shock, has managed to tell me that she sent a picture of her bare backside to her friend Lizzy Knowles on Snapchat because Lizzy told Em that the girls in their group were all going to compare tan-lines after the summer holidays.

8

'What's a Snapchat?'

'Mum, it's like a photo that disappears after like ten seconds.'

'Great, it's gone. So what's the problem?'

'Lizzy took a screenshot of the Snapchat and she said she meant to put it in our Facebook Group Chat, but she put it on her wall by mistake so now it's there like forever.' She pronounces the word 'forever' so it rhymes with her favourite, 'Whatevah' – lately further abbreviated to the intolerable 'Whatevs'.

'Fu'evah,' Emily says again. At the thought of this unwanted immortality, her mouth collapses into an anguished 'O' – a popped balloon of grief.

It takes a few moments for me to translate what she has said into English. I may be wrong (and I'm hoping I am), but I think it means that my beloved daughter has taken a photo of her own bare bum. Through the magic of social media and the wickedness of another girl, this image has now been disseminated – if that's the word I want, which I'm very much afraid it is – to everyone in the school, the street, the universe. Everyone, in fact, but her own father, who is upstairs snoring for England.

'People think it's like really funny,' Emily says, 'because my back is still a bit burnt from Greece so it's like really red and my bum's like really white so I look like a flag. Lizzy says she tried to delete it, but loads of people have shared it already.'

'Slow down, slow down, sweetheart. When did this happen?'

'It was like seven thirty but I didn't notice for ages. You told me to put my phone away when we were having dinner, remember? My name was at the top of the screenshot so everyone knows it's me. Lizzy says she's tried to take it down but it's gone viral. And Lizzy's like, "Em, I thought it was funny. I'm so sorry." And I don't want to seem like I'm upset about

9

it because everyone thinks it's really hilarious. But now all these people have got my like Facebook and I'm getting these creepy messages.' All of that comes out in one big sobbing blurt.

I get up and go to the counter to fetch some kitchen roll for Em to blow her nose because I have stopped buying tissues as part of recent family budget cuts. The chill wind of austerity blowing across the country, and specifically through our household, means that fancy pastel boxes of paper softened with aloe vera are off the shopping list. I silently curse Richard's decision to use being made redundant by his architecture firm as 'an opportunity to retrain in something more meaningful' – or 'something more unpaid and self-indulgent' if you were being harsh, which, sorry, but I am at this precise moment because I don't have any Kleenex to soak up our daughter's tears. Only when I make a mess of ripping the kitchen paper along its serrated edge do I notice that my hand is shaking, quite badly actually. I place the trembling right hand in my left hand and interlink the fingers in a way I haven't done for years. 'Here is the church. Here is the steeple. Look inside and see all the people.' Em used to make me do that little rhyme over and over because she loved to see the fingers waggling in the church.

''Gain, Mummy. Do it 'gain.'

What was she then? Three? Four? It seems so near yet, at the same time, impossibly far. My baby. I'm still trying to get my bearings in this strange new country my child has taken me to, but the feelings won't stay still. Disbelief, disgust, a tincture of fear.

'Sharing a picture of your bottom on a phone? Oh, Emily, how could you be so bloody stupid?' (That's the fear flaring into anger right there.)

She trumpets her nose on the kitchen roll, screws up the paper and hands it back to me.

10

'It's a belfie, Mum.'

'What's a belfie for heaven's sake?'

'It's a selfie of your bum,' Emily says. She talks as though this were a normal part of life, like a loaf of bread or a bar of soap.

'You know, a BELFIE.' She says it louder this time, like an Englishman abroad raising his voice so the dumb foreigner will understand.

Ah, a belfie, not a belfry. In my dream, I thought she said belfry. A selfie I know about. Once, when my phone flipped to selfie mode and I found myself looking at my own face, I recoiled. It was unnatural. I sympathised with that tribe which refused to be photographed for fear the camera would steal their souls. I know girls like Em constantly take selfies. But a *belfie*?

'Rihanna does it. Kim Kardashian. Everyone does it,' Emily says flatly, a familiar note of sullenness creeping into her voice.

This is my daughter's stock response lately. Getting into a nightclub with fake ID? 'Don't be shocked, Mum, everyone does it.' Sleeping over at the house of a 'best friend' I've never met, whose parents seem weirdly unconcerned about their child's nocturnal movements? Perfectly normal behaviour, apparently. Whatever it is I am so preposterously objecting to, I need to chill out, basically, because Everyone Does It. Am I so out of touch that distributing pictures of one's naked arse has become socially acceptable?

'Emily, stop texting, will you? Give me that phone. You're in enough trouble as it is.' I snatch the wretched thing out of her hands and she lunges across the table to grab it back, but not before I see a message from someone called Tyler: 'Ur ass is well fit make me big lol!!! 😂'

Christ, the Village Idiot is talking dirty to my baby. And 'Ur' instead of 'Your'? The boy is not just lewd but illiterate. My Inner Grammarian clutches her pearls and shudders. *Come off it, Kate. What kind of warped avoidance strategy is this? Some drooling lout is sending your sixteen-year-old daughter pornographic texts and you're worried about his* spelling?

'Look, darling, I think I'd better call Lizzy's mum to talk about wha—'

'Nooooooo.' Emily's howl is so piercing that Lenny springs from his basket and starts barking to see off whoever has hurt her.

'You can't,' she wails. 'Lizzy's my best friend. You can't get her in trouble.'

I look at her swollen face, the bottom lip raw and bloody from chewing. Does she really think Lizzy is her best friend? Manipulative little witch more like. I haven't trusted Lizzy Knowles since the time she announced to Emily that she was allowed to take two friends to see Justin Bieber at the O2 for her birthday. Emily was so excited; then Lizzy broke the news that she was first reserve. I bought Em a ticket for the concert myself, at catastrophic expense, to protect her from that slow haemorrhage of exclusion, that internal bleed of self-confidence which only girls can do to girls. Boys are such amateurs when it comes to spite.

All of this I think, but do not say. For my daughter cannot be expected to deal with public humiliation and private treachery in the same night.

'Lenny, back in your basket, there's a good boy. It's not getting up time yet. Lie down. There, good boy. Good boy.'

I settle and reassure the dog – this feels more manageable than settling and reassuring the girl – and Emily comes across and lies next to him, burying her head in his neck. With a complete lack of self-consciousness, she sticks her bottom in the air. The pink Victoria's Secret shorts offer no more cover than a thong and I get the double full-moon effect of both bum cheeks – that same pert little posterior which, God help us, is now preserved for posterity in a billion pixels. Emily's body may be that of a young woman, but she has the total trustingness of the child she was not long ago. Still is in so many ways. Here we are, Em and me, safe in our kitchen, warmed by a cranky old Aga, cuddled up to our beloved dog, yet outside these walls forces have been unleashed that are beyond our control. How am I supposed to protect her from things I can't see or hear? Tell me that. Lenny is just delighted that the two girls in his life are up at this late hour; he turns his head and starts to lick Em's ear with his long, startlingly pink tongue.

The puppy, purchase of which was strictly forbidden by Richard, is my proxy third child, also strictly forbidden by Richard. (The two, I admit, are not unrelated.) I brought this jumble of soft limbs and big brown eyes home just after we moved into this ancient, crumbling-down house. A little light incontinence could hardly hurt the place, I reasoned. The carpets we inherited from the previous owners were filthy and sent up smoke signals of dust as you walked across a room. They would have to be replaced, though only after the kitchen and the bathroom and all the other things that needed replacing first. I knew Rich would be pissed off for the reasons above, but I didn't care. The house move had been unsettling for all of us and Ben had been begging for a puppy for so long – he'd sent me birthday cards every single year featuring a sequence of adorable, beseeching hounds. And now that he was old enough not to want his mother to hug him, I figured out that Ben would cuddle the puppy and I would cuddle the puppy, and, somehow, somewhere in the middle, I would get to touch my son.

The strategy was a bit fluffy and not fully formed, rather like the new arrival, but it worked beautifully. Whatever the opposite of a punchbag is, that's Lenny's role in our family. He soaks up all the children's cares. To a teenager, whose daily lot is to discover how unlovable and misshapen they are, the dog's gift is complete and uncomplicated adoration. And I love Lenny too, really love him with such a tender devotion I am embarrassed to admit it. He probably fills some gap in my life I don't even want to think about.

'Lizzy said it was an accident,' says Em, stretching out a hand for me to pull her up. 'The belfie was only supposed to be for the girls in our group, but she like posted it where all of her other friends could see it by mistake. She took it down as soon as she realised, but it was too late 'cos loads of people had already saved it and reposted it.'

'What about that boy you said was coming round? Um, Tyler?' I close and open my eyes quickly to wipe the boy's lewd text.

'He saw it on Facebook. Lizzy tagged my bum #FlagBum and now everyone on Facebook can see it and knows it's like mine, so now everyone thinks I'm like just one of those girls who takes her clothes off for nothing.'

'No they don't, love.' I pull Em into my arms. She lays her head on my shoulder and we stand in the middle of the kitchen, half hugging, half slow-dancing. 'People will talk about it for a day or two then it'll blow over, you'll see.'

I want to believe that, I really do. But it's like an infectious disease, isn't it? Immunologists would have a field day researching the viral spread of compromising photographs on social media. I'd venture that the Spanish flu and Ebola combined couldn't touch the speed of photographic mortification spreading through cyberspace.

Through the virus that is Internet porn, and in the blink of an eye, my little girl's bare backside had found its way from our commuter village forty-seven miles outside London all the way to Elephant and Castle where Tyler, who is what police call 'a known associate' of Lizzy's cousin's mate's brother, was able to see it. All because, according to Em, dear Lizzy had her settings fixed to allow 'friends of friends' to see whatever she posted. Great, why not just send it directly to the paedophile wing of Wormwood Scrubs?

4.19 am: Emily is asleep at last. Outside, it's black and cold, the first chill of early autumn. I'm still getting used to night in a village – so different from night in a town, where it's never truly dark. Not like this furry black pelt thrown over everything. Quite close by, somewhere down the bottom of the garden, there is the shriek of something killing or being killed. When we first moved here, I mistook these noises for a human in pain and I wanted to call the police. Now I just assume it's the fox again.

I promised Em I would stay by her bed in case Tyler or any other belfie hounds try to drop in. That's why I'm sitting here in her little chair with the teddy bear upholstery, my own mottled, forty-something backside struggling to squidge between its narrow, scratched wooden arms. I think of all the times I've kept vigil on this chair. Praying she would go to sleep (pretty much every single night, 1998–2000). Praying she would wake up (suspected concussion after falling off bouncy castle, 2004). And now here I am thinking of her bottom, the one that I trapped expertly in Pampers and which is now bouncing around the worldwide web all by itself, no doubt inflaming the loins of hordes of deviant Tylers. *Uch.*

I feel ashamed that my daughter has no sense of modesty

because whose fault is that? Her mother's, obviously. Mine – Emily's Grandma Jean – instilled in me an almost Victorian dread of nakedness that came from her own strict Baptist upbringing. Ours was the only family on the beach that got changed into swimwear inside a kind of towelling burqa, with a drawstring neck my mum had fashioned from curtain flex. To this day, I hardly glance at my own backside, let alone offer it up to public view. How in the name of God did our family go, in just two generations, from prudery to porn?

I desperately need to talk to someone, but who? I can't tell Richard because the thought of his princess being defiled would kill him. I flick through my mental Rolodex of friends, pausing at certain names, trying to weigh up who would judge harshly, who would sympathise effusively then spread the gossip anyway – in a spirit of deep concern, naturally. ('Poor Kate, you won't *believe* what her daughter did.') It's not like laughing with other mums about something embarrassing Emily did when she was little, like that Nativity play when she broke Arabella's halo because she was so cross about getting the part of the innkeeper's wife. (A dowdy, non-speaking role with no tinsel; I saw her point.) I can't expose Em to the sanctimony of the Muffia, that organised gang of mothers superior. So, who on earth can I trust with this thing so distressing and surreal that I actually feel sick? I go to my Inbox, find a name that spells 'unshock-ability' and begin to type.

From: Kate Reddy
To: Candy Stratton
Subject: Help!
Hi hon, you still up? Can't remember the time difference. It's been quite a night here. Emily was lured by a 'friend' into posting a photo of her naked derrière on Snapchat

which has now been circulated to the entire Internet. This is called a 'belfie', which I'm old enough to think might be short for Harry Belafonte. Worried that heavy-breathing stalkers are about to form a queue outside our house. Seriously, I feel Jurassic when she talks to me. I don't understand any of the tech stuff, but I do know it's really bad. I want to murder the little idiot and I want to protect her so badly.

I thought this parenting lark was supposed to get easier. What do I do? Ban her from social media? Get her to a nunnery?

Yours in a sobbing heap,

Kx

A Technicolor image pings into my head of Candy at Edwin Morgan Forster, the international investment company where we both worked, must be eight or nine years ago. She was wearing a red dress so tight you could watch the sashimi she ate for lunch progressing down her oesophagus. 'Whad you lookin' at, kid?' she would jeer at any male colleague foolish enough to comment on her Jessica Rabbit silhouette. Candace Marlene Stratton: proud, foul-mouthed export of New Jersey, Internet whizz, and my bosom buddy in an office where sexism was the air that we breathed. I read about a discrimination case in the paper the other day, some junior accountant complaining that her boss hadn't been respectful enough in his use of language. I thought: Seriously? You don't know you're born, sweetie. At EMF, if a woman so much as raised her voice, the traders would yell across the floor, 'On the rag are you, darling?' Nothing was off limits, not even menstruation. They loved to tease female staff about their time of the month. Complaining would only have confirmed the sniggerers' view that we couldn't

17

hack it, so we never bothered. Candy, who subsisted on coke back then – the kind you gulped from a can *and* the kind you snorted up your nose – sat about fifteen feet away from me for three years, yet we hardly spoke. Two women talking in the office was 'gossiping'; two men doing exactly the same was 'a briefing'. We knew the rules. But Candy and I emailed the whole time, in and out of each other's minds, venting and joking: members of the Resistance in a country of men.

I never thought I would look back on that time with affection, let alone longing, only suddenly I think how exciting it was. It tested me in a way that nagging kids to do their homework, cooking nine meals a week and getting a man in to do the gutters – the wearisome warp and weft of life – never does. Can you be a success as a mother? People only notice when you're not doing it right.

Back then, I had targets I could hit and I knew that I was good, really good at my work. Camaraderie under pressure; you don't realise what a deep pleasure that is until it's gone. And Candy, she always had my back. Not long after she gave birth to Seymour, she headed home to the States to be near her mom, who longed to babysit her first grandchild. It allowed Candy to start an upmarket sex-toy business. *Orgazma: for the woman who's too busy going to come* (or maybe the other way around). I've only seen Candy once in the years since we both left EMF, although, forged in the heat of adversity, ours are the ties that bind. I really wish she was here now. I'm not sure I can do this by myself.

From: Candy Stratton
To: Kate Reddy
Subject: Help!
Hey Sobbing Heap, this is the Westchester County

24-Hour Counselling Service. Calm down, OK. What Emily did is perfectly normal teen behaviour. Think of it as the 21st century equivalent of love letters tied with a red ribbon in a scented drawer . . . only now it's her drawers.

Count yourself lucky it's just a picture of her ass. A girl in Seymour's class shared a picture of her lady garden because the captain of the football team asked to see it. These kids have NO sense of privacy. They think because they're on the phone or computer in their own home it's safe.

Emily doesn't realise she's walking butt-naked down the information superhighway looking like she's got her thumb out and she's trying to hitch a ride. Your job is to point that out to her. With force if necessary. I suggest hiring some friendly nerd to see how much he can track down online and destroy. You can ask Facebook to take obscene stuff down I'm pretty sure. And restrict her privileges – no Internet access for a few weeks until she's learned her lesson.

You should get some sleep, hon, must be crazy late there?

Am here for you always,

XXO C

5.35 am: It's now so late that it's early. I decide to unload the dishwasher rather than go back to bed for a futile hour staring at the ceiling. This perimenopause thing is playing havoc with my sleep. You won't believe it, but when the doctor mentioned that word to me a few months ago the first thing that popped into my head was a Sixties band with moptop hair: Perry and the Menopauses. Dooby-dooby-doo. Perry was smiling, unthreatening, and almost certainly wearing a hand-knitted Christmas jumper. I know, I know, but I'd never heard of it before and I was relieved to finally have a name for a condition that was giving me broken nights then plunging me down a mineshaft of tiredness straight after lunch. (I'd vaguely wondered if I had some fatal illness and had already moved on to touching scenes by the graveside where both kids cried and said if only they'd appreciated me while I was still alive.) If you have a name for what's making you scared you can try to befriend it, can't you? So Perry and I, we would be friends.

'I can't afford to take an afternoon nap,' I explained to the doctor. 'I'd just like to feel like my old self again.'

'That's not uncommon,' she said, typing busily into my notes on the screen. 'Classic textbook symptoms for your age.'

I was relieved to have classic symptoms; there was safety in numbers. Out there were thousands, no, millions of women who also walked around feeling like they were strapped to a dying animal. All we wanted was our old self back, and if we waited patiently for her she would come. Meanwhile, we could make lists to combat another of Perry's delightful symptoms. Forgetfulness.

What did Candy say in her email? Find some nerdy guy who can track down Emily's belfie and wipe it? 'Perfectly normal teen behaviour.' Maybe it's not so bad after all. I take a seat in the chair next to the Aga, the one I bought on eBay for £95 (absolute bargain, it only needs new springs, new feet and new upholstery) and start to make a list of all the things I mustn't forget. The last thing I remember is a dog with no sense of his own size jumping onto my lap, his tail beating against my arm, silky head resting on my shoulder.

7.01 am: The moment I wake I check my phone. Two missed calls from Julie. My sister likes to keep me up to date on our mother's latest adventure, just to make it clear that, living three streets away in our Northern home town, it's she who has to be on call for Mum, who has so far refused to adopt any behaviour which might be called 'age appropriate'. Every Wednesday morning, Mum prepares all the vegetables for Luncheon Club, where some of the diners who she calls 'the old people' are fifteen years her junior. This fills me with a mixture of pride (look at her spirit!) and exasperation (stop being so bloody independent, will you?). When is my mother going to accept that she too is old?

Since I decided to 'swan off' as my sister calls it – aka taking the difficult decision to move the family back down South so I could be near London, the place most likely to give me a well-paid job – Julie has become one of the great English martyrs, giving off a noxious whiff of bonfire and sanctimony. Never misses a chance to point out I'm not pulling my weight. Even though, when I speak to Mum, as I do most days, she tells me that she hasn't seen my younger sister for ages. I think it's terrible Julie doesn't drop in to check on Mum, seeing how near she is, but I can't say so because, in the casting for the play of our family, I am the Bad Daughter Who Buggered Off and Julie is the Unappreciated Good Daughter Who Stayed Put. I do my best to change the script; I bought Mum a computer for her birthday and told her it was from both of us, Julie and me. But making me feel guilty is one of the few bits of power my twice-divorced, vodka-chugging sister gets to wield in her hard and helpless life. I get that. Rationally, I do, and I try to be understanding, but since when could the power of reason unpick the knots of sibling rivalry? I should call Julie back, and I will, but I need to get Emily sorted out. Emily first, then Mum, then prepare for my interview with the

21

headhunter this afternoon. Anyway, I don't need Julie's help to make me feel guilty about getting my priorities wrong. Guilt is where I live.

7.11 am: At breakfast, I tell Richard that Emily is sleeping in because she had a bad night. This has the virtue of being a lie that is perfectly true. It was certainly bad, right up there with the worst nights ever. Completely drained, I move through my morning tasks like a rusty, scrapyard android. Even bending over to pick up Lenny's water bowl is such an effort I actually make encouraging sounds to get myself to straighten up. ('Come on, *ooff*, you can do it!') Am making porridge when Ben descends from his lair looking like a wildebeest tethered to three kinds of electronic device. When he turned fourteen, my lovely boy's shoulders slumped overnight and he lost the power of speech, communicating his needs in occasional grunts and snide put-downs. This morning, however, he seems weirdly animated – talkative even.

'Mum, guess what? I saw this picture of Emily on Facebook. Crack-ing photo.'

'Ben.'

'Seriously, the bottom line is she got thousands of Likes for this picture of her . . .'

'BENJAMIN!'

'Well, well, young man,' says Richard, looking up briefly from his frogspawn yogurt, or whatever it is he's eating these days, 'it's good to hear you saying something positive about your sister for a change. Isn't it, Kate?'

I shoot Ben my best Medusa death-ray stare and mouth, *'Tell Dad and you're dead.'*

Richard doesn't notice this frantic semaphore between mother and son because he is absorbed in an article on a cycling website. I can read the headline over his shoulder. '15 Gadgets You Never Knew You Needed.'

The number of gadgets cyclists don't know that they need is very extensive, as our small utility room can testify. Getting to the washing machine these days is like competing in the hurdles because Rich's bike gear occupies every inch of floor. There are several kinds of helmet: a helmet that plays music, a helmet with a miner's lamp clipped to the front, even a helmet with its own indicator. From my drying rack hang two heavy, metal locks that look more like implements used during the torture of a Tudor nobleman than something to fasten a bike to a railing. When I went in there yesterday to empty the dryer, I found Rich's latest purchase. A worryingly phallic object, still in its box, it claimed to be 'an automatic lube dispenser'. Is that for the bike or for my husband's chafed backside, which has lost its cushion of fat since he became a mountain goat? It sure as hell isn't for our sex life.

'I'll be late tonight. Andy and I are riding to Outer Mongolia,' (at least that's what I think he said). 'OK with you?'

It's a statement not a question. Richard doesn't look up from his laptop, not even when I put a bowl of porridge in front of him. 'Darling, you know I'm not eating gluten,' he mutters.

'I thought oats were OK? Slow release, low GI aren't they?' He doesn't respond.

Same goes for Ben who I can see is scrolling through Facebook, smirking and communing with that invisible world where he spends so much of his time. Probably charting the global adventures of his sister's bottom. With a pang, I think of Emily asleep upstairs. I told her everything would seem better in the morning and now it is the morning I need to think how to make it better. First, I have to get her father out of the house.

23

Over by the back door, Richard starts to put on his cycling gear, a process fraught with zips and studs and flaps. Picture, if you will, a knight getting ready for the Battle of Agincourt with a £2,300 carbon fibre bike taking the part of the horse. When my husband took up cycling three years ago, I was totally in favour. Exercise, fresh air, anything so I could be left in peace on eBay picking up 'more junk we don't need to clutter up this ruin', as Richard calls it. Or 'incredible bargains that will find a place in our magical old house', which I prefer.

That was before it became clear that Rich wasn't just cycling for fun. Seriously, fun did not come into it. Before my unsuspecting eyes, he morphed into one of those MAMILs you read about in the Lifestyle section of the papers, a Middle-Aged Man in Lycra who did a minimum of ten hours in the saddle every week. On his new regime, Rich rapidly lost two stone. I found it hard to be delighted about this because my own extra pounds were clinging to me with greater tenacity every year. Unlike Richard's saddlebags, mine were no longer removable (if only you could unhook the panniers of spare flesh!). Until my late thirties, I swear all it took was four days of eating only cottage cheese and Ryvita and I could feel my ribs again. That trick doesn't work any more.

Rich had never been fat, but he was always cuddly in a rumpled, Jeff Bridges kind of way, and there was something about the soft ampleness of his body that matched his good nature. He looked like what he was: an amiable and generous man. This angular stranger he studies in the mirror with intense interest has a taut, toned body and a heavily lined face – we have both reached that age where being too thin makes you look gaunt instead of youthful. The new Richard attracts lots of admiring comments from our friends and I know I should find him attractive, but any lustful thoughts are punctured instantly by the cycling gear. What Rich most resembles when he wears his neck-to-knee stretchwear is a giant turquoise condom. Horribly visible, his penis and testicles dangle like low-hanging fruit.

The old Rich would have appreciated how ridiculous he looks and enjoyed sharing the joke. This new one doesn't smile much, or maybe I don't give him much to smile about. He is permanently in a grump about the house or 'Your Money Pit' as he calls it, never missing an opportunity to get in a dig at the lovely builder who is skilfully helping me coax the sad old place back to life.

As he fastens his helmet, he says: 'Kate, can you get Piotr to take a look at the bathroom tap? I think the washer he used was another of his post-war Polish cast-offs.'

See what I mean? Another sideswipe at poor Piotr. I would say something sarcastic back, like how I'm amazed that Richard even noticed something about our house when his mind is on much higher things, but suddenly feel really bad that I haven't told him about Emily and the belfie. Instead of snapping, I go over and give him a guilty goodbye hug, whereupon my dressing gown gets snagged on a Velcro pocket flap. There are an awkward few seconds when we are stuck together. It's the closest we've been for a while. Perhaps I should tell him about last night? The temptation to blurt it all out, to share the burden, is almost overwhelming, but I promised Emily that I wouldn't tell Daddy, so I don't.

7.54 am: With Richard and Ben safely out of the house, I go upstairs to check on Em, bearing a mug of brick-red tea with one sugar. Since she started her juicing regime, she won't allow any sugar to pass her lips, but surely sweet tea counts as medicine in an emergency? I can only push her door so far before it jams on a pile of clothes and shoes. I squeeze through the gap and find myself in what looks like a room vacated in a hurry after an air raid. Debris is spread over a wide area and on the bedside table teeters an art installation made of Diet Coke cans.

The state of a teenager's bedroom is such a time-honoured source of mother–daughter conflict that I guess I should have been prepared for it, but our fights over this disputed territory are never less than bruising. The latest, after school on Friday, when I insisted that her room be tidied *right now*, ended in furious stalemate:

Emily: 'But it's *my room.*'

Me: 'But it's *my house.*'

Neither of us was prepared to back down.

'She's so stubborn,' I complained later to Richard.

'Who does that remind you of?' he said.

Emily is sprawled diagonally across the bed, duvet twisted about her like a chrysalis. She has always been a very active sleeper, moving around her mattress like the hands of a clock. When she's asleep, as she is now, she looks exactly like the toddler I remember in her cot – that determined jut to her chin, the flaxen hair which forms damp curls on the pillow when she's hot. She was born with these enormous eyes whose colour didn't settle for a long while, as if they were still making up their mind. When I lifted her out of the cot each morning, I used to chant, 'What colour are your eyes today? Browny bluey greeny grey?'

They ended up hazel like mine and I was secretly disappointed she didn't get Richard's perfect shade of Paul Newman blue, though she carries the gene for those so they may yet come out in her own kids. Unbelievably, my mind has already started straying to grandchildren. (I knew you could be

26

broody for a baby, but broody for your baby's baby? Is that a thing?)

I can tell Emily is dreaming. There's a movie running behind those busy, fluttering eyelids; hope it's not a horror film. Lying on the pillow next to her head are Baa-Sheep, her first toy, and the damn phone, its screen lit up with overnight activity. '37 unread messages,' it says. I shudder to think what they contain. Candy told me I should confiscate Emily's mobile, but when I reach out to take it her legs twitch in protest like a laboratory frog's. Sleeping Beauty ain't going to give up her online life without a struggle.

'Emily, sweetheart, you need to wake up. Time to get ready for school.'

As she groans and turns over, burrowing deeper into her chrysalis, the phone dings once, then again and again. It's like a lift door opening every few seconds.

'Em, love, please wake up. I've brought you some tea.'

Ding. Ding. Ding. Hateful sound. Emily's innocent mistake started this and who knows where it will end. I snatch the phone and put it in my pocket before she can see. *Ding. Ding.*

On the way downstairs, I pause on the landing. *Ding.* Looking through the ancient mullioned window onto a still-misty garden a line of poetry comes, absurdly, alarmingly, into my head. 'Send not to know for whom the belfie tolls. It tolls for thee.'

8.19 am: In the kitchen, or what passes for one while Piotr is building an actual kitchen, I quickly post the breakfast stuff into the dishwasher and open a tin for Lenny before checking my emails. The first one I see is from a name that has never previously bothered my Inbox. Oh, hell.

27

From: Jean Reddy
To: Kate Reddy
Subject: Surprise!

Dear Kath,

It's Mum here. My first email ever! Thank you so much for clubbing together with Julie to buy me a laptop computer. You girls do spoil me. I've started a computing class at the library.

The Internet seems very interesting so far. Lots of funny cat pictures. Am really looking forward to keeping up with all the grandchildren. Emily told me she is on a thing called Facebook. Please can you give me her address?

Love Mum xxxx

So yesterday, I Googled 'Perimenopause'. If you're thinking of doing it, one word of advice. Don't.

Symptoms of Perimenopause:
- Hot flushes, night sweats and/or clammy feeling
- Palpitations
- Dry and itchy skin
- Irritability!!! *must me, I'm the Komodo dragon of irritability!!*
- Headaches, possibly worsening migraines
- Mood swings, sudden tears
- Loss of confidence, feelings of low self-worth
- Trouble sleeping through the night
- Irregular periods; shorter, heavier periods, flooding
- Loss of libido
- Vaginal dryness *+ BALDING PUBES*
- Crashing fatigue
- Feelings of dread, apprehension, doom *☹*
- Difficulty concentrating, disorientation, mental confusion
- Disturbing memory lapses *✓*
- Incontinence, especially upon sneezing or laughing
- Aching, sore joints, muscles and tendons
- Gastrointestinal distress, indigestion, flatulence, nausea
- Weight gain
- Hair loss or thinning (head, pubic, or whole body); increase in facial hair
- Depression *— No kidding!!*

What does that leave? Oh, right. Death. I think they forgot death.

2

THE HAS-BEEN

I made Emily go to school the day after the night her bottom went viral. Maybe you think I was wrong. Maybe I agree with you. She didn't want to, she pleaded, she came up with every reason under the sun why it would be better if she stayed home with Lenny and caught up on some 'homework' (binge-watching *Girls*, I'm not that stupid). She even offered to tidy her room – a clear sign of desperation – but it felt like one of those times when you have to stick to your guns and insist that the child does what feels hardest. Get back in the saddle, isn't that the phrase our parents' generation used before making your child do something they don't want to became socially unacceptable.

I told myself it would be better for Em to run the gauntlet of crude jokes and smirking whispers in the corridors than throw a sickie and hide her dread under the duvet at home. Just as when the seven-year-old Emily came off her bike in the park, the gravel cruelly embedded in her scraped and bloody knee, and I knelt before her and sucked the tiny stones out of the wound before insisting that she got back on again in case the instinctive aversion to trying what has just hurt you were to bloom into an unconquerable fear.

'NO, Daddy, NO!' she screamed, appealing over my head to Richard who, by then, had already bagged the softer, more empathetic parent role, leaving me to be the enforcer of manners, bedtimes and green vegetables – tedious stuff lovely, tickly daddies don't care to get involved with. I hated Rich for obliging me to become the kind of person I had never wanted to be and would, in other circumstances, have paid good money to avoid. But the moulds of our parental roles, cast when our kids are really quite small, set and harden without our noticing until one day you wake up and you are no longer just wearing the mask of a bossy, multi-tasking nag. The mask has eaten into your face.

Come to think of it, you can probably date everything that went wrong with modern civilisation to the moment parent became a verb. Parenting is now a full-time job, in addition to your other job, the one that pays the mortgage and the bills. There are days when I think I would love to have been a mother in the era when parents were still adults who selfishly got on with their own lives and drank cocktails in the evening while children did their best to please and fit in. By the time it was my turn, it was the other way around. Did this vast army of men and women dedicated to the hour-by-hour comfort and stimulation of their offspring cause unprecedented joy in the younger generation? Well, read the papers and make up your own mind. But this was our story, Emily's and mine, Richard's and Ben's, and I can only tell you what it felt like to live it from the inside. History will pass its own verdict on whether modern parenting was a science or a fearful neurosis that filled the gap once occupied by religion.

31

Yes, I made Emily go to school that day, and I nearly made myself late for my interview because I drove her there, instead of making her ride her bike. I remember the way she walked through the gate, head and shoulders down as if braced against a gale, although there was no wind, none at all. She turned for a second and gave a brave little wave and I waved back and gave her a thumbs-up, although my heart felt like a crushed can inside my chest. I almost wound down the window and called after her to come back, but I thought that, as the adult, I needed to give my child confidence, not show that I, too, was anxious and freaked out.

Did it start then? Was that the root of the terrible thing that happened later? If I'd played things differently, if I'd let Em stay home, if I'd cancelled the interview and we'd both snuggled under the duvet, watched four episodes of *Girls* back to back and let the caustic, jubilant wit of Lena Dunham purge a sixteen-year-old's fearful shame? So many ifs I could have heeded.

Sorry, I didn't. I had to find a job urgently. I reckoned there was enough money in the joint account to last us three months, four at most. The lump of money we put by after selling the London house for a profit and moving up North had shrunk alarmingly, first when Richard lost his job, then after the move back South when we rented for a while until we found the right place. One Sunday lunchtime, Richard casually revealed that not only would he be earning next to nothing for two years but also that, as part of his counsellor training, he was now in therapy himself twice a week, for which we would have to pay. The fees were monstrous, maiming: I felt like ringing the therapist and offering her a potted history of my husband in return for a fifty per cent discount. Who knew every quirk and wrinkle of his personality better than I did? The fact Rich was spending our food-shopping money on sessions where he got to complain about me only fuelled my sense of injustice. To make up the difference, I needed a serious, main-breadwinner position, and I needed it fast or we would be homeless and dining on KFC. So, I made my daughter get back in the saddle, just as I took myself back to work when she was four months old and had a streaming cold, the phlegm bubbling in her tiny lungs. Because that's the deal, that's what we have to do. Even when every atom of our being is shrieking, 'Wrong, Wrong, Wrong'? Even then.

10.12 am: On the train to London, I'm supposed to be going through my CV and reading the financial pages in preparation for my meeting with the headhunter, but all I can think about is Emily, and Tyler's foul, disgusting message to her. What does it feel like to be the object of such salivating lust before you've even lost your virginity? (At least I assume Em is still a virgin. I'd know if she wasn't, wouldn't I?) How many of those kinds of messages is she getting? Should I notify the school? How would the conversation with the Head of Sixth Form go: 'Um, my daughter accidentally shared a picture of her bottom with your entire pupil body'? And what further problems might that cause Em? Isn't it better to play it down, try to carry on as normal? I may want to kill Lizzy Knowles. I may, in fact, want her entrails hung above the school gate to discourage any future abuse of social media that mortifies a sweet, naive girl. But Emily said she didn't want her friend to get in trouble. Best let them sort it out themselves.

I could call Richard now and tell him about the belfie, but it will distress him and the thought of having to comfort him and deal with his anxiety, as I have done for the whole of our life together, is too exhausting. No, easier to fix it myself, like I always do (whether it is a new house, a new school or a new carpet). Then, once everything is OK for Em, I will tell him.

That's how I ended up being a liar in the office and a liar at home. If MI5 were ever looking for a perimenopausal double-agent who could do everything except remember the password ('No, hang on, give me time, it'll come to me in a minute'), I was a shoo-in. But, believe me, it wasn't easy.

You may have noticed that I joke a lot about forgetfulness, but it's not funny, it's humiliating. For a while, I told myself it was just a phase, like that milky brain-fug I first got when I was breastfeeding Emily. I was so zombified one day, when I'd arranged to meet my college friend Debra in Selfridges (she was on maternity leave with Felix, I think), that I actually put wet loo paper in my handbag and threw the car keys down the toilet. I mean, if you put that in a book no one would believe it, would they?

This feels different, though, this new kind of forgetfulness; less like a mist that will burn itself off than some vital piece of circuitry that has gone down for good. Eighteen months into the perimenopause and I regret to say that the great library of my mind is reduced to one overdue Danielle Steel novel.

Each month, each week, each day it gets slightly harder to retrieve the things that I know. Correction. The things that I know that I knew. At forty-nine years of age, the tip of the tongue becomes a very crowded place.

Looking back, I can see all the times my memory got me out of trouble. How many exams would I have failed had I not been blessed with an almost photographic ability to scan several chapters in a textbook, carry the facts gingerly into the exam room – like an ostrich egg balanced on a saucer – regurgitate them right there on the paper and, Bingo! That fabulous, state-of-the-art digital retrieval system, which I took entirely for granted for four decades, is now a dusty provincial library staffed by Roy. Or that's how I think of him anyway.

Others ask God to hear their prayers. I plead with Roy to rifle through my memory bank and track down a missing object/word/thingummy. Poor Roy is not in his first youth. Well, neither of us is. He has his work cut out finding where I left my phone or my purse let alone locating an obscure quotation or the name of that film I thought about the other day with the young Demi Moore and Ally Somebody.

Do you remember Donald Rumsfeld, when he was US Secretary of Defense, being mocked for talking about 'Known Unknowns' in Iraq? My, how we laughed at the old boy's evasiveness. Well, finally, I have some idea what Rumsfeld meant. Perimenopause is a daily struggle with Unknown Knowns.

See that tall brunette coming towards me down the dairy aisle in the supermarket with an expectant smile on her face? Uh-oh. Who is this woman and why does she know me?

'Roy, please can you go and get that woman's name for me? I know we have it filed in there somewhere. Possibly under Scary School Mums or Females I Suspect Richard Fancies?'

Off Roy shuffles in his carpet slippers while Unknown But Very Friendly Tall Brunette – Gemma? Jemima? Julia? – chats away about other women we have in common. She lets slip that her daughter got all A*s in her GCSEs. Unfortunately, that hardly narrows it down, perfect grades being the must-have accessory for every middle-class child and their aspirational parents.

Sometimes, when the forgetfulness is scary bad – I mean, bad like that fish in that, that, that film* (*'Roy, hello?'*) – it's like I'm trying to get back a thought that just swam into my head then departed a millisecond later, with a flick of its minnow's tail. Trying to retrieve the thought, I feel like a prisoner who has glimpsed the keys to her cell on a high ledge, but can't quite reach them with her fingertips. I try to get to the keys, I stretch as hard as I can, I brush aside the cobwebs, I beg Roy to remind me what it was I came into the study/kitchen/garage for. But the mind's a blank.

Is that why I started lying about my age? Trust me, it wasn't vanity, it was self-preservation. An old friend from my City days told me this headhunter she knew was anxious to fill his female quota, as laid down by the Society of Investment Trusts. He was the sort of well-connected chap who can put a word in the right tufty, barnacled old ear and get you a non-executive directorship; a position on the board of a company that's highly remunerated but requires only a few days of time a year. I figured if I had a couple of those under my belt, to supplement my financial-advice work, I could earn just enough to keep us afloat while Richard was training, while still taking care of the kids and keeping an eye on Mum and Rich's parents as well. On paper, everything looked great. Hell, I could do two non-execs in my sleep. Full of hope, I went to meet Gerald Kerslaw.

11.45 am: Kerslaw's office is in one of those monumental, white, wedding-cake houses in Holland Park. The front steps, of which there must be at least fifteen, feel like scaling the White Cliffs of Dover. Apart from the occasional party and meeting with clients, I haven't worn a decent pair of shoes in a while – amazing how quickly you lose the ability to walk in heels. On the short journey from the Tube, I feel like a newborn gnu; tottering on splayed legs, I even stop to steady myself with one hand on a newspaper vendor's stand.

'Alright, Miss? Careful how you go,' the guy cackles, and I am embarrassed at how absurdly grateful I am that he thinks I'm still young enough to be called Miss. (Funny how rank old sexists become charming, gallant gentlemen when you're in need of a boost, isn't it?)

It's hard to comprehend how swiftly all the confidence you built up over a career ebbs away. Years of knowledge brushed aside in minutes.

'So, Mrs Reddy, you've been out of the City for how long – seven years?'

Kerslaw has one of those stentorian barks that is designed to carry to the soldier mucking about at the back of the parade. He is bawling at me across a desk the size of Switzerland.

'Kate, please call me Kate. Six and a half years actually. But I've taken on a lot of new responsibilities since then. Kept up my skillset, provided regular financial advice to several local people, read the financial pages every day and . . .'

'I see.' Kerslaw is holding my CV at a distance as if it is giving off a faint but unpleasant odour. Ex-Army, clip-on Lego helmet of silver hair; a small man whose shiny face bears the stretched look of someone who had always wanted to be three inches taller. The pinstripes on his jacket are far too wide, like the chalk lines on a tennis court. It's the kind of suit only worn by a family-values politician after their cocaine-fuelled night with two hookers has been revealed in a Sunday tabloid.

'Treasurer of the PCC?' he says, raising one eyebrow.

'Yes, that's the parochial church council in the village. The books were a mess, but it was quite hard to persuade the vicar to trust me to manage their one thousand nine hundred pounds. I mean, I'd been used to running a four hundred million-pound fund so it was quite funny really and . . .'

'I see. Now, moving on to your time as Chairman of the

Governors at Beckles (is it?) Community College. Of what relevance might that be, Mrs Reddy?'

'Kate, please. Well, the school was failing, about to go into special measures actually, and it took a huge amount of work to turn it around. I had to change the management structure, which was a diplomatic nightmare. You can't believe school politics, seriously, they're much worse than a bank, and there was all the legislation to adhere to and the inspection reports. So much red tape. An untrained person hasn't got a hope in hell of understanding it. I instigated a merger with another school so we'd have the money to invest in frontline staff and bring down classroom sizes. It made Mergers and Acquisitions look like *Teletubbies*, quite frankly.'

'I see,' says Kerslaw, not an atom of a smile on his face. (Never watched *Teletubbies* with his kids, obviously.) 'And you were not working full-time in that period because your mother was unwell, I believe?'

'Yes, Mum – my mother – had a heart attack, but she's much better now, made a full recovery thank goodness. I'd just like to say, Mr Kerslaw, that Beckles Community College is one of the fastest improving schools in the country, and it's got a terrific new head who . . .'

'Quite. So what I need to ask you is: if one of your children were to be ill when a board meeting was scheduled, what would you do? It's vital that, as a non-exec director, you would have time to prepare for the meetings and, of course, attendance is compulsory.'

I don't know how long I sit there staring at him. Seconds? Minutes? I can't promise that my jaw isn't resting on the green leather desktop. Do I really have to dignify that question with an answer? Even when such questions are supposed to be illegal now? It seems that I do. So, I tell the headhunter prat with his trying-too-hard red silk jacket lining that, yes, when I was a successful fund manager, my children were occasionally unwell, and I had always arranged backup care like the conscientious professional I was and that any board could have the utmost confidence in my reliability as well as my discretion.

The speech might have gone down better had a phone not chosen that exact moment to start playing the theme from *The Pink Panther*. I look at Kerslaw and he looks at me. Funny kind of ringtone for a stuffy old headhunter, I think. It takes a few moments to realise that the jaunty prowl of a tune is, in fact, coming from the handbag under my chair. Oh, hell. Ben must have changed my ringtone again. He thinks it's funny.

'I'm terribly sorry,' I say, one hand plunged into the bag, frantically searching for the mobile, while the rest of me tries to remain as upright as possible. Why does a handbag turn into a bran tub when you need to find something fast? Purse. Tissues. Powder compact. Something sticky. *Uch*. Glasses. Come *on*! It has to be here somewhere. Got it. Switching the errant phone to Silent, I glance down to see one missed call and a text from my mother. Mum never texts. It's as worrying as getting a handwritten letter from a teenager. 'URGENT! Need your help. Mum x'

I hope that my face remains both smiley and calm, and that Kerslaw sees only a highly suitable non-exec director opposite him, but my imagination starts to pound. *Oh, God*. The possibilities swarm:

1. Mum has had another heart attack and crawled across the floor to get her mobile, which has ninety seconds' battery life left.
2. Mum is wandering around Tesco, utterly bewildered, hair uncombed, wearing only her nightie.

3. What Mum really means is: 'Don't worry, they're really very nice in intensive care.'

'You see, Mrs Reddy,' says Kerslaw, steepling his fingers like an archdeacon in a Trollope novel, 'our problem is that, while you undoubtedly had a very impressive track record in the City, with excellent references which attest to that, there is simply nothing you have done in the seven years since you left Edwin Morgan Forster which would be of any interest to my clients. And then, I'm afraid to say, there is the question of your age. Late forties and fast approaching the cohort parameter beyond which . . .'

My mouth is dry. I'm not sure, when I open it, whether any words will come out. 'Fifty's the new thirty-five,' I croak. *Don't break down, Kate, whatever you do. Let's just get out of here, please don't make a scene. Men hate scenes, this one especially, he's not worth it.*

I get up quickly, making it look like the decision to terminate the interview is mine. 'Thank you for your time, Mr Kerslaw. I really appreciate it. If anything comes up, I'm not too proud to go in at a considerably more junior level.'

The door seems a long way away. And the pile on Kerslaw's carpet is so lush it feels like my heels are sinking into a summer lawn.

12.41 pm: Back on the pavement, I call my mother and could almost cry with relief when I hear her voice. She's alive.

'Mum, where are you?'

'Oh, hello, Kath, I'm in Rugworld.'

'What?'

'Rugworld. Better choice than you get in Allied Carpets.'

'Mum, you said it was urgent.'

'It is, love. What d'you think I should go for? For my lounge. The sage or the oatmeal? Or they've got wheatgrass. Mind you it's very dear. Seventeen pounds ninety-nine a square metre!'

One of the most crucial interviews of my entire life has just been derailed because my mother can't decide what colour carpet she wants.

'The oatmeal would go with everything, Mum.' I hardly know what I'm saying. The roaring traffic's boom, my feet screaming to be let out of their stilettos, the sickening thump of rejection. I'm too old. Outside the cohort parameter. Old.

'Are you all right, love?'

No, I'm not. Very much not all right, pretty bloody desperate actually. All my hopes were pinned on this interview, but I can't tell her that. She wouldn't understand; I'd only make her worry. The years when my mother could cope with my problems are past. At some indiscernible moment, on a day like any other, the fulcrum tips and it becomes the child's turn to reassure the parent. (One day, I will be consoled by Emily, hard though that is to imagine now.) My father's death five years ago was the tipping point. Even though my parents were long divorced, I think Mum secretly thought Dad would come crawling back when he was old enough or, more realistically, skint and immobile enough, to stop acquiring girlfriends younger than his own daughters. This time, though, it would be her who would have the upper hand. After he was found dead in the bed of Jade, a glamour model who lived in a flat above his favourite betting shop, it was only ten months before Mum had a coronary of her own. A broken heart isn't just a metaphor, it turns out. So, you see, my mother can no longer be confided in, or leant upon, or burdened; I am careful what I say.

'I just had an interview, Mum.'

'Did you? Bet it went well, love. They couldn't ask for anyone more conscientious, I'll say that for you.'

'Yes, it was really good. It all came back to me. What I need to do.'

'You know best, love. I'll go for the oatmeal, shall I? Mind you, oatmeal can be a bit bland. I think I fancy the sage.'

After my mother has gone off quite happily to not buy a carpet, I take first a deep breath and then a decision. I told Kerslaw I wasn't proud, but it turns out I was wrong: I am proud, he has rekindled it. Ambition was there like a pilot light inside me, awaiting ignition. If I'm too old, then I'll bloody well have to get younger, won't I? If that's what it takes to get a job I could do in my sleep, then I'll do it. Henceforth, Kate Reddy will not be forty-nine and a half, a pitiful has-been and an unemployable irrelevance. She will not be 'fast approaching that cohort parameter' which doesn't apply to over-promoted dicks like Kerslaw or men in general, only to women funnily enough. She will be . . . She will be forty-two!

Yes, that sounds right. Forty-two. The answer to life, the universe and everything. If Joan Collins can knock twenty years off her age to secure a part in *Dynasty*, I can sure as hell knock seven off mine to get a job in financial services and keep my own dynasty going. From now on, against all my better instincts, and trying not to imagine what my mother would say, I shall become a liar.

*Finding Nemo. *Roy finally retrieved name of film about amnesiac fish.*

42

3

THE BOTTOM LINE

Thursday, 5.57 am: My joints are raw and aching. It's like a flu that never goes away. Must be Perry and his charming symptoms again. (Just like when I woke at three with a puddle of sweat between my breasts even though the bedroom was icy cold.) I'd much rather turn over and spend another hour in bed, but there's nothing for it. After my ordeal at the hands of the evil, pinstriped headhunter, Project Get Back to Work starts here.

Conor at the gym agreed to stretch the rules and gave me his special Bride's Deal, for women who want to look their best on the big day. I explained that I had pretty much the same goals as any newly engaged female: I needed to persuade a man, or men, to commit and give me enough money to raise my kids and do up a dilapidated old house. There would be a honeymoon period in which I would have to lull them into thinking I would always be enthusiastic, wildly attractive and up for it.

'Basically, I need to lose nine pounds – a stone would be

even better – and look like a forty-two-year-old who is young for her age,' I explained.

'No worries,' said Conor. He's a New Zealander.

So, this is where I prepare for re-entry into a real job. By real, I mean a decently paid position, unlike my so-called 'portfolio career' of the past few years. Women's magazines always make the portfolio career sound idyllic: the heroine, in a long, pale, cashmere cardigan worn over a pristine white T-shirt, wafts between rewarding freelance projects whilst being home to bake scrumptious treats for adorable kids in a kitchen that is always painted a soothing shade of dove grey.

In practice, as I soon found out, it means doing part-time work for businesses who are keen to keep you off their books to avoid paying VAT – even to avoid paying you at all. So much time wasted chasing fees. For someone who works in financial services I have a weird phobia of asking people for money – for myself anyhow. I ended up with a handful of overdemanding, underpaid projects, which I had to fit in around my primary role as chauffeur/shopper/laundress/ caregiver/cook/party planner/nurse/dog-walker/homework invigilator/Internet killjoy. My office, aka the kitchen table, was covered in a sprawl of paperwork, not wholesome baked goods. My annual earnings did not run to cashmere, and the white T-shirts grew sullen in the family wash.

All successful projects begin with a stern assessment of the bottom line followed by the setting of achievable goals. With everyone still safely asleep, I lock the bathroom door, pull my nightie over my head in a single movement ('a gesture of matchless eroticism', a lover once called it) and examine what I see in the mirror. This is what forty-nine and a half looks like. My breasts have definitely got lower and heavier. If you were being critical (and I certainly am), they look slightly more like udders than the perky pups of yore. Actually, I got away quite lightly. Some of my friends lost theirs entirely after childbirth; their boobs inflated, but once the milk dried up they shrivelled like party balloons. Judith in my NCT group got implants after twin boys sucked her dry and her husband couldn't bear what he charmingly called her 'witch's tits'. He went off with his PA anyway and Judith was left with two sacks of silicon so heavy she developed back problems. My boobs kept both their size and shape but, over the years, there's been a palpable loss of density; it's the difference between a perfect avocado and one that's gone to mush in its leathery case. I guess that's what youth means: ripeness is all.

I shiver involuntarily. It's freezing in here, even colder in the house than it is outside because Piotr hasn't got around to upgrading the plumbing yet. To tell you the truth, I'm scared of what he's going to find when he takes up the floorboards. The ancient radiator beneath the window emits a grudging amount of heat; its gurgling and plopping suggest serious digestive difficulties.

I drape a towel around my shoulders and focus again on the body in the mirror. Legs still looking pretty good: only a touch of crêpey ruching around the knees as though someone has taken a needle and pulled a line of thread through them. Waist has thickened, which makes me more straight-up-and-down than that curvy young woman who never struggled to attract attention and who never, not for one moment, thought about the sly magic her body made to draw men to it.

I always had slight, rather boyish hips. They wear a jacket of flesh now; I pinch it between thumb and forefinger till it hurts. That needs to go for a start. The skin below my neck and across my collarbone looks cross-hatched as though a painter has scored it with a knife. Sun damage. Nothing to be done about that – at least I don't think there is. ('*Roy, remind me to ask Candy, she's had every procedure known to man.*') Nor can I fix the C-section scar. It has mottled and faded with time, but the surgeon's hasty incision – she was in a hurry to get Emily out – created a small, overhanging belly shelf which no amount of Pilates can shift. Believe me, I've tried. I used to be so scornful of those celebrities who combine an elective C-section with a tummy tuck. Why wouldn't you wear your birth scars with pride? Now I'm not so sure, nor so self-righteous. The stomach itself is pretty flat, though the flesh is puckered like seersucker here and there.

And the bottom line? I turn around and try to get a glimpse, over my shoulder, in the mirror. Well, it's still roughly in the right place and no cellulite, but . . . butt butt butt. Put it this way, I won't be taking a photo of it and sharing it with my Facebook friends.

All of this is no surprise, no cause for shame; this is what time does to a body. So small, so mercifully infinitesimal are the changes that we barely notice, until, one day, we see ourselves in a photograph on holiday, or glimpse a reflection in a speckled mirror behind a bar and, for a split second, we think, 'Now, who *is* that?'

Certain things about ageing still have the power to shock, though. My friend Debra swears she found her first grey pubic hair the other day. Grey pubes, seriously? *Uch*. Mine are still dark, though definitely sparser – must we really add balding pussy to the list of menopausal mortifications? – and the hairs on my legs grow back much slower these days. Saves on waxing anyway. All the follicle activity has moved to my chin and neck where seven or eight dastardly little bristles poke through. They are as relentless as weeds. Only tweezers and eternal vigilance on my part prevent them forming a Rasputin tribute beard.

The face. I've saved the face till last. The light in here is kind. Soft, sifted, southerly light from a garden that is still dreaming. Too kind for my purposes. I yank the cord on the nasty fluorescent strip above the mirror. One virtue of eyesight deteriorating with age is you can't see yourself very well; at least that twisted old bitch, Mother Nature, got that bit right. Generally I console myself that, as everyone keeps telling me, I look young for my age. Comforting to hear when you're thirty-nine. Not so much now I'm nearly that number which shall not be mentioned.

Viewed in the unsparing, acid-yellow glare, my reflection reports that I have an incipient case of Muffin Chin. The jawline is a little lumpy, like cake mix before the flour's thoroughly blended, though at least it's not the dreaded wattles. For some masochistic reason, I Googled 'wattle' the other day: 'a fleshy caruncle hanging from various parts of the head or neck in several groups of birds and mammals'. My dread is that the caruncles are coming to get me. With two thumbs, I scoop up the skin under my chin and pull it back. For a second, my younger self stares back at me: startled, wistful, pretty.

The eye area isn't bad at all – thank you, Sisley Global Anti-Age cream (and I never smoked, which helps) – but there are two sad-clown grooves either side of my mouth and a frown, a small but determined exclamation mark – ! – punctuating the gap between my brows. It makes me look cross. I trace the vertical wrinkles with my fingernail. You can get Botox or Restylane injected into those, can't you? I never dared. Not that I have any ethical objection, none at all, it's just superstition. If you look fine why get work done and run the risk of looking freakish?

I would prefer to see a familiar, lightly creased face in the mirror than look like that actress I spotted in a café the other day. She was on TV a lot in the Seventies, starred in all the Dickens and Austen adaptations – the kind of artless, natural beauty poets compose sonnets to. I don't know what she's had done, but it's as though someone tried to restore the bloom of her apple-cheeked youth and ended up making her look like she has a mouth full of Brazil nuts. Her cheeks were bulging, but unevenly, and one corner of that rosebud pout was turned down like it was trying to cry but the rest of the face wouldn't let it. I was trying hard not to stare, but my eyes kept darting back to check out the disaster. Rubbernecking that sad rubber face. Better to stick with the face that you know than risk one that you don't.

I put out the cruel light and scramble into my gym stuff. Can hear Lenny whining downstairs; he knows I'm up. Need to let him out for a wee. Before going downstairs, I give the woman in the mirror one final, frank, appraising look. *Not too bad, Kate, give yourself some credit, girl.* There's definitely work to be done, but we're hanging in there. We who were once hot may yet be hot again (well, let's aim for lukewarm and see how it goes). For now, I'll just have to rely on concealer and foundation and hope the personal trainer can help me pass for my new age.

6.14 am: Starting as I mean to go on, with two spoons of cider vinegar in hot water (lowers blood sugar and suppresses appetite, probably because it makes you retch). This is also a fasting day, when I am allowed a maximum of five hundred calories. So here I am preparing a sumptuous breakfast of one solitary oatcake and wondering whether to go crazy and have a teaspoon of hummus. The calorie content of the oatcake is written on the side of the box in letters so small they are only legible to tiny elves equipped with an electron microscope. How am I supposed to follow sodding Fast Diet when I can't even read kcals? Go to fetch my reading glasses from The Place Where Reading Glasses Are Always Kept so Kate Doesn't Forget Where Her Reading Glasses Are. Not there. (*'Roy, are you up yet? Roy?? Where did I put my glasses? I need my glasses. Can you find me my glasses, please?')

No answer. Damn. Nibble small piece of oatcake and wonder if I can get away with drinking any of Emily's green slime, the making of which has created a pile of washing-up that is filling my sink. Open the fridge and pick up various tempting items, then put them right back again. Pause by the bread bin where yesterday Richard put a crusty, Italian artisanal loaf he picked up at the Deli. Crusty Loaf, Crusty Loaf, how you call to me!

Self-control, Kate. And lead us not into temptation and deliver us from gluten. I am meant to be exchanging the wasteland of midlife elasticated leggings and quiet despair for the waist-land of pencil skirts and professional possibility.

From: Candy Stratton
To: Kate Reddy
Subject: Headhunter Humiliation
You go for one interview and Midget Prick says because you're 49 you need to get euthanised and YOU BELIEVE HIM? SERIOUSLY!? What happened to that fabulous woman I used to work for? You need to get to work on your résumé and start lying big time. Anything you know that you can do, tell them you've done it in the past 18 months, OK? I'll give you a great reference.

And get a hairdresser to do you some highlights. Not Clairol over the side of the bathtub. Promise me.

XXO C

6.21 am: About to leave for the gym when, somewhere, there is the unfamiliar sound of a phone ringing. It takes me a couple of minutes to realise it's the landline. Takes twice that to track down the actual phone, which is chirruping forlornly to itself behind some sections of plasterboard that Piotr has stacked against the kitchen wall. Who could be ringing this early? Only cold callers and what Richard insists on calling 'The Aged Ps' use the house phone these days, now that everyone has a mobile. Yes, even Ben. It was impossible to hold out any longer once he turned twelve. He claimed it was 'child abuse' to deny a kid a phone and he was going to 'call the government'. Plus, he added, there was no way he was going to show me how to transfer my files onto a new laptop if he didn't have a mobile. Hard to argue with that.

The phone is covered in a thick layer of chalky builder's dust. Sure enough, the caller is an Aged P talking very politely to an indifferent answerphone. Donald. I hear his Yorkshire accent, once so rich and thick you could have cut it like parkin, now papery and fluting in his eighty-ninth year. When Richard's dad leaves a message, he speaks slowly and carefully, pausing at the end of each sentence to allow his silent interlocutor time to respond. Donald's messages take forever. 'Come on, Dad, spit it out!' Richard always shouts across the kitchen. But I love my father-in-law, his air of musing wistfulness like Sir Alec Guinness; he addresses the machine with such courtesy it's a reminder of a lost world where human spoke unto human.

I listen to Donald with half an ear while rummaging in the fruit bowl for a breakfast kiwi. Better than a banana, surely. Can't be more than forty calories. Why does this always happen? Like hand grenades when I brought them home from the supermarket two days ago, the kiwis have turned to mush; it feels faintly obscene, like I'm palpating a baboon's testicle.

50

'Terribly sorry to disturb you so early, Richard, Kate. It's Donald here,' says my father-in-law unnecessarily. 'I'm calling about Barbara. I'm afraid she's had a falling out with our new lady carer. Nothing to worry about.'

No, please God, no. After two months of negotiation with Wrothly Social Services, which would have exhausted the combined diplomatic skills of Kofi Annan and Amal Clooney, I managed to secure a small care-package for Donald and Barbara. That meant someone would help with the cleaning, bathe Barbara and change the dressing on her scalded leg. It's a pitiful amount of time they've been allocated, so short that the carer sometimes doesn't even bother to take her coat off, but at least there's someone checking in on them every day. Richard's parents insist they don't want to downsize from the family home, a stone farmhouse on the side of a hill, because it means leaving the garden they have tended and loved for forty years; they know some of the trees and shrubs as well as they know their own grandchildren. Barbara always said they would move 'when the time was right', but I fear they missed that particular window, probably about seven years ago, and they are now stuck in a rambling place they refuse to heat ('Can't go throwing your money around') with a vertiginous staircase – the one Ben fell down the Easter he was three.

'We do hate to be a burden . . .' the voice continues as I'm lacing up my trainers. Check the clock. Going to be late for first training session with Conor. Sorry. I know if I was a good, self-sacrificing person I would pick up the phone, but I simply cannot face another *Groundhog Day* conversation with Donald.

'. . . but you see Barbara seems to have caused offence yesterday when she said that Erna didn't have good enough English to understand what was what. Barbara made Erna a cup of tea and Erna said "Thank you", and Barbara said "You're

51

welcome", but Erna *thought* she said, "You *will* come", and that Barbara was giving her orders, but she wasn't, you see. Erna was rather rough with Barbara, I'm afraid. She left in quite a huff and she hasn't been in for a few days. I'm happy sorting Barbara's bandage myself, as I do remember my First Aid, thank goodness, but she won't let me into the bathroom with her and you know that's how she burnt her leg in the first place. She runs the hot tap and then she forgets to put in cold.'

A man who, almost seventy years ago, navigated a Lancaster bomber through the treacherous skies over occupied Europe – he was three years older than Emily is now, a thought that always makes me want to cry – sounds resigned to his fate: calm, composed, stoical and utterly utterly helpless.

'If it's not too much trouble . . .'

Oh, all right, all right. Just coming.

'Hello, Donald. Yes, it's Kate. No, not at all. You're not a bother. Sorry, no, we haven't got your messages. We don't always check the . . . Yes, it's better to call the mobile if you can. I did write our numbers on the calendar for you. Oh, dear. Barbara caught the carer smoking in front of the Bishop of Llandaff?' (Hang on, what's a senior Welsh clergyman doing in my mother-in-law's herbaceous border?) 'Oh, the Bishop of Llandaff is a type of . . . Yes, I see, and Barbara doesn't believe you should smoke by the dahlias. No, quite. Yes, yes. I can see that. And she'd prefer a carer from the area if possible. OK, I'll give social services another call.'

They're bound to have a non-smoking, English-speaking, dahlia-friendly home help at short notice, aren't they?

Eventually manage to hang up after promising Donald that we will pay a visit once the kids are settled back in school, once Emily's exams are out of the way, once I have a new job and a functioning kitchen and once Richard can take time out from his twice-weekly therapy sessions and cycle races. I make that the Twelfth of Never.

Text Conor to say sorry, I've had a family problem, and I will definitely see him at the gym on Friday. If I'm ever allowed to have some time for myself. Is that really too much to ask?

7.17 am: 'Dear God, listen to this, Kate.' Rich is sitting at the kitchen table. He looks up from the paper, squinting in the sharp light streaming in through the windows. Beautiful big Georgian windows, a gracious pair, but one sash mechanism is broken so you can't open it, and the sills are riddled with rot.

'Can you believe it?' Rich sighs. 'It says, "Hackers access one hundred thousand Snapchat photos and prepare to leak them including under-age nude pics". Darling, do the kids have this Snapchat thing?'

'Um, *drner*.'

'Luckily we know Emily isn't going to be posting pictures of her genitals for public consumption, but lots of parents haven't got a clue what their kids are up to on social media.'

'*Ingggmr*.'

'I mean it's totally inappropriate.'

'Mmmm.'

Since his midlife crisis took hold my husband has started subscribing to progressive left-wing periodicals and using words like 'inappropriate' and 'issues around' a lot. Instead of saying poverty he says 'issues around deprivation'. I don't know why no one says 'problems' any more, except maybe problems have to be solved, and they can't be, and issues sound important but don't demand solutions.

'I've got therapy first thing,' Rich says, 'then I'm straight into lectures. Joely at the drop-in centre wants me to help get this meditation facility off the ground. We're thinking of crowd-funding it.'

Your average menopausal male can generally be relied upon to purchase a leather jacket and the services of six-foot Russian blondes. Mine buys a book called *Mindfulness: A Practical Guide to Accessing the Calmer, Kinder You.* After being let go by his ethical architecture firm, he decides to take the opportunity to retrain as a counsellor and starts fretting about the health and safety deficiencies in Bolivian tin mines when we can't even staunch the pong from the soil pipe in the downstairs loo of our Tudorbethan hovel. (How I wish I'd never heard the term soil pipe, which is basically Victorian for 'shithole'.) Honestly, it's hideous. I'd rather he got a Harley-Davidson and a girlfriend called Danka Vanka.

Richard is so het up about the global epidemic of inappropriateness that he has no idea what is going on in his own home.

'We put those parental controls on the kids' phones and iPads, didn't we?' he asks me.

(Please observe the tactical use of the marital 'we'. Richard doesn't mean did 'we' put parental controls on the kids' electronic devices. He wouldn't know a parental control if it punched him on the nose. What he means by 'we' is me, the wife, who gets shared credit so long as things are going well. As soon as things go wrong, you can bet the question will be, 'Did *you* organise those parental controls?')

'*Course* we have parental controls, darling. Fancy a bacon butty?'

Richard looks down at his Lycra-sheathed six-pack before capitulating. 'Go on then, won't say no if you're making one.'

Over twenty years, the bacon sandwich has never failed as distraction, bribe or tranquilliser dart for my partner. Given a choice between a blow job and a bacon butty, let's just say Rich would definitely hesitate. If he ever goes vegetarian, or even vegan – as looks increasingly likely judging by the tragic woven bracelet on his left wrist – our marriage is doomed. Anyway, I am telling the truth for a change. The kids do have parental controls on their technology. What I'm not telling Richard is that after Emily's bottom went viral I called Joshua Reynolds, the village computer prodigy who is now in his late-twenties doing postgraduate work in physics at Imperial. (His mother Elaine told our Women Returners group that the infant Josh could re-route the US Navy from his buggy or something.) One of those disappointed, mousy women who only lights up in her offspring's reflected glory, Elaine was thrilled when I called to ask for Josh's number, explaining that I needed help with some Internet problems. I figured Josh was young enough and, let's face it, sufficiently on the spectrum, not to think it was at all weird that I wanted to spy on my own daughter, or that I needed his help tracking down and destroying evidence of her naked backside wherever it might have got to.

In fact, on the phone, Josh was gratifyingly unsurprised, which instantly made me feel better. He said he would see what he could come up with regarding social media but, in the meantime, he told me how to get into the history on Emily's laptop. I scrolled down the recent purchases and found that Madam had used *my credit card* to download 'How to Use a Proxy to Bypass Parental Control Filters'. I mean, what are you supposed to do? It's like I'm a Stone Age person living with Bill Gates.

7.23 am: Emily is upset. I made the mistake of pointing out that to produce one pint of her green juice she creates six miles of washing-up, presently still festering, unwashed in the sink. There is a heap of vegetable waste – apple cores, feathery celery stalks, bleeding beetroot carcasses – that would feed a drove of pigs for a week.

'It's such a mess, darling. Could you at least put the juicer in the dishwasher?'

'I *know*,' she snaps, 'I *know*. I'll do it, *OK*?'

'And you can't live just on that green juice, sweetheart. You need some solid food inside you. Please at least have some eggs. I'll make them for you.'

'What part of *juice diet* don't you understand, Mum? It's a seven-day cleanse.'

'But you can't get through a school morning on a glass of slime, love.'

'You're on a bloody diet permanently, but when *I* do it it's not healthy. I don't need any more of this crap . . .'

There are tears in her eyes as she veers away from my outstretched hand and checks her phone.

After the belfie catastrophe, I did confiscate her mobile for twenty-four hours, exactly as Candy suggested, but it was as if Em had been bereaved. Removal of Internet access seemed to distress her even more than her backside going viral. She sobbed inconsolably and begged me to give it back. I know I should have stuck to my guns, I know, but I couldn't bear to cause her yet more distress. Take away a teenager's phone and you remove the threat of dangers which are invisible to the maternal eye, plus the constant pressure on a girl to peacock herself for the peer group, then get crushed when she doesn't get enough Likes. Unfortunately, you also take away their life, or the only part of their life they care about. I couldn't do that to her, not when she's still so churned up.

Storming out of the kitchen, Emily slams the door into the

56

hall with such ferocity that the old brass lock shudders loose and hangs there, dangling from two nails. I go over and try to press it back in, but the wood is so badly splintered that the nails have nothing to hold them in place. (*'Roy, please add a locksmith to my to-do list.'*)

This is the way our relationship has been for the past eighteen months. The little girl who was desperate to please, who was so angelic she looked like she'd tumbled out of a Pears Soap poster, the poppet who invited me for tea in her Wendy house: that little girl is no more. Instead, there is this exasperated and exasperating young woman who is aggravated by my every suggestion – sometimes, it seems, by my very existence. She tells me I am 'Soooo annoyyyingg'. I need to 'Back off'. 'Just chill, will you?' 'Stop worrying, Mum, I'm not a baby any more.'

Stop worrying? Sorry, darling, I'm your mother; that's kind of the job description.

As my own hormones recede, my daughter's are surging in. She is buffeted about by them and we all have to surf that tide with her. This belfie business has made it ten times worse. Emily has barely spoken to me for the past three days; any time I try to raise the subject she runs upstairs, like she did just now, and locks herself in the bathroom. When I knock on the door, she claims her period's started and she feels sick, or her tummy hurts, but close observation of Tampax supplies tells me she's only just finished her period. I haven't even told Em that I've hired Josh Reynolds to carry out what he calls a 'seek and destroy mission'. I just wish I knew what the repercussions have been for her at school, but I can't find out unless we're talking, can I? Obviously, I am to blame for the entire sixth form, the school choir and three million people on Facebook having seen the photo she took of her bare bottom, complete with its very own hashtag: #FlagBum. I understand that she is taking out her distress and anger on me. As my *Parenting Teens in the Digital Age* book says, my daughter knows that I love her unconditionally, so I am a safe place to put those feelings. Intellectually, I get that. Doesn't make her behaviour towards me any less hurtful though. Emily can wound me like no one else.

7.30 am: When she comes back down for breakfast, Em is wearing full Cleopatra make-up, her eyes given raven wings by flicks of kohl. She either looks amazing or like jailbait, depending on your point of view. *Pick your battles, Kate, pick your battles.*

'Mum?'

'Yes, darling.'

'Lizzy and some of the other girls are going to see Taylor Swift for her birthday.'

'Any relation to Jonathan?' asks Richard, not bothering to look up from his iPad.

'Who's he?'

'Jonathan Swift. Famous satirist during the eighteenth century. Wrote *Gulliver's Travels*,' says Rich.

'Mum, puhlease can *I* get a Taylor Swift ticket? She's so cool, she's like the best singer ever. Izzy and Bea are going. *Everyone's* going. Mu-um, *please.*'

'It's not *your* birthday,' objects Ben, not bothering to look up from his phone.

'Shuddup, will you? Little brat. Mu-umm, tell Ben to stop it, will you?'

'Emily, don't kick your brother.'

'Jonathan Swift suggested that children should be boiled and eaten,' muses Rich to himself.

Sometimes, just occasionally, my husband makes me laugh out loud, and reminds me why I fell in love with him.

'I think Swift was definitely onto something there,' I say, placing scrambled eggs on the table. Richard is washing his bacon butty down with a glass of some weird energy drink which looks like that purple Dioralyte we gave the kids when they were dehydrated from vomiting.

'Emily, you've got to eat something, darling.'

'You just don't get it,' she says, pushing the plate of egg away from her with such venom that it tips over the edge of the table and smashes onto the floor, scattering fluffy yellow florets over the terracotta tiles.

'*Everyone's* like going to the O2 to see Taylor Swift. S'not fair. Why are we poor?'

'We are not poor, Emily,' says Richard in that slow, soft, vicar voice he has adopted since starting his course. (Oh, please, not the South Sudan lecture.)

'There are children in the Horn of Africa, Emily . . .'

'OK!' I jump in before Rich can build up a head of sanctimony. 'Mummy's going to get a full-time job very soon, so you can definitely go and see Taylor Swift, darling.'

'*Kate!!!*' protests Richard, 'what did we say about not negotiating with terrorists?'

'What do *I* get?' wails Ben, looking up from his phone.

Lenny, seizing this optimal moment of family friction, snarfs up the scrambled egg and licks the floor clean.

Rich is right to be cross. Extortionate concert tickets are not part of our agreed budget cuts, but I sense that Emily's distress – panic even, did I detect panic in her eyes? – is about more than Taylor Swift. The girls she mentioned are all part of the Snapchat group that Lizzy Knowles shared the belfie with. The last thing Emily needs is to miss their outing. If Rich can blow one hundred and fifty quid a week talking about himself, and Ben's new braces will require us to take out a second mortgage, then surely we can find the money to help Em be happy?

7.54 am: When the kids have gone upstairs to do their teeth and get their stuff together, Richard briefly raises his eyes from his cycling website and notices me – me as a person, that is, not as diary secretary and rinser of Lycra – and says, 'I thought you were at the gym today.'

'I was, but your dad rang really early. Couldn't get him off the phone. He was on for twenty minutes. He's really worried about your mum. She's obviously pissed off the new carer. Told her that her English wasn't good enough after she caught her smoking by the Bishop of Llandaff.'

'What?'

'It's a flower. Passive smoking harms dahlias apparently. You know what your parents are like about the garden. And the carer sounds hideous. Donald mentioned a bruise on Barbara's wrist, although that could be a fall. The whole thing's a mess, but now they haven't got anyone going in again.'

'For fuck's sake.' Richard allows himself a very non-Dalai Lama reaction and I'm glad. Like most couples, our relationship has been held together by a common outlook on life, and by laughing at or despising those who don't share it. I neither much like nor recognise Mr Wholefoodier Than Thou who is currently occupying the body where my lovely, funny husband used to live.

'Mum's impossible,' he says. 'How many carers is that they've gone through? Three? Four?'

'Barbara's really not well, Rich. You need to get up there and sort things out.'

'Cheryl can do it. She's nearer.'

60

'Cheryl has a full-time job and three sons doing twenty-seven after-school activities. She can't just drop everything.'

'She's their daughter-in-law.'

'And you're their son. So is Peter.' (Don't you hate the way families assume it's always the women who should take care of the elderly parents, even if a son lives nearer? That may just be connected to the fact that we always do.)

At least Rich has the grace to look sheepish. 'I know, I know,' he sighs. 'I thought Mum seemed fine in Cornwall. That was only two months ago.'

'Your father's good at covering things up.'

'What kind of things?'

'You've seen how forgetful she is.'

'That's perfectly normal at her age, isn't it?'

'It's not normal to ask your fourteen-year-old grandson if he needs a wee wee. She genuinely thinks Ben is in kindergarten. She needs proper help. We can't just leave your dad to cope, Rich. He's amazing but he's almost ninety for God's sake.'

'Could *you*? I mean, would *you* mind going, Kate? I would go, you know I would, but I can't take a break from therapy right now. This is such a crucial time in my personal development. I know you're job hunting and it's a big ask, darling, but you're so good at these things.'

'Are you kidding?'

That's what I am about to say, anyway, but something in Rich's expression makes me pause. For a moment, he looks like Ben did that time in the middle of the night when he was kneeling on the bathroom floor next to the toilet bowl and admitted he was scared of vomiting.

Rich has always been horrified by anything to do with illness or doctors. Like most men he believes he's immortal and I guess there's nothing like witnessing your parent's decline into

61

dementia to dent that treasured myth. Despite his phobia, if I'm ill Rich always forces himself to be a good nurse. When I got salmonella from a cheap chicken, not long after we first met, he refused to leave me alone in my grotty shared flat though a combination of paper-thin partition walls and thunderous visits to the loo should have dealt a lethal blow to our budding romance. I remember thinking, between bouts of retching, how tenderly devoted this new boyfriend was. Not at all like the emotionally shut-off public schoolboy I had imagined him to be. If Rich's passion could survive hourly explosions from all orifices, he must be a keeper. I had had better lovers, men my body was helplessly in thrall to, but wanting someone who was also kind to me? Now, that was a first.

When did we stop being kind to each other, Rich and I? All the pressure and upheaval of the past few months has made us scratchy and inconsiderate. I need to do better.

'OK,' I say, 'I'll see if I can go up to Wrothly and check in on Barbara and Donald before they invite me to interview for new Governor of the Bank of England.'

Richard smiles (haven't seen one of those for a while) and swoops in for a kiss. 'Brilliant. You'll get a job offer, darling,' he says. 'Once that headhunter guy sends out your CV you'll be beating them off with a stick.'

I haven't told him how badly things went with Kerslaw. Don't want to worry him.

Josh Reynolds to Kate

Hi Kate, Josh here. I've notified Facebook that the pic of Emily breaches their Community Standards and it should be taken down by now. As she's sixteen she no longer qualifies as a child & won't get highest priority. Although she's not recognisable in the pic – you can only see her back and her bum which won't identify her – I've zapped everything I could find and I've set up notifications which will alert me next time a pic of Emily's bum is shared. I'll kill it, natch. There are ways in which I can make Lizzy Knowles's online life very unpleasant 😼 but you didn't hear me say that, OK? If you want me to do what can't be mentioned, let me know. You know if this is revenge porn you can get police involved. Do you want to do that? Thanks for asking me. It was fun!

Kate to Josh Reynolds

Thanks so much, Josh. Brilliant job. Really appreciate it. No, not revenge porn. Just teenage girl stuff. Not serious. Don't want police involved!! Let me know how much I owe you.

9.47 am, Starbucks: With breakfast cleared, the site of the Green Juice Massacre swabbed down, the dishwasher mumbling to itself and Candy's stern advice in mind, I have taken myself into town to work on my CV in a café. I can pretend to be 'telecommuting', instead of sitting at the kitchen table waiting to be ambushed by family members.

My mission today is to produce an attractive new CV, omitting my date of birth and any other incriminating details. Instead of admitting to 'time out', as prospective employers will see it, I must repackage what I have learned and achieved since I left Edwin Morgan Forster, as a mother, wife, daughter, daughter-in-law, loyal friend, school governor, PTA member, penniless yet imaginative house restorer, eBay addict, and inspired (and only slightly crooked) investor of parish church's 1,900 quid (just call me Bernie Madoff!). It's a cinch. Apply Harvard Business School model to position of Household Servant and General Dogsbody. Here goes:

- **Over the past six years, I have built up an impressive track record in Conflict Resolution.** (Translation: Wrestled Xbox out of Ben's hands after three hours solid on *Grand Theft Auto IV*. Got him to agree to consume at least one green vegetable a day plus Brainy Teen fish oil capsule in return for more time on *GTA IV*.)

- **Financial management and capital projects: I have considerable expertise in this area after helming several challenging schemes.** (You can say that again. The Money Pit, aka 'period gem' is eating giant bites out of our meagre savings account and I am driving increasingly hard bargains with suppliers to get the job finished.)

- **International negotiating skills honed on domicile issues in the UK.** (Bloody au pair Natalia and her cocaine-dealer boyfriend.)

- **Time Management and Prioritisation: I have balanced the complex needs of different individuals and developed routines while learning to prioritise multiple tasks and meet strict deadlines.** (Of course I have. Am I not a mother? Do I not manage the lives of two adolescents and one male in midlife meltdown whilst keeping an eye on elderly relatives, walking the dog, trying to keep up with friends, carving out time to exercise, doing the garden and watching *Homeland* and *Downton Abbey*? Feel free to add to this list, it's endless.)

- **Grown a highly productive business start-up.** (Planted beautiful Cutting Flower Garden guided by Sarah Raven book on same. Also, purchased huge smelly composting bin and learned to identify weeds. To my surprise, I have become a gardener.)

- **Due diligence work on complex UK legislation.** (Fought tooth and nail to get non-existent care package from local authority for Donald and Barbara, who get frailer by the day.)

- **Pioneering research in Human Resources with special emphasis on staff development and motivation.** (Spent days tracking down and hiring highly rated private tutor, fighting off several Tiger Mothers, to get Ben into the only local secondary school without a record of drive-by shootings and dreadful exam results. Told Emily she could have two tickets for the Reading Festival if she got nine good GCSEs. Result!)
- **Built strong knowledge base in transport.** (Personal chauffeur to two teenagers with active social, musical and sporting lives. Regularly take Ben and his drum kit to orchestra, jazz group, etc. Drove Emily to events around the country until she decided swimming was giving her Popeye shoulders. If you want my advice, never let your kids take up swimming; you always have to set off at dawn, usually in fog, and then you have to sit on an orange plastic seat in some repellently warm building that stinks of chlorine and wee – you can actually feel the bacteria multiplying in the soupy air. Plus, you have to maintain a keen interest during forty lengths of butterfly stroke. Seriously, choose any other sport.)

'Oh, hello, Kate? Fancy seeing you here.'

I glance up from my laptop to find a blonde around my age smiling expectantly at me.

***'Uh-oh. Roy, are you there? We have a woman in her forties, possible school mum, but wildly overdressed for a latte in Starbucks (Missoni coat, Chanel shades). Clearly loaded, judging by the number of bags she's carrying. How do I know her?'*

'Oh, hello.' I smile back and hope Roy shows up fast with her name. 'Hello! Um, I'm just updating my CV.'

'So I see. Very impressive. Job hunting, are we?' (*'ROY?? Get a move on, will you! Please tell me who she is.'*)

'Er. Yes, well, with the kids getting a bit older I thought I'd stick a toe in the water. See what's out there, you know how it is.'

She smiles again, revealing lipstick on her top teeth, which have been expensively whitened. Too white – more Dulux gloss than Farrow and Ball.

Oh, here comes Roy, back from the stacks and a little breathless. Thank God. *Roy says that I put my glasses in the drawer next to the Aga.

'WHAT? I don't need to know where my glasses are, Roy. That was earlier. What I would now like you to focus on is retrieving this woman's name.'

'By the way,' the woman says, 'I'm so glad Emily can come to Taylor Swift.'

**'It's Lizzy Knowles's mum,' says Roy. 'You know, mum of that little cow that sent Emily's bum everywhere. Cynthia Knowles.'*

Good job, Roy!

I've only met Cynthia a couple of times. After a school concert when both our daughters sang in the choir. And then at one of those charity coffee mornings where a well-bred mummy provides chocolate chip cookies no one eats, because we're all fasting or eating protein only, and you pay her back by buying some jewellery you don't want, and can't really afford, but it's rude not to because the mummy, who is married to Someone in The City, is trying to find something she can Do For Herself. So, you hand over your money to this hugely wealthy woman, which she then gives to charity, when she could perfectly well have written a large cheque. Oh, and nine days later the 'silver' earrings you bought at the coffee morning turn green and pus starts coming out of your left earlobe.

'We'll take them to the O2, of course,' Cynthia is saying. 'Christopher will drive them down in the Land Rover. Lizzy wants Korean BBQ afterwards. She said Emily's a definite. Did she mention the ticket price?'

You know what? Meeting Cynthia, mother of the girl who has hurt my daughter so hideously, I don't feel like being polite. My inner maternal dragon would prefer to breathe fire at her and scorch those perfect caramel highlights to cinders. Does she even know about the belfie that Lizzy accidentally-on-purpose shared with the whole school and all the paedophiles of England? Or are we playing Let's Pretend I Have Perfect Children, which is a favourite game of women like Cynthia because to admit otherwise would be to admit their whole life has been a tragic waste of time?

'Yes, that's absolutely fine,' I lie. How much can it be? More than £50? £60? No wonder poor Em was so frantic to get our agreement at breakfast. She'd already accepted Lizzy's invitation.

'And I hear you're on the waiting list for our brainy book group, Kate?' Cynthia continues. 'Serena said that you'd expressed an interest. We like to think we're a cut above your average book group. Usually choose one of the classics. Very occasionally a novel by a living author. Booker Prize shortlist. No chick lit. Such a waste of time, all that shopping and silly women.'

'Yes, isn't it.' Who does Cynthia Knowles with her carrier bags: two L.K. Bennett, one John Lewis and one Hotel Chocolat think she is – Anna sodding Karenina?

'Such luck bumping into you. Just tell Emily to give Lizzy a cheque for ninety pounds for the ticket.'

Ninety pounds! Make strenuous effort not to let jaw drop or emit squeak of dismay.

'I think Lizzy just wants Topshop vouchers for her birthday,' she goes on. 'No presents per se. Good luck with the job hunting!'

Cynthia stalks off to the far corner of the café to join a group of the yummiest mummies imaginable, taking her skinny latte and most of my morale with her. Why do women like her get to me? Probably because they get to play domestic goddesses on hubby's Platinum Amex. Not a life I ever wanted – although, recently, I must admit the idea of being a kept woman has developed a certain appeal.

Bit late for that, Kate. Most of the guys who could keep you in the style to which Cynthia is accustomed are (a) on Wife Number Two or (b) picking up debt-ridden students on Sugar Daddy websites so they can rub their slack, saggy bodies on prime young flesh. *Uch.* For Wifey Number One, hanging onto her position is a full-time job: gym, Botox, yoga, nutritionist, even vaginoplasty to get her pre-baby pussy back so hubby's floppy dick isn't wanging about in a wind tunnel that three babies' heads have passed through. No thank you.

And yet, glancing across the café at Cynthia and her gaggle of mums, I feel a corkscrew of envy in my gut. Always slightly dreaded the whole school-gate thing; in truth, I was dismissive of those women whose life revolves around coffees and play-dates. But now that Ben is too old to be picked up any more, I miss the ready companionship that that ritual provided and all the pleasant, eager, worried women I could discuss my kids with. They were a bulwark against the loneliness of parenting, if only I'd known it. Anyway, need to get this magnificent CV finished. Just a few final points.

- **Oversaw the establishment of a major hydro site.** (Weekly laundry, handwashing Rich's pongy cycling gear so it doesn't 'go bobbly'.)

- **Provided sustainable nutritional support for staff in line with industry standards.** (Always kept snacks for kids to eat in car on way home from school, thus avoiding total meltdown. At least one cooked meal a day for four people, making approximately ten thousand hot dinners in the past seven years, without any thanks or acknowledgement of what it takes to cater said dinners.)
- **Turned around declining private company through regular programme of cuts and aggressive streamlining to offset threat of double-dip recession.** (Went on Fast Diet and started going to gym again. Hopefully on track to fit into my old office clothes.)
- **Strove for a consistent improvement in the bottom line.** (Slightly smaller bum as a result of excruciating squats.)

If any of the above strikes you as vaguely fraudulent or unethical, well, I'm sorry, but what are the words you'd use to describe the fact that women take care of the young and the old, year in year out, and none of that work counts as skills or experience, or even work? Because women are doing it for free it is literally worthless. As Kerslaw said, we have nothing of interest to offer, except everything we do and everything we are. I am not by nature a political person, but I swear I would march to protest the vast untold work done by all the women of this world.

3.15 pm: Fighting the urge to go upstairs and sleep. Can hardly put 'afternoon napping' down as part of my skillset on application form, although it's the one thing I excel at these days. Probably Perry's fault. With my CV immensely improved (although I'm not sure I'd dare show it to my Women Returners group) I brace myself for a call to Wrothly Social Services. Sadly, it's too early for alcohol.

'Your call may be assessed for training purposes.'

Here we go. You know when you've pressed five for one department and then you've pressed one from the Following Range of Options, although you think you may have misheard, and that maybe you needed three? And then you've pressed seven for Any Other Queries, and your hopes are getting up that you might be about to interact with an actual human being, when a recorded voice says, 'Sorry. We are experiencing a high volume of calls. Your call is important to us, please hold the line'? And the phone rings and rings and rings and you picture a cobwebby office with a skeleton sitting in a chair at a desk and the phone on the desk it rings and rings and rings? Well, that's what it feels like to be calling Wrothly Social Services.

By now, surely everyone has figured out that these multiple options are not designed to be helpful; they are supposed to act as a deterrent whilst giving the illusion of progress and choice. Even 'your call may be used for training purposes' is basically a threat, telling you to behave yourself or else. A mere twenty minutes elapse until I get through to someone in the right department, who then asks if he can put me on hold while he speaks to a colleague, who may or may not have access to Barbara's case notes. I am almost tearfully grateful for this basic courtesy.

'Hello? Can I help you?'

The voice does not sound at all helpful. In fact, she sounds as though she may recently have graduated from a bespoke Unhelpfulness training course – the one they send American border security staff on.

I know, let's baffle her with politeness and friendliness.

'Good afternoon, thank you so much. It's great to talk to an actual person.'

No response.

'So, I'm ringing on behalf of my mother-in-law, she has a burns injury . . .'

'Barbara Shattock?'

'Yes, that's right. Great. Thank you so much. I spoke to my father-in-law earlier and he says that, unfortunately, there was a misunderstanding between Barbara and Erna, the carer you so kindly sent to help them.'

'I'm afraid that your mother-in-law has been reported in connection with a possible hate crime,' says the voice.

'What? No. That can't be right.'

'Mrs Shattock racially abused one of our carers.'

'Sorry? No. You've got that wrong. You don't understand. Barbara, she's eighty-five. She's very confused. She's not herself.'

'Mrs Shattock accused her carer of not being able to speak English. At Wrothly, we take hate crime very seriously.'

'Hang on. What hate crime? Erna is Lithuanian, isn't she? She's not a different race to Barbara. Do you even know what racism is?'

'I'm not trained to answer that question,' the voice says flatly.

'But you're making a very serious allegation.'

There is an icy silence into which I burble and plead: 'I'm really sorry if there's been a misunderstanding, but it's simply not in Barbara's nature to upset someone like that.'

That is a blatant lie. As long as I've known her, more than twenty years now, Barbara has been the princess of passive aggression, the empress of undermining. The world is full, as far as Barbara is concerned, of people who are Simply Not Up To It. The list of Simply Not Up To Its is long and ever-expanding. It includes news anchors with sloppy diction, women who 'let themselves go', tradesmen with dirty boots who don't show sufficient respect to Axminster carpets, pregnant weather-girls, politicians who are 'basically Communists', and the fool responsible for a misprint in the *Daily Telegraph* crossword. A mistake in her favourite crossword and Barbara will act out the mad scene from *Lucia di Lammermoor*, calling for the head of the idiot who introduced an error into Twenty-Two Across.

As the lesser of her two daughters-in-law, it was established early on that I was Simply Not Up To It. I was hardly the girl Richard's mother hoped her son would marry and she did very little to conceal her disappointment. Every time we visited, Barbara would ask without fail, 'Where did you get that dress/blouse/coat, Kate?' and not in a way which indicated she wished to go out and purchase one for herself.

One Christmas, I was in the pantry looking for tinned chestnuts when I heard Barbara say to Cheryl, the preferred daughter-in-law, 'Kate's problem is she has no background.'

It stung, not just the snobbery, but because Barbara was right. Compared to the comfortable, well-established Shattocks, my own family had a hasty, provisional feel. We were the Beverly Hillbillies, the supermarket's basic range, and I know Barbara sensed it from the moment Rich first took me home. Luckily, he was so in love he didn't notice her dig at my unmanicured hands. (I'd been decorating a junk-shop chest of drawers and the residue of grey-green paint looked like dirt beneath my fingernails.) I could put up with having my family patronised, my cooking dismissed and my choice of clothes derided, but the one thing I could never forgive Barbara for is that she has always made me feel like a bad mother. And I'm not.

Yet, here I am defending Barbara to the woman from social services because Barbara is no longer in any fit state to tell this woman that she is Simply Not Up To It. Which she clearly isn't.

'Has it occurred to you that it might be quite upsetting if you're an elderly lady and the person washing you is a bit rough and she can't understand what you're saying? Are we allowed to say that? Oh, I see, we're not allowed to say that. Pardon me.'

Uch. When did we become this nation of hateful automatons, unable to deviate from the official script to respond to genuine need and upset? All friendliness gone now, I channel my steeliest professional self and suggest that the voice gets another carer around to help Barbara and Donald asap.

'Otherwise, Mrs Shattock might seriously hurt herself at which point Wrothly Social Services will be obliged to comment. On the evening news.'

'I am not trained to answer that,' I hear the voice say, followed by the dialling tone.

Well, that went well.

To: Candy Stratton
From: Kate Reddy
Subject: Headhunter Humiliation
Hi hon, thanks for the pep talk. I did a new CV as you suggested. Might enter it for Pulitzer Prize as piece of groundbreaking, experimental fiction. It's not really lying if you know you can do all the things you haven't done, is it?

I've been going to these Women Returners meetings. Don't laugh. They're really sweet and it's making me realise how much luckier I am than those who quit when they had their first baby. Desperately trying to lose weight and get myself into shape, but I'm just so damn tired and wrung out the whole time. Hard not to raid the biscuit tin when you're knackered! Not sleeping cos of night sweats. I have hog's bristles sprouting out of

my chinny chin chin. I'm so blind I can't read the calories on any foodstuffs, which I'm not supposed to be eating anyway as I need to get into my Thin Clothes because I gave my Fat Clothes to the charity shop the last time I lost weight and swore I would never be fat again. Plus, I need to take a nap every afternoon. I have the energy of a heavily sedated sloth.

Missed my gym session today with Conan the Barbarian because I was talking to Richard's dad about Richard's mum, who clearly has Alzheimer's, but no one can face having that conversation so we are all pretending it's fine until she burns the house down. Oh, and the council is accusing Barbara of a HATE CRIME because she didn't like the surly, non-English-speaking 'carer' they sent to bathe her. Excuse me, she's eighty fucking five! If you can't be a difficult old bitch then, when can you be?

I never know when my period's coming these days and I'm scared the deluge will happen when I'm out. Just like I was scared when I was 13 and my period started in the middle of a chemistry test. So I prefer to stay in and watch property-porn shows and fantasise about life in a neglected French chateau being renovated for me by Gérard Depardieu (circa *Green Card*, not since he got bigger than an actual chateau) with his large, capable yet tender hands, TOTALLY FREE OF CHARGE.

Be honest. Does this sound like the kind of mature, together person anyone in their right mind would want to employ?

Your (VERY) old friend,

Kxx

4

GHOSTS

Women Returners. They sound like the ghosts in some horror movie, don't they? You can practically see the trailer with that grave, apocalyptic, male Hollywood voice booming, 'Women Returners! They're back! Rising from the dead and rejoining the workplace! If only they can escape the Mummy's Curse and rely on someone else to take the lasagne out of the freezer and give Grandma her statins!'

I don't know about ghosts, but some of the women in our Returners group definitely have a haunted look about them. Haunted by the careers they gave up – in some cases so many years ago that they might as well be a different person altogether. Haunted by all those Might Have Beens. Sally, sitting on my right today, used to work for a big Spanish bank in Fenchurch Street. A small, sunken person in an outsize cable-knit cardigan, Sally only has to say Santander or Banco de España in a perfect Spanish accent and you glimpse the spirited, flirtatious person that she must have been twenty years ago, when she was running her own department with a squad of

Juans and Julios doing her bidding. Sally's nostalgia for those days is so acute that sometimes I can't bear to watch the dormouse-bright eyes in that lined face. During the group's first few meetings, Sally was shy, almost painfully reticent, swathed in an unseasonally warm fleece when the rest of us were still in linen trousers and summer dresses.

Kaylie, the group leader – a large, expansive Californian with a wardrobe built exclusively around turquoise and orange (to be fair, it probably worked better in San Diego than it does in East Anglia) – did her best to draw Sally out. By Week Four, Sally volunteered that once her two sons and a daughter had flown the nest (Antonia graduated two years ago; Spanish and History at Royal Holloway), she did think it would be 'good to get back out there'. Sally said she got a part-time job, which she still has, working as a cashier at Lloyds Bank in the scuzz-iest street in the pretty, prosperous market town where we meet.

'You know the one, it's all charity shops and doner kebabs,' Sally said. We nodded politely, but we didn't know it.

Over time, the branch manager began to notice that Sally was unusually competent. (She played down her years in London on her application because she was worried it might look boastful or intimidating and they wouldn't employ her.) The manager gave her more responsibility: totting up at the end of the day, handling foreign currency. They get a lot of Turkish lira conversions because of the kebab shops.

'I suppose it is a bit beneath me,' she told the group, sounding not in the least bit convinced that anything was beneath her, except possibly the ground, 'but I like my colleagues. We have a laugh. It gets me out of the house. And now that Mike is retired . . .'

'You'd like to be at home more?' Kaylie beamed her best facilitator smile.

'Oh, no,' said Sally quickly, 'now that Mike is retired I want to be at home less. Drives me potty having him in my kitchen.'

'I know how you feel,' said Andrea. 'I sometimes think I'll go mad if I don't get out of the house.' Andrea Griffin joined the graduate training scheme of one of the UK's big four accountancy firms straight from university. By the time she was thirty-seven, she'd made partner. Not long after, her husband John had his accident; a lorry smashed into his car on a fogbound M11. Luckily the helicopter was available – it's the same one Prince William pilots now – and they flew him straight to the head injuries unit at St George's. Took John a year to learn to talk again.

'The first words that came back to him were the filthiest swear words you can imagine,' Andrea said. Her freckly chest flushed a little at the thought of her husband, a decent sort who used to say 'Blimey' and 'Well I never!' at moments of great surprise, reduced to a scowling wreck who told his mother-in-law to go fuck herself. The insurance company finally paid up in January, after a ten-year legal battle, and now that they can afford 24/7 care for John, Andrea can relinquish some of her responsibilities. 'Started to think it might be nice to use my brain again,' she said when Kaylie asked us to share what we hoped to get out of the Returners workshop. 'If I've still got a brain,' Andrea laughed. 'The jury's still out on that one. It's all a bit daunting, to be honest.'

The room we meet in is in the modern annexe of the old town library. What it lacks in atmosphere it makes up for in strenuous attempts to remove actual books from what one poster depressingly calls 'The Reading Experience'. Why is everything in here on a screen? I remember how Emily and Ben adored their bedtime stories, then gulped down *Harry Potter*, even making us queue up at midnight outside the local bookshop to buy the latest instalment. Now they are practically soldered to their keyboards. Emily might still pick up a novel from time to time and breeze through seventy pages before something more compelling intervenes – usually a make-up tutorial on YouTube by Zooella or Cruella or someone. She's obsessed with make-up. Ben is wary of anything too long to be read on the screen of a phone.

The decor in here is that folksy Scandinavian look which seems to have taken over all British public spaces. There is a noisy pale-wood floor and uncomfortable, sloping bony chairs with leaf-print cushions and matching pale-wood arms. The coffee from the machine by the entrance is disgusting, so people pick one up from Caffè Nero next door. Sally brings a flask and so does Elaine Reynolds (mum of belfie-tracker Josh). We've been meeting here every Wednesday afternoon for five weeks now. There were fifteen of us to begin with, but two women swiftly decided it wasn't for them and then, a fortnight ago, a third dropped out because her daughter was hospitalised with anorexia after failing to meet her weekly outpatients' target of 0.5 kg weight gain.

'Of course, it doesn't rule out Sophia going to Oxford,' Sadie said, as though there might actually be someone among us who urgently needed reassurance on that score. Sophia was already garlanded with 10 A*s at GCSE, as we'd been told several times, and her mother clearly saw the girl's stint in an eating disorders unit as a minor bump on the road to academic glory, rather than a possible hint that it was precisely that route which had brought about her recent crash.

'They can still sit their exams in there,' Sadie continued. 'There's no problem with that. I'm making sure Soph gets her AS coursework in on time. Compare *Atonement* with *The Go-Between*. It's not exactly Shakespeare, is it? I'm reading both novels, of course, so I can help the poor darling as much as I can.'

Everything about Sadie, from her figure to her dark bobbed hair, from her matching taupe bag and loafers to her South African accent, was clipped, with no unnecessary waste. The person she most reminded me of was Wallis Simpson – immaculate without being in any way appealing. Or human. I found myself wondering what it must be like to have such a controlled and controlling creature as a mother. Looking across the circle, I could see that Sally was having exactly the same thought. She rolled her lips back and forth as if she were setting lipstick on an invisible tissue, and her eyes glistened with what might easily be mistaken for concern, but was actually closer to disdain.

To be perfectly honest, I wasn't sure about joining the Returners. I mean, I've never cared for the lazy assumption that women have shared preoccupations and views, like we're some kind of endangered minority group. There are good, decent and feeling women, sure, millions of them, but there are also Sadies who would leave your child for dead by the side of the road if it meant getting an advantage for her kids. Why do we insist on pretending otherwise? Just because she has ovaries and a vagina (probably steam cleaned), doesn't make Sadie my 'sister', thanks very much.

Like so many of the all-female events that I've attended, there is something mildly apologetic about Women Returners. With no men in the room, we are free to be ourselves, but maybe we are so out of practice that we tend to overshoot and end up giggling like nine-year-olds or, inevitably, talking about the kids we actually have. Women get so easily bogged down in anecdote; instinctive novelists, we make sense of our lives through stories and characters. It's wonderful, don't get me wrong, but it doesn't make us any good at single-mindedness, at shutting out the day-to-day stuff and going for what we want. Imagine a group of men ending up talking about their wife's mother's heart bypass. Never happen, would it?

Today will be different, however, because a man, a well-known employment consultant called Matthew Exley, is here to talk to us about how best to market our skills. 'Call me Matt' is clearly enjoying being the only ram in a flock of ewes. He begins with some research. Studies show, Matt says, that if ten criteria are listed for an advertised job and a man has seven of them, the man would be willing to 'have a go'. By contrast, if a woman has eight, she will say, 'No, I can't possibly apply for the job because I don't meet two of the criteria.'

'Now, ladies, what do we think this is telling us?' Matt beams encouragingly at his flock. 'Yes, Karen?'

'I'm Sharon,' says Sharon. 'It's telling us that women tend to undersell themselves. We underrate our capabilities.'

'Spot on, Sharon, thank you,' says Matt. 'And what else can we deduce? Yes, the blonde lady over there?'

'That men generally assume they'll be good at things they're rubbish at because their experience of the workplace proves that mediocre men are consistently given positions beyond their capabilities, while highly able women have to be twice as good as a man to have any chance of being given a senior position for which they are infinitely better qualified?'

Every so often at Women Returners, I'm sorry to report that a cynical, world-weary and, quite frankly, abrasive voice ruptures the happy bubble of feelgood reinvention and shared sisterhood.

'Ah.' Matt looks to Kaylie for support in dealing with this party pooper.

'C'mon, Katie,' smiles Kaylie valiantly with her too-white teeth. (You guessed it was me, didn't you?) 'I think you're kinda taking all the negatives onboard. We've talked before about how women are tough on themselves. I know how perfectionist you are, Katie. What Matt is trying to say is that we need to give ourselves permission to think that, even if we're not the perfect candidate for a job, then being a seven or eight instead of a ten may be good enough.'

'That's right,' says Matt with obvious relief. 'Your CV doesn't need to be a perfect fit to have a shot at a job.'

'Sorry, but I think what Kate was trying to say . . .' It's Sally speaking now. The group turns with interest to its shyest and most tongue-tied member. 'Correct me if I'm wrong, but I think what Kate was saying is that the reason men have a lot of confidence applying for jobs is because the odds were, and to some extent still are, heavily stacked in their favour. They think they have more chance of succeeding because they actually do. You can't really blame older women for having low self-confidence when that reflects the opinion the world has of us.'

'I hear you, Sally,' says Matt.

(In my experience, 'I hear you' is a phrase used only by those who are completely deaf to any sound but their own voice.)

'But things are much better than they were even five years ago,' he goes on. 'Employers are much more aware of the qualities that women returners can bring to the office. You will all have noticed that work–life balance has moved up the political agenda and many firms are beginning to see that a more, shall we say, enlightened approach to taking on older females, who have taken time out from their careers, may not damage their business. Quite the contrary, in fact!'

'I'm sure you're right,' says Sally uncertainly. 'My friend's daughter took nine months off work from an investment fund with her second baby and no one batted an eyelid. That would have been unheard of when I was at the bank. Even four months' maternity leave . . . Well, your job might still be there when you got back, but someone else would have the title. You might be allowed to assist him. My bank sent me to the Middle East when my boys were very small, to see if I would give up, probably.'

'When I told my boss I was pregnant with my second,' Sharon chips in, 'he went fucking mental. He said, "But, Sharon, sweetheart, you've already had a baby."'

Everyone laughs. The secret, subversive laughter of the servants below-stairs at *Downton Abbey* discussing their masters' funny little ways.

'Listen, guys,' says Kaylie, 'I think Katie is being way too pessimistic. Like Matt says, firms are more open than ever to the idea that activities outside of the office can give you transferable skills. Seriously, the Mum CV is now a big thing in recruitment.'

I look around the circle at the women's eager faces. They nod and smile at Matt, grateful for his assurances that the employment they left during the years of raising children will welcome them back, that the 'skills' of nurturing and running a small country called Home are transferable. Maybe that's true if you've been out of the loop three years, five max. Privately, I think the ones who are in the worst position are those who kept no work going at all, who gave up every last bit of personal independence. When the chicks fly the nest, at eighteen, they take with them their mother's reason for being. And the women turn to look at the men they've lived with for the past twenty-four years and they realise the only thing they have in common any more is the kids, who have just left home. The child-rearing years are so busy, so all-consuming it's easy to ignore the fact your marriage is broken because it's buried

82

under the Lego and the muddy dungarees and the PE bags. Once the kids are gone there's no place for your relationship to hide. It's brutal.

At least my freelance stuff gave me a slender handrail to hold onto in a rapidly changing jobs market. Plus, I'm one of the younger ones here, and even I will have to lie about how old I am to stand a chance of getting back into my industry.

I think of how I felt sitting in Gerald Kerslaw's office with my own 'Mum CV'. Watching his eyes flick down my activities outside the office for the past six and a half years. Work for the school, work for the community, for the church, backbone of society, carer for young and old. I felt small. I felt diminished, irrelevant, unregarded. Worst of all, I felt foolish. Maybe 'Call me Matt' is right and attitudes are changing, but, in my line of business, a forty-nine-year-old who's been out of the game for seven years might as well walk through the Square Mile ringing a bell and shouting, 'Chlamydia!'

Matt asks for one final question and I raise my hand. Bravely, he picks me. 'As ageism is clearly a major problem in the workplace, whether we like it or not, would you ever recommend that those of us who are in our forties, fifties and sixties should lie on our CV?'

His brow puckers, not with genuine thoughtfulness but in that mature frown which men adopt to indicate that they are busy pondering. If he had been wearing glasses he would have pushed them to the end of his nose and looked over them in my direction.

'Lie?' Nervous neigh of laughter. 'No. Although I wouldn't necessarily foreground your age. There's no requirement to write down a date of birth any more. Put it this way, I certainly wouldn't make your age an issue if it doesn't need to be. Or the particular years when you were at school and university;

people can count, you know. Anyway,' (a consoling smile), 'I wish you all the very best of luck.'

I'm putting my card in the machine to pay for the car park, when I feel a hand on my arm. 'I just wanted to say well done in there.' It's Sally the mouse.

'Oh, thank you. You're very sweet, but I was awful. Much too cynical. Kaylie's trying to give us all a boost and there's me sounding off about institutionalised sexism like Gloria Steinem with rabies. Just what everyone needs.'

'You were telling the truth,' Sally says, cocking her head to one side in that intelligent, birdlike way I've noticed.

'Maybe, but who wants the truth? Highly overrated, in my experience. It's just . . . Oh, look, I went to a headhunter in London the other day to see if he could come up with anything for me. It was . . . Well, he made me feel like some hideous old peasant woman turning up to flog goat turds in Fortnum & Mason. It was terrible. Funny thing is, I didn't even want to come to our group in the first place. You know that saying about not wanting to belong to any club that would have you as a member? I thought it was all a bit pathetic. I mean, Women Returners?'

'Revenant,' says Sally.

'Sorry?'

'The French for ghost is *un revenant*, which literally means 'a returner'. One who comes back. As in, from beyond,' she says.

I told her that was spooky. She laughed. She said ghosts generally are spooky. I said, 'No, I meant it's such a coincidence because I was only thinking earlier that returners made us sound like we were back from the dead; I didn't know it was

French for ghost.' She said her French was rusty – shameful really when she had half a degree in it. I said, 'Don't worry, you sound like Christine Lagarde to me.' I said sometimes I felt like the ghost of my former self. There was no way back to that person I used to be. That it was all over for me. 'Not for you, Kate,' she said. And we kept talking and talking, and we would have liked to have gone for tea at some point, but it turned out we both had dogs we had to get back for and then it turned out that we walked our dogs in the same country park and so we went and collected the dogs and walked them on our favourite walk together and sat on our favourite bench at the top of the hill. And that was how Sally Carter became my very dear friend.

5

FIVE MORE MINUTES

7.44 am: 'Mum, have you seen *Twelfth Night*?' Emily looks pale and her hair needs a wash.

'I think you had it in the living room last night, love, when you were doing your homework. Or it could be in that pile on the chair under Lenny's toys. Are you going to take a shower?'

'Haven't got time,' she shrugs, 'got choir practice then we're getting our revision timetable.'

'What, already? You've barely started the course. That's a bit soon?'

'Yeah, I know, but Mr Young said two kids in the year above got Bs last year and they don't want that happening again.'

'Well, you should wash your hair before you go in. Make you feel fresher, sweetheart. It looks a bit . . .'

'I *know*.'

'Em, darling, I'm just trying to . . .'

'I *know, I know*, Mum. But it's like I've got so much on.' As she turns to go out of the door I notice that her school skirt has got tucked in her knickers at the back, revealing a ladder of nasty cuts up her thigh.

'Emily, what's wrong with your leg?'

'S'nothing.'

'You've hurt yourself, darling. It looks horrid. Come here. What happened?'

'*S'nothing.*' She tugs furiously at the back of her skirt.

'What do you mean *nothing*? I can see it's bleeding from here.'

'I fell off my bike, Mum. OK?'

'I thought you said your bike was being mended.'

'Yeah, I rode Daddy's.'

'You rode Bradley Wiggins to school?'

'Not that one. The old, cheaper one. It was in the garage.'

'You fell off?'

'Mmmmmm.'

'What happened?'

'There was gravel on the road. I skidded.'

'Oh, no. And you hurt your poor leg. And you've grazed the other one. Lift your skirt up again so I can see properly. Why didn't you tell me, love? We need to get some Savlon on that. It looks nasty.'

'Please stop, Mum, OK?'

'Just let me take a look. Hold still a minute. Pull the skirt up, I can't see properly.'

'GO A-WAY. JUST STOP. PUHLEEEASE!' Emily lashes out wildly, knocking my glasses off and sending them flying to the floor. I bend down to pick them up. The left lens has popped out of its frame.

'I can't stand it,' Emily wails. 'You always say the wrong thing, Mum. *Always.*'

'What? I didn't say anything, my love. I just want to look

at your leg, darling. Em. Emily, please don't walk out of the room. Emily, please come back here. Emily, you can't go to school without eating anything. Emily, I'm talking to you. EMILY?'

As my daughter exits the house trailing sulphurous clouds of reproach and leaving me to wonder what crime I have committed this time, Piotr enters. He is standing just inside the back door with his bag of tools. I blush to think of him hearing our screaming match and seeing Emily knock my glasses off. I can't believe she actually hit me. She didn't mean to hit me. It was an accident.

'Sorry. Is bad time, Kate?'

'No, no, it's fine. Really. Come in. Sorry, Piotr. It's just Emily had an accident, she fell off her bike, but she thinks I'm making a fuss about nothing.'

Without being asked, he takes the glasses out of my hand, retrieves the missing lens which is on the floor next to Lenny's basket, and begins to work it back into its frame. 'Emily she is teenage. Mum she's always say wrong things, isn't it?'

Despite wanting rather badly to cry, I find myself laughing. 'That's so true. A mother's place is in the wrong, Piotr. Wrong is my permanent address at the moment. Would you like some tea? I've got some proper tea today, you'll be pleased to hear.'

In his new spiritual incarnation, Richard has acquired a wide range of tranquillity teas. Rhubarb and Rosemary, Dandelion, Lemon, Nettle and Manuka Honey, and something in a urine-coloured box called Camomindfulness. On the recommendation of Joely at the counselling centre, in February he presented me with Panax Ginseng, said to be good for hot flushes and night sweats. A thoughtful present although, if you were being picky, perhaps not totally ideal for the red-hot lover's message of Valentine's Day. (After receiving a set of Jamie Oliver saucepans for Christmas I thought we'd reached a low point in the history of Rich's gifts to me, but clearly there is plenty of floor below that to fall through.) It takes a lot to perturb Piotr, whose temperament feels as generous and easy as his countenance, but even he recoiled when I said we had run out of builders' tea and offered him Dandelion instead.

'In my contree, dantyline means wet bed like children's,' he smiled, revealing a mouth of characterful, uneven teeth of the kind that have pretty much died out among the British middle classes.

Piotr's English is bad, yet strangely appealing. I feel no need to correct it, as I do with Ben and Em, because (a) that would be horribly patronising and (b) I love the mistakes he makes because they are so expressive (which I guess is horribly patronising). That's what happens with the kids, isn't it? You correct their errors and their speech gets better and better until, one day, they don't say those funny, sweet things any more. I can't press Rewind and hear Ben say, 'I did go'd fast did I Mummy' or a five-year-old Emily ask if she can come with me to the 'Egg Pie Snake Building' (Empire State sounds so dull by comparison) or have 'piz-ghetti' for dinner. Or tell me, 'I'm not a baby I'm a togg-er-ler.' Sometimes I think I wished away their childhood so life would be easier; now I have the rest of my life to wish it back.

I put water in a saucepan and olive oil and butter in a casserole on the Aga. Kettle not working again while Piotr has the electricity switched off. Methodically, I start preparing the onions, carrots and celery for bolognese, our family's all-purpose comfort food. It's the Marcella Hazan recipe and I know it so well that her quaintly formal words float into my head as I chop. The addition of milk 'lends a desirable sweetness'. Perfectly true, it's the magic ingredient you could never guess.

In the larder – a tiny, pitch-black cupboard leading off the utility room – I grope for tinned tomatoes in the dark and my hand finds a Hammer Horror cobweb. It's the size and shape of a tennis racquet. *Uch*. Fetch some kitchen wipes and start to clean down the slatted wooden shelves.

I always dreamt of having an Aga. Visions of home-baked bread, delicious stews murmuring to themselves on the range and maybe even an orphaned baby lamb being gently brought back to life in the warming drawer. Unclear where I was going to find a lamb, except in the meat aisle of Waitrose, and therefore well past the point of reviving, but the daydream persisted. Now, I realise my Aga fantasy was of the pristine magazine kind that comes equipped with its own Mary Berry. Ours is a malevolent old beast encrusted with the splashed fat of half a century and has only two temperatures: lukewarm and crematorium. You know, I really don't think it likes me. Shortly after we moved in, I put a cauliflower cheese in the top oven; ten minutes later I prised open the heavy door to take a peek and found a petrified forest with these perfect little charred florets like mini oak trees.

Richard, who was cross, hungry and partial to cauliflower cheese, said it looked like one of those art installations that would have a pretentious title like *The Physical Impossibility of Dinner in the Mind of Someone Starving*. It's since become one of his favourite Calamity Kate anecdotes, and I can't help noticing he finds it much funnier when he's telling other people than he did at the time.

Not that I'm in any position to complain. Am still trying to convince Rich that this house was a fantastic buy. We agreed that in order to move to Commuterland, so I could get into London and back every day, we would have to downsize and find a place with lower outgoings. (No way could we afford to buy in the capital, not after a period up North. I checked on Rightmove and our old house, the Hackney Heap, is worth £1.2 million now.) We'd just had an offer accepted on a four-bedroom new-build, convenient for the train station, when I took the agent's advice that I should 'just pop in' and see a 'charming period gem of considerable potential, in need of sensitive updating'.

Fate and the weather conspired against me. It was one of those glittering, glad-to-be-alive days when a bitingly clear cobalt sky makes you feel your soul has left your body and is soaring heavenward. If only it had been raining. Maybe I would have seen that a patchwork of ivy and moss covering three exterior walls, a rickety tiled roof and two chimneys, each the size of a four-by-four, did not, as I preferred to believe, suggest an enchanted castle just waiting to be released from a spell of cruel neglect.

'Exactly how much will it cost to hack through the foliage to free Sleeping Beauty, and what will the brickwork be like underneath once we get her out?' These were not among the questions I asked as I stood on the terrace at the back, marvelling at the honeyed stone in which the house was constructed three centuries ago. The view down the garden was like an Impressionist painting – a vivid splash of green lawn fringed with mascara smudges of pine and beech. I could practically hear the strains of Vaughan Williams's 'The Lark Ascending' as I drank in this quintessentially English scene; the imagined music was so potent it drowned out the whooshing of the nearby M11, which would become a roar once the trees had shed their leaves and we had signed the contract. *Caveat emptor.*

We did go back to check out the new-build property, Rich and I. How bland and cramped it seemed with its specially made, teeny, doll's house furniture (a cynical developer's trick to make the rooms look bigger, or so a designer friend told me). The agent said the developer was prepared to meet us halfway and would pay the stamp duty, such a huge saving that Rich gave a low, appreciative whistle. But I had lost my heart to another and found only fault where there were bargains and benefits to be had. I wanted the period gem with the gracious proportions and the fine old staircase, its mahogany handrail just visible through layers of chipped paint.

The rival agent said that because it was a renovation project which 'very few people have the imagination to take on' (i.e. no one but you is nuts enough to even attempt it), the owner was 'prepared to consider knocking a significant amount off the asking price' (they were desperate to sell, it had been on the market more than a year and there was a grave shortage of suckers prepared to share a bath with a daddy-long-legs and her nineteen children). I was able to clinch the deal with Richard by pointing out that the house was in the catchment area of a superb secondary school. Result! True, some persuasion-sex may have been involved, but I had my dream property, and that was orgasm enough.

Except Richard pretty much hated the house from Day One. He calls it 'Gormenghastly', and not affectionately either. Anything that goes wrong – oh, let me count the ways! – demonstrates that I made a poor decision and causes him to crow in a rather unpleasant manner. On the first evening we spent here, he actually produced a DVD of a Tom Hanks movie called *The Money Pit*, which is about a couple who try to restore a hopelessly dilapidated house. It was funny until I plugged in an electric heater to warm up the freezing sitting room and all the lights fused and the TV went *phffft*.

I wish I could say that I've proved my doubting husband wrong. Despite Piotr's heroic efforts, and almost constant house calls from Polish guys bearing ladders, hammers and saws, every day seems to bring more bad tidings of damp and decay. The financially devastating news of a sagging bathroom floor came in tandem with the emotionally devastating news of a sagging pelvic floor from the person once called my Obs who is now just my Gynae.

'Kate, pan it's burn.'

'Sorry?' Piotr makes me jump. He's right beside me in the larder.

'Cooker it's fire,' he says. 'Careful please.'

I run into the kitchen. The casserole is belching thick smoke. Damn, I forgot. Don't know what I was thinking.

'Roy, really, why didn't you remind me I was heating the oil for the Spag Bol? ROY! We can't keep forgetting things like this. Last week, it was the bath that overflowed.'

I would douse the pan in the sink, but there is no sink any more because Piotr has taken it out to the skip. Besides, isn't there something about not pouring water on boiling oil, or is it the other way around? Grab the casserole and run into the garden where a light drizzle tamps down the sizzle and spit. Before going back indoors to start again, and heat up more oil and butter, I spend a minute drinking in the view. The leaves are particularly lovely this year, shades of fierce apricot and shy primrose from Nature's Autumn Collection that continue to astonish. (*'Roy, please remind me to plant those tulip and daffodil bulbs.'*) Yes, I'm prepared to concede that it might have been better to do the sensible thing and downsize. Not only can we not afford the renovations, until I find a job, I have also used up any remaining capital I had in my marriage. In some ways, a relationship is like a savings account: during the good times, you both pay in, and in the lean times there's enough to see you through. Right now, I'm heavily overdrawn.

I should have listened to Richard. (*Perhaps you should tell him that, Kate; climbing down never came easy, did it? Stupid pride again.*) I can't really explain why I made us buy the house except that something in me railed against the thought of life contracting, getting smaller instead of bigger. Before you know it, you're in a wheelchair-access bungalow in sheltered accommodation wearing incontinence pants. I'm already doing a little wee every time I sneeze. Sorry, but I did not want to 'go gentle into that good night'. I wanted to take on one more challenge, if only to prove that I'm still alive and capable of thinking big.

In the kitchen, Piotr reunites me with my mended glasses, but not before breathing on them and wiping them with a proper, old-fashioned handkerchief, which he produces with a conjuror's flourish from the pocket of his jeans. I haven't seen a laundered handkerchief like that since my grandfather died. As he leans in to place the specs on my face, I get a pungent wash of cigarettes and sawn wood. I'm so happy when he's here because it means we're making progress. I'll definitely have a kitchen in time for Christmas. And because he lends – *'what was it again, Roy?'* – that's it: a desirable sweetness.

Kate to Emily

Hi sweetheart. Hope you're OK. Just been making you Spag Bol for dinner. So sorry about your accident and your poor leg. Let's cuddle up tonight and watch some *Parks and Rec*?
  Love you, Mum

Emily to Kate

I'm good!!! Can Lizzy & some friends come over? Don't worry bout me 🏃🖼 Love u xx

1.11 pm: It is a truth universally acknowledged, that a single woman over thirty-five in search of a mate must never reveal her

94

age in a dating profile. At least, that's what Debra tells me over lunch.

I've just confessed to my oldest friend that I'm lying about my age to try and get a job. Deb reports that she does the same if she wants to get a man.

'Seriously, you never give your true age?'

'Never, ever *ever*,' says Deb. Stabbing miserably at the last rocket leaf on her plate, she picks it up and pops it in her mouth before licking the dressing from her finger. We both ordered salad and sparkling water, no bread, because our thirty-year college reunion, which for so long felt a safe distance away, is approaching fast. But now Deb starts doing urgent, smiley semaphore at the waiter, indicating she wants wine.

'What if you look amazing for your age?' I ask.

She gives a bitter laugh – a harsh, cawing sound I can't remember hearing before. 'That's even worse. If you look good for your age you'll probably be vain enough to give it away. So you arrange to meet up, he takes you for dinner, you have a few glasses of wine, candles, it's getting romantic and he says, "God, you're gorgeous", and you're feeling relaxed and prob-ably a bit drunk and you really like him and you think "this one's sensitive, not shallow like some of the others", so you get carried away and you say, "Pretty good for fifty, huh?"'

'Well, it's true you do look fabulous,' I say. (She is terribly changed since the last time we met, on my birthday. She looks so red and puffy. It's a drinker's face, I realise for the first time. Oh, Deb.)

'Doesn't matter,' Debra says, wagging a cautionary finger. 'So the guy does a charming, funny double-take and he gives a wolf whistle and he agrees that you are, indeed, incredibly well-preserved for fifty. No one could possibly guess. I mean, Totally Amazing. Then you see it. The panic rising behind his eyes. And he's thinking, "Omigod, how did I not notice that? The lines around her mouth, the scrawny neck. She *definitely* looks fifty. And I'm only forty-six, so she's an older woman. Plus, she lied on her profile". Oh, waiter, waiter, sorry, can I get a glass of wine here? Sauvignon Blanc. Join me, Kate, please?'

'I can't, I've got Women Returners later.'

'Then you definitely need alcohol. Two glasses of white, please. Large? Yes, thanks.'

'And then what happens?'

'And then he throws you back in the sea and goes fishing for a younger one.'

'Well, at least you know he's not the man for you if he's going to reject you just because of your age.'

'Oh, Kate, Kate, my sweet deluded girl, they're *all* like that.' Another mirthless cackle. Deb reaches across the table and taps me affectionately on the nose, which hurts a bit. It's the part of the bone where Ben bit me when he was taking his first steps. I knelt down to catch him in case he fell and he staggered towards me like a tiny drunk, tried to kiss my mouth and got my nose instead. A tiny, tooth-shaped scar marks the spot.

'What you don't understand, darling, in your married bliss with Ricardo, is that when guys get to our age they hold all the cards.'

(It's the perfect opening to tell her how bad things are between me and Richard, but I don't, not yet. I can hardly bear to tell myself.)

Deb knocks back her wine with a complaint about the small measures, then reaches out her hand and pours most of my untouched one into her own glass. 'A man of forty-eight isn't interested in a woman the same age. Why would he be when he can maybe pick up someone in the twenty-nine to thirty-six category? A fifty-year-old man can still tick, "May want children one day". What can I tick? "May need a hysterectomy if I keep bleeding like a stuck pig"? Anyway, cheers, my dear!' She clinks both glasses together, hands me my almost empty one and takes several gulps from her own.

I've known Debra since our third week at college when we got chatting in the bar and found out that we shared the same boyfriend. We should have been sworn enemies, but we decided we liked each other much better than the boy, who was doubly dumped and would forever after be known as Two-Time Ted.

I was bridesmaid when Deb married Jim. I was godmother to their first child and chief mourner at the divorce after Jim went off with a twenty-seven-year-old broker from Hong Kong when Felix was six and Ruby was three. Deb feels guilty because Felix suffers with anxiety and blames himself for the break-up of the marriage. He has a lot of trouble fitting in at school and Deb keeps moving him (three times in the last five years), probably because it's easier to believe the school's the problem than your child. Deb often refers to Felix's ADHD diagnosis as if it explains everything. I think (though would never say) that, with Jim not around, she found it hard to control the boy's behaviour and she spent a fortune on PlayStations and every gizmo you can imagine to keep him happy while she worked. I was horrified, last Christmas, at the size of the TV Deb gave Felix, so much bigger than their family one. She spends almost nothing on herself. Felix, now seventeen, looks exactly like Jim, which can't help. Deb loves her son although, increasingly, I suspect she doesn't like him very much.

'Go on, tell me about "Women Returners", then?' I can practically hear the ironic quotation marks Deb puts around my support group.

'I know you think I don't need it.'

97

'You don't need it, Kate. You just need to get yourself out there and stop sublimating all that ambition of yours into renovating some crazy old house.'

'I thought I was bringing life back to a period gem of considerable potential in need of sensitive updating.'

'Is that you or the house, darling?'

'Both. Can't you tell?'

She laughs properly, like herself this time, a warm, generous sound which is incongruous in this fashionable palace of steel and glass. I love Deb's laugh; it reminds me of so many times we've shared.

'Suit yourself,' she says. 'Can't think of anything worse than sitting in a room with a lot of women moaning that they're past it and nobody will employ them. Do you want coffee? How many calories in a flat white, do you reckon?'

(Hang on, I read that the other day. Paging Roy. *"Roy, can you please get me the number of calories in a flat white? Full fat and semi-skimmed. Roy, hello? You're not allowed a lunch break by the way. Being my memory valet is a full-time job.'*)

Last time I spoke to Richard about finding a position at a good firm in London, he said, 'It'll kill you doing that journey twice a day. You're not as young as you were. Why don't you find something local like Debra did?'

Is that really what he wants for me? Deb quit her job at one of the top London law firms a couple of years after Jim shacked up with the Asian Babe (who is friendly, tactful, sweet with the kids and super-bright – basically your total nightmare). Felix had become obsessive about not having peas too close to the sweetcorn or ketchup on his plate, and he bit any nanny who forgot this diktat. Finding a form of childcare that was happy to be bitten on a regular basis proved impossible. 'I did not *give up*, Kate, I bloody well surrendered to the inevitable,' Debra booms when she's had too many, which is quite often lately. In midlife, all the women I know, apart from the 'My Body is a Temple' high priestesses, are intimates of Count Chardonnay and his cheeky sidekick Pinot Grigio. Every day, around 6.35 pm, when habit sends me to get wine out of the fridge, I think 'Empty calories!' and sometimes I am good and listen to that health warning, but other times it's easier, and kinder somehow, to grant myself admission to the buzzy warmth and instant sense of well-being. 'God, I hate it when they call it giving up work,' Deb always says when she's onto her third glass.

Me too. So, the legendary, beautiful redhead (think face of Julianne Moore, curves of Jennifer Lopez) with the Cambridge First, on track to become a partner in a London firm earning gazillions, is now festering in a solicitor's office above Hot Stuff Indian restaurant in the high street of a provincial town, resolving leylandii disputes for homicidal octogenarians and growing big and blowsy from drowning her sorrows. All of Deb's recent emails begin, 'Shoot me!'.

I need something better than that. Don't I?

Debra is growing louder and more belligerent, so I change the subject and tell her about Emily's belfie. Our disasters are small gifts we can give to our friends who suffer because they believe our lives are easier than their own.

'Oh, they're all doing it,' Deb snorts. 'Sexting. Some kid in Ruby's year got himself arrested. Sent a pic of his willy to a girl aged fourteen. Huge hoo-ha at the school – said he was guilty of child abuse or something ridiculous. He's been suspended, poor thing. The girl didn't even complain. Teacher saw her laughing and sharing the dick pic with her friends; now it's this huge deal because she's underage.'

'I think I'm pretty broad-minded,' I say, 'but can you imagine?'

'Very easily, darling. If you give kids phones that do all that naughty stuff why wouldn't they? It's just too tempting. I mean, *I* have.'

'You've done what? Deb. No. You *haven't*. Please tell me you haven't.'

'Only knockers.' She smiles and cups her breasts in her hands, thrusting them upwards in her straining blouse till they look like two quivering panna cotta. 'Getting your tits out, that's pretty entry-level stuff for online dating, Kate darling. Consider yourself lucky you're off the market and don't have to display your wares to new suitors.'

'I feel sorry for them,' I say, suddenly realizing how helpless and angry I feel about the belfie. 'Emily and Ruby, they're supposed to be the freest most liberated generation of girls who ever lived. Then, just as equality's in sight, they decide to spend every minute slapping on make-up and posing for selfies and belfies like they're courtesans in some *fin de siècle* brothel. What the hell happened?'

'Dunno, beats me.' Deb tries to suppress a loud burp and fails. 'Shall we get the bill?' She turns and flags down a scurrying waiter. 'I do know Ruby goes out wearing next to nothing then, if some poor guy wolf whistles at her, suddenly it's, "Oh, no, it's sexual harassment." I tried to tell her that the male brain is programmed to respond to certain parts of the female anatomy. Most boys like Felix and Ben can act in a civilised fashion, if they're properly brought up by women like you and me, but enough boys won't be civilised and then you're in big trouble because, surprise fucking surprise, rapist Rob hasn't read your student guide to inappropriate touching.'

We fall silent for a moment. 'The kids say I'm from the past,' I say.

'We *are* from the past, thank God,' Deb booms. 'I'm bloody

glad we grew up before social media, darling. At least when we went home from school we were by ourselves, or with family who treated us like part of the furniture. There was no one poking us every ten seconds to admire their perfect bloody life. Imagine having every little bitch who was hateful to you at school joining you in your bedroom via your phone. I felt crap enough about myself already. I didn't need an audience, thanks very much.'

'Probably every generation of parents must feel like this,' I say cautiously. It's been so much on my mind, but I haven't tried to put it into words before. 'It's just that this . . . this . . . this *gulf* between us and the kids, their world and the one we grew up in, it's . . . I don't know, Deb, it's all happened so quickly. Everything's changed and I don't think we've even begun to understand what's going on. Or what it's going to do to them. How is Ben supposed to learn empathy for other people when he spends half his life carrying out drive-by shoot-ings in some virtual-reality world? Did I tell you I found out Emily actually downloaded something to help her bypass the parental controls on their devices?'

Typically, Deb is delighted, not appalled. 'Genius! She sounds a highly resourceful woman, just like her mummy.'

It's time to go. She has drained my wine glass and we've argued over the bill. (Can't remember who paid last time. I ask Roy, but he's still busy looking up the number of calories in a flat white.)

As the guy by the door hands us our coats, I ask Deb to be honest with me. 'Do you think I can pass for forty-two?'

She grins. 'God, yes, no problem. I'm thirty-six, darling. If I ever bring a boyfriend to meet you we need to get our stories straight, OK? Or he'll think "how come these two were in the same year at university and there's a six-year age difference?"

101

Now, you be honest with me, Kate. Do you think I can get away with thirty-six?'

(No. I don't. Whatever thirty-six looks like, Deb is no longer it, and neither am I.)

'Course you can. Never better. Love what you've done to your hair.'

Debra is halfway down the street when she turns and yells at me: 'College reunion! Don't forget, I'm going to be two stone lighter.'

'And fifteen years younger!' I shout back, but the traffic drowns out my reply and she is gone.

5.21 pm: Just had a lovely long walk with Lenny to shake off the Women Returners meeting. He was desperate to go out when I got back from lunch; now he's fast asleep and lying on his back in his basket by the Aga, all four paws wide apart, fluffy white tummy unprotected. Something almost unbearably touching about an animal's utter trustingness. No sign of Richard. Ben's got football, but I'm sure Em said she was having friends over.

Upstairs, I find three girls sitting on Emily's bed in complete silence, heads bent over their mobiles like they're trying to decode the meaning of the *I Ching*. One is Lizzy Knowles, daughter of Cynthia and hateful sharer of the belfie; the other – pale, pretty, auburn – is Izzy, I think.

'Hello, girls. Why don't you, you know, have a nice chat? Face to face with eye contact,' I say, peering round the door at this eerie dumb-show. My tone is only very lightly mocking. Emily looks up and shoots me her special 'You'll have to forgive my mother, she's mentally impaired' glare.

'We *are* chatting. We're *texting*,' she hisses.

I feel like Charles Darwin observing finches on the Galapagos

Islands. Where is all this communication without speaking going to end? My great-great-grandchildren will be born with prehensile texting thumbs, no vocal cords and zero capacity to read human facial expressions. I am struggling to see any of this as evolution for our species, if evolution means progress, but at least Em isn't by herself. Whatever friction the belfie caused in the peer group must have been fixed. At least, that's what I hope. I tell the girls there's Spag Bol downstairs if they want it. Only Lizzy responds. 'Thanks, Kate, we'll be down later,' she says in the coolly condescending manner of Lady Mary Crawley addressing Mrs Patmore, the *Downton Abbey* cook. I give Lizzy my best and most ingratiating smile; my daughter's fragile happiness is in that girl's hands.

5.42 pm: By the time Ben gets in, I've put carrot sticks and hummus on the kitchen table for him to eat. Piotr has removed all the old worktops; it's like living in a shed, but it should be over soon. Ben grunts, ignores the healthy snack, gets some crisps from the cupboard (who bought those?) and disappears into the living room. A few minutes later, I hear the voice of another boy in there. Where did he come from?

5.53 pm: 'Benjamin, dinner time.'
  'Ben? *Now*, please. Spaghetti's ready.'
  'Five more minutes. We're nearly at half-time.'
  'Who is?'
  'We are.'
  'Who's we?'
  'Me and Eddie.'
  'When did he come round? I didn't hear anyone come in.'
  I walk into the living room, adopting the voice of maternal sternness. 'You know the rule, Ben. If you want your friends to—'

Ben is alone, hunched on the sofa, clutching a handset, thumbs a blur. On the TV, someone in red takes a corner. Players rise in mayhem, the ball goes in, the crowd explodes and Ben keels over sideways as if shot, laughing into a cushion. Other cackles answer him, from nowhere; I recognise the voice of Eddie, saying, 'That's *sick*,' but I can't tell where it's coming from.

'Is that real?' I ask, genuinely not knowing whether it's a football match onscreen, with actual swearing fans telling the referee to fuck off, or whether it's millions of digital dots. Not quite sure how real I am myself, most days. Maybe I should get someone to design a digital me, who gets on with cooking dinner, ordering shower tiles and all the boring jobs no one notices I'm doing, while the real Kate can concentrate on the life I really want, with time on my nicely manicured hands, firming up the abdominals and the plunging pelvic floor, and much less need to swear.

'Kind of.'

'Where's Eddie?'

'At home, Mum, don't be stupid.'

'Please don't call me stupid, Benjamin. Your real dinner is on the table and it's getting cold.'

'OK. Five more minutes.'

'It was five minutes ten minutes ago.'

'Extra time. Maybe penalties. I can't pause it. We'll lose the whole game.'

I give up. Emily is upstairs with friends and they're not speaking. Ben is downstairs speaking with friends, but they're not here. They're miles away, in another part of town. The kids are right: I am from the past. But they are from some Mad Max, post-apocalyptic future where mankind has dispensed with the civilities and physical interaction of all previous centuries. It scares me, it really does, but trying to wean them off their screen addiction seems futile. Like switching off the wind or the rain. If there's a heaven, and my kids ever get there, their first question to St Peter will be, 'What's the password?'

Hunger finally draws Ben to the table, where he tucks in with gratifying enthusiasm. I love to watch my boy eat his favourite meal; it must be some atavistic thing. Between mouthfuls of spaghetti, which he shovels in rather than twirling on a fork – the Battle for Table Manners has been lost – he explains that upstairs Emily and her friends are scrolling through Facebook and Instagram, sharing any videos or photos that they like. Talking is strictly optional in that process, apparently. It means showing each other something someone else has said, written, or photographed, not forming their own original thoughts or stories. I can't help thinking of Julie and me creating a whole universe in our bedroom with just Lego and a single Sindy doll.

'You do meet some people IRL,' Ben says. 'Is there any more Parmesan?'

'I'll get it. What's IRL?'

'Mu-um, you know IRL.'

'I don't, sorry.'

'In Real Life.'

'I see. In real life?'

'Yeah, but mainly it's not IRL 'cos basically you're like online the whole time.'

'How about school? Is school IRL?'

'You're not supposed to have phones in class,' Ben admits cautiously, 'but people do. Basically, that's what social life is like now for my generation.' (I've never heard him come out with anything so philosophical or grown-up before. I didn't know he even knew the word 'generation'. Result! Must stop thinking of him as seven.)

As he's leaving the table, Ben says did I know that the boys at school gave Emily the Rear of the Year Award because of the pic of her bum going viral, and she had to go to the nurse because she threw up in assembly?

No, I did not know.

9.37pm: Bedroom is dark, but my daughter's face is illuminated by her phone. She is scrolling through photos. There are so many of them, an immense number, screen after screen. Up closer, I see they are nearly all selfies; in none of them is she smiling. She's making that weird duckface, the one all the girls pull now. Halfway between a pout and a pucker, it makes her lips look huge, outsized in her face. And she sucks in her cheeks – a come-hither, glamour-model pose. Emily is constantly watching these online make-up tutorials; she's got really skilled at it, much better than I am actually. But it does look like she's painting an older, more sophisticated woman onto that sweet, heart-shaped face.

I really dislike the selfies, this gallery of narcissism, and the way Em stares at them so avidly, as if she were an addict and the drug is herself. In my mother's family album at home there are only three or four snaps of me at Emily's age: one with Julie on holiday in Colwyn Bay; one as a bridesmaid in a too-tight, fuchsia satin dress (I'd sprouted breasts between the fitting and the wedding); one of me and my dad by the veg patch in the back garden, him stripped to the waist and grinning at the camera, as devilishly handsome as Errol Flynn, and me prim and awkward beside him in a knitted tank top over a cheesecloth shirt with an awful straight fringe and National Health specs (you'd never think we were related). Emily takes more photos of herself in a single week than exist of me from half a lifetime. It makes me deeply uneasy, though I know I'll get my head bitten off if I say anything.

'Ooooh, you look so pretty. Look at you, gorgeous girl!'

Em shrugs away the compliment, turning on her side and pulling the duvet up over her shoulder.

'Is everything OK at school, love? You know I got the son of this nice lady in my Women Returners group to take your belfie off the Internet. Josh Reynolds. He's a computer genius; he was at your school ten years ago. He says he's zapped all the ones he could find.'

'Please don't, Mum.'

'I know you don't want to talk about it, love. I understand. I just want you to know that Josh is going to block the belfie if anyone ever tries to share it again.'

'Didn't tell Dad?'

'No, of course I didn't.'

I can see Em's shoulders start to heave under the duvet.

'Oh, darling, it's OK. Don't cry.' Climbing on the bed next to her, I stroke her wet face. 'What is it? Is it the belfie? Have people been mean to you?'

'No. Just I'm really really stressed, Mummy. School's so hard. I'm not the cleverest, I'm not the prettiest, I'm not the sportiest. I'm not the anythingest.'

'Oh, sweetheart. You *are* good at things, you know you are. So good at Music and English. It's natural to feel like that. And the girls came round today, didn't they? And you're all going to Taylor Swift, that'll be so nice. Did you give Lizzy the cheque?'

She nods. 'We can't afford it.'

'Course we can afford it. We're just being a bit careful until Mummy finds a job, that's all.'

She rolls over and buries her face in my neck. 'Sorry I knocked your glasses off, Mum.'

'Doesn't matter, love. I was just worried you'd hurt yourself, that's all. I know I was being a nuisance. Is your leg better now?'

'S'fine.'

'Can I have a look?'

'Noooo.' Her body stiffens and she jerks away again.

'OK, OK. But let me know if you need any cream to put on it? Oh, look who's here! Baa-Sheep.'

Emily's beloved companion – she carried him around by his right arm for her first three years on Earth – is definitely showing signs of age. His white fleece is now a smutty grey, though, thankfully, Baa-Sheep's power to comfort is undiminished. I tuck the toy next to her face; she kisses him and I kiss her. Oh, help. All the problems she had when she was little, they seem like child's play now.

'Good night. Sleep tight.'

'Don't let the bedbugs bite,' Emily whispers.

11.01 pm: Am shattered, but so much to do before I take myself off to bed. Get Ben's football kit out of the washing machine and put it in the dryer, ready for the morning. At least he managed to bring a pair of socks home this time, that's something, although the name tapes reveal that one sock belongs to a different boy – a giant by the look of it. I think of Joe Barnes's mum out there somewhere, washing my Ben's odd sock with the same wry shrug.

I let Lenny out into the garden for a final wee. This takes a while because he loves being out at night; maybe his sense of smell is heightened? I must ask Sally; she knows that kind of thing. (*'Roy, please please can you remind me to plant those bulbs?'*) The dog is following one of his urgent scent trails around the containers on the patio then breaking into a run as he gets to the lawn beyond. I soon lose sight of him; all that my eyes can make out is the distant silhouette of three Scots pines and a single glimmering silver birch that looks like a fork of lightning against the pewter sky.

'Lenny, LENNY!' I call and call, scanning the dark lawn for a flicker of movement. 'Lenny, don't do this to me, please. I've got enough on my plate with your sister.' (Do I really think of Lenny as Emily's naughty little brother? I'm afraid I probably do.) Oh, please God, let him come back. I can't face Lenny getting lost, not on top of everything else.

Take deep gulp of cold air and try to whistle. So much for Lauren Bacall's 'Just whistle'; there's no 'just' about whistling in my experience. Lenny is a lot less biddable than Humphrey Bogart and has a fascination with the river on the far side of the wood at the bottom of our garden. I purse my lips and make a feeble peeping sound. Just then, Lenny is at my feet, an old tennis ball in his mouth hung about with tendrils of weed and drool. Hugely pleased with himself, his tail thumping a personal round of applause.

'Oh, good boy. Clever boy! We'll get Emily sorted, won't we, boy? Everything's going to be all right.'

Midnight: Rich is fast asleep: claimed he rode twelve miles tonight. The bassoon section of the Snore Orchestra is warming up nicely, which isn't ideal background music for me to drop off. I plug my phone in to charge and am just about to flick the Ringer Silent switch when a sweet-sounding chord announces a new email has landed. I recognise the name of the sender, a contact from my City days. That's strange. Wonder why she's getting in touch now?

From: Miranda Cullen
To: Kate Reddy
Subject: Hello stranger

Hi Kate,

Long time no see. I was in NYC last week and I bumped into Candy Stratton at a women's networking thing. She said you were looking for a job? She gave me your email. Funnily enough, I had lunch with someone today who said her friend was going on maternity leave from Edwin Morgan Forster of all places! New name, new building, new staff, but same old, same old basically. It's marketing, business development, bit of admin. Too junior for you but might be a way in? I think Maggie said the person you need to contact in HR is a Claire Ashley. Worth a try?

Good luck, Miranda x

There are 153 calories in a flat white made with semi-skimmed milk (214 in full-fat variety). You need to walk forty minutes to burn 153 calories. Roy gives me this information about ten hours after I drank the coffee. He needs to speed up.

6

OF MICE AND MENOPAUSE

Today is my seventh session at the gym this week. Even God got to rest on the seventh day, but God was only trying to create the world, not restore a middle-aged female body to a state of battle readiness. I'd like to see how long that would take Him.

What can I tell you? Everything hurts. I have pain in parts where I didn't know I had parts. But this is a good thing. Finding the old me, the leaner, keener, meaner me, within this sad and sagging sack is the object of the exercise, and, boy, am I exercising. When Conor, my trainer, said we would be doing Tabitha, I thought, 'Oh, that sounds nice. Maybe some cat-like stretches (tabby cat, I suppose)?' Turned out it was Tabata, some new Japanese fitness torture where you do a series of exercises eight times for twenty seconds with ten seconds' rest in between.

The worst is the lunges, where you have to bend one knee and stretch the other leg out behind you in a kind of masochist's curtsey. Conor's instruction to 'lay on the floor' sounds relaxing, but I now realise that that is code for stomach work, even more hellish than the lunges, if such a thing were possible.

'Pill your billy bitten to your spain, Kite.' (It's a New Zealand accent, you need to hear it.)

I'm trying, I'm trying. My belly button has not connected with my spine for many years. In fact, the pregnant Lycra bulge I see when I survey the length of my stomach from the supine position strongly suggests that the two named body parts may no longer be in the same postal district.

Conor is great, though. A Kiwi of few words, he is excellent at ignoring my panted excuses and yelps of anguish. Every morning, he says a combination of three things: 'Awesome', 'You are in the zone' and 'Set your own goals and I'll help you get there.' My goal is to be able to climb successfully out of the driver's seat of my car when every single muscle is screaming, 'You must be fucking kidding me!' On the plus side, it can't be long before I qualify for a blue disability parking badge.

All of the above is in preparation for my interview on Thursday. Claire Ashley, head of Human Resources at EM Royal, as Edwin Morgan Forster is now called, said they were 'very interested' in considering me for the position and thanks so much for my email. (How many times have I read and reread Claire's three-line email, examining it for any nuances I may have missed?) Alternately, I tell myself not to get too excited (it's not a great job) then I get excited (it's a job!). A rather lowly marketing position trying to bring in new business, that's pretty much what Miranda said in her email, and at my old investment management firm of all places, but an opening, nonetheless.

Somewhere, a heavy, glass door sighs in its airlock and a

woman approaching fifty sprints to get her fingers in the gap before it closes.

7.48 am: Back from the gym. Absolute agony and, thanks to lunges, now walking with thighs splayed apart like John Wayne in a gunfight. Even squatting down to sit on the loo is excruciating; will soon have to pee standing up. Take a shower, as hot as I can bear, to soothe angry muscles. Decide that I haven't left enough time to go to the hairdresser to get my colour done *and* fit in a leg wax before the interview. So will have to shave legs myself, for the first time in yonks, risking the wrath of beauty therapist Michelle, who believes that self-shaving is the work of the devil and promotes rampant hair growth. I locate my long-lost Ladyshave under the sink and scream. Has a pirate been in my bathroom? The head is clogged with a clump of dense black hairs. A whole beard's worth. Trust me, there are few sights more disturbing than unknown hairs in your shaver.

Richard appears at bathroom door in a new towelling bath robe and asks what I'm making such a fuss about. I say that my shaver has been abused by werewolves.

Rich laughs lightly before explaining that the culprit is none other than himself.

'You used *my* shaver. How about using *your* shaver?'

'Not for my face, darling,' Rich says, pointing downwards. Dear God. My husband's legs look like chicken drumsticks – deathly, almost bluish, pale skin with dark dots where the hairs used to be.

'You shaved your *legs*?' For a second, I wonder if this heralds the start of Rich transitioning to a woman. Honestly, at this moment nothing would surprise me.

'Marginal gains,' says my husband.

Apparently, some study has shown that the aerodynamic

113

improvement offered by hairless legs could save five seconds in a 40 k bike race ridden at 37 kph or something. Plus, if he falls off, it's easier to treat the wound.

For some reason, Rich thinks this explanation will be reassuring. His enthusiasm for cycling seems to be moving beyond the worryingly obsessive into something unhinged. It's only when my smooth-legged spouse has left the bathroom that I realise something else. I've been naked during our whole conversation and this has had no noticeable effect on him or the front of his new bathrobe. None whatsoever. What, not even a flicker of interest from my old friend who used to dance with hope if even a hint of areola peeped out of my own dressing gown?

From: Candy Stratton
To: Kate Reddy
Subject: Sex
Hi hon, just checking you got the testosterone patches? Trust me, they're the best. All that perimenopausal crap will go away. Put some lead in your pencil as you get back to the office. It works for the guys, right?
Bonus is you don't have to join all those fifty-year-olds queuing at the doctors to get hormone pussaries to keep them juices flowing!
XXO C
PS I meant pessaries, but I kinda like pussaries. Whaddya think – shall I apply for a patent?

Yes, I did get the testosterone patches from Candy. She sent them by Fedex as soon as she heard I'd got an interview. A typically generous and crazy gesture. The unopened yellow box with the More Mojo label and a picture of an ecstatic Cindy

Crawford type standing on a perfect white American beach sporting a perfect white sweater and a full keyboard of Steinway teeth is in the drawer next to the furious old Aga. Every time I yank open the drawer (broken) to pull out a wooden spoon, I see 'Cindy' beaming at me. 'Get your mojo back!' begins the small print. 'Small transparent patches worn on the skin could help with a range of problems, including depression, anxiety, persistent tiredness, reduced sex drive, poor sense of well-being and loss of confidence.'

Is that all? How about raising teenage boys from the dead in time for school, training a dog not to chew your newly upholstered sofa, tiptoeing round a stressed-out daughter, paying a builder to discover yet more intractable problems in your decrepit old house, oh, and grabbing the attention of a husband who is more hairless than a Thai ladyboy and no longer gets erect at the sight of his wife's naked breasts. Can you help with that, Mojo Cindy?

I actually flinched when I first opened Candy's parcel and saw all of my symptoms written down like that. Am I really such a cliché? The middle-aged mammal who once had a tiger in her tank and now has a slightly hesitant vole.

The thought of all those hormones going out like the tide, leaving my body arid and dried out. *Uch.* 'Barren' was the word my grandmother used when a woman couldn't get pregnant. Such a cruel word, 'barren' – biblical in its harshness. Like a land that can't be tilled. Like a seed that can't be sown. You don't think about being fertile when you are fertile, do you? Not once in the past thirty-five years did I wake up and think, 'Yay, I'm fertile!' Periods were a monthly chore to be got through, a headache in every way – often a skull-splitting migraine in my case, just like my mum had – and the cue for frequent outbursts. I was a pre-menstrual monster, flying into a rage if someone so much as dropped a spoon on a tiled floor. Sudden loud noises I found particularly intolerable. What bliss to be free of all that dumb biology. And yet and yet . . . Poor sense of well-being? Check. Weight gain? Sadly. Depression? No. No, I'm just tired, that's all. Reduced sex drive?

What sex drive? Signals from down below are now so intermittent it's like one of those black-box flight recorders lost on the bottom of the Pacific Ocean. Teams of men with advanced radar systems could be sent out to locate my libido and never be seen again. Come to think of it, when did Richard and I last have sex?

Oh, please no. It couldn't be, could it? Yup. It was New Year's Eve. Another cliché. Starting the year as we meant to go on, except we didn't – go on, that is. Rich never stopped wanting to but, eventually, he stopped trying because whenever he moved onto my side of the bed I hardly gave him a warm welcome. Didn't feel so much as a bat-squeak of desire. What ever happened to that magic, electrical connection between lips and loins?

'As long as there's nothing wrong in That Department, a marriage will survive,' Barbara, my mother-in-law, boomed at me one day in Ladies' Underwear in M&S. I remember laughing like a fiend, so preposterous was the idea that Rich and I would ever have problems in That Department. I would never have believed that my young, hungry body would close the department and shut up shop altogether.

So back in June, six months since I'd last had sex, I went to the doctor like all the dried-up lady hags Candy mentioned in today's email. I'd never seen that particular doctor before. She was wearing one of those stripy, boxy Breton tops that suit no one, except possibly a Breton fisherman. She stared at the screen for some time before saying, 'You're forty-nine? Periods?'

'Yes. I mean intermittently. None for a couple of months then one or two. Then none again.'

'Perfectly normal at your age. When did your mother have her menopause?'

'Not quite sure.'

'Is she still alive?'

'Yes. Yes, very much so.'

'Better ask her. So any discomfort during intercourse?'

'Er, well, we haven't tried for a while.' Embarrassed laughter. 'But I don't think so, no.'

'*Tch tch tch.*' The doctor clucked her tongue and I believe she may have wagged her finger at me like a teacher whose pupil has failed to complete their coursework. She turned to the computer and started typing. 'You do know what they say, Mrs Reddy? Use it or lose it.'

Wednesday, 3.15 pm: Sometimes, when Kaylie is in the middle of one of her tooth-rottingly sweet Hallmark-card homilies to our Women Returners meeting, I amuse myself by going round the circle and planning makeovers for all the members of the group. Elaine Reynolds, for instance. Nice face, good bones, but needs to lose the straggly, salt 'n' pepper hair halfway down her back, and get a decent cut. She thinks that long hair, probably much the same since student days, keeps her youthful but, sadly, beyond a certain point it has the opposite effect. I can imagine not wanting to ask the hairdresser to cut it off, though – we're at an age when hair comes out in scary amounts if you just run your hand through it. Or maybe that's just me. I've given up my bedtime brushing ritual in the unscientific hope that the hair that's still there will stay put if I don't disturb it.

I remember my wonderful friend Jill Cooper-Clark telling me that she could put up with the cancer and the mastectomy;

it was the loss of her auburn crowning glory that was truly devastating. Jill, who was married to Robin – he was my boss back then – will have been dead eight years next spring. She is often in my thoughts, probably more so now because she gave up her career to take care of Robin and the boys and was thinking of going back full-time when she found the lump. Dear Robin is retired now, but still doing some trustee work in the Channel Islands. Come to think of it, Jill would have been forty-nine when she got the diagnosis; a death sentence, really. The cancer spread like a forest fire; there was no stopping it. If force of character alone were enough to survive cancer, she would be alive now. Jill is one of those people you carry in your heart, and time and death don't change that; maybe that chamber of the heart just gets more crowded as you get older.

'Now, maybe Kate would like to share with us her hopes and her strategies for her interview tomorrow? We are all so excited for you, Katie.'

Kaylie is looking at me with that same bright expectation I see in Lenny's eyes when he knows I am eating toast and a crusty corner will soon be coming his way – because his mistress thinks that if she gives a corner to the dog she won't, technically, have eaten any toast. Normally, I am highly allergic to our leader's Californian can-do credulousness, but this afternoon I feel strangely touched, tearful even, as Kaylie and all the other women in the group smile and murmur encouragement.

Our group's only successes so far are Janice, who, before our course really got going, was accepted onto an accountancy firm's returners' scheme, and Diane who, after seventeen interviews, was offered a job in an admin capacity when the original, first-choice candidate turned it down. When Diane discovered what the salary was (£18,000 pa), she turned it down too, but now isn't sure that was wise. 'Beggars can't be choosers,' she says flatly. Strictly speaking, I am the first of our clapped-out sorority to have a real shot at a professional job.

'Well, Kaylie,' I return the hopeful smiles with one of my own, 'my strategy, such as it is, is to be thin enough by six am tomorrow to get into my Paule Ka navy work dress, which I last wore to do a presentation in 2007. So, sadly, I won't be having one of the delicious brownies Sharon has brought in today. Please save me one, Sharon! I will be bearing in mind the things we've talked about as a group: not apologising for the experiences and skills I've built up outside the office environment and feeling confident that a career break has given me a new perspective which will be extremely valuable, particularly to those male colleagues who have never had to create a Mary Poppins costume for World Book Day with ten minutes' notice. Oh, and finally, just in case that's not enough to get the position, I will be knocking seven years off my age.'

There is an explosion of laughter followed by applause and cheers.

'Way to go, Katie,' beams Kaylie. 'Way to go!'

'They didn't believe me. The lying about my age bit. They thought I was joking.'

Sally and I are sitting on our bench on the crest of our hill. It's practically the only hill in East Anglia so you can't miss it. It's beautiful up here. We come most days to walk the dogs, the view spread out before us like a giant patchwork, with embroidery of trees and houses and a distant church spire. We watch as Lenny and Coco, Sally's Border Terrier, play together. Lenny is all clueless, blokeish enthusiasm; Coco is more fastidious and definitely in charge. She pretends to be annoyed when

Lenny gets too rough, but then yaps and looks longingly if he beats a retreat. The dogs are getting acquainted, building trust, and so are their owners. Gradually, bit by bit, Sally and I colour in the outlines of our lives.

I haven't made a new friend for a long time, not a good new one anyway, and I'm impatient for Sally to know everything about me, my family, my life, so I hardly stop talking. Sally is more reserved, a quality I noticed the first time I saw her at Women Returners; she reveals herself slowly in acute observations, wry humour, gentle suggestions.

'Are you quite sure, Kate? The lying about your age, I mean. Might it not cause problems down the line?'

'Yes, it might,' I say. 'But I've thought about it and I don't think I've got much choice. Realistically, forty-two is the upper age limit to put on an application form in my industry after a long break, particularly as I have to go in at a more junior level, where most staff will be in their early thirties. If I claim I'm forty-two, they'll just see me as older; I'm afraid that almost fifty would be a synonym for "dead".'

Sally nods. 'I used to love *National Velvet* when I was little. Remember Elizabeth Taylor pretending to be a boy jockey and winning the Grand National? And Barbra Streisand dressed up as a boy, didn't she? What was that film?'

There is a moment of silence while Sally and I ask our respective elderly archivists to go and fetch the answer. (*'Roy? Film where Streisand dresses as a boy? Hello?'*)

'I can't think of a film where someone lies about their age, can you?' asks Sally.

'No, but Dustin Hoffman was a young actor dressing up as a menopausal woman in *Tootsie* because he needed a job, so just think of me as doing the same sort of thing in reverse. Not sure I could pull off being a man. If I don't get this job

120

at EM Royal I might have to give it a go, though. I could let my chin hairs grow instead of plucking them. Wouldn't take long to get a nice little beard going. What d'you think?'

Sally and I are laughing so much that Coco and Lenny have come back to the bench and started barking, mistaking their mistresses' mirth for distress.

'You'd make a gorgeous guy, Kate,' Sally says.

'Well, never say never.'

Last week, I called up the CFA customer support to check if my Investment Management Certificate was still valid. I need that qualification to be allowed to work in finance. The woman who answered the phone asked, 'What year were you born?' When I said 1965, she made this noise. It wasn't a snort of disbelief, but it wasn't far off.

'Am I rather old to be doing this?' I asked the woman, hoping she'd say something kind to reassure me.

What she said was, 'We have had a few people older than you,' as though I was one of those sixty-year-olds who go to Spain to get impregnated.

It wasn't the woman's fault. She was being honest. By their standards, I'm practically an ancient monument. If I get the job – a big if – I can start right away because it turns out my IMC *is* still up to date, even if its owner is a bit rusty. If the firm gives me something more permanent I will have to get my PCIAM – that's Private Client Investment Advice and Management – but I can study for that on evenings and weekends. I don't need that immediately as I won't be doing my old job. If I was still a fund manager, it wouldn't be legal.

We have started walking again now, down the other side of the hill and along the path that skirts the ploughed field; the leaves underfoot are chocolate brown, the size and the shape of hands. The colour in the trees is still glorious, because we have had such a dry autumn, Sally says, but in a few days the branches will be bare. Walking ahead of me, in single file with Coco, Sally says she hates those drop-down things travel companies make you do, where you have to scroll down till you reach your year of birth.

'Just seeing how far the years go back, to 1920, and already how far I have to go back to get to me – to 1953. And I suppose you can see a time when your own date of birth will be pushed further and further down the chart, as the years behind it gradually disappear, and the people with them.' She turns and grins at me. 'Goodness, that's a cheerful thought. Shall we talk about something else?'

I realise that I'm hesitant about mentioning Perry to Sally. Stupid really. After all, she must have gone through the whole damn business herself. But it still feels taboo somehow. Why can't we be honest about this huge change in our bodies? I mean, I know why you wouldn't want to tell a man; they recoil from women's bits at the best of times. But I haven't even talked about it to a single friend, except Candy on email. It's almost as if we fear admitting to other females that we've lost sexual power, that we're out of the contest we've been in since our teens. Surely, I can talk to Sally?

'I've been feeling pretty grim lately,' I say with a pre-emptive grin. 'Think it's probably that boring old Time of Life thing.'

Sally turns to look at me. 'Oh, poor you. No need to suffer in silence, Kate. I'll give you the number of a gynaecologist I went to on Harley Street. I felt absolutely dreadful at your age and he put me on HRT.'

'Oh, I don't want to take HRT,' I say quickly. 'It's not that bad, I'm OK, I can manage – honestly.'

'He'll make you feel much better,' Sally says, tugging Coco

away from a pile of dried horse poo. 'They call him Dr Libido, I believe.'

'Oh God, he'd have to be an Antarctic explorer to find *my* libido. It's probably in the same pack ice as Shackleton's ship. Let me buy you a coffee, Sal?'

'No, my turn. Wasn't it Shackleton who said, "Difficulties are just things to overcome, after all?" Now, let's go to the caff and you can tell me more about what you're wearing tomorrow. I haven't been in an office for so long I can hardly remember what you do.'

Sometimes, when Sally is talking about her years at the Spanish bank, I glimpse a different woman. Clearly, it wasn't easy in what was a highly macho environment, even by banking standards. They deliberately sent her to the Middle East a lot when Will and Oscar were still really small.

'I used to go back to my hotel room and cry. I think my boss sent me there expecting me to fail, so they could get rid of me after I had the boys, but I was determined to make a success of it and I did bring in a lot of business, which surprised them.' She mentions a Spanish colleague from the bank who was with her in Egypt, and in Lebanon. 'They thought I needed a man to chaperone me, but those countries were much more liberal then. You never saw women wearing the veil, certainly not in the cities. Beirut was idyllic, so sophisticated, we absolutely loved it.' She takes out her phone and shows me a picture of a gamine brunette, a look of Audrey Hepburn about her, wearing shorts and a white broderie anglaise top tied in a double knot on her tiny, tanned waist. She's standing on a wall next to the sea and she is giving the camera a look of such impish glee. 'I think that must have been Jiyeh, maybe 1985 or '86.'

Of course. The woman is Sally. It took me a few seconds to

connect that joyful sprite with the woman sitting opposite in the fleece and squidgy dog-walking hat. Sal is sixty-one now.

'You look insanely happy,' I say and she nods.

'I adore the heat.'

We've only just taken a seat in the café, a low wooden structure tucked in the lee of the hill, when Sally's phone starts ringing and dinging. Texts and voice messages demanding her attention. There's no reception further up so they all come at once.

'Do you mind if I check those, Kate? Sorry, I bet it's the kids.' She says there's one from Will, no, two from Will, asking what he can do about his lost passport and where will he find clean underpants. Oh, and there's a text from Oscar: he's suffering from post-traumatic stress after being dumped by his long-term girlfriend, and he didn't get into work on time, so they fired him. And there's one from Antonia. Sally reads it out to me: 'Mum, can you find my brown boots please? Probs bottom my wardrobe. Love you x'.

She places her palm briefly on her forehead as though checking her temperature. 'I despair,' she says. Will, aged thirty-one, is still wandering around thinking he has a future as a war reporter, or maybe a professional cricketer; meanwhile he's living at home with Sally and Mike working in Clink and Son, the estate agents. Oscar, who is twenty-nine, has done two degrees and endless postgraduate work in International Relations and Conflict Resolution, and is currently living in a vile flat in Forest Gate, smoking far too much weed, which is causing him acute anxiety (although he denies it), and is expecting his parents to supplement his income as a Deliveroo biker. 'Although it sounds like he's even lost that job now.'

Antonia is the most academic of the three. She graduated with a 2:1 in Spanish and History and is now on her third

124

(maybe it's her fourth) internship, where she basically pays some PR agency to give them the opportunity to exploit her.

After a bad blip in her second year of college – probably a series of panic attacks, Sally thinks, though nobody's quite sure – Antonia is on anti-depressants (really helpful once they kicked in). She recently announced on Facebook that she is bisexual, which Sally is fine about, except there's no sign that she's having sex of any kind with anyone, male or female, and her mother does fret about that at 3 am, the hour when mothers wake and wonder if their children are happy.

'Honestly, Kate, I sometimes think I've produced a trio of wimps,' Sally grimaces. (Her face is becoming more animated as she knows me better. I think back to the dormouse I first saw at Women Returners.) 'They really should be independent by now, shouldn't they? Not texting me every day saying, 'Mum, I've got a cold.'

She takes a sip of coffee and pushes the carrot cake towards me. 'I hear so many parents saying the same thing. Where did we go wrong? Half of the boys' mates are still drifting, can't settle to anything. None of them are married. It's like we were on their cases the whole time when they were growing up, in a way our parents never were on ours – never had the time or the inclination to be, quite frankly. And then, when we try to get off their case, they get anxious and they can't cope and we end up resenting it because part of us is thinking, "Excuse me, this is *My* Time now, young man". Is that horribly selfish of me?'

I push the cake back at her, but not before inhaling a heavenly waft of the fragrant icing. 'Of course it's not selfish. You've done so much for them, Sal. Life just seems to be harder than when we were starting out. We always knew we could get a job, didn't we, and a flat didn't cost twenty times your salary.'

'Don't get me wrong, Kate,' Sally says, 'they're great kids.' She passes me her phone. The screensaver is a picture taken at a recent family wedding. 'That's Will in the middle, he's got his arm around, well, obviously, that's Osky on the left, and Antonia, look at her, she's a real titch compared to the boys.'

The two brothers, fair and broad like a pair of Norwegian oarsmen, are so alike they could be twins. 'Oh, Sal, wow! Look at them. Tall, blond and handsome. Is Mike fair, then?'

Her husband used to be fair like the boys, Sally confirms, but he's grey now.

'And Antonia, what a beauty. She's dark like you, Sal. Look at those brows. Emily spends ages painting in her brows to get them that dark. She's the spitting image of that actress. Oh, what's her name?' (**'*Roy, can you take a look in Movie Stars for me, please? Willowy, dark actresses?*') 'You know the one. She's in lots of those, that director, his films. I love them. You know. What's she *called*?'

'Some people say Antonia's a bit like Keira Knightley?' Sally prompts.

'No, darker, the actress I'm thinking of is much darker. It'll come to me.'

7.19 pm: Homework. No, not school homework – that guerrilla war between parents and kids which makes our involvement in Iraq look like tea at Claridge's. If I had a pound for every time I've coaxed and cajoled and yelled and threatened the kids to please even track down the *bag* where their homework might be hiding, I wouldn't need a full-time job. Sadly, there isn't a minimum wage for the Homework Monitor. When I think of the wages of Motherhood, I see that jar on the kitchen windowsill in my mum's house, full of 1ps and 2ps with the occasional silver 10p winking among the copper – the small change of a life lived for others. Even when she had next to nothing, my mum always put coins in that jar for charity.

I never wanted that life. I saw what it did to her, totally dependent on my father, who was a drunk with a whim of iron. Whatever happened, I would always make sure I had my own money, not something called 'housekeeping' counted out onto the blue Formica table on a Friday night before Dad went down the pub. Mum's awful gratitude, the little pantomime of coquetry as she went to take the cash and put it in her purse and received a pat on the bottom from him, The Almighty Provider.

So for more than twenty years I worked and I was paid well for that work, and I stood on my own two feet. Never thinking what it would feel like to have your legs pulled out from under you. People talk about giving up work as if it's a holiday or a change of scene, but in my experience it was more like a death – a small death, but a profound loss nonetheless. When you don't have a pay cheque, a month feels very different – contourless, void. After I finally left Edwin Morgan Forster, and we moved to Yorkshire for Richard's job, the vicar handed me an application form to fill in to become Treasurer of the Parish Church Council. First question: 'What is your personal income for the past year?' I hesitated – seconds, days – before circling 'None'.

I waved goodbye to the vicar and drove down the lane to collect Emily and Ben from school, but I couldn't see for crying. Pulled over into a lay-by and wailed, proper big, ploppy tears like I hadn't wept since my grandfather died. Tears that pooled at my breastbone and leaked into my bra. *None.* It was such a humiliation to actually write it down. To see it in writing. None. How had I got to this strange, frightening place where my personal income was nothing?

127

Focus, Kate. You've got homework to do. Tonight, it's me I have to nag to start revising. Interview tomorrow for a lowly job with the investment fund that I started all those aeons ago. Mustn't mention that detail of course, or the fact that the fund is now worth about £200 million less than when I ran it. I am a humble supplicant with an impressive, if mainly fictional, CV. With a little help from Women Returners, and from Candy, Debra and Sally, I have managed to perfect a cover story for the six and a half years when I took 'time out'. Also, I have a new age – the age that I was when I left that very office, funnily enough. Must Remember: I am forty-two. (*'Roy, I hope you're getting this; we can't afford to make any slip-ups, OK?'*)

Plus, I've got a crib sheet of all the new acronyms that have been coined since I left EMF, for example:

SANE
Which countries: South Africa, Algeria, Nigeria, Egypt.
What does it tell us: what were considered the African continent's most likely growth powerhouses.

'What's *SANE*?' snorts Richard, standing by the dining-room table and peering over my shoulder. 'There's nothing sane about where you used to work, darling. They're all certified madmen. We're seeing a lot of them seeking counselling now. Big growth area, burnt-out capitalists.'

'Needs must.' I smile and touch his hand. It feels essential to avoid the 'As you're becoming a counsellor paid in aduki beans and string someone needs to earn enough to pay the mortgage' argument. Not tonight.

'Emily, can you please lay the table and don't disturb Mummy. She's revising for her interview.' Richard, who is dressed in the stripy butcher's pinny I bought him for his birthday, said he would cook dinner to give me time to prepare. A typically kind, thoughtful gesture that causes more work than if he'd done nothing at all.

You see, when Rich cooks he can't be Delia, or even Nigella; he is Raymond Blanc – stock made from bones bought at the butcher, complicated sauces with three stages each. Even frozen peas have to be done with onion and pancetta. The result is always an absolutely delicious dinner that takes ten minutes to eat and three days to clear up. I do my best not to resent this, really I do.

9.35 pm: Ben is in his pyjamas and testing me. He will do anything to avoid going to bed – apart from his homework, of course.

'OK, what's PIIGS, Mum?'

'Um, Portugal, Italy, Ireland, Greece and Spain.'

'Cor-rect!' My son beams encouragement. 'Why are they pigs?'

'Because they were the Eurozone's weakest, most debt-laden economies when we had this really bad financial crisis a few years ago. It's very hard to make a currency like the Euro work when it's used by strong countries like Germany and also by much poorer ones like the PIIGS.'

'Are *we* PIIGS?' he asks anxiously.

'No, love, we're sort of DOGS. Debt-ridden but overall good strategy for recovery. *Woof-woof!!*'

Ben barks back and leans in for a hug. A rare concession these days. I still remember the little boy who shouted with astonished joy when I told him I was leaving my job at EMF. 'Are you going to be A Real Mummy now?' he asked. Had I not been a real mummy to him while I worked?

I kiss the top of his head. 'Hey, bed now, Mister! You know I probably won't get this job, don't you?'

'You will,' he says, turning away so I can't see his face. 'You're really clever, Mum.'

10.10 pm: Have carefully laid out clothes for the morning on the laundry basket in the bathroom. Tights not laddered? Check. Shoes, two of, matching. Check. New, flattering, indigo, velvet jacket from M&S. (I allowed myself one new item of clothing for morale boost.) Check.

The mirror reveals that Project Get Back To Work has already trimmed some flesh off my saddlebags and I can see a waist, though, sadly, not the one I had in 2002. An improvement, definitely, but I still need some extra help. Cutting open the packet with nail scissors, I slide out my new Shaper Suit. It looks like some macabre garment stitched from dead human flesh by a serial killer in a Hannibal Lecter film. Cost a hundred quid, insanely, but it does feature a 'zoned-compression option'. Not quite sure what that is, but I want one.

Wriggle head-first into elasticated, calamine-lotion-coloured sack, but it's so tight I can't pull it down over my hips. It feels like I'm trying to stuff too much meat back inside a sausage skin. Can't move in here. Or find opening for arm. Starting to panic.

Don't panic, Kate! You are in your own bathroom and therefore perfectly safe. I need both arms to tug the Shaper Suit down over my rear end. Unfortunately, one arm is stuck by my side as cannot find a second armhole. Where is it? Must be here somewhere. I can feel the sweat starting to pour down inside the Shaper Suit and gather where the garment has got stuck on my stomach, just above the C-section scar. Perhaps the zoned-compression option is too compressed? I decide to take the suit off and start again, but I can't. Am trapped. Literally can't move. Just wondering whether I should call for help when I hear Emily's voice close by, in the bathroom. She must be right next to me.

'Mu-um? *Urrgh*. What are you wearing? Like that's totally weird. I can only see your pubes. Where are you?'

'*Hernneuf.*'

'Da-ad, come and see Mum, she's like stuck in like this weird straitjacket like a crazy person. It's hilarious. Is that your Halloween costume? Oh, where's my phone, I need to get a picture of this.'

After a combined rescue effort by my husband and daughter, I escape from the Shaper Suit. It's not easy explaining to your slender-as-a-wand teenager why Mummy would want to squeeze into a punishment corset belonging to a less emancipated era. But squeeze I must.

I manage to get the Shaper Suit on properly the second time and the navy Paule Ka dress and jacket fit like a glove. Only it's so tight that breathing is optional. Think about what long-term damage to vital organs is being inflicted by my vanity/fear. Also, how on earth will I manage to go to the loo?

None of that matters. The only thing that matters, right now, at this decisive moment in my personal history, is that I look the part. For tomorrow, Kate Reddy is back in uniform and ready for covert operations.

7

BACK TO THE FUTURE

Thursday, 7.25 am: I get to the station early. Interview isn't until 11.30. Journey to Liverpool Street on semi-fast train takes forty-eight minutes. Estimated walk from Liverpool Street to offices of EM Royal, approximately six minutes. Time allowed for safe arrival at office, including total collapse of rail network, unforeseen major weather event, terrorist attack, snow, ladder in tights necessitating emergency stop at M&S plus Any Other Disasters: four hours and five minutes. Should be enough.

As I step off the train, I am hit by the twin sensations of smell – that signature London elixir of ambition and grime with prickly top-notes of sweat – and speed – even though the train has stopped, the capital is forging ahead, insisting that you leap aboard or get trampled by the hordes. I'm overwhelmed. It's as if, after being locked in a cellar where I've mushroomed into middle age and grown accustomed to the dark, I am now suddenly released into all this light and noise and energy. In the country, I curse other drivers for pootling along, for their tragic indecisiveness at junctions; here it's me who's the dithery slowcoach. For one paralysed second, I think I might turn around and go straight back home again, but I'm swept along in the great tide of commuters, powerless to move any way but forward, towards the ticket barrier. My eyes narrow and grow watery in the searing brightness of this world outside the cellar. The City's adrenalin used to course through my veins when I was young and hungry, but can it ever be my lifeblood again?

With more than two hours to kill till I'm expected at EM Royal, I head for Michael's café by Petticoat Lane market. Candy and I used to escape there to jump-start our weary brains with pungent shots of Turkish coffee and flirt with Michael's three Cypriot sons, who had a winning combination of outsize biceps and long, feminine eyelashes. The café is far enough from the office and sufficiently scruffy that it won't be patronised by anyone likely to be interviewing me. I walk up and down the street searching for it. I could have sworn I could find it in my sleep, but it's hard to get my bearings. The news-agent's and the greengrocer next door have been replaced by a Starbucks and one of those temporary 'pop-up' shops selling 'artisanal vegan food' – whatever that is. Turnip root covered in sun-baked organic mud presumably.

'Roy, have I got the address right? I'm sure Michael's was here. How can I have forgotten? Can you remind me, please?'

Secretly, I'm looking forward to old man Michael and the boys recognizing me, saying I haven't changed, espresso on the house for the beautiful lady! They always made Candy and me feel like queens; indiscriminate waiters' flattery, it meant nothing, but I could do with some of that particular soul-tonic brand of nothing this morning. Roy dawdles back from the map room and says the café is six shops along from The Queen Victoria pub, on the corner of the market. That's what I thought. I'm not going mad. I retrace my steps and end up standing outside the galvanised-steel windows of what looks like a stage set for a miniature French flea-market, full of quaint bric-a-brac, statues speckled with age, bird cages. The sign over the window says 'Pierrot le Food'. Peering through the glass, I spot a marble counter and an espresso machine.

Once inside, I instantly get what kind of place this is; a cross between a diner and a carefully curated museum. Richard would love it. There's a small selection of fashionable salads – kale, broccoli, pomegranate seeds, chickpeas – all made from ingredients which were previously only fed to cattle, but have since been elevated to 'happy' foods favoured by the rich and miserable. For breakfast, you can get dairy-free and gluten-free porridge with chia seeds – it's surely only a matter of time till they perfect the first porridge-free porridge – and a glass of coconut water costs six quid. Pretty steep for a slug of chilled semen.

The coconut water and chia seeds of my youth were aloe vera and aduki beans, but that was long ago when fat was still the enemy, not sugar. Now, you're encouraged to eat butter only you're not allowed bread to spread it on, which is a bit like saying you can hug Ryan Gosling without using your arms.

I ask the dark-haired girl behind the counter if she can direct me to Michael's. 'So silly of me, I know it's around here, just can't seem to find it.'

The girl shrugs and shouts, 'Goran?' From behind a tall display of porcelain toilet bowls and African violets, a man emerges and talks to the girl in a foreign language – Latvian? Slovenian?

'Michael's was 'ere, this place, but close-ed,' he says to me, making 'closed' two words. 'Gone maybe five year. Owner he die-ed, maybe, am not sure.'

It's worse than the senility I feared; time has trodden on my memories and erased them. I thank the guy and turn for the door, nearly knocking over a polystyrene bust of Venus de Milo. It's too depressing to stay in this exorbitant place where so much has been spent trying to confect a charm that money can't buy. Michael's had it for free. That's the story of twenty-first-century London: gut all the old places with character, then pay some designer mega bucks to put it back again. Well, I'm so ancient I can now look at a shop-front and see its previous incarnations; I know what the palimpsest of history would show for this place, and the fact I'm one of the few left who carries that knowledge fills me with sadness. I hurry away from that thought, straight across the street and back towards Broadgate where I'll be just two minutes from the interview.

Why were you expecting things to have stayed the same, Kate? You know full well the financial district is one big pop-up shop; places and people are cruelly culled when they've outlived their usefulness, or don't make money any more. Beneath this very pavement is a Roman villa where wealthy women wearing the finest togas had a healthy eating plan based around baked dormice, until the next fad came along. Poor Michael. He was probably finished off by a catastrophic rent-hike in a city where even the scuzziest area is no longer safe from becoming desirable and a Full English Breakfast comes with a side order of irony.

Thank goodness the Broadgate Champagne Bar is still open, and there's a notice on a stand outside saying it does breakfast. That's new. I should probably eat something to calm my churning, interview stomach. I am shown to a table overlooking the ice rink, which they built to emulate the one at Rockefeller Center and also to give the illusion that people who work round here might be allowed to have fun. As soon as I sit down I realise what a bad idea this is. Why didn't I think about it before, or was I letting my subconscious do the driving?

The last time I saw Jack we skated together here. The very last time. This memory is so strong I don't need Roy's help to fetch that one. It comes crowding in, breathless and laughing, just like Jack turning up at the office with two pairs of skates and insisting I join him. Me protesting that I couldn't skate, him saying he was skater enough for the both of us and all I had to do was lean on him. 'You're not gonna fall, Kate. I've got you. Just let go.'

Jack. Six years and nine months since I saw him. Who's counting? They say that time's a great healer, don't they? I expect they mean well, but I'm afraid they're lying through their teeth.

The waiter puts a cafetière in front of me and I ask if he can bring cold not hot milk, then I turn to look at the ice where a young couple are doing delighted circuits, just as we did.

I was determined to hate Jack Abelhammer at first sight. Isn't that how all the best love stories begin? This American client had been handed to me by my boss, Rod Task, as a kind of booby prize. The other team leaders at EMF all got bonuses that year – bonuses which my highly successful fund paid for, I might add – but I got Abelhammer instead. I was furious. Like so many women I always entered salary negotiations full of resolve to be properly rewarded for my performance this time and somehow, twenty minutes later, left the room with twice the work and no extra money. There has to be a word for that, doesn't there? Apart from WTF, I mean.

Anyway, my initial contact with Jack was almost comically terrible. First, he yelled at me down the phone on Boxing Day because some Japanese stock we'd bought for him had gone through the floor. (And a very Merry Christmas to you too, you rude, workaholic Yank!)

After that first debacle, I referred to him as the Appalling Abelhammer. When the Japanese stock recovered a few weeks later, he did send me a polite, somewhat contrite email but, unfortunately, Candy emailed me at exactly the same moment suggesting we had a girls' night out to drown our sorrows. 'I don't need to be drunk to be disorderly,' I replied. Except it wasn't Candy's email I was replying to, was it? Too late, I'd already pressed Send. TFD. Total Fucking Disaster. Back then, the kids were still small and waking me two or three times a night and the days at work were stressful and long. I was a dead woman walking, basically. Making silly mistakes, such as accidentally promising a major client you've never met a wild, alcohol-fuelled night, was par for the course.

My life felt like one damn absurdity after the next. So it was no great surprise, when I finally got to meet the Appalling Abelhammer in his vast corner-office in New York, that our nanny should text me during the meeting to say that Emily and Ben had nits. Of course they had nits! I started scratching immediately, and couldn't stop. We had dinner that evening, Jack and I, at a seafood restaurant in the East Village and I had visions of these lice abseiling down my hair – it was long back then – into Abelhammer's clam chowder. Do I really remember what he ate?

Oh, I remember everything. Even when I am old and grey and full of sleep and sitting in one of those high-backed plastic chairs in a care home with a too-loud TV and the sweet stench of urine, I know that every moment I spent breathing the same air as Jack Abelhammer will be vivid bright, stored in some time capsule of memory that the passing of the years cannot corrode. Age shall not wither what I felt for him.

That first night, we talked about anything and everything – how great Tom Hanks was in *Apollo 13*; a particular part of Provence Jack loved which has its own micro-climate so you can sit outside in a T-shirt in winter; his steadfast devotion to hideous, American plastic cheese, despite a gourmet palate; the matchless, breathy vocals of Chet Baker; the mysterious allure of Alan Greenspan. With his $2,000 suit and salt 'n' pepper buzz-cut Jack was cartoon-perfect Central Casting for your classic Harvard Business School product. I'd met plenty of those and they all spoke the same stunted language of money. Their speeches were like prefabricated sections of a chicken coop, one business cliché bolted onto the next. Jack was different. Irish on his mother's side (I'm Irish on my father's), he had the hereditary gift of the gab and a matchless frame of reference for everything under the sun, from highbrow to lowbrow, quoting reams of movies and poetry, flatteringly expecting me to get the references, which mainly I did. It was exhilarating trying to keep up; I felt parts of me that had been dormant since college begin to wake, as bulbs start to murmur and stir when the sun strikes the frozen earth. Almost anything was material for Jack's wry, dark wit – facts and figures, personal tragedies and disappointments, all brought to their knees in service of whatever laugh he hoped to extract at the end of a story. His mother, he told me, was the classic all-American homemaker, but bright with it. A cleverness which led first to boredom, then bourbon – copious amounts in the afternoon so she was often plastered by the time Jack got home from high school, once heating up a meat pie for dinner, which turned out to be apple.

Even this he made into comedy, but I have a theory about men who, as small boys, have witnessed their mother's distress, and been unable to help her. Ever after they are afraid of female emotion, of getting too close to it, so they wall themselves in and pull up the drawbridge. Maybe that explained why there didn't seem to be a Mrs Abelhammer, or any kids. I didn't probe too deeply because I was enjoying the fierce kick of being with Jack and chose not to mention my own children that night. Shameful, in a way, but I hadn't felt so alive, so powerfully myself for a long long time. Over coffee, Jack said that he'd got it, he knew who I reminded him of.

'Who?'

'Samantha in *Bewitched*.'

Of all the heroines in all the world, he had to choose mine. *Bewitched* was the first US show, along with *Scooby-Doo*, that I saw as a child. Samantha was a typical American housewife who just happened to have supernatural powers, sanity, the perfect home, luscious blonde hair, a certain buoyant, insouciant can-do smile and the ability to always get her way. Although her husband, the hapless Darrin, thought he was running the show, events were actually manipulated by a witchy twitch of Samantha's nose. But only when she needed it as a Hail Mary pass if her wit, diplomacy, and feminine wiles came up short that time. Looking back, I can see how I was captivated by a woman using her subversive, secret powers to take control of her life in a way my own downtrodden mother never did. So great and so enduring was the influence of *Bewitched* that I actually thought about calling my baby girl Tabitha, like Samantha, but Richard swiftly vetoed it, saying it was a stray cat's name.

'But I *loved* Samantha,' I exclaimed, as Jack asked the waiter if he could get the check.

'How could you not love Samantha?' he said.

He had a slow-release George Clooney smile that reached his eyes before the mouth was fully engaged. Eyes which glistened with amusement as we talked. He made me feel funnier and more beautiful than I had any right to feel. Bewitched?

'Fraid so.

I wasn't looking for anyone. Are you joking? I was a working mother who needed at least twenty-seven hours in a day to get through all her chores and duties, instead of the frankly pitiful and inhumane allocation of twenty-four. Richard and I still had sex back then, and when we did it was good, but not sufficiently amazing that I wouldn't have preferred an extra hour's sleep. I had a crazy demanding job and two children I adored but saw too little of. When I was at work I felt guilty about the kids and when I was at home I felt guilty about work. Time off for myself felt like stealing, so I rarely took it. Like every other mother on the planet, I was doing the jigsaw of family life in my head whilst living with a husband who thought that collecting the dry cleaning *and* taking his offspring to the park on Sunday merited a Purple Heart/Victoria Cross. As Debra used to joke, the only good thing about our situation was we were Far Too Knackered to Commit Adultery. I repeat, the last thing I needed was a love interest.

But whatever spark was lit that night in New York would not die down. When I got back to London, Jack emailed me almost hourly. I'd never been addicted to anything in my life – having an alcoholic for a father will do that to you – but I became hooked on seeing the name Abelhammer in my Inbox. Actually got tetchy withdrawal symptoms if I didn't hear from him for half a day. (They say that the dopamine response fires up in the brain with the receipt of keenly anticipated emails in the same way it does for heroin, and I'm not surprised.) Oddly, the lack of physical proximity meant we became closer than if I'd been able to touch him. We got to know each other through an old-fashioned epistolary courtship, albeit the letters were electronic. I guess we were among the first humans in history to establish such instant intimacy while thousands of miles apart, and it was seductive – God, it was amazing, actually – the way, with just a few keystrokes, he could make me

140

want him. And the fact he seemed to admire and want me in return gave me a confidence I'd never had before, nor since really.

One morning at the Hackney house, I got up really early and switched on the computer. There was a very brief email from Jack. Subject: Us. It said: 'Houston, we have a problem.'

He didn't need to spell out what the problem was. We had fallen in love and that was hellishly difficult – as implausible and impossible as bringing a broken spacecraft back safely to Earth, even if Tom Hanks was at the controls.

We were fine, Jack and I, so long as we existed in that rarefied atmosphere where lovers live, and the world goes away. But I was the mother of young children, responsible for their happiness, married to a lovely man I couldn't imagine hurting. Our relationship, Jack's and mine, would burn up on re-entry to real life, I was sure of that; even our love, invincible as it felt, would not be a shield against all the pain and anger that would be unleashed if we tried to be together. Turned out I was neither selfish enough, nor brave enough, to obey my heart's anguished instructions.

So, I left my job at Edwin Morgan Forster, made a huge effort to put things right with Richard, moved up North, away from the city to which I had given my youth, oh, and I changed my email address because I knew I wouldn't have the willpower to resist if I ever saw his name in my Inbox. You know, I saved Jack's last email, couldn't bear to delete it – the one after he knew that it was over, that I'd gone for good. I half expected him to be angry and reproachful; instead he was encouraging, dammit. Said he couldn't believe that I wouldn't return to work in triumph one day. He did allow himself one bittersweet quip: 'The great thing about unrequited love, Kate, is it's the only kind that lasts.'

He was right, in a way. Separation ends a relationship, but not unrequited love, which struggles on in the survivor's mind, asking, 'What if?'

'You're not gonna fall, Kate. I've got you. Just let go.' Should have? Could have? Would have? I felt such loyalty to Richard, to his love for me and the children, to that family I believed we were creating together. I couldn't walk away, not even for that testosterone-rich burst of springtime that was the aptly named Abelhammer. I never found out about *the* hammer, but, oh, how I longed to find out! Instead, I stayed to lay more bricks in the fortress called home.

Too often, now, I find myself thinking I've been bricklaying solo. For a man so scoldingly self-righteous about being 'present' all the time, Richard has been notably absent. Where does he go? When he is there, he seems distant, on his invisible bike pedalling away from me. I played it safe, for all the right reasons, and maybe I lost. What if? What if Jack skated up to this window right now, tapped on the glass and beckoned me to come with him . . .

'Can I get the check?' I say to the waiter. 'Oh, sorry. May I have the bill, please?'

As I walk across the piazza towards my old and – please God, let it be – my new workplace, a voice within me keeps repeating: forty-two, forty-two, forty-two. I must remember to be exactly the same age that I was six years and nine months ago, when I walked out of this glass tower for what I thought was the last time. *Forget time, Kate. Wipe it out. Be who you were.*

Easier said than done. Just as I'm struggling to wind back the clock, another voice, hidden and unbidden, comes to my aid. I know it at once, like a warm whisper in my ear. Jack. 'C'mon, Katharine. How hard can it be?'

8

Old and New

12.41 pm: How did the interview go? It went fine, thank you. Better than I could have hoped, actually, although I was so nervous I felt like throwing up into one of the bonsai trees they have everywhere in black granite pots. I'm not generally a vomit kind of person (managed to get through two pregnancies with almost no morning sickness), but so much was riding on this. Come to think of it, the queasiness could have been the Shaper Suit constricting my stomach to the size of an almond, or maybe Candy's testosterone patch with its surge of Man Juice was kicking in. I stuck one on the night before for luck.

There was a panel of four: three men and a woman. They would ask a question, then all three of the men would look down and make copious notes while I answered. It meant that I ended up talking to the crowns of three balding heads, and to Claire, the HR director on the end, who looked interested – kind even.

'Why do you think you are right for this role, Kate?' (Because

I am so desperate for a job in my industry, any job, that I will be your pathetically grateful slave and work harder than three younger guys combined?)

'Can you tell us about your experience to date?' (Well, up to a point, I can. Please do read my most imaginative CV.)

'Tell us about your weaknesses?' (Uh-oh, trick question. Carefully select 'weakness' that will be a strength in their eyes – 'bit of a perfectionist', 'workaholic tendencies', 'never leaves till the job's done', 'won't take no for an answer', etc.)

'Are you comfortable with a target?' (Are you kidding? Give me a target and I am Jason Bourne's psychopath auntie.)

'Are you talking to any other firms?' (No, I am yours and yours alone! True, though not for reasons they would find comforting.)

'What is your take on the markets this morning?'

'So, I'm particularly interested in oil. We've seen oil prices fall by nearly fifty per cent in the second half of this year with crude oil from US shale disrupting the global market. And those price drops coming after several years of relative calm in the world-wide crude markets when rising output in America was balanced by growing oil demand around the globe. The critical question now for us is where is oil trading? And what impact is its decline likely to have on global equities. (That should shut them up. I didn't even take a breath. Please note sly use of 'us', as if I'm already part of the team. Sports metaphors always get big Brownie points also.)

'Kate, what would a typical day look like for you?'

'Er, expect to get in by eight at the latest, unless I have a breakfast meeting. Aggressively pursue new leads, liaising with contacts in law and accountancy firms. Hand-holding calls with existing clients to reassure them that their wealth is safer with us than anywhere else.' (I don't add: despite inexplicably shit performance of the fund.) 'Lunch at desk or with clients. New business pitches in the afternoon. Dinner and a night at the opera/theatre/charity event, building relationships, encouraging investment, making clients feel loved. Home late to find that no one has walked the dog, loaded the dishwasher, bought milk, cleaned up Lenny's poo by the back door or even noticed that Mummy has a job.' (Obviously, I left out that last part too.)

After a while, I got bored of the three male faces disappearing every time I spoke. When one of them asked, 'Are you familiar with the implications of the latest US non-farm payrolls?' I watched all their heads go down again, pens poised, expectantly awaiting my response, and I said, 'Not a clue.'

All three bald heads popped up instantly, like in that Splat the Rat game, and their expressions registered concern and disbelief. ('Did the candidate just say, "Not a clue?"')

Now not quite so confident, I said, with what I hoped was an engaging smile, 'Just kidding' and obediently reeled off the relevant facts on the US non-farm payrolls. As you do.

'Tell us, Kate, what do you see as the outlook for PIIGS and the European government bond market following the Greek debt crisis?' The question comes from the man in the middle with the dead-shark eyes. Hooray, Ben tested me on PIIGS last night.

'So there is likely to be some degree of contagion pushing European bond yields higher and the Euro lower. Ironically, a weaker Euro will benefit European equities longer term, with the exception of the European banking sector.' Thank goodness I did my homework.

'What *I* would like to know about, Kate', said Claire, addressing me directly for the first time, 'are your interests outside work. It's so important that you can talk to clients, make them want to spend time with you.'

145

'Of course. Well, naturally, I do have a wide range of, mmmm, interests.' Desperately try to buy time while thinking of anything non-child, non-dog, non-Polish builder, non-sweaty-cycling-gear related.

At that precise moment, for reasons still unknown, Roy came up trumps, bringing me answers on a silver salver. 'So, yes, I'm passionate about the theatre, with a particular interest in Shakespeare. I was only reading *Twelfth Night* again last night,' (well, I saw it on Emily's bed), 'because I know The Globe is doing a new production, and we have a membership there. Terribly important to support the arts, isn't it? I've steered several clients towards successful sponsorships in the past. I also enjoy architecture, particularly the restoration of historic buildings using authentic materials. I like to keep up with trends in computer gaming; the interactive nature of that is particularly fascinating. And I'm a keen reader – Hilary Mantel, Julian Barnes and this year's Booker prizewinner.' (Give me a break. It's on my bedside table, OK?) 'Lately, I've even tried to, um, start dabbling in fiction myself.'

From: Debra Richards
To: Kate Reddy
Subject: New job?
Well? Have you rejoined the Rat Race? Must I suffer alone? Pls send news soonest.
    D xx

From: Candy Stratton
To: Kate Reddy
Subject: Interview
Don't keep me in suspense, honey. Bet you blew them away, or blew them anyhow. Is it still OK to make BJ

jokes if you are the last woman in NYC who 'identifies as heterosexual'? I get confused.

If you don't get this job, you will get the NEXT one. Cross my heart and hope to diet.

XXO C

Sally to Kate

Have been thinking of you all day. So much hoping it's good news and the testosterone patch(!) your friend gave you worked. Coco pining for Lenny. Saturday afternoon any good? Sx

Richard to Kate

What time are you back? Piotr moved my bike stuff to get to the fusebox and I can't find the Kryptonite lock. Emily said something about her art folder? Hope interview went OK. R x

Tuesday, 6.28 am: It's my Assessment at the gym and I am really not in the mood, but Conor wants to record my progress. Need to get back in plenty of time to take Ben plus drum kit to school for Christmas concert rehearsal. (Christmas already? I haven't even started to think about it.) As I haul myself out of bed, I can feel the three-hundred-year-old oak boards beneath my feet sloping away. Piotr says he can level the floor if we take the boards up, get the joists replaced and then re-lay them, but the quote was vertiginous, dizzying. Can't afford it, not while Richard's retraining and I don't know when – if – I will be gainfully employed. (Still no word from EM Royal.) Getting to the bathroom from my own bed each night is a bit like being on board HMS *Victory* in a gale.

Richard says that a modern floor would be much cheaper

and all the bedroom furniture would not be tilting drunkenly and our bed would not be on a steep slope with its legs propped up on bricks so we can sleep on a vaguely flat surface. But I love the boards. I feel protective towards them; their generous width, their gnarled richness, the injuries which time has inflicted on them, the living that has happened on them, the stories they could tell. OK, they are ancient and sagging and a nightmare to maintain, but then so is my pelvic floor. And you don't see me replacing that with a cheap, modern re-tread.

6.43 am: Drive in dark to gym wearing newly purchased three-quarter-length leggings, which looked sporty and youthful in the shop. In spirit of New-Me optimism I bought the smaller size, which are *too* small, so stretch leggings only just reach my kneecaps. I look ridiculous: like Big Bird minus the insouciance. To compensate have worn my longest T-shirt and dog-walking fleece. Conor is waiting for me in brightly lit Cardio Room. A large TV on the wall is helpfully showing Ariana Grande (size zero and pipe-cleaner legs) on a spin bike.

'No worries,' says Conor. The assessment is just to figure out my level of motivation and commitment to exercise and diet. He is going to use calipers to measure my fat. No worries. The calipers are like crab claws pinching my midriff, but I feel no pain as the subcutaneous blubber acts as a protective layer. ('I am the walrus! Goo goo g'joob.') Conor asks me how much I weigh. I think of a worst-case scenario and knock off a couple of pounds. Sadly, my guess is nowhere near high enough. Conor adjusts the scale, notch by dismaying notch, away from my delusions of Grande. Seeing my disappointment, he sweetly asks if I'd like to remove some clothing as that might help. I decline, protectively pulling the fleece, coated in Lenny's hair, tightly around me. Let my shame stay covered.

I really don't want to embarrass this genial giant, but I could weep with frustration. For years, I tell Conor, my weight hovered under nine stone. Then came two large babies and a lot of clearing up (OK, eating) kids' food. I put on a few pounds, but that was just about OK while I was still killing myself doing fourteen-hour days. After I left work, and with no office clothes to fit into, I stopped watching what I ate. Since the Perimeno – well, over the last year or so – I seem to have ballooned for no reason. Now, after weeks of self-denial and strenuous working out, with barely a grain of sugar passing my lips, I still weigh more than in my worst nightmare.

Conor says that, at my age, the body will take longer to respond. It's not realistic to compare me to my thirty-year-old self. 'Your body is changing, Kate, no question, just that the scales aren't reflecting that yet. Muscle weighs more than fat, remember. Be patient.'

He leads me to the static bike and off I go, mesmerised by Ariana Grande pedalling away in full make-up, hair extensions flying. One good thing about being nearly fifty (*note to Roy: 'please remind me there was one good thing about turning fifty'*) is I know that, for me, such a look is unattainable. And I don't care. What bliss, finally, not to care. Can't help wondering if airbrushed, uber-skinny perfection is what girls like Emily feel compelled to achieve, and how that must make them feel. Em is going to see Taylor Swift with Lizzy and the other girls at the weekend. I thought she'd be happy about it, but she's been shutting herself away in her room, yelling at me if I try to go in. When I went to say goodnight last night, there was a PRIVATE notice on her door.

7.56 am: Ben is crashing about the kitchen when I get back, complaining that we don't have any cereal. We do have cereal.

We just don't have chocolate-filled Addict, or whatever it's called, which I have strictly forbidden after watching a recent documentary on child obesity. Ben has inherited his father's wiry physique, but a certain deadly kind of fat can accumulate around the vital organs apparently. Visceral fat. Ha! Didn't need Roy for that one. It even sounds like a poisonous dart. I've probably got that as well.

'Not having that granola crap,' he bellows like a stricken bison.

'Please, Ben . . .'

'How'm I s'posed to find stuff in this mess?'

'It will be lovely by Christmas. Clever Piotr will have finished our new kitchen, won't you Piotr?'

I raise my voice to reach the prone form of our builder. All that is visible of him is denim legs poking out from under the sink, or where the sink would be if we had a sink. The button of his jeans is undone and his black T-shirt has ridden up over his taut stomach revealing a band of pale skin and curly dark hairs beneath which . . .

No, Kate, don't go there. What are you thinking?

Piotr's head emerges from the cupboard and he gives us both a cheery little wave. 'Trust Mum, Ben, Christmas mother she always does perfect.'

8.10 am: Driving Ben to school and doing breathing exercises. Exhale on a count of ten. We were early, but now we're late because Ringo Starr forgot his drumsticks and we had to go back to get them and the traffic is insane. He's next to me, in the passenger seat, scribbling, a pad of lined paper open on his knees. 'Please do your belt up, sweetheart. Is that homework?'

'*Gnnnn.*'

'You really need to get your act into gear now, you know.

This constant leaving your homework until the last minute, it's not good enough any more.'

Ben sighs with a fourteen-year-old's infinite weariness at the vast, fathomless stupidity of his elders.

'Seriously, Mum, no one works hard at my age. Except the Asian kids.'

I flinch. 'What kind of attitude is that? If the Asian kids can work, why can't you?'

I picture a future where Indians and Chinese are running all the multinationals and the UK is one giant call-centre manned by white slacker-boys – like mine – with very poor English and mismatched socks. All too plausible, sadly.

'Nobody starts working till second year of GCSEs, Mum.'

'Well, I worked hard at your age. I had to. No one was spoon-feeding me and making my life easy. We had a French verbs test every Monday morning and God help you if you didn't . . .'

Glance over and see that Ben is playing a tiny invisible violin, the plangent soundtrack to Mummy's growing-up-poor, hard-luck story that my kids love to mock.

'Can you stop that? I'm being serious.'

'Don't take it out on me because you're stressy about not getting your job, OK? It's not fair.'

'We don't know I didn't get the job,' I protest, but my boy has already jumped out, got his drums from the boot and is lugging them towards the school hall. He doesn't turn to wave.

I hate parting from him that way more than I can say. I just hate it.

To: Candy Stratton
From: Kate Reddy
Subject: Interview

Still no word from EM Royal. Finding it really hard tbh. Will officially give up hope tomorrow, burn Women Returners' handbook and throw myself on pyre of dead career.

In other news, since wearing your testosterone patches I have felt first frisson of sexual desire in over a year. For my Polish builder.

I would get rid of him, but I need a kitchen by Christmas. What do I DO?

Kxx

From: Candy Stratton
To: Kate Reddy
Subject: Woo hoo!
Easy. Pole dancing! I knew you had it in you.

Do NOT give up hope. It's only been three working days.

XXO C

There now follows an anxious period of limbo while I wait to hear if I got the job. I am keen to find any excuse to remove my new, disconcertingly horny self from temptation presented by Piotr, who is lying on his back fiddling with my plumbing. You wish.

Decide this is a good moment to go and see Barbara and Donald, check how they're doing and placate obnoxious sister-in-law at the same time. Ben has fixed my phone so the *Psycho* shower-scene music plays if Auntie Cheryl rings. (Bad boy, yet somehow very good.) Richard says he still can't get away. Something urgent to do with a mindfulness retreat. (Isn't an urgent mindfulness retreat a contradiction in terms?) It infuriates me that Rich the trainee counsellor is so caring about the whole damn world but happy to abandon his own parents. I feel like telling him I'm not putting up with his excuses but, as Donald's answerphone messages get more effusively apologetic, I have started to fear the worst. I can combine a trip to Wrothly with a visit to my mum, who lives fifty miles away.

Donald admitted that the electric blanket we got them a few years back has packed up, so I pop into the department store in town to get a new one. My parents-in-laws' house is so cold, a heated blanket counts as a necessity not a luxury.

'Would you like one of our brand-new store cards?' the assistant asks. Indeed, I would. Other middle-aged women turn to alcohol, toy boys or colouring-in books: John Lewis is my drug of choice. They say that heroin makes the cares of the world go away. That's what happens to me in the soft furnishings department of John Lewis. I fill out the form and am amazed and embarrassed a few minutes later when the man returns and tells me that my application for a store card has been rejected. Says he isn't allowed to give me a reason, but when I demand to see the manager, he mutters under his breath that it has something to do with my credit rating.

Go online, check credit rating and find that it is the lowest it could possibly be, short of my actually being deceased. Actually, a dead person would have a better credit rating.

'Roy, can you think of any unpaid bills I have? Sorry, Ben? What has Ben got to do with my credit rating??'

2 pm: Leeds station. As I approach the gates, I see Donald is standing just beyond the barrier waiting for me. You couldn't miss him. For a man of almost ninety, he is remarkably upright, with that posture people used to call military bearing. (What do we have instead, a computer crouch?) Not as tall as when I first met him, but you can see what a fine figure of a man

153

he was. He's wearing his tweed coat, the one with the brown suede collar – not the kind of coat you see much any more. Donald insists on taking my case from me and there is a moment, one of those delicate moments you get with elderly people, when you hesitate because you're not sure if you should insist on carrying your own bag, as it's clear you are more capable of doing it than they are. But to do so would be to deprive Donald of his natural role, being the gentleman. And I don't want to do that, so I thank him and yield the case to his trembling hand.

On the winding road to Wrothly, memories ambush me at every turn. Like the first time Richard took me home to meet his parents. We were having sex about three times a day back then. We only got out of bed to eat and go to work. Barbara knew full well we lived together, in a tiny flat above a laun-derette in Hackney, but she showed me to a small bedroom containing a chaste single-bed with a frowning, brown-wood headboard. (It was the room in the house where all the bad ornaments and crappy lamps end up because no one has the heart to throw them away.) Rich crept along the corridor when he thought everyone was asleep, and there was much hilarity as he tried to fuck me without rattling the bed, whose screeching springs were Barbara's unpaid informants. I could be wrong, but I think there might have been so much laughter that, in the end, we gave up and talked instead.

Then, there was the December we brought baby Emily here. I know exactly when it was: 1997, because Em will soon be seventeen. There was snow on the hills, and it felt magical to be bringing this new person to meet her grandparents. At the first sight of the perfect rosebud in her pink bonnet and matching matinee jacket, Barbara welled up. She only had sons, which was difficult, I suspect, for such an immensely feminine woman.

Although she never did soften towards me, she has been Emily's champion ever since and won't hear a word against her.

'Nearly there. No need to hold onto the seat, Kate,' says Donald. I relax my grip and do my best not to be alarmed that my father-in-law drives not with one hand, but with one finger on the wheel. I suppose he has known this road for longer than I've been alive.

It's a shock when he unlocks the back door and we step straight into the farmhouse kitchen. Barbara's kingdom, from which she ruled her family as a benign despot, looks like a student bedsit. Every surface is covered with crockery, saucepans, utensils, cans of food. My nostrils twitch at the pungent stink of wee. I look towards the dog basket for the culprit. The basket is still there, next to the range, but, I suddenly remember, they had to have Jem put down in the spring; the Collie's back legs had gone.

'Look who I've brought to see you, love. Kate's come to see us, isn't that marvellous?'

Barbara sits in a high-backed, checked armchair that used to live in the sitting room. I recognise other bits of furniture from the rest of the house in here. It's like a junk shop.

'She's having a good day today, aren't you Barbara?' Donald speaks loudly, partly for my benefit, partly for his own, perhaps, and partly to get a response out of the old lady. Barbara is unrecognizable from the summer, when we all had a week together in Cornwall. The speed of the deterioration is terrible. Her hair, always immaculately curled after a weekly visit to the hairdresser, lies flat on her scalp.

'Say hello, Barbara. Poor Kate will be thinking you don't know her! She's come all this way to see us.'

Not knowing what else to do, I sit on the stool by her knee and hold Barbara's hand; it's curled in on itself like a claw. She

155

stares at me with a look of childlike curiosity, her eyes like those misty marbles I coveted at school.

'I'll make us a nice cup of tea, shall I? Barbara, I'm saying to Kate, I'll make us a Nice Cup of Tea? Or would you prefer coffee, Kate? I know Richard used to drink coffee before he started having all those peculiar teas to go with his new ideas. Camomile, is it?'

'Tea'd be lovely, Donald. Just normal, thanks. Richard's really sorry he couldn't be here, but he's on a training course.' So glad he didn't come. I flinch to think of what Rich would feel seeing his parents amidst the ruins of their life.

'I can see you looking at Jem's basket, Kate. I should chuck it out, but it's . . . Well, Barbara sometimes thinks Jem's still with us, don't you, love? Sixteen years we had him. Couldn't ask for a better companion. I do miss our walks,' he says. 'Gets you out the house does a dog. But it wouldn't be kind to take on another animal. Not at our time of life.'

I take my mug of tea from Donald and look for an empty place to set it down, but there isn't one. Another memory: Barbara with a dishcloth, remorseless as a windscreen wiper, always cleaning the work surface, and woe betide you if you put so much as a toast plate down for a few seconds or a wine glass without a coaster. She didn't like anything on her work-tops. It made it so hard bringing the kids here when they were little; clearing up instantly because the slightest spillage upset Grandma.

Donald notices me looking for a place to put the mug. 'We thought, Kate, as Barbara doesn't always know which cupboard things are in any more that it would be helpful to put everything on the work surface so she can see it. If she needs a pan for soup, she doesn't have to think which cupboard it's in, it's right there.'

'Oh, what a good idea,' I say. 'What a good idea, Barbara, putting things on the top so you know where they are. Does that help you find what you need, Barbara? I could do with that in our house to be perfectly honest with you.'

'Margaret, the new carer, she'll be here in a minute,' Donald says. 'I say Margaret's coming, Barbara, you like Margaret, don't you?' The old lady smiles.

Donald takes me aside. I'm not sure why as Barbara can't hear us and, even if she could, she probably wouldn't understand. Margaret, he says, is a very nice woman. Better than Edna, the foreign one, who Barbara didn't get along with at all.

'Erna?'

'That's her. Quite abrasive, she was. A smoker.'

Barbara seems to like Margaret, in so far as anyone can tell what Barbara likes any more, and I think back to the heated exchange I had with the woman at Wrothly Social Services about providing a new carer. At least I've been of some small help in what I now realise is a dire situation, much worse than Donald could bring himself to say on the phone.

It's a relief when Margaret arrives in person and creates a cheery bustle, taking Barbara off for a shower and instructing Donald to go and fetch a prescription from the chemist. I'd like to call Richard to tell him what I've found here, but there's no mobile signal. Nor can I find the house phone. Instead, I fetch the Hoover and a mop, fill a bucket with hot water and Flash, and I begin to clean, furiously, just as Barbara would clean, if she were here.

'They can't go on like this much longer,' Margaret says when she's putting her coat on, about to leave. 'Donald's wonderful with her, but it's not fair on him. If they sell this place they'll have enough to go somewhere decent where they'll both be looked after. Need to get it on the market, but it wants tidying up first. You will tell your husband?'

The next morning, Donald insists on driving me to the station, although I don't want him to leave Barbara, not even for ten minutes. He lugs the case to the barrier and plants a wet, whiskery kiss on my cheek. 'Not a great deal to be said for old age,' he says, speaking normally, now he doesn't have to mega-phone for Barbara as well. 'We've probably had enough, Barbara and me. Make the most of being young, Kate, love,' he says.

'I'm not young,' I protest, but the old gentleman has turned away and is walking towards the car park, the collar of his tweed coat pulled up high against the bitter wind. On the train to my mother's, the hills a blur of green through the window, I find myself thinking that I could never have imagined a time when I would miss Barbara condescending to me, and finding fault. But I do miss her. Seeing her as she is, missing presumed alive while squarely in the centre of her own domain, is like beholding the Ghost of Christmas Future and it's frightening. Resolve to make the most of my time with Mum, even when she's infuriating me with her dithering over carpets.

That's the thing about parents, isn't it? They drive you mad for years with their tedious *Groundhog Day* anecdotes about Joy in the post office whose Dachshund, Dookie, is losing his hair. And did I tell you the funny story about Michael Fish the weatherman? Yes, seven hundred times, actually.

And you think, I don't know Joy in the post office from Adam and perhaps Dookie the bald Dachshund has delighted us long enough and might go and play in the traffic. Then, one day, something happens, something that changes everything. A fall, a stroke, some tiny cog in the brain thrown out of whack and, all at once, you find yourself nostalgic for those boring, infuriating anecdotes. The years when things would go on as they always had and always would. The years before you knew what comes next.

One of the privileges of youth is that knowledge is kept from you. And so it should be, if you ask me, because it's just so fucking sad.

Haven't been able to check my emails since Donald collected me from the station yesterday. The signal is better now. Glance down the Inbox. One from Candy. Two from Debra (Subject: Shoot Me!). One from Emily demanding to know where I've put her black suede boots. (*My* suede boots, Madam!) One from Ben asking if I can collect him from football. (Has he even noticed I'm not there?) One from Richard saying he and his annoying colleague are organising a meditation retreat in Anglesey in December (What? They'll bloody freeze.) One from a hypoallergenic dog-food supplier: 'We miss you!' One about my dire Experian Credit Rating. One from the phone company about 'unusual levels of spending'. What unusual spending? (*'Roy, didn't I ask you to get onto this?'*) Another email promises to help me conquer the 'dread of exposing your bingo wings as we enter the festive season'. Thanks for that. Oh, and, finally, finally, one from Claire Ashley. The one I've been waiting for. *Go on, open it, Kate. Get it over with.*

From: Claire Ashley
To: Kate Reddy
Subject: EM Royal Vacancy
Dear Kate, I am delighted to inform you . . .

She's delighted? Imagine how *I* feel. Oh, thank you, thank you. Quickly scan the rest: the money's good, better than I thought.

The job is Maternity Cover, for six months in the first instance, with the possibility of staying on should my performance prove satisfactory. Start date: immediately, if it's convenient.

Yes, oh, yes, that is most convenient.

From: Kate Reddy
To: Candy Stratton
Cc: Debra Richards, Sally Carter
Subject: Older Female in New Job Shock
Yaaaaaaaaaaaaaaaaaaaaaaaaaaaaaaaaaaaaayyyyyyyyyyyyy!

*Yentl. Roy is pretty sure that's the film where Barbra Streisand dresses as a boy.
**Roy thinks the actress Sally's daughter reminds me of is Penélope Cruz.

9

GENUINE FAKE

Monday, 7.44 am: Like a Time Traveller, I step out of the lift into my former workplace. It feels so strange, simultaneously familiar and disorientating. As I follow Claire Ashley past the serried rows of desks, I am quite sure everyone on the floor must be staring at me, reading the anxious tickertape of thoughts scudding across my brain. Looking me up and down, thinking, 'Wow, she's changed, and not for the better. Rough couple of years, huh?'

Luckily, I know that's not true. There are no familiar faces here. They've gone, all of them. After changing hands twice in the years since I left, Edwin Morgan Forster is technically no more – new owners, new branding, new name – but the fund I set up is still the same. Ironically, it's for my own fund that I will be working, although my new boss and his team have no idea about the connection, and I intend to keep it that way. I have landed this job on false pretences – the firm believes I am the same age I was when I left here almost seven years ago (who says you can't hold back Time?). There's a risk, a very small one, that someone could come out of the woodwork and identify me. What the hell, I'm going to hold my nerve and PUA: Proceed Until Apprehended.

Claire gestures through the vast wall of glass to the square, seven storeys beneath us. A lot has changed, but I see the skating rink, the champagne bar and the serrated Victorian arches of Liverpool Street station, where my train got in over an hour ago. I killed some time in one of the thirty coffee shops which have sprouted up since I left, the new girl about to start school with butterflies in her tummy. Making sure I had my pens, my pencil case, my lipstick in the damson Mulberry bag – a knock-off Debra brought back from holiday in Turkey last summer. She took a picture of the proud sign outside the bag shop: 'Genuine Fakes'. You'd never guess that the bag's not the real thing. Nor me, I hope.

Everyone in here looks so much younger than I remember; perhaps it's just that I'm not young myself any more and don't realise it. After the financial crisis of 2008, they cleared out most of the older guys, and the rest, seeing the writing on the wall, jumped before they were pushed. Some of them moved to smaller firms, nicely distant from the lingering stench of risky lending, or they used their redundancy money to seed start-ups in St James's, making sure they had an office to go to. They couldn't possibly be at home (who knows what went on at home?).

It's as though this place went through a great war – a vast, man-made disaster really – and an entire generation was wiped out (and, with them, trillions of dollars). The faces I see are too fresh to recall any of it. And that suits me just fine. Funnily enough, I feel like a veteran of my own war coming back to the battlefield, peering through the smoke of time at the ghosts of people I used to work with.

Claire has paused by a horseshoe-shaped arrangement of desks and starts making the introductions. A strikingly pretty blonde with princess-length hair, maybe late twenties, Alice Someone, is immediately friendly and welcoming. I am shown to a seat next to her. A couple of guys – Troy? Jamie? – who are studying a screen nod at me then look away. Another thing that's sprouted since I was last here is facial hair. Never would have predicted the Great Beard Revival, not in a million years. All of the young guys have one, or long, sculpted sideburns. Claire hails a burly, bespectacled chap with a thatch of curly red hair who is dashing past. She introduces Gareth, the Welsh head of Research, who has the short, stocky build of his coal-mining ancestors. 'You'll be working closely with Gareth, of course. Oh, and here's Jay-B now; he's been looking forward to meeting you, Kate.'

My new boss is the physical opposite of Welsh Gareth. Spare and reedy, he wears a Tintin quiff in his hair which is as black and shiny as his conquistador beardlet and his very pointy Prada shoes. I recognise the type immediately. Self-styled hipster, metrosexual, spends a fortune on scruffing products and Tom Ford Anti-Fatigue Eye Treatment. Probably got a penthouse in Clerkenwell – no, it's Shoreditch these days, isn't it? – with a built-in vivarium where he keeps fastidious small reptiles like himself. I think Claire mentioned that Jay-B is thirty, which means that he was born the year that I went to university. That can't be right. I mean it's not natural, is it?

I realise I was sold to Jay-B as a well-spoken blonde who, despite being forty-two (*memo to Roy: Do Not forget we are forty-two!*) still presents well and could be useful in marketing and business development, selling to high-net-worth individuals and private family offices. A notoriously tough sell. It's the young wide boys who market to chains of stockbrokers and make the big bucks. I'll be courting the old buffers, family trusts and some of the new-money brigade, the up-and-comers

163

still regarded with suspicion. Still, if I do well, it's decent money and money is what we need right now. Our family is experiencing its own liquidity crisis. I think of Emily's face when she said that Lizzy was going with Bea and Izzy to the Taylor Swift concert. After I wrote that cheque for ninety pounds to Cynthia Knowles to pay for Em's ticket, Emily said that *Everyone* was giving thirty-quid Topshop vouchers to the birthday girl.

'Really? Thirty each? On top of the concert ticket?'

'You can't get much in Topshop for less than that,' Emily said, staring at her shoes, not wanting to look at me, knowing it was too much, but also daring me to query the price of admission to Lizzy's club. I remember being her age, the agony of exclusion, the need to belong, as urgent as the need to urinate. Julie and I, we never had the right clothes or the right toys when we were growing up. Once, I was invited to play tennis with three girls from the nicer part of town and all I had was this racquet Mum got with Green Shield Stamps – a stick with a bit of plastic netting basically. The other girls' racquets made a satisfying *pock* when they struck the ball; mine gave a defeated twang like a busted bluegrass guitar. I never ever want my daughter to feel she's not just as good as anyone else.

'So, Kate – take a seat.' Jay-B ushers me into his corner office, floor-to-ceiling windows on both sides. Am I imagining it? No, I'm not. This was once the mighty Rod Task's lair. My old boss. I can still hear the abrasive Australian yelling at me to 'Get out there and kick the fucking tyres, Katie!' He was a nightmare – sexist, racist, think of any bad 'ist' you can mention and that was dear old Rod. Last thing I heard from Candy, Rod was back in Sydney and had been involved in a bull-shark attack on the Great Barrier Reef. Significant blood loss and heavy biting, but the poor, stunned shark was expected to recover.

Jay-B sees me glance outside. 'Helluva skyline. Shard's the

fourth tallest building in Europe now. That whole area down by London Bridge, you wouldn't recognise it. Couple of the big accountants moved down there. Next to Borough Market. Great foodie place.'

I suddenly remember that a fox was living at the top of the Shard when it was being built. Imagine his – or her – terror as their home got higher and higher. Hope they didn't have cubs. My new boss glances down at what I presume are notes from the interview panel.

'O-kay, I see you've built strong client relationships in the past. That's what we've brought you in for, Kate. Some of the team, they're great sales people, but they haven't always got the life experience that enables them to handle some of our, well, our more mature investors. We've got a couple of merry widows, for example, who need their hands holding.'

'Oh, I'm great with old ladies,' I say, thinking of Barbara in her high-backed chair gripping my fingers. Thinking of my mother, still trying to choose between green and beige carpets.

'Fantastic. Fantastic. And it says here you've got two kids.' Jay-B has raised one impeccably waxed eyebrow, as though children were some kind of exotic perversion. 'How old are they, then?'

'Oh, they're sixte—'

NO! What are you thinking? Remember you're forty-two, for heaven's sake. Emily can't be sixteen going on seventeen. That means you would have had her when you were twenty-five. Round here that makes you a child bride.

I should have thought of this before. Attempt rapid mental arithmetic but brain feels like fudge. (*'Help me, please, Roy. How old are my kids?'*)

'So. Emily. Emily, she's my daughter and she is eleven. Yes, she's eleven. And Benjamin, that's my son, he will be, he will be eight next birthday.' I tell Jay-B their ages with what I hope is a proud maternal smile, rather than a look of blind panic.

'It's high time I got back to work. I'm really looking forward to getting stuck in.'

Phew. The lie comes more easily than I imagined, almost as easily as it did when I was an undercover working mother in this office all those years ago, trying to act like I didn't have kids at all.

Well, you know what that doctor said. Use it or lose it.

2.30 pm: First meeting with the whole team. Chance to impress. Eleven guys around the table, all spraying ideas, and two women (me and Alice). With his quiff and his head cocked to one side, Jay-B looks like a cross between Tobey Maguire and a quizzical parrot.

'Yeah, thanks, Troy. Was there something you wanted to contribute, Kate? Just in case some of you guys don't know, this is Kate Reddy, our newbie. Kate will be covering while Arabella's off on maternity. Sorry, Kate, please shoot.'

The thing is, I went in with this really good idea I thought Jay-B might buy. But the moment we sat down my mind flicked like a switch to School Frequency, remembering I hadn't returned the bloody form for Ben's German exchange student. Friedrich? (*'Roy, can you please find name of the German boy coming to stay in March?'*) And when it switched back to the Work Frequency three seconds later, the idea was gone. *Poof!* Just like that, gone.

There I am with twelve pairs of eyes on me and I plead silently with Roy.

'*Please, Roy, this is our first day back at work in almost seven years. Please go and fetch me that brilliant idea I had to impress The Boy with. It's got to be in there somewhere. Forget Friedrich.*' Christ, this Perry memory-pause is really getting me down. I need to be firing on all cylinders. '*ROY?*'

And I just sit there like a carp out of water, mouth opening and closing. Thinking of Barbara who believes Jem the dog is still alive. Thinking of Ben's exchange student, the one I'd forgotten. (Cedric? Yes, Cedric, I'm pretty sure.) Thinking of Conor telling me my body's taking longer to respond because it's older. 'No worries.'

'Sage!' The word just pops up, from a chaos of Joely's menopausal tea and Mum's carpets.

'I'm sorry?' says Jay-B, not sounding the least bit apologetic. 'What's sage got to do with anything?'

Take a deep breath, fight down the panic. Then, suddenly Roy, bless him, is back with the missing thought and I'm up and running: 'Oh, you know, Warren Buffett. The Sage of Omaha. Buffet has this really great idea. Make a list of your twenty-five top goals then go through it and circle the top five and act on *those*. They will be the investments you really believe in.'

'Like it, Kate,' says The Boy, tapping on his phone. 'Top Five. Joe, can you make a note of that? Top guy, Warren Buffett.'

7.05 pm: Would anyone like to ask Mummy how her first day back at work went?

No, fine. I understand that people have better things to do than pay homage to the breadwinner. Richard just waved at me, scooting through the kitchen on his way to the shower, after chucking a pungent Lycra top on the floor of the utility room. Emily yelled at me when I put my head round her door. Apparently, I interrupted a vital eyeliner tutorial and she got a black streak down the side of her face. Ben is in the living room playing some horrible new video game, which I don't recognise and am quite sure I didn't pay for. (*Did we buy that game for him, Roy?*) The only one pleased to see me is Lenny, who practically leapt into my arms when I came through the door and has stuck by my side ever since. Sally calls him Velcro Dog. Am grateful to inspire such unqualified adoration in at least one member of the household. Later, I need to do some work, looking through client profiles so I can be on top of things if The Boy throws a question at me tomorrow. First, I need to make dinner and then it's time for my tranquilliser of choice.

8.39 pm: My mother rings at the precise moment I sit down to watch *Downton Abbey*, which I have recorded specially to unwind after work. You know, sometimes I wonder whether there is some vast global conspiracy to prevent me having a moment to myself. Perhaps my parents, in-laws and kids are all fitted with earpieces, like Carrie in *Homeland*: 'Hey, looks like she's poured herself a glass of wine and is lowering herself onto the sofa and assuming a TV-watching position. Uh-oh. Are you gonna interrupt her or am I? Over!'

'Thing is, Kath, I can't decide about the curtains. Do you think I should go for the biscuit or the sage?'

Not this again.

'I don't know, Mum. What do you prefer?'

'Well, they're both nice, but the biscuit's a bit washed out. It goes with everything though, doesn't it, biscuit?'

'Yes, but green is very fresh and pretty . . .'

'Oh, I don't like GREEN.' My mother shouts suddenly as though an intruder had frightened her.

'Okay, but you said sage was one of the options, that's all.'

'Did I? No, I don't like green. Very bilious is green. Julie's got oatmeal in the front room.'

'Oh, that's nice.'

'Terrible. Looks like she's made the curtains from Shredded Wheat. What do you reckon to biscuit then?'

'Um . . . Lovely. Very, er, biscuity.'

Gulp of wine. Although I'm on the wagon in the run-up to the college reunion, I'm permitting myself a drink tonight to celebrate first day back at work. Lower eyelids like shutter on a camera. Open them to see the Dowager Countess of Grantham pulling that face she makes before launching one of her Wildean witticisms. Maggie Smith's mouth looks like a drawstring purse. Is that what they mean by pursed lips? Downton's Lady Grantham is supposed to be a snobbish harridan. I like her far more than Lady Mary, a creature of 'motiveless malignity'. Who said that? (*'Roy? Roy? Need you to check a quote. "Motiveless malignity?" Macbeth maybe.')

Where was I? Oh, yes, I love Lady Grantham. She makes me think old age might be a wicked pleasure, not just decrepitude and ever more fearful forgetfulness. Like poor Barbara with all her kitchen stuff out on the worktop. Plus, unlike my mother, Lady G does not deliver punishingly long monologues about curtains and carpets.

Suddenly, there is a squawk from the phone. 'I don't want that Gordon Brown taking my money,' says my mother.

'Gordon Brown isn't the Prime Minister any more, Mum.'

'Isn't he?'

'No. Gordon Brown went ages ago. Have you taken your tablets today, Mum?'

'Course I have. I'm not senile yet, you know.'

'I know you're not.' As I say it, I get a pang thinking of Barbara, who really is senile with no tablets that can fix it. 'You're doing brilliantly. I can't believe how well you bounced back after the heart bypass. You know that I've got a new job, Mum. The one I told you about. It's a bit scary getting back in the saddle after all these years. I feel old and clapped-out to be honest.'

'Don't go overdoing it, Kath,' says my mother. It's her reflex reply, always was. Don't think she really heard what I said. Not sure she can take my worries onboard any more. Hate to think what would happen if she found out about Emily's belfie. Her head would explode. Hell, *my* head is exploding!

'You always were a one for doing too much,' my mother says. 'Do you think sage walls would go better with the new carpet?'

Hold phone slightly away from ear, just close enough to catch my mother talking me through the many different greens in the paint chart. Centre Court Green. Sherwood Green. Olive Green. Seasick Green. Why bother? I know she'll end up picking magnolia, the default colour of the English imagination.

Take another gulp of wine and resume watching *Downton*. What I really need is a Mrs Hughes to take care of the house and Anna, that lovely ladies' maid. A Carson to strike a gong and summon recalcitrant children to dinner would also be fabulous. Wonderful, capable Mrs Hughes could oversee the mad manor, and she wouldn't mind a bit that Piotr has removed the kitchen sink, so we are having to get water from the teeny basin in the cloakroom and the kettle won't fit under the taps so you have to use a glass to fill it. Anna, meanwhile, could update my back-to-work wardrobe, sew on missing buttons, adjust the seams, etc.

'Will you be wanting the blue day-dress, Milady, which makes you look like you could actually be forty-two, even though your half-century is approaching like a train? Or would you prefer the nine-year-old black Joseph jacket you can no longer button up over your once fabulous and now frankly sagging bust?'

'Oh, Anna, be a dear and pull in my corset a notch.'

'Yes, Milady.'

9.31 pm: Enter Richard with another uplifting herbal brew. Instead of joining me on the sofa, he stands there regarding the TV screen with a look of immense pain.

'I don't know why you watch that rubbish, Kate,' he says. 'It's a ludicrous parody of what society was like in the Twenties. Do you really think an earl would waste his time advising his cook about a memorial to her deserter nephew?'

'I don't want a documentary about *Das Kapital*, thanks, Rich. I want to relax. Can you get me another glass, please?'

He takes the empty wine glass with evident distaste and hands me the 'I'm A Feminist' mug in exchange.

'Joely says that alcohol can exacerbate menopausal symptoms.'

'Like what?'

'Well, mood swings.'

'Oh, please. Spare me the clean-living lecture.' I expect Joely's idea of stress is figuring out what flavour Whiskas to feed her nine cats. 'I'm just trying to unwind after my first day back in the office which no one seems even vaguely interested in.'

'Mu-um?'

'Yes, darling, what is it?' Emily comes and sits next to me, leans in close and starts twiddling my hair, wrapping a strand around her forefinger, like she used to do when she was a baby drinking her milky bottle.

'Mum, Lizzy can like get me this fake ID from her sister Victoria who's got the same hair as me, we look really similar, so I can go out with them on Friday night. Pleeaaaase, Mum.'

Here we go. Round Twelve of the 'Why Can't I Get Fake ID?' battle. Em is desperate to be in the cool group at school, but I won't let Emily use fake ID, so she will never be allowed into clubs or the cool group. Ergo, I am an evil witch.

'Darling, how many times? I said no, OK?'

She pulls away, taking a strand of my hair with her. *Owwww.* '*Whyyy*?'

'Because it's not suitable, that's why.'

'You never think *anything's* suitable.'

'How about illegal?' says Richard soothingly. 'Mummy's right, darling, I'm afraid underage drinking is illegal.'

Richard now assumes his traditional role as Mother–Daughter Peacemaker on the Iran–Iraq border. It makes quite a tableau: my daughter is standing up to me, my husband's standing up for me and, most important of all, they're both standing in front of the bloody telly.

'Will everyone please get out of the way so I can see Mr Carson? All I want to do in this world is spend one hour watching a functioning household in 1924.'

10.33 pm: I go up to Emily's bedroom to apologise for sticking to my principles and not letting her use fake ID to get into a club. You might think it should be the other way around, and it's Emily who should be apologising to me, but there you would be wrong.

Just my luck to be a mother at a time when teenagers are able to speak to their parents in a way no previous generation in history has allowed. I can remember my dad accusing me of being an ungrateful little tyke, and I probably was. But my kids have so much more to be thankful for than we did. Rich and I have observed and nurtured their fledgling emotions, taken pains to get to know them as individuals, made sure they eat a balanced diet, frequently bust the budget to deliver most requests on the Letter to Santa. We have never smacked them – well, maybe that time at Luton airport when Emily got on the luggage carousel. We have read them millions of words from carefully selected books and taken them to Suffolk and Rome and Disneyland Paris, not left them in the back of the car with a packet of smoky bacon crisps – which is what happened to Julie and me while our parents were in the pub. (The car's cream plastic ceiling had turned saffron from Dad's chain-smoking.) And guess what? Em and Ben grew into teen-agers, just like we did, only much ruder and a lot less grateful. I mean, how is that fair?

Emily is lying on the bed scrolling through her selfies. She won't look at me.

'Darling, I'm sorry about the ID thing, we just can't let you break the law, it's not safe.'

'S'NOT THE ID,' she wails. 'So much work. I mucked up my French. Can't cope.'

'Look at me, Em. Look at me. You've just started a new course and that's stressful for anybody, OK? Mummy just started a new job and I'm worried I can't manage.'

'You're not.' Em has stopped crying and I can tell she's listening.

'I am. Of course I am, sweetheart. I have to prove myself in front of all these new people and I haven't done a scary job like this one for a long time, not since you and Ben were little. Do you know I'm the old lady in my office?'

'You're not old,' Emily objects, half sitting up and her hand on my arm. 'You're really young for a middle-aged woman, Mummy.'

'Thanks, darling. I hope I am. Are you behind with your homework, love?'

Emily nods. I thought as much. The door between us that's been slammed shut is briefly ajar and I must lose no time in getting inside, before she closes it again.

'Well, we can fix that.'

'We *can't*, Mum.'

'Yes, we can. Is it an essay?'

'*Twelfth Night*. Mr Young gave me an extension, but I can't do it. Got to get it in by Wednesday or I get detention. There's like so much. I can't. I caaaaaaan't.'

173

'OK, so how about you send me what you've done so far, and Mummy will take a look at that, pull it together, yes? I bet it's really good. Then you can hand something in and you'll be back on track. Everything will feel better once you've caught up, I promise, darling. Now, let's put the phone away, shall we? It'll keep you awake, my love, it's bad for your brain. Can I take your phone out of the room? No. OK, so I'll put it down here. You can see it. It's just there. It's charging. No, I'm not going to take it away. Sleep now. Sleep, my angel.'

Midnight: Going through some client files to try and get myself up to speed. Brian the brewery baron sounds interesting. Arabella's notes say that Brian's a 'bit of a handful': that's industry code for sex predator. Am dropping off, but before I sleep must look at *Twelfth Night*. I did the play at school so hopefully it will all come back. ('*Roy, can you get out thoughts about Shakespearean comedies for me, please?*')

I never wanted to become one of those crazy, ambitious Sadie mothers, the kind who write their kid's coursework when they're in an anorexia unit.

Just look at yourself, Kate.

Richard always says our parents wouldn't have had a clue what subjects we were doing at school. It's true. Now, it feels like we're practically taking the kids' exams for them. Is that why everyone's so bloody stressed? The parents are stressing the kids out because perfect grades are achievable if they behave like lab rats, negotiate the maze and open the correct boxes. The kids are stressing the parents out because they duly behave like lab rats, who open the right boxes then all end up going mad and gnawing off their own feet. No one dares be the first to ask if the experiment is worth it.

I know I shouldn't be doing this for her, but Emily seems

so worried. If I finish this essay she'll be back on track. It's just this once, isn't it?

12.25 am: 'So, City superwoman, you didn't end up telling me. How was your first day?'

Richard has come to bed in a pair of baggy grey sweatpants. I'm guessing they're yoga trousers. I slide Em's copy of *Twelfth Night* under the duvet. Rich believes that children should 'build resilience'; don't think he'd approve of me writing an essay for her. Besides, I don't want to risk another argument. He isn't wearing anything on his top half, revealing an almost hairless, wiry torso. The hair on his head is grey and wispy. This is how a super fit man who has cycled several thousand miles and eschews all refined carbo-hydrates looks; like an emu having a bad experience of chemotherapy. Obviously, I bury that unkind thought as soon as I've had it. (Does Richard look at me and think, 'What happened to that fit blonde I married?' Wouldn't blame him if he did.)

I tell him the office was surprisingly OK. 'Most of the guys on the desk are blanking me until I prove I won't be a passenger, which is fine. Nice girl called Alice. My immediate boss is a cocky little hipster. Jay-B. About the same age as Ben with roughly the same social skills, but, unlike Ben, he probably has his own pedicurist. I don't need any help with the client stuff, but some of the new technology is totally beyond me. What's a dongle?'

'Wasn't he in *The Banana Splits*?' Rich says.

We both laugh. Encouraged by his reaction, and thinking that, to make the most of Candy's testosterone patches, I should at least make an effort, I inch towards Rich's side of the bed. But, with a single movement he has turned over and switched off his lamp. I place my hand on his shoulder. So cold.

'M'night.'

'Night.'

Once I'm convinced he's asleep, I retrieve *Twelfth Night* and start to read.

Throughout our life together, I had always been able to reach Richard, to restore that closeness I told myself was our default setting. No matter how great the irritation, how furious the argument, all it took was a glance, an allusion to some shared story grown shiny with the retelling. The way Rich had ordered cuttlefish pasta the very first time we went out together and got black ink on his teeth, making him look like a tramp, never failed to make us laugh. Over time, the date's hopeless lack of romance had itself become romantic, part of our mythology as a couple. This larder of memories, of sex, of life, of family that we had built up, could always be called upon in the leaner times of our relationship. The briefest of kisses on the back of his neck, his hand resting on my waist and we were our selves again, Richard 'n' Kate, Kate 'n' Richard. Everything we had built together over twenty years was there to be tapped into, summoned as evidence that we were made to last.

I hadn't realised how much I counted on that trick working until the time came when it didn't. We lay side by side in bed, just as we had always done, but there was a vast prairie of distance between us. Awake, sleepless in the dark, eyes wide open and often drenched in night sweats with Richard snoring beside me, I increasingly thought of us not as a couple, but as twin solitudes. Together yet apart. We might as well have lain in separate tombs. The loneliness was far more acute than any I recalled feeling when I was alone. It was easy – all I had to do was reach out and touch his back, but I couldn't reach out across that nine-inch chasm. The will was there, at least sometimes it was, but my arm would not obey the instruction. I was no longer sure who I would be touching. Yes, that was it.

We hadn't had sex since New Year's Eve, after the Campbells' party. And that had been awful – had felt, in fact, like carpentry. When, at last, his wilting penis hardened to the point that he could, he stuffed it inside me with his hand and I cried out because I was dry down there, and it hurt. He was drunk and he hadn't waited for me to be wet, but why would he when we'd never needed a lubricant before? He hadn't even kissed me. Kissing would have helped release the juices. But the kissing stops at some point in a marriage, although the sex may go on for a long time after.

At each thrust, I could feel the vagina walls chafing, being rubbed raw, and my mind strayed to the medicine drawer in the bathroom and what cream I might use in the morning to make it not sore. There was one old sachet of Cymalon, from the time when we made love frequently and I always ran straight to the loo to pee away the bacteria. As my husband moved on top of me, I could picture that creased sachet, tucked in a side-pocket of my Cath Kidston washbag. I could have said 'Stop', could have pushed him off me, protested about the lack of foreplay, but it was easier to pretend my cry of pain was pleasure and to cry out some more so he would come quickly, and it would be over.

Roy says 'motiveless malignity' is actually a description of Iago in Othello, *not Macbeth, who was motivated by his wife. Lady Macbeth obvs going through perimenopause and therefore not responsible for violent mood swings, bullying of husband, child murder, etc.*

10

REBIRTH OF A SALESWOMAN

The first few days back at work were surprisingly uneventful. Jay-B gave me lots of client reports to do and I was grateful for the monotony and for the opportunity this simple task afforded me to observe my new colleagues; to figure out who might be a potential ally and where I would have to watch my step. As a freelance, I was used to working alone and I'd forgotten what a complex, seething ecosystem an office can be. Last time I sat here, it was as a boss; it was many years since I'd been this low down the food chain. Mine was the *Benjamin Button* of careers; age and status had both gone backwards. It definitely took some getting used to.

Within a couple of hours, I'd figured out that Jay-B, lording over the flies like a Banana Republic dictator, was over-promoted. Must have accelerated up the greasy pole when they had a clear-out of the old guys after the crash. He was good, but not nearly as good as he thought he was, which is almost more dangerous than being bad. In a crisis, the only thing

Jay-B would save was his own skin, and his hair products; that quiff took serious maintenance.

Troy was unofficially Number Two on the team. Jay-B should have appointed someone older to balance out his lack of experience and gravitas, but I reckon he relied on Troy's brashness and trodden-puppy subservience to make himself look good. Classic rookie error. Honestly, when I saw what that kid had done to My Fund I could smite my head on the desk. Smote? Smite? Whichever, it infuriated me, but I wasn't there to take charge, or to point out their mistakes, just to collect a pay cheque. I decided to adopt a strategy of asking Troy for help when I didn't need it because Troy was the kind of jerk who enjoyed patronizing the ladies, and it cost me nothing to give him that simple satisfaction. Honestly, Troy could not have been more thrilled with his clueless new sidekick.

Otherwise, it suited me to say very little. Alice, in the next chair, chatted away, but I made only guarded replies. I wanted to disclose the bare minimum of personal information, until I got used to being forty-two and to never having worked here before. It takes time to get into character, ask Dustin Hoffman. After a couple of easy-peasy days, I did find myself wondering if it had been absolutely necessary to lie about my age and then I overheard Claire Ashley talking to Troy about Phil, a guy in Treasury, who they were thinking of moving across.

'Oh, God, he's a bit past it,' groaned Troy. 'He's not going to have enough energy and appetite, is he?'

'Hey, Phil's two years younger than me!' said Claire, playfully thumping Troy on the shoulder.

Alice told me Claire was forty-one, so Phil could be described as 'past it' at thirty-nine. As I told Sally before my interview, forty-two was practically a Zimmer frame and fifty has a Do Not Resuscitate notice taped to its forehead.

Tuesday, 1.01 pm: Things are so undemanding in my new role that it is easy for me to switch between a client report on one screen and Emily's *Twelfth Night* essay, which I am correcting and expanding, on the other. There was only one sticky moment when Troy appeared at my shoulder and said loudly, 'Who the hell's Sir Toby Belch?'

'Oh, thanks, Troy,' I said, grateful-minion smile on full beam. 'You spotted a typo. It's Toby Welch, actually; he's a big noise at Feste Capital. New outfit. Thought we should try and get to him if we can.'

Troy's grin exposed ratty, pointed little incisors, too small for his wide, almost feminine mouth. He was pleased to have taught the new girl another lesson. Once he was a safe distance away, I returned to my argument about how *Twelfth Night* shows that sometimes deceit is the only way to go. Emily's essay was coming along nicely, if I say so myself.

Sod's Law that Jay-B should then throw my first presentation at me, for this very afternoon. Put it another way: Troy was handed the pitch by Jay-B and Troy has pushed it on to me in what he is pretending is a huge personal favour, but I strongly suspect is a toxic game of Pass the Parcel. Why do the words poison and chalice spring to mind? Ridiculously short notice too, but I can hardly say no. Here's a chance to prove I'm not just middle-aged desk fodder, but someone Jay-B can send out to firefight if necessary.

From the little that Troy has told me I have to pitch to portfolio analysts for a Russian family in Mayfair, taking Gareth from Research and Alice, my marketing colleague, with me because no Investment Managers are available. Unclear if any of the Russian family members will be present, also unclear who the competition is – who else will be pitching for this dubious privilege? We were asked to take part in this Beauty Parade at the last minute for reasons no one can quite explain. Maybe someone pulled out, having decided they didn't much like the look of it?

Troy's exact words to me were: 'We've got this Russian, it's not ideal, but the lawyer says he's got forty million to invest. He's been working with him for years and they say he seems fine.'

Anyway, no use dwelling on the negatives. Here's a chance to see if the old girl can come out of retirement and show the kids how it's done. We've got half an hour to pitch, including fifteen minutes for questions. No time for thorough research on the client, let alone paying an outside company to do the due diligence and dig up any possible dirt. I set Alice to Googling Vladimir Velikovsky and his family while I call the lawyer who tipped us off about this 'opportunity'. He's out to lunch. Pick up the phone to call Compliance in the building, and then it comes back to me. I'm new. It's always better to see people in person, make them feel more valued, plus they don't know me or trust me yet. Alice says Compliance is on the fifteenth floor.

The lifts are busy taking people to lunch, so I take the stairs. Two steps at a time. (Conor would be proud of me!) At the desk, I introduce myself to Laura, the Compliance Manager, and put on my friendliest, most trustworthy face. Then I outline the situation with the Russians. Laura wrinkles her nose, as if she has just opened a drawer and found yesterday's tuna sandwich. She says that, as the client is 'from a higher risk jurisdiction' (translation: probably total crook), Compliance would like to do enhanced due diligence on this one.

'How much time do we have?' she asks. 'Start of next month OK?'

'We have about twenty minutes till the cab comes.'

Laura is aghast. Says that, under the circumstances, she would say she is 'marginally unhappy' about me attending the meeting.

OK, but 'marginally unhappy' is still not a definite 'No', is it?

Presentations were always my forte; I need to grab this pitch if only to prove to Jay-B that I'm not some deadbeat temp just keeping the seat warm for Arabella's maternity leave. Tell Laura cheerfully that I very much doubt we'll win. And I really don't want to let down the lawyer who gave us the tip-off. The lawyer has said that Mr Velikovsky is 'fine', which is one up on being 'marginally unhappy' with him, I suppose. Although the legal definition of 'fine', in these circumstances, may well turn out to mean 'not hitherto proven to have fed any business associates to his pet shark'.

2.03 pm: In the taxi on the way to Berkeley Square, Alice shares her Google findings with me and Gareth. Vladimir Velikovsky made an estimated £350 million or more buying gas at a preferential rate from some allies of Vladimir Putin and selling it on at a higher price. There are only two photographs in the public domain. In one, he is posing in the snow, with a Kalashnikov slung over his shoulder, behind a huge, black, dead, and rather cross-looking bear. All I can see of him – the hunter, not the prey – is a pair of mirrored ski-goggles and a voluminous padded parka. The second image shows him beside Mrs Velikovsky, Kristina, a former Miss Belarus, who looks as if she herself has just bagged some big game of her own. You could cut yourself on her cheekbones.

'What did she see in him, I wonder?' demands Alice. 'She's insanely beautiful.'

'Go on,' chuckles Gareth, 'take a guess.'

'I'm sure Mr Velikovsky is perfectly charming,' I say. 'Have they got kids, Alice?'

'Two boys and a girl, as far as I can tell,' says Alice. 'I think the oldest must be about eleven. Oh, and he likes pizza and vodka.'

'The son or the dad?'

'Almost certainly both.'

A gentleman of exquisite taste, then, Mr V. It's not much to go on, but it'll have to do. As we get out of the cab, and Gareth is paying the driver, I get this sharp, crampy twinge in my stomach. Just nerves probably. *Come on, silly, it'll all come back to you.*

Alice has Nurofen to hand, and I throw two of them into my mouth as security men in black leather jackets and dark glasses open the front door. Tom Cruise would have entered through the roof.

2.30 pm: The meeting is in a ballroom on the first floor of one of those seven-storey London Georgian houses. All of the original features have been painstakingly ripped out and replaced with aluminium industrial staircases, which look like a New York fire escape, and those open, pebble-edged gas-fires that were fashionable for about five weeks and now appear both silly and chilly – the exact opposite of what you want in a fire. The house must be Grade 2* listed, if not Grade 1. The heritage people would have a fit if they saw what's been done to it, but the owners need not trouble themselves with petty things like listed building consent. With wealth of this order, the world asks *you* for permission, not the other way around.

It's so peaceful up here; the cars in the square below seem to be in a silent movie. It's the kind of hush that only several billion can buy, outside of a monastery or a tomb. There is a boardroom table with a white Carrara-marble top, and behind the table sits a trio of our would-be clients: non-speaking, non-smiling, and, to judge by their expressions, non-alive.

The trio goes as follows. Large, Little, Tsar. The one on the left is a bruiser – looks like he spends his evenings and weekends doing some actual bruising. If Russians played rugby, that would be fine, but ask this fellow whether he likes to be hooker or prop and he would thump you. He hunches forward, eyebrows one single line of black thatch. In the middle is a trim, slim, compact figure, who appears to have popped straight out of a box. Crisp cuffs, starchy collar, beady eyes a-glitter behind wire frames. Probably the numbers guy. And so to the Tsar: noble bearing, neatly trimmed beard – looks like he should be sporting the Order of the Silver Sable, First Class, on a ribbon round his neck. A Savile Row suit that costs more than my car. May well be distantly related to British royal family. May well, if I'm honest, be Prince Michael of Kent.

So, which of them is the dreaded Velikovsky, master of beauty contestants and slayer of bears? My money's on Prince Michael, although my money carries about as much weight in this room as my degree in History. None of the three rose at our approach, or made any sign of greeting; none has introduced himself yet, nor do any of them, it would seem, feel the urge to do so. Perhaps they are three-in-one, like God. All in all, it's National Mateyness Day.

Deep breath. As I'm about to start speaking, I do a double-take. That painting on the wall behind them, of an odalisque lounging around, with her harem pants and her almond eyes – the world's most beautiful slacker – could almost be a Matisse. The colours are dazzling enough. Then I remember where I am. *Don't be thick, Kate. Of course, it's a Matisse.*

'Good afternoon, gentlemen, it's great to be here and thank you for giving us the opportunity to tell you a bit about EM Royal. To start with, allow me to give you a little bit of background. At EMR, we have an exceptional research team. Gareth Bowen, our head of Research, is here today to give you an insight into how we do things. My colleague, Alice Myers, will talk you through investment strategy. We are extremely proud of our performance. We've got two hundred and fifty million pounds of assets under management. Our fees are very competitive and, believe me, our service is second to none.'

I soon relax and start to enjoy myself. It comes back to me. *You're good at this, Kate, really good.* Compared to the swashbuckling presentations I used to do a decade ago (one, notably, standing on a desk on the 105th floor of the World Trade Center, alas), it's a cinch. The muscle memory kicks in.

'Gentlemen,' I say, 'please look on our fund as a high-performance kicker to run alongside your more conventional investments. Think of us as your Cristiano Ronaldo.' I can feel Alice stiffen slightly beside me. The trio opposite smiles nervously, wondering where this comparison is going. 'Well, Ronaldo without the tantrums or the hot-pink shorts.'

They are still laughing when I feel it happen. Oh, God. Not just bad period pain, not just the trickly inkling that a period has started. More like a melting glacier in one of those time-lapse films that show the history of the Earth in five seconds. It's as though a land mass has crumbled in my womb and fallen away completely. Something catastrophic is happening down there. I need to get to the loo immediately.

Luckily, I've just reached a point in my spiel where I can hand over to Gareth, so I don't feel like a complete fraud when I say, 'Excuse me just a moment. I'll leave you in the capable hands of Gareth, our legendary research supremo. Gareth and

Alice will answer any questions you may have. Gareth, over to you.'

Gareth and Alice look like I have just handed them a small nuclear device, but I can't worry about that now. Get up and perform a kind of crab-like skedaddle across the vast room, trying to keep my thighs together in case anything drops onto the paler than pale Danish-wood floor. Thank God I wore black opaque tights because I thought it was just another work day, not the sheer hold-ups I usually wear to look the business for a pitch.

I stumble through the heavy door into the ladies' cloakroom. It is the most beautiful I have ever been in. The walls are lined with hand-painted silver chinoiserie paper featuring the palest-pink magnolia trees and darting hummingbirds so lifelike it feels like a bird could fly onto my hand at any moment. The washbasin is a ceramic barge, almost bigger than our entire bathroom at home, and on the windowsill there blooms a dense field of white orchids. I practically fall onto the loo. Safely sitting down, and with my knickers and tights around my ankles, I get a chance to assess the damage. It's unspeakable. Who knew this much blood could come out of one person? It's not just blood either; there are liver-like clots. I feel faint just looking at them. For a moment, I wonder if I'm having a miscarriage. Then, I remember that I haven't had sex since New Year's Eve. Can't be pregnant. Momentary relief. Doesn't last long. Oh, God, please help me, somebody help me. I feel hot and sick, but I can't stay here like this, I can't. This haemorrhage is not in our promotional material, that's for sure. *Come on, Kate, come ON!* Time to dump that Loch Ness monster into the toilet and mop myself up.

Gingerly I remove first my tights and then my knickers, flush as much of the abbatoir mess as I can flick off down the loo, and place a big wodge of loo paper between my thighs. Carefully rising from the toilet, I put my pants and tights in the vast basin, run hot water in a torrent and pump in as much soap as I can get out of the silver dispenser. Swirl around briskly then leave to soak. Allow the loo paper to absorb the accumulated bloody mess between my thighs for a few seconds then flush down the loo. Repeat the process. Flush away again. Repeat process five times till loo paper has run out. Look around for new roll of paper. No roll to be found and I can still feel stuff trickling out of me.

I check my handbag, even though I know for a fact there's no Tampax in there. Damn. Periods have been so light and infrequent for months now I don't bother. Not that a tampon would be any match for the crimson tide. In desperation, I take a beautiful monogrammed linen hand towel, with VV in one corner, hand-embroidered for bear-hunting oligarchs, and fold it into an emergency sanitary napkin. I place that between my legs in a kind of hammock. Now what I need is something plastic for a protective layer, to prevent any leaks – shower cap, bag for disposing of sanitary products, something like that? I look everywhere, down by the side of the loo, under the sink. Nope. All that's here is liquid soap and about thirty giant orchids. Well, desperate situations call for desperate remedies.

I retrieve my tights and knickers from the basin, let the vile water out, and rinse them again. I wouldn't say they were clean, but they'll have to do. Wring them dry as best I can, then step quickly back into the damp knickers. Now I take the biggest orchid leaf I can find – its shiny green surface is waterproof and, when it's flipped over, forms a perfect dug-out canoe – and I slip it into my pants so it can hold Mr Velikovsky's hand towel snugly in place. Then I pull on the tights, which, amazingly, look fine. Now kneel on the floor and clean any splashes of blood with gold-handled, monogrammed loo-brush. I feel like the murderer at the scene of my own crime.

How long have I been in here? Seems like hours, but probably only minutes. *Come on, Kate, get it together. Maybe there's still time to rescue the pitch?* Check myself in the Venetian glass mirror, dappled with age, which hangs over the washbasin. Cheeks very flushed. Quickly apply powder from compact. Touch up lipstick. The towel feels bulky between my legs, like I'm wearing a soggy nappy, but don't think it can be detected through my skirt. I pray it can't. Leave loo and return to the meeting room. I can hear Gareth's warm Welsh tones and feel reassured. It's going OK. Apologise quickly to everyone, in light, bright voice, mention something about seafood for lunch, then I pick up the pitch where I left off, thanking Alice and Gareth for their contributions. There is bewilderment in Alice's eyes, but that glorious smile is fixed in place. Good girl. I see the Russians relax. Under my skirt I can feel the knickers, unpleasantly damp and cold, and under the knickers the orchid leaf, waxy and stiff, like a biodegradable sex toy. Doesn't matter, so long as the bloody tsunami is kept at bay and nothing leaks.

'Mrs Reddy?' The bruiser speaks. It's like listening to a cement mixer. 'Mr Velikovsky, he would like to ask you something.'

'Yes, of course. Please fire away.'

'Mr Velikovsky, he would like to know if you can get his son into Eton College. Sergei he likes mathematic.'

'Ah, well, Mr Velikovsky,' I say, staring fixedly at the Matisse, since I still don't know whom I should be addressing, 'we can offer clients assistance in a variety of different ways. I'm afraid that it's not possible simply to obtain a place at Eton any longer; there is a demanding admissions process, which of course is a tribute to the quality of the school.' (No harm in a plug. The Velikovskys of this world, currently buying up entire parishes of London, can't get enough of such traditional British fare; the only hitch is that not all of it can be bought, not even for ready cash. That annoys them, and makes them want it all the more.)

'Your son may well be in a position to sit that test, but bear in mind that there are many other excellent schools which I'm sure would look very favourably on a child of Mr Velikovsky.' (Basically, pick any cash-strapped ancient boarding school in need of a new science block, and Vlad's your uncle.)

'Needless to say, I would be more than happy to advise Mr and Mrs Velikovsky on the matter of bespoke tutoring services for Sergei. Some of these are available for as little as five hundred pounds an hour.' I give a slight smile, which is returned by the Tsar. He's the one. Must be. He certainly gets the joke. (Offer men like him, or their partners, anything that smacks of a genuine bargain and they will rear back in horror. Why should *they*, of all people, even dream of saving money? Give them some utterly ridiculous quote, on the other hand, and they perk up. Only the best will do, whether it's a yacht, a wife, or the Oxford graduate with impeccable manners who will very patiently coach Sergei in the future perfect of *avoir*. The future can always be perfect, if you've got the cash.)

There is a pause. Then the man in the middle gets to his feet, followed hurriedly by the other two. He comes round the table and approaches me, eyes sizing me up, flicking from my toecaps to my earrings with a sort of shameless candour, as if he were about to purchase me or put me up for sale. The Tsar and the brute hover behind him, radiating respect. If Napoleon had ever ditched the conquest of Europe and retrained as a chartered accountant, he would have been Vladimir Velikovsky.

189

'Miss Reddy.' Virtually no accent. The international, border-scorning voice that is firmly rooted in the First Class Lounge at Heathrow, and nowhere else. 'I believe we understand each other. You have gathered, correctly, that I am something of an Anglophile. And when you admire something, well . . .' He trails off, spreads his hands, and smiles. Ice caps may be melting in the Arctic, but the pack ice of the Velikovsky smile remains as hard as stone.

He takes another step towards me. Oddly, in defiance of the laws of perspective, he seems to be getting smaller the closer he comes. The top of his head is, I would estimate, somewhere around the level of my nipples, which probably suits him just fine. The man with the hundreds of millions is a borderline dwarf. Just for an instant, the walls of the mansion fall away. I am no longer attending a business meeting in Mayfair. I am in *Game of* bloody *Thrones*.

'I think', the munchkin resumes, 'that we could do business together. Perhaps, Miss Reddy, you and your—' he glances at Gareth and Alice, as if struggling to suppress the word 'serfs', then turns back to me, '—and your colleagues would be so kind as to run through the particulars of your proposed investments one more time. Perhaps even twice. Please forgive my caution; over the years, I have found it constructive to', a momentary pause, 'take pains.' Did he say that to the bear? Something tells me this guy hasn't just taken pains, I bet he's given his fair share too.

Twenty minutes later, we walk out into Berkeley Square. A nightingale may well be singing, for we have a firm commitment from the Russians to invest. I apologise to my colleagues for leaving them in the lurch like that.

'Kate, you were awesome,' says Alice.

'What's a bespoke tutoring service when it's at home?' demands a chuckling Gareth.

'Buggered if I know. Like helping my kids with their home-work and charging them a small fortune for it. Not a bad idea, actually. Taxi! TAXI!'

As I climb into the back of the cab, a wave of heat passes from my chest to my face. Whether it's a hot flush or a blush of shame I cannot say.

4.38 pm: We won the pitch. That's the good news. The bad news is that when we get back to the office, Troy, who clearly set me up to fail, does not bother to hide how pissed off he is. The New Girl, Troy's gormless apprentice, has clinched the deal when any fool could see she didn't stand a chance, which is why he gave it to her in the first place. So that *she* could fuck up instead of *him*.

'Is Velikovsky a drugs baron? Has he bumped anyone off?' Troy demands. 'Do we really want to be associated with him? Did you OK it with Compliance, Kate?' On and on, like a pesky wasp at a picnic.

Jay-B strolls out of his office and, to my quiet fury, seems to take Troy's side, saying that if Velikovsky turns out to be the gangster that everyone thinks he is, the risk to our business could be 'reputational'. Russian money is notoriously flaky, etc. Even if Velikovsky comes in for forty mill, he could walk out a year later. (Catastrophe for the bottom line, my arse. It's the Alpha Males closing ranks to squidge the Beta Female.)

Alice rolls her eyes at me and swigs from a can of Diet Coke. Gareth says he's going for a sandwich and does anybody want anything. I thank Troy for registering these strong and perfectly valid concerns. Perhaps making them *before* we went to the pitch might have been even more helpful, but still.

Troy stares at me. Like Vlad without the muscle. Or the power. He's weak and wounded, so Handle With Care.

'OK,' I smile at Troy, 'you could well be right. Let's wait for the enhanced due diligence report on Velikovsky, then see what the head of Risk has to say. Agreed?'

Stomach suddenly cramps, like a labour contraction, and I have to grab the back of a chair to stop myself crying out. Not again, surely. I give it a minute and the pain recedes. Tell Alice I'm popping to M&S for some sushi. Sprint across the piazza. Once in the store, I scoot up the escalator to Ladies' Underwear, buy a three-pack of pants in a large, comforting size, plus black opaque tights and only remember the sushi as I'm running out. On the way back, I stop off in Boots and consider the sanitary protection display. Never needed anything except Tampax before, except when I brought the babies home from the hospital. I pick up a pack of maternity pads 'for postpartum care' and hurry back.

Make a bit of a fuss depositing the sushi on my desk, and loudly offering Alice some, to prove I haven't gone AWOL, then head straight for the loos. In the cubicle, I remove my damp tights and knickers and place both in the M&S bag. Amazingly, the orchid leaf has done its job. Decide to keep the mono-grammed Velikovsky hand towel, aka emergency sanitary napkin, which I roll up small, put in the Boots plastic bag and then my handbag as a war trophy. With toilet paper, I pat dry any part of me down there that still feels damp. The clean-up part of the operation over, I pull on a pair of the roomy new pants – clean, oh, blissfully clean – tuck the wodge-like maternity pad down the front and hastily wriggle into the black tights. I hear the door swing open and a voice calls: 'Kate, are you OK?' Alice.

'Fine, absolutely fine. Be with you in a min. Do you want to start Googling high-end vodkas?'

Laughter. 'Will do.'

I need to get back to my desk and make things right with

Troy. Can't afford to show sign of weakness, not at this stage. Am sliding the lock on the cubicle door when I get a whiff of something bad: the rusty odour of dried blood. Damn. Fumble in my bag for perfume and spritz several generous squirts of Mitsouko between my legs, just in case, and a couple into the handbag for good measure. Troy already smells blood. No need to give him ammunition.

Kate, this is madness, what are you doing?

Sit down again and just give myself a moment, perched on the loo seat. My heart is racing. What the hell just happened to me? Back there in the oligarch palace with Velikovsky's vaginal volcano. I feel . . . what do I feel? A combination of shame and fear. That my body has let me down, sacrificing me on the altar of middle age. That suddenly I've been taken back into a primitive world of animal helplessness, one we spend the whole of our adult lives trying to put behind us. My body, once so loyal, so reliable. Fear and humiliation. *Please don't let me down. Not now. I need you to work so I can work.*

Must make appointment to see that gynaecologist and actually go to it this time. ('*Roy, can you please remind me? Urgent!*')

Check phone. Donald has left a Voicemail (must be bad, Donald never calls my mobile), Debra has emailed (Shoot Me!) and there's a text from Ben, which I answer quickly from the loo seat.

Ben to Kate
Lift

Kate to Ben
Remember I'm at work, sweetheart. If you want me to come and fetch you later from Sam's can you at least ask nicely? 'Lift'

is an elevator, not a word designed to persuade your mother to get in the car and pick you up! xx

Ben to Kate
K

Kate to Ben
What is K? That's not even a word.

Ben to Kate
OK

Kate to Ben
Mummy has had a really tough day and

Delete that. Self-absorbed adolescent male doesn't wish to know about his mother's problems. He wants her to be stable, strong, smiley, cook pasta, give the illusion she doesn't go out to work and exists solely to make his life wonderful. He must never be troubled by the thought of that awful wreck in the oligarch's palace. At the thought of Ben, and what I'm putting myself through just to give him and Emily a good life, and how I'm making such a bloody mess of it, the dam finally breaks.

No. Sorry. Dry your tears. That's quite enough bodily fluids for one day.

Kate to Ben
I'll pick you up from Sam's house. Have fun! Love you xxx

Before I leave the toilets, I drop the carrier bag containing my soiled stuff in the bin, making sure to push the orchid leaf as far down as it will go. Wash my hands thoroughly, carefully apply lipstick and return to my desk.

Right, now where was I?

What a day that was.

First there was me breezily saying I'd write Emily's *Twelfth Night* essay for her by tomorrow. That was when I thought I'd have almost nothing to do. Next came that bloodbath at the Russian palace. Then, when I was safely back at my desk, I had a whispered phone conversation with Donald, who said that Barbara has started to tidy up fanatically, just like she used to when she was herself, only much worse.

'The doctor says you often see patients with dementia displaying exaggerated characteristics of their old personality. Barbara's trying to put everything away. She's hidden my teeth and I can't get her to tell me where they are. What do you think, Kate, love?'

'I don't know, Donald. Maybe look in her dressing-gown pocket or her coat?'

'What's that? Can't hear you. Can you speak up, Kate, love?'

('No, I can't speak up because I'm at work and they think I'm talking to a client, not a senior citizen in Yorkshire whose wife has kidnapped his dentures.')

Once I'd got Donald off the phone with a promise I'd call him back when I got home, I listened to a curt voicemail from Julie. Said Mum needs more help in the house, and we'll have to pay, so what am I going to do about it? Last time I saw Mum, only a few weeks ago, she seemed fine. It's almost like my sister is deliberately laying it on thick to punish me for moving away and doing well. In fact, that's exactly what she's doing, but such is my guilt at moving away that I don't protest, or even try to point out that it doesn't feel like I'm doing well.

I surrendered the moral high ground when I moved back down South, and Julie knows it.

All in all, though, it wasn't such a terrible day – those Russians had taken the bait for a start – just an exhausting one. My resources were drained, my defences were down, my resistance was low. And let's not forget the long shadow in which I was living, the shadow of that particular birthday. Do you know it's a scientifically proven fact that human beings behave worst and most recklessly when their age ends in nine – twenty-nine, thirty-nine, forty-nine, all dangerous years? Maybe we think, 'It's now or never.' And that, of course, had to be the moment it happened.

7.21 pm: Still at office. Just about to leave work. Have to get back to collect Ben from Sam's. Email the stuff I've done on Em's essay to my home address. Check work Inbox one last time to see what assault course Jay-B has in store for me the next day. And there it is. A name I never thought I'd see again. Never wanted to see again. (As soon as I saw the name I knew that was a lie.)

From: Jack Abelhammer
To: Kate Reddy
Subject: Hello again

Oh, Lord, it's him. It's really him. Who knew that a name could summon so much emotion? How awful and how amazing. Hello Jack, my love.

11

TWELFTH NIGHT
(OR WHAT YOU WON'T)

I didn't want to think about him. I could think of nothing else. I got home, I went to collect Ben from Sam's and, while Sam's nice mum, Hannah, was chatting to me on the doorstep, I made all the right shapes with my face – at least I hope I did. I didn't hear a word she said. His name was tapping through me like Morse code. Jack. Jack. Jack.

It was almost as though, by thinking about him over breakfast at the ice rink, I had summoned him, like a genie. That chapter of my life had been closed for a very long time and, as soon as I let the book fall open, Jack emailed me. Can you know that someone is longing for you? Can you sense that a person who rejected you is wild with all regret? Obviously not, but life has its own strange logic and what is coincidence feels like it was meant to be.

Anyway, I needed to put Abelhammer out of my mind and get Emily's essay done for the morning. Richard was out (some workshop again), which was a big relief. First, though, I had some washing to do. I boiled a kettle and carried it to the utility room. Clambered over the bike-accessories assault course and got to the sink which I filled with the piping hot water, then added some from the tap. I immersed the Velikovsky hand towel, and a skein of bright red blood bloomed in the water. It grew and grew like an atomic cloud until the sink was literally a blood bath. I washed the towel again, and then again, before hanging it on the drying rack. The VV in one corner was so densely and lavishly embroidered it felt like moss to the touch.

I had got through the ordeal at the oligarch's palace, God knows how, but I had. All that remained was to finish Emily's essay. She had already started, so my task was to fill the gaps, and expand where necessary. Funnily enough, the topic turned out to be, well, rather topical.

From: Emily
To: Kate Reddy
Subject: Help!!
Hi Mum, this is what I wrote so far. I don't know if it's any good but it's kind of like what I want to say and I wish I could of have had more time. I'm just a bit stressy. Please do any corrections or adding bits that are better.
Love you, Emxxxxx

'The most perceptive characters in *Twelfth Night* are the best at fooling others.' How far would you agree with this statement?'

Most of the main characters in the play are either deceiving people or they are being deceived. By the end of Act One, there is a love triangle. Duke Orsino is in love with Olivia; Viola (dressed up as Cesario) is in love with Orsino; and Olivia is in love with Cesario (who is really Viola)—

Well done, Em. I can never remember who wants to get off with whom. Usually I end up doing a drawing with arrows in it.

Whether this means that the characters are perseptive—

EMILY! CHECK YOUR SPELLING! AND IF YOU MUST SPELL A WORD WRONG, TRY NOT TO PICK A WORD THAT IS SPELT CORRECTLY IN THE TITLE OF THE ESSAY. Honestly. The idea that a child of mine, my own flesh and blood, cannot learn to spell properly, or, worse still, cannot be bothered to spell . . . She would probably say I don't know how to text properly. That I write essays on text when you're supposed to send five words at most, three of them abbreviations and one of them an emoji. And she'd be right.

—are perceptive, however, is open to question. Even Olivia, who is not in disgiuse—

EMILY!!!

—not in disguise, is worried that she is fooling herself and letting her feelings get out of control:

'I do I know not what, and fear to find
Mine eye too great a flatterer for my mind.'

As for Viola, even though she is an expert at pretending, she criticises herself and her gender—

Bloody gender. When did people stop calling it sex?

—for being weak and vulnerable to being made fools of:

> 'Disguise, I see, thou art a wickedness,
> Wherein the pregnant enemy does much.
> How easy is it for the proper-false
> In women's waxen hearts to set their forms!'

This is quite sexist in my opinion because it says that women are like victims when it's men as much as women who get taken for a ride—

This is an A level essay, darling, not an episode of Holby City.

—who are taken in by deception. In fact, the men are even bigger fools in the play. Orsino is much higher in society than Malvolio, but both of them are equally duped.

Probably the cleverest person in *Twelfth Night* is Maria, the maidservant of Olivia. She does not come up with the idea of taking the piss out of—

For God's sake. Please.

—making fun of Malvolio just for the sake of it but (a) because he has been spoiling the fun she has with Sir Toby Belch and Sir Andrew Aguecheek and (b) because she knows exactly how to get at Malvolio. She is clever and she analyses his personality and says that he is 'the best persuaded of himself' and believes that 'all that look on him love him; and on that vice in him will my revenge find notable cause to work.' It is exactly because she knows where Malvolio is at that she gets him to look like such a loser.

Not great, but I'll let it pass. Can't stay up all night. I've got my paid job to go to in the morning.

This is backed up by the other smart people in the play. Viola recognises that she and the Fool are very similar because both of them have used their wits to have a laugh at other people's expense. This talent, like all intelligence, does not match people's status in society. Feste is called the Fool, but is not a total dork;

DORK? Please. Never use that word!

—Feste is called the Fool but is actually very bright and one posh person (Viola) wears a sort of cammerflarge—

Nice try.

—a sort of camouflage that successfully fools two posh people (Orsino and Olivia). In fact, although there are loads of characters in the play Viola is probably the heroine because right from the beginning just after she lands in Illyrria,—

Nearly. Ilyrria? Illirya? (*'Roy? Help!')

—in an unfamiliar country, she realises that it's only by becoming somebody else that she will get anywhere in life:

'Conceal me what I am, and be my aid
For such disguise as haply shall become
The form of my intent.'

And there the essay grinds to a halt. Attagirl, Em. Not bad at all, sweetheart. Plenty of shrewd insights to make up for the dodgy spelling. She really should have more confidence in herself, but girls like Emily set themselves impossibly high standards so they never feel good enough. What was it she said to me? 'I'm not the cleverest, I'm not the prettiest, I'm not the anythingest.' It's the disease of the day. Wish I could wiggle my nose, like Samantha in Bewitched, *and make her see how irrelevant most of the things that worry her will be in a few years' time. Sadly, the one gift you can't give your child is perspective.*

I read Emily's last paragraph again. Does my daughter know, or at any rate sense, that by now she is hardly writing about Shakespeare at all? That she is, in fact, writing about her own desperate attempts to fit in, that all teenagers must put on 'motley' to be in with the cool kids? That Emily's daily make-up tutorial on Instagram is teaching her how to contrive a cat-eyed mask, to disguise herself and her gripping fear that she is not perfect. And making her think that being imperfect is somehow not OK, rather than the human condition. And what will future historians make of the fact that, at the start of the twenty-first century, when Feminism seemed to have won the argument, girls like Emily tried their hardest to look like the courtesans of a previous age when women had almost no power except their looks and the ability to attract a man of status? What the fuck is that about, actually?

Let's not even mention her menopausal mother, who, for the sake of a job, in new and hostile territory, must disguise her age as if it were her sex, in an effort to become, if not a man, at least one of the boys, and a forty-two-year-old *boy to boot? Forsooth.*

The essay needs an ending. Let me put on the cammerflarge of my beloved child and, God (or the teacher, Mr Young) forgive me, while I add something that Emily probably doesn't know.

All this must be set in the context of a time when women were not even allowed to appear on stage. So, all their parts were taken by boys. This means that the Cesario who was watched by spectators in 1602 was in fact a boy pretending to be a woman pretending to be a man. And Olivia, who fell for him, was a male actor, falling for a male played by a female played by another male. Perhaps *Twelfth Night* still speaks to us four hundred years after it was written because, in many ways, we still haven't figured out what girls are allowed to be, or how they are allowed to look, or if the only way they can be taken seriously is to act like a man. If that seems confusing, maybe it's because it really is confusing, and we are still confused at the start of the twenty-first century. If William Shakespeare was alive today, I don't think he would be shocked that so many young people say on their Facebook page that they 'identify as bisexual'. In conclusion, that is why, as Ben Jonson said, Shakespeare was 'not of an age, but for all time.'

1.12 am: Finished. It's crazy late, but at least Emily will have something to hand in tomorrow. Today, actually. She wouldn't speak to me when I got in from work – no change there – but maybe doing this essay for her will help. If I can't give her the confidence she lacks, then at least I can get her out of a detention.

The period drama seems to be over, thank goodness; only some light spotting now, although I really must go and talk to someone about it. (*'Roy, what happened about the gynaecologist? Did we call yet? Please can you remind me?'*)

I run the hottest bath I can bear, then, from the cupboard under the sink I take out the Jo Malone Lime Basil and

Mandarin; barely an inch left at the bottom of the bottle. I've been saving it for a special occasion; its glorious scent reminds me of better, stronger days; days when I took so much for granted, such as a well-behaved womb and being able to afford my favourite bath oil. When I climb in, the water is so hot my body momentarily mistakes it for cold. Lie back, and start soaping myself. Pubic hair is stuck together in matted clumps by the dried blood. I am pulling each clump apart, teasing out the rusty residue, separating the individual hairs, when one finger comes to rest on my clit. I try an experimental circular motion, then press down hard, just to see. Anybody there? Making myself come was never a problem, particularly if I thought of a certain strapping American. There was a song Jack played me on the jukebox at the Sinatra Inn all those years ago. 'The Very Thought of You'. How true, that song. The *mere idea* of him was enough to make my nipples stiffen, my body convulse. How can someone do that to you when they're not on the same continent? I think of Jack's email waiting patiently in my Inbox. I can't open it. I mustn't open it. Even if he thinks he wants to see me, that woman he cared for, she's a ghost; her invisibility date is fast approaching. I want him to remember me as I was.

'How easy is it for the proper-false in women's waxen hearts to set their forms.' *Love's a delusion, Kate, forget it.*

*Illyria. Roy belatedly supplies the proper spelling.

204

12

CATCH-32

6.09 am: Black Friday. Sounds like the anniversary of a terrorist attack but, no, it's supposed to be merry, merry, merry! 'The day when Christmas really begins', according to hideously chirpy woman on the radio. Am up early to get some shopping done online because, sadly, I no longer believe in Father Christmas. There is no Father Christmas. Nor is there a crack team of present-wrapping elves and eight non-pooping, flying reindeer. There is just me – one disillusioned mother of a Christmas – and a very knackered Mastercard. (*'Roy, did you figure out what happened with my credit rating? Urgent!'*) The thing is, Christmas always feels ages away then, one morning, you wake up and it's careering towards you like a carjacked Nissan Sunny in a high-speed police chase.

That's what Black Friday's for: a call to arms for Mother Christmas. And even though my kids are bigger now, no longer spending their entire year in a countdown to the Big Day, Christmas always takes me back to that feeling of dread that I might let my chicks down. Get your bargains right now, madam, says every single ad on Earth, or you are doomed to flounder in full-price, gift-less purgatory and disappoint all your children, who still want to believe in Santa Claus, even though their dad's sole contribution is to ask, at 8.27 pm on 24th December: 'What have we got for Emily?'

Thank God I've already ordered Ben's PlayStation 4. It's so popular, apparently, that it's impossible to get one now. Totally sold out. For once, I am ahead of the game like proper organised mother. Ben told me it's the only thing he wants because it offers a dualshock wireless controller. Me neither.

Yes, I am aware that I should not be feeding my son's electronics habit, but I'd just got my first pay slip in seven years – Hallelujah! – and this new sense of agency made me want to buy Ben and Em something special to celebrate. When the kids were little, and I did a lot of business trips, I always brought them home a guilt gift. Emily ended up with Barbies in the national dress of thirteen different countries, mainly because I had no time for shopping and used to snatch one up at the airport when I was running for Departures. Not long ago, when we were getting ready to move house, we donated the entire Barbie collection to the charity shop and Em said they made her feel weird, probably because she knew each Barbie meant Mummy was absent. I confessed I felt the same; the dolls were symbols of the guilt I could never quite shake when I was trying to live two lives simultaneously. Looking back, I don't know how I did it: the breakneck switching between international flights and needy toddlers, the dark business suit dodging sticky hummus hands. The person who managed all that seems remote from me now, like an actress in a film. I both miss her terribly and feel relieved by my narrow escape.

'The UK is bracing itself for seven days of hot hot deals!' hollers hideous chirpy woman. I switch her off, pat Lenny who is eager for breakfast ('Just a minute, boy'), open a tin and put a saucepan of water to boil on the Aga when I hear furious bellowing from upstairs. What now?

7.12 am: 'We are not going to find it any faster if you shout at me like that, young man. EXCUSE ME, what did you call me?'

The Zika virus is swarming across the Americas, we are either going to be killed by airborne plague or bearded jihadist nutters, but what matters, what really matters, is that Ben's left football boot is missing. And this is my fault. Because, in my given role as Mother of Teenagers I'd Cheerfully Murder, everything is now my fault, even things I have never seen nor heard of or simply forgotten – which, let's face it, is increasingly likely. (*'Roy, have you seen Ben's football boot?'*)

'I put it here,' Ben says, gesturing furiously at the floor, or where the floor should be if it weren't covered in stuff. My son is apparently engaged in a competition with his sister to see whose bedroom can have the least visible carpet area.

'Ben, I tidied and hoovered in here on Sunday.'

'D'uh! Well, that's why I can't find anything,' he protests, shrugging his shoulders and simultaneously raising his outstretched arms to the ceiling like Chandler, his hero from *Friends*. (Both my kids baulk at learning a foreign language, but they speak fluent US sitcom, a flip sarcastic tongue against which mere reason is powerless.)

'Please don't say "D'uh" to me, Benjamin. I am trying to help. If you would only keep track of your—' My domestic sermon is interrupted by more furious bellowing. This time, it's from downstairs.

7.17 am: 'CRAP, why does this SHITTY printer never work?'

'Emily, please don't swear.'

'I'm not. I've got to print my sodding History coursework. SHIT!'

'Did you hear me? I said, don't swear.'

Emily narrows her eyes dangerously. 'You're such a bloody hypocrite, Mum. You swear. Daddy swears.'

'He does not.'

My daughter gives one of her most contemptuous equine snorts. If she had hooves, they'd be pawing the ground. 'Every time Dad hits his head on the beam by the back door, which is literally like seven times a day, he says, "Fuck this bloody house."'

'EMILY!'

'Emily said fuck! Emily said fuck!' chants Ben, who has descended from his room to revel in his sister's disgrace.

'Benjamin, what is that you're playing?'

'*Mortal Kombat*,' he mumbles.

'What did you say?'

'S'not violent, Mum,' he adds hastily.

'"*Mortal Kombat*" *isn't violent*? Do you think I'm stupid or something? Get off that thing *now*. Give it to me! I said, *give* it to me. Right, young man, all your technology privileges are withdrawn for one week.'

'She's been reading that book again,' Emily smirks at her brother.

'Yeah. *Parenting Teens in the Digital Age*,' says Ben with unwelcome accuracy.

My squabbling, obnoxious children have a rare moment of truce, united in mirth against the common enemy. Me.

'Did I miss something funny?' Richard has appeared in the doorway carrying a wicker basket of what look like nettles. Here comes Mrs bloody Tiggy-Winkle.

'Mum's losing it over nothing,' says Emily.

'Yeah, she needs help,' adds Ben.

'Well, Mummy's got a lot on her plate with the new job,' says Richard soothingly, pecking our hideous, foul-mouthed daughter on the cheek and ruffling Ben's hair. 'I'll give you both a lift to school and we'll let Mum get her train, shall we?'

Here we go again. Daddy gets to be the good cop. Mostly, I accept that's the deal, but this morning I could throw the coffee machine at Rich for not backing me up.

Furious now, and overwhelmed by the unfairness of the kids making me the enemy, when *I* was the one up at dawn buying their Christmas presents, I turn on them. 'Hey, I have news for you two. Copernicus rang. He says you're not the centre of the universe.'

Ben looks at his sister. 'Who's Copper Knickers?'

Emily runs out, across the hall and into the kitchen, slamming the door behind her. I hear the loose brass lock clatter to the floor. Again.

'EMILY? Emily, come back, please. You left a page on the printer.'

7.43 am: After I've fed Lenny and remembered to fill his water bowl, I notice the voicemails from my mother. Three within the space of thirteen minutes. Oh, here we go again. Mum has already started fretting about the arrangements for Christmas. As I listen to the first message, my heart sinks.

'Shall I book Dickie into kennels, Kath? I don't want to bring him and be a nuisance.'

I know that she wants to bring her little dog so, in conversation after conversation, spread over weeks, I will assure her that it's fine to bring Dickie, it would be a *pleasure* to receive the doubly incontinent Dachshund for our Yuletide festivities. ('Oh, I don't think so, love. I don't want him spoiling your carpets.'

'Really, it's OK, we haven't got any carpets he can spoil, Mum.')

The phone calls will go on and on, eating up hours I simply don't have. My mother is very happy to talk through every possible permutation of the arrangements before changing her mind: and her indecision is final. When you're getting on, as Mum is, your world contracts, so an event which is several weeks away, like going to stay with your daughter's family for Christmas, fills your every waking thought. For me, it's just another hurdle in the calendar; for Mum it's like climbing K2. The elderly require the same patience you give to small children – gentle encouragement, repetition, endless reassurance – only, what feels endearing in the young can be plain irritating in the old. With both to attend to simultaneously, you are the squished ham in the sandwich, piggy in the middle. I think that's why I've kept Roy so busy lately, sending him to hunt down words I can no longer pull up. Between the pitched battles with cursing children and the monotonous loop of conversation with the elderly, I struggle to complete a single thought of my own.

I decide to call Mum back later. Piotr will be in soon. He's starting really early these days, finishing late, and walking Lenny for me until I can find a dog-walker. The man's a saint. I look forward to seeing him because it means that we really will have a functioning kitchen for Christmas, just like I promised Richard.

Speaking of which. Need to order turkey at upmarket organic butcher as highly recommended by Sally. ('*Roy, can you remind me to order a KellyBronze, please?*')

Settle down at the laptop only to find Inbox flooded with Black Friday reminders. 'Deals you won't want to miss!', '4 Magical Days of Offers', Black Friday up to 50% off and free delivery!' 'For a Christmas less ordinary get your decorations and tealights now!' Unscented tealights. Ten-hour tealights. Bumper shimmer tealights. Midwinter Night's Dream tealights. How on earth did humanity manage before the tealight came to brighten our lives and, by way of a bonus, burn down half our homes?

One more unexpected delight of Black Friday is every merchant I've ever bought anything from decides to message me simultaneously. It's a ghostly rosary, a list of my mortal-spending sins. Suddenly, I spot an email from the supplier of Ben's PS4. I begin to read:

Good Morning Kate,
You placed an order with us on 1 November for PlayStation 4. Unfortunately, we were unable to process your payment due to a reset password.

I shout back at the screen, despite the fact there's nobody to hear: 'NOOOO! But you *told* me I had to reset my password.'

It is not permitted to use a password previous used.

'*What???* That's not even English. Previous used? You said the system didn't recognise my password so how can I not be allowed to use it? What are you talking about?'

Order is cancelled. Please contact Customer Services with any further queries.

'You have *got* to be kidding me. *Please* don't do this. I need Ben's present.'
'Sorry, Kate, is bad time?'
I jump and turn to find Piotr standing just a few feet away from me. Mortified to think of him hearing me raging aloud at invisible Internet cow.

211

'No, it's fine. Come in. Sorry, Piotr. It's just I bought Ben's Christmas present and now it's a disaster because they're saying they've cancelled my order because I used a password I'd used before but they said they didn't recognise that password so I thought it would be OK to use that password again because if I used a new password I knew I'd just forget it.'

This doesn't make sense, not even to me, but Piotr nods and smiles. 'Yes, Kate. Internet not like shop with real person. Try again maybe? Let me help you. Too much open on laptop. See we can close here and here – and here. Now, we can start new.'

Up close his eyes are the green of a rockpool at low tide. I need to get dressed for work. 'Thank you, Piotr.'

From: Candy Stratton
To: Kate Reddy
Subject: You
Hey, what's with the radio silence? I worry when you go quiet on me, honey. Need full update on how you're dealing with working for that Boy running YOUR fund, the one you set up when he was still in diapers. What happened with Emily's butt pic?

Breaking news: think I have found solvent male in New York of the opposite sex who doesn't identify as pansexual, doesn't repulse me and is not on a Witness Protection Programme. Yay!

XXO C

8.27 am: I am going to be late for work. Hideously late. I called a cab and made it do a detour, via Emily's school, where I left the final page of her History coursework with Reception. Jumped back in the cab and we headed for the station, but, by

212

then, the traffic had really built up. Every single traffic light turned red as we approached it. Every bloody one. Just my luck, it was RED NOs day.

Am finally on the train. I manage to fight my way to my preferred window seat and take out *Parenting Teens in the Digital Age* by Dr Rita Orland. The book the kids find so hilarious. Dr Orland says you must not regard this phase as one in which your lovable child becomes an unpredictable monster. 'Your child is not only good when they're not doing bad things.'

Closing my eyes, and pressing my head back against the seat, I ask the Goddess of Mothering for forgiveness. I keep losing it with the kids, when I don't mean to. Ben said I need help, didn't he? Maybe I do. Perry is turning me into an absolute harridan. As though from a distance, I observe that I've started to cry. The two passengers sitting opposite look and then quickly look away again. I sympathise. There's something so naked about someone crying in public, isn't there? All this weird random weeping: is it me or is it Perry, or are we one and the same now? I've got to stop; it's becoming a habit.

I think of Emily struggling to print out her History. So anxious and stressed. She's right, the printer *is* shitty. *All* printers are shitty, designed to flash up mystifying symbols indicating they're out of ink, or jamming paper for no reason. Thinking about what the school day ahead holds for Em, I regret that stupid quarrel we just had, especially my part in it. Sometimes I act, I know I do, like my love for her is conditional – on tidiness, on good behaviour, on improved grades – but that simply isn't the case. However much she may distress or anger me – and, boy, does Emily know how to press that button – my frustration with her is always to do with love.

Kate to Emily

Hi darling, hope you got to school OK. You left a page of your coursework at home. I gave it to Nicky at Reception – she knows you're going to collect it. Hope you have a good day. Pls let me know if there's anything you specially want for Christmas? Love you. xxxx

From: Kate Reddy
To: Sally Carter
Subject: Guilty Secret

Hi Sally, so sorry I had to cancel our walk again. Feeling a bit overwhelmed with the new job tbh. I'd forgotten how tiring it can be. I'm shattered and surrounded by all these kids half my age then I get home and have my own kids to deal with!

I need some advice from someone who's a bit further along the Motherhood track. Would you be horrified if I told you I helped write Emily's English essay for her? I know it's cheating and I shouldn't do it, but Em hasn't been herself since that dreadful business with the belfie I told you about. I'm worried that she isn't coping with her A levels and all the pressures from social media. For the first time since Emily was a newborn, I feel like I don't know what I'm doing as a mother.

Why do they call it Sweet Sixteen by the way? She's sour and vile to me most of the time. Plus, big college reunion is looming and I planned to look totally fabulous and successful which now seems unlikely as:

(a) Will probably lose new job as I can't figure out how to work the 'dongle' thing the IT guy gave me, even though he wrote it all down.

(b) Appear to be growing Robinson Crusoe whiskers

214

while the hair on the top of my head is coming out in handfuls. Seriously, what kind of merciful God would make middle-aged women bearded AND bald?

Typing this on my phone on v v crowded commuter train. Hope it makes sense. Please can we rebook dog walk for tomorrow or Sunday afternoon? Lenny will never forgive me!

Kate x

From: Sally Carter
To: Kate Reddy
Subject: Guilty Secret

Dear Kate, please don't reproach yourself. I can imagine how tiring it is settling into the new routine. Everyone at Women Returners is longing to hear how it's going. You do realise you are now the Poster Girl for midlife employment!

Can I urge you to book in with that gynaecologist in Harley Street I mentioned? He's a real lifesaver. I had an undiagnosed underactive thyroid and I felt exhausted and freezing for three years and my hair fell out. Now take thyroxine every morning, but still have to wear lots of layers as you may have noticed.

As for feeling guilty about Emily's essay, please don't. Parents doing their kids' coursework is the middle class's guilty little secret. In fact, doing the work yourself is jolly noble of you. Oscar said that his mate Dominic's mother paid a UCL English graduate a small fortune to do Dominic's A level coursework as he's thick as a brick, not like Emily. Apparently, none of the Russian kids at St Bede's would dream of doing their own work. They have a different tutor for each subject. It's a total racket.

Antonia started being hideous to me around the age of fourteen and didn't stop till she was twenty-two. She still has her moments! Emily will come back to you, just hang in there. Believe me, you have nothing to worry about with the college reunion. You have achieved far more than most of us. In my experience, those occasions always cause panic and self-loathing and then you go along and rather enjoy yourself.

Kate, I really think you should do something for your fiftieth. I know you want to pretend it isn't happening, but you may feel miserable and regret it if you don't. Please say if I can organise something, however small. I've got a lot more time on my hands now than you and I would actually enjoy it. I used to be good at parties in a previous life.

There are some very dark things in the world and I feel we should celebrate the good and the joyful whenever we can.

Coco says Wuff!

Sally xx

11.01 am: Thank heavens for Alice. I texted her to say I'd been delayed and she bamboozled the morning meeting, saying I was at breakfast with a really promising contact. She even texted me the details of the imaginary person I hadn't met. That girl could really go places.

Lateness apart, everything is going according to plan in Project Undercover Almost-Fifty Woman. Except for the hot flush I just had in Jay-B's office. Pretended I'd had allergic reaction to the lemongrass perfume sticks on his desk. Am now seeking refuge in the Ladies, pressing a bottle of cold water to my cheeks until the heat has left them.

Come out of the cubicle to find Alice putting on her make-up. I give her a hug to thank her for covering for me. 'No problem, Kate. Normally, I'm the one who's late,' she says.

Alice is wearing the same purple dress and taupe jacket she wore yesterday so obviously stayed over last night with the boyfriend. Been with Max on and off since they were at school, or so she told me. Incredibly handsome, wealthy family, done some modelling, not settled yet to any job in particular, holidays in the Maldives and Val d'Isère with his parents. When she showed me Max's picture on her phone I knew I was being invited to bow down before his god-like perfection, as Alice clearly does. What I saw was one of those pointlessly good-looking, spoilt public schoolboys who is nowhere near committing to anything, let alone the girl who has worshipped him since they were fifteen.

How old is Alice: twenty-eight? Thirty? With her long blonde hair and candid, searching blue eyes, she's a dead ringer for her namesake in Wonderland. One of the hardest things about being back at work is seeing all these younger women who I still think of as me. But when I watch Alice in the mirror, I realise with a pang that I am not her, not any more. Her peachy face is untroubled by broken nights or blazing rows with teen-agers; her figure is as slender as a reed – as mine once was – and effortlessly so, without need of brutal, twice-weekly gym sessions with Conor and no pudding or cheese. Ever.

What does Alice see when she looks at me? An older woman (she doesn't know how old) but pretty 'well-preserved', I guess. Although she has no idea of the cost of preservation – and why should she? I never gave it a second's thought when I had a face and body like hers and assumed that youth would last for ever. Please please don't let me become one of those jealous old baggages like Celia Harmsworth, the head of Human Resources who made life hell for me when I was Alice's age.

Let me lift up my sisters! There are some things I don't envy, though. Like her on-off relationship with Narcissus and his magnifying mirror.

'Stayed over with Max last night,' Alice admits with a rueful smile, as though she read my thoughts.

'I guessed,' I say lightly, taking out my own lipstick. 'Don't you keep a change of clothes at his place?'

She shrugs. 'Max is a bit funny about me leaving my stuff there.'

'Really?' (Uh oh. Don't like the sound of that.)

'Yeah. Normally he stays at mine, but he had tennis this morning.'

'Have you thought about moving in together? I mean, you've been going out a long time?'

Alice rolls her eyes. 'Oh, Max is hopeless like that. Says he loves me, can't live without me yadda yadda, but not ready to make the commitment.'

'You do know what Beyoncé says? If he likes it he should put a ring on it.'

'Oh, Kate!' Alice grimaces. 'You sound just like my mum. Guys now, they're not like that. They don't need to settle down.'

'How about you? You need to think about yourself, Alice.'

That's the trouble with girls of Alice's generation. They see an ad on the Tube for freezing your eggs and they think that biology has been vanquished, and pregnancy indefinitely postponed. It's a con and the fertility clinics are full of its victims, handing over thousands to recreate what Mother Nature provided gratis.

Shall I give Alice the lecture? Oh, what the hell. I tell my young colleague that I've seen the pattern too often for comfort. Girl goes out with same guy till their late twenties, hangs in there waiting for him to take it to the next stage. The guy doesn't bother because he's getting regular sex and free food, and men don't initiate anything unless they want sex or food, or a woman insists it happens. Then, at the age of thirty-one, he falls for someone younger, fresher and much more impressed with him. Within seven months, they're married and expecting twins – it's always twins – and he emails the old girlfriend saying he's really grateful that she helped him to grow up and realise what he really wants from a relationship. (Gee, thanks. It was nothing!) The girl now needs to find a new guy to have a baby with. 'But that won't happen overnight, and she really has to start trying within the next couple of years in case she has problems getting pregnant. Trouble is, men run a mile from women who are giving off Let's Make Babies signals,' I tell Alice, 'so, basically, it's Catch-32.'

She drops her mascara wand into the basin, her mouth frozen in that slack 'O' girls make when they are concentrating on applying eye make-up.

'I thought it was *Catch-22*?' she says.

'For men, maybe. For women, it's Catch-32, the age by which you really should have signed up the prospective father of your children. Or the chances of you having any start diminishing by the month.'

'Wow. Are you trying to scare me, Auntie Kate?' There's mockery in those blue eyes and maybe a flicker of fear.

'Not scare, Alice. Just giving you the information you need to make good choices, darling. Remember what I said about always doing your due diligence to check out whether someone's a safe bet?'

'I thought that was clients, not boyfriends?'

'Same principle. Men and clients should be assessed for decency, probity and long-term viability before you invest in them. OK, here endeth the lesson. Sorry, Alice, it's just I've seen too many girlfriends left high and dry by bast— Forget I said anything. I'm sure Max isn't one of those. Shall we go and run

219

through that presentation to Brian the Bolsover-brewery-baron?'

Alice can't hear me. Her hands are plunged in the new Dyson dryer, so powerful it's moving her skin around like water. Glance down at the back of my own hands; a lack of elasticity there is one sign of ageing you can't hide. Ah, hands and neck, the downfall of the genuine fake.

As Alice picks up her bag, she says Jay-B mentioned at the meeting earlier that he wants me to go and woo Grant Hatch, some mega financial adviser. Huge business for us if it came in.

'Hatch is supposed to be a nightmare. Jay-B must really trust you,' says Alice with a grin.

For the very first time, I allow myself to think: maybe I can pull this off. Maybe it's going to be all right.

From: Kate Reddy
To: Candy Stratton
Subject: You

Hi hon, work going OK. Think I am winning The Boy over slowly. They let me do a pitch to Russian oligarch. Poison dwarf. Just your type. Halfway through the bottom fell out of my world or, rather, the world fell out of my front bottom (that's British for vagina btw). I thought I was dying, or at least having a miscarriage. Scary. Really must book to see gynaecologist. They call him Dr Libido! Maybe he can make me human again. Here's hoping.

Great news about solvent, non-serial killer boyfriend. It's been minutes since you had a husband. You know that green satin dress, the one I wore to your last wedding? Well, I was counting on wearing it to my college reunion. Way too tight. Am living on Lite cherry yogurt and Diet Coke.

It's taking sooo long to shift the damn weight. Menopause really stinks. Any suggestions that don't involve scalpels?

K xxx

PS Got email from Jack A

From: Candy Stratton
To: Kate Reddy
Subject: JACK'S BACK!!
Katie, are you fucking kidding me? The great love god ABELHAMMER, who could give you an orgasm discussing commodity prices from Cleveland? How could you not TELL ME? What did he say?

To get into reunion dress you need Vaser lipo to zap the fat pouches. No big deal. Get it done over lunch.

Sorry to hear about the haemorrhage at the oligarch's palace. Yuck. It happens. When I told Larry I was through the menopause he said, 'Thank God. No more Crime Scene periods.'

Obviously, I divorced the insensitive bastard.

Mail me back NOW. Need to know what Jack said.

XXO C

PS Front Bottom? WTF?

From: Kate Reddy
To: Candy Stratton
Subject: JACK'S BACK!!
I didn't open Jack's email. Too dangerous.

From: Candy Stratton
To: Kate Reddy
Subject: JACK'S BACK!!

Open the box, Pandora! What's the worst that can happen?

From: Kate Reddy
To: Candy Stratton
Subject: A certain American
Well, I could unleash feelings for a certain American which I have been suppressing successfully for 7 years. And I don't want to feel those feelings because then I'll realise how little I feel these days which would be unbearably sad and I am nearly 50 and am reconciled to nobody ever fancying me again or kissing me on the lips or having sex again, except at New Year and birthdays which is OK actually. I am not unhappy.
K xx

I sent the email. I know, it was what Emily calls TMI. Too Much Information. But I pressed Send anyway. Old friends are one of the few good things about getting older. You can't have old friends when you're young, can you? All the friends worth having have stuck around, and you can tell them practically anything. Candy knows me almost as well as I know my self. But she was wrong about me and Jack. That door was nailed shut. To open it would be madness. Like Lot's wife, I could not look back.

From: Candy Stratton
To: Kate Reddy
Subject: A certain American
Objection, Your Honor. Not unhappy is not the same as Happy. Open the email. And book the lipo.
XXO C

Absolutely not. Must stay strong. I go to my Inbox, scroll down and down till I find Jack's unopened email. I look at it for a while, lost in thought, my finger hovering over the Delete key.

8.09 pm: Managed entire day at work where I ate only three packets of Juicy Fruit gum and an apple. Hunger is making me hangry. Not helped by Richard deciding to cook a big wholemeal pasta dish for dinner.

'Sure I can't get you some, Kate? You need to keep up your strength, darling.'

Why do men never understand diets? Almost as if Rich is deliberately undermining my resolve to get into the green dress.

'I've got treacle sponge and custard for pudding,' he adds treacherously.

'Yum,' says Ben. 'Why isn't Mum eating anything?'

'Mum's on a diet for her college reunion,' says Emily, reaching for the salad. 'She needs to look hot because she'll be seeing all these guys who fancied her when she was nineteen.'

'Mum hot? Mum hot?' repeats Ben, trying out this outlandish concept.

'Your mother certainly was hot,' says Richard. 'Is hot,' he adds quickly. 'Sure you won't have a spelt roll with your salad, Kate?'

'How many times? I'm not eating carbs.'

(*'Roy, please remind me. Must book lunchtime lipo to fit into green dress. Assert control over own body and mind and feelings and Inbox.'*)

Perhaps I could take a peek at Jack's email. What harm could it do? NO, frailty thy name is woman! *Do NOT open Jack's email.*

8.38 pm: Looking for my laptop to do some more Christmas shopping when I hear a familiar voice coming from the living room. It can't be. Mum?

223

Emily and Ben are sitting on the sofa, Lenny wedged between them, Skyping my mother on my computer.

Emily smiles and beckons me over. 'Mum, come and say hi to Grandma. Auntie Julie's new boyfriend just showed her how to Skype.'

'Oh, hi, Mum.'

'Hello, Kath, love, CAN YOU HEAR ME?'

'Yes, Mum, we can hear you fine. You don't have to shout. Are you OK?'

'I'm fine love. I left some messages on your phone about Christmas. Think I'll book Dickie into kennels. Fancy being able to see you like you're on the television.'

'Hey, Grandma, what's the news on the street? What's going *down*?'

This is Ben, of course, who ribs rather than reveres his adoring grandmother to an extent that I would never have dreamed of as a child. Annoyingly, he gets away with it. Even *more* annoyingly, she actively enjoys being teased.

'My street is lovely, thank you, Ben. I've been out doing lots of weeding and planting in the garden, and I—'

'Planting weed, Grandma? You can get two years for that. Might let you off if it's your first offence.'

Ben and Emily now go through the motions of a polite elderly person smoking a joint – eyebrows up, lips pursed, thumb and forefinger describing a delicate 'O'.

Emily is giggling like a two-year-old. Seizing the moment, she cries out, 'How's the Internet, Grandma?'

I glare at her, to absolutely no effect.

'Oh, it's marvellous. I could be on it all day if I'm not careful.'

'Sick,' says Ben.

'Who's sick? Are you poorly again, Emily? You know when you weren't feeling well, love, I said you should go to the doc—'

224

'We're fine, Grandma, all of us,' Emily replies, cutting my mother short before she can launch into what is, against stiff competition from Dickie, her favourite cause for concern. 'What sort of thing have you been looking at online?'

'I found an awful lot of sites about cats and who they look like. That was really good. But since I've got my grandchildren here now, and you're both the computer experts, how do I get onto Bookface?'

Which is more than my children can stand. They clutch each other in uncontainable mirth and fall off the sofa. Lenny starts barking.

'Um, Mum, it's actually called Facebook.' I decide to help.

'That's the one. Mavis, well, her nephew Howard says it's wonderful, and now she's on it too.'

I have never met Mavis, but over the past two years, for some reason, she has become an oracle whose lightest word is taken by my mother as a universal truth. If Mavis casually recommended space travel when they bumped into each other in Tesco, my mother would immediately send a stamped addressed envelope to NASA, requesting further information and departure dates.

'I'm not sure about that, Mum.'

'No, it's ever so useful, love. It reminds you about birthdays, and I need reminding, at my age. But what I don't know is whether you have to put your actual face on the computer.'

'You can put any body part, Grandma,' says Ben wickedly.

I take a swipe at him and he ducks. Emily hisses and, as her hands form involuntary claws, the sleeves of her T-shirt ride up and reveal her arms. What, has she got scratches on her arms now as well? Is that from the bike accident?

Ben looks triumphant, having managed to offend everyone.

225

Then, as usual, he pushes his luck too far, adding, 'Even your bottom—'

'Mum, it's not that,' I say, cutting Ben off. 'It's just that, once you're on it, you may, you know . . .'

'May what, love?'

'You may end up seeing things or learning things about people that aren't very nice.' I try a weak smile on Emily. She's looking down at the floor.

'Oh, I'm tougher than I look, love.' Which is perfectly true. I wish I could say the same of myself.

'Talking of which,' my mother goes on, 'I was looking up medical symptoms, there's ever so many places that tell you . . .'

'Don't do that, Mum. Once people start that, they get themselves in a terrible state.'

'Oh, I know. Mavis's cousin Val, she had this rash, and she looked it up online and it said she might have contracted HGV.'

'That's what I mean.'

'Unprotected sex with a lorry,' says Ben out loud.

'Ben! I'm warning you.'

'What was that, cheeky boy?' my mother laughs.

'Just saying I hope you're not ill, Grandma,' he says, in a mime of dutiful sweetness. Emily sticks two fingers down her throat, right in front of him.

'Are you all right, Emily love? You're looking a bit peaky. Don't you think she looks pale, Kath? Hope you're not over-doing it at school, love.'

'I'm fine, Grandma, don't worry,' says Em quickly.

'She's fine, Mum. The lighting's not very good in here. We haven't had the electrics done yet.'

'Is it still that Polish Peter you've got doing the work?'

'Yes, Piotr, that's right. He'll have it done by the time you're here at Christmas.'

226

'Lovely. I don't know whether to bring Dickie, Kath. I'm worried he'll spoil your carpets.'

Deep breath, Kate.

'He won't, Mum. Really, please don't worry about that. Just come and enjoy yourself.'

'I've got to go now, I've got a walnut cake in the oven; it's for the coffee morning tomorrow. The last one raised sixty-four pounds. For Help the Aged.' Says she, who is pushing seventy-six.

'Sounds wonderful, Mum. Take care.'

'And you, love. It's lovely to see you all. Emily, Ben. Isn't technology wonderful? Goodnight and God bless.'

For a moment, as their grandmother's face disappears, Emily and Ben lie across me, one on each breast, as they did when they were little. They're heavy now, too heavy really, but I don't ask them to move. We stay there a bit, in the half-dark, holding each other close.

'Grandma's heart's much better,' says Ben, breaking the silence.

'She's really strong, isn't she, Mum?' says Emily.

'Yes, of course she is,' I say, fervently praying that's the case. 'She's incredible, your grandmother.'

How very much they love her, as she loves them. The sweetest, most uncomplicated love of them all. Don't want to think about how we nearly lost her, when she had the heart attack four years ago, or what it will mean for all of us when she's gone.

9.36 pm: After hour-long online battle, successfully placed new order for Ben's present. And it's in stock! There is a God, if not a Father Christmas. Our Father Christmas is out at a visualisation seminar with Miss Batty Herbal Teas.

10.20 pm: Staring at self in bathroom mirror. After six or seven weeks of applying testosterone patches, side effects include:

- (a) Rough, coarse patches on my face.
- (b) Alarming growth and strengthening of existing hairs along chin-line and neck. New outcrop of fine black hairs around – oh, the horror! – nipples.
- (c) Being very snappy & liable to lash out for the smallest thing.
- (d) Swearing like a trooper.
- (e) Ready to have sex with pretty much anything – furniture, household implements, Polish builder.

Do men feel like this all the time? If so, how is it sensible to let them run the world?

Midnight: As I'm turning out the light, email arrives from supplier of Ben's Christmas present.

> **Good Evening Kate,**
> **Apologies for the delay in dispatch, we have had a supply interruption. We expect new stock of your item to arrive 29 December. We will then dispatch your item ASAP. Merry Christmas!**
>
> Nooooooooooooooooooooo.

Emily to Kate
Mum, soz I wz rude today. Thanks for bringing my history to school. Can I hve 50 to my Xmas party? Love you xx

WHAT CHRISTMAS PARTY? (*'Roy, did we agree to a Christmas party?'*)

13

THOSE STUBBORN AREAS

NOVEMBER

Hell hath no fury like a woman who is nine pounds overweight less than a week before her college reunion. Was simply not ready to face the boyfriends of my youth as a middle-aged frump. In flattering light I could once pass for Nicole Kidman. Now I look more like Mrs Doubtfire. Hadn't I promised myself I would approach this landmark occasion like a mature adult, accepting of my body and of who I am at forty-nine, about to be fifty? In the prime of life, a proud survivor, knocked about by the flow and eddy of time, sure, and not to be mistaken for that fresh-faced girl staring so anxiously out of the Freshers' photo. She was right to be anxious; she still had that awful pageboy cut that Denis at Fringe Benefits in the precinct gave her, loosely based on Lady Diana. Very loosely. It made me look like a medieval minstrel. Never trust a Northern hairdresser called Denis who pronounces his name D'knee. As in the Blondie song.

So, I thought I was ready for the reunion. For seeing people

I hadn't seen for a quarter of a century – my God, that's more years than we had been alive when we first met. I was, in that hideous phrase, well-preserved. (Preserved like what? Like pickled onions? Like fish? Can youth, like berries, ripen and be kept from rotting?) I had a new job, an old house full of 'potential', two teenage kids not in jail, and I was happily married. (Well, married. I mean, who is happily married?) I was in a good place. Until I tried on the dress.

You know how you rely on a particular dress or outfit to get you through an occasion you are dreading? When I first worked in the City, I spent every penny I had on a designer suit in Fenwick's; it was worth it. My Armani armour. I would pull that suit on in the morning, like a knight getting ready for a jousting tournament. The navy fabric, jersey I think, was yielding but cut just right, nipping me in at the waist, but affording plenty of protection both front and back. I felt invincible in that suit, which was just as well, given the flak that I took from the guys in the early days. I could never bear to throw the suit out. Then some charity, Dress for Success, asked female executives in the firm if they would donate clothes to be used by women who were trying to get back into employment. I gave my navy suit. I liked to think of it working its magic on some other scared girl who needed to look unafraid.

It never occurred to me back then that, one day, I too would be an anxious woman trying to get back into employment. The circle of life, eh?

Clothes can do that for you, which is why I'd chosen my outfit for the college reunion with such care. An emerald dress I'd splashed out on for Candy's most recent wedding in the Hamptons. Richard refused point blank to attend. 'I'll come to the next one,' he said. (Rich doesn't care for Candy's more-is-more attitude to life and husbands.)

At my age, you need some help lifting and separating, not to mention cantilevering. The emerald dress was the Isambard Kingdom Brunel of frocks, a miracle of structural engineering. It put my boobs and belly back to where they were twenty-five years ago.

At least two ex-boyfriends who were going to be at the reunion had seen me naked between 1983 and 1986. I wanted my breasts to be in the same general area where they last saw them.

I'd had the emerald frock specially dry-cleaned at Five Star in Islington, which does steaming and hand-finishing. It glinted a jealous jade in its polythene chrysalis, hanging on the wardrobe door. I was ready for the reunion, oh yes I was! And then I tried on the dress.

The zip gritted its teeth and went up an inch, but it refused to budge over the flob of flesh below my waist. That marsupial pouch which had never really shifted since I was pregnant for the second time. No amount of pinching fabric together and pulling and pleading would shift it. Nor would the Shaper Suit do the job.

'You've got lots of other dresses, darling,' said Richard, as though there were comfort in numbers.

'I'm wearing *that* dress,' I snapped, slamming the bathroom door and shedding hot, humiliated tears in front of the mirror. So much for maturely accepting my body at forty-nine and a half. I was going to get into that dress by Saturday if it killed me.

It nearly did.

Monday, 11.03 am: Damn, buggeration. Jay-B calls me into his office, just as I am planning to scoot out unobserved, jump into a cab and dash across town for my carefully scheduled 'procedure'. He says my meeting this afternoon with Grant Hatch is crucial.

'I know you appreciate that Hatch owns one of the biggest financial advisers, Kate. Self-made multi-millionaire, tricky customer, but he used to work here as a trader years ago. If we can get our fund onto his platform, y'know, if his guys are recommending us to their clients then, basically, it's jam all the way.'

'I get that,' I say. 'It would be great to get him onboard. Just wondering, why me? I mean, I'm flattered, but I'm new here and there are more experienced people.' (Please, please can Jay-B give this one to someone else because I will still be recovering from lunchtime lipo?)

Jay-B's cheek twitches. He's not going to let me off the hook. 'Well, it looks like you worked your charms on Velikovsky, Kate, and Grant, he's a bit of a ladies' man.'

Oh, dear God. Two of the most ominous words in the English language. Ladies' Man.

'Put it this way, I think you got what it takes to make Grant happy. Not gonna lie, though. He's a rough diamond.'

There are two other worst words, right there. All we're missing now is serial killer.

Thanking Jay-B profusely for this fantastic opportunity with the Rough Diamond Ladies' Man, I walk backwards at speed out of his room, practically bowing like one of the King of Siam's thirty-nine wives. Then, before he has a chance to call me back, I sprint out of the building to the cab rank.

11.33 am: On the way to Knightsbridge, I get an email from Debra. (Subject: Shoot Me!) Says she was on a break with the kids in Marrakesh when she texted a highly promising neurologist she'd met on some dating site with: 'I've just had the most wonderful tagine.'

Unfortunately, and unbeknownst to Deb, predictive text changed 'tagine' to 'vagina'. Says she was puzzled when the neurologist suddenly got very keen and responded with several horny texts about wanting to taste her tagine. Now she's in a bind.

Kate, I really like this guy. He could be The One. He's solvent, sane, single, well, divorced twice, no kids. You know how impossible it is to meet anyone without baggage. I want to tell Stephen I had a wonderful tagine, not vagina, but now he thinks I'm this hot bisexual and suddenly he's really into me. What shall I do?

How the hell should I know? I feel a flash of irritation with Deb and her many disasters. I seem to have become the on-call agony aunt since she started 'dating' – a nerve-wracking American import that came into vogue after I was safely married. Suddenly, it's like women of my age are all fifteen again and wearing hot pants and spraying Silvikrin on our feathery Farrah Fawcett cuts. 'Should I text him?' 'What is the optimum amount of time to leave before texting him back?' As if love were an algorithm.

'Will he hate me if we don't shag on the first date?' Thirty years ago, the question was, 'Will he think I'm a slut if I have sex with him too soon?' Honestly, I'm struggling to see this as progress.

The pursuit of love is exhausting and mostly ridiculous. Debra has, once again, made a fool of herself. Meanwhile, my unread email from Jack lies in wait in my Inbox. I didn't delete it as I intended to. But I don't look at it, I've disciplined myself not to. Even though it calls to me when I'm falling asleep and the moment I wake up. And most of the minutes in between. I don't know how much longer I can resist.

11.59 am: I may have abandoned any remaining feminist principles, and gone and done something I swore I would never do, but at least I now understand how all those models and actresses 'bounce back' into shape after pregnancy. It's not superhuman willpower, it's not 24/7 breastfeeding, it's not spinach shakes or Pilates, it's not even good genes or airbrushing. No, it's a procedure. I panicked and put my name down for it at a bijou clinic in a leafy mews off Hyde Park. Candy said in her email that 'lunchtime lipo' was a cinch. And cinch is what I'm after: a cinched waist so that I can pour myself into the emerald green dress for the reunion.

The clinic's brochure, so glossy you could use it as a mirror to touch up your lipstick, promises to painlessly streamline what it calls, with exquisite tact, 'those stubborn areas'. As I ascend the vertiginous open staircase, made of giant Fox's Glacier Mints, I just know that I shouldn't be here.

What are you doing, Kate? Is your fear of looking frumpy at your reunion so great, is your self-respect so fragile that you would pay the price of a John Lewis cooking range to have the pouch beneath your waist sucked out by a fat-guzzling Hoover thingy?

Sadly, that does appear to be the case.

The two women seated behind the clinic's Reception desk are like air hostesses from a previous era, when flying made you feel like a glamorous globetrotter rather than a galley-slave with an overpriced tub of Pringles and no room to breathe. Immaculate make-up fixed with shimmery powder, intoxicating wafts of perfume. All they lack is those jaunty little hats with a badge, which is a pity. They ask me to take a seat and offer a dizzying choice of beverages. Because I'm nervous I opt for the one I want least. Liquorice. Is that really a tea? Think about changing my order and asking for cappuccino, which would be comforting, but, no, I am here to have my stubborn areas recontoured. It's probably frothy coffee that got them so bloody stubborn in the first place.

There are three other people sitting in the waiting area, and we are all studiedly avoiding each other's eyes. Despite the soothing, Zen-like decor and the piped music there is a sticky shame in being here. Everyone wants to stay young, but no one wants to be caught in the act of trying to stay young through artifice. It has to be our guilty secret, as 'undetectable' as the clinic's work.

When one of the receptionists comes over to collect the man behind the newspaper opposite, I glance up from an article on shortening your big toe (all the rage, mysteriously) and realise that it's a famous actor. Well, famous in the Eighties, less so now. The sandy hair has been strenuously backcombed, perhaps to disguise how little there is of it left. Once handsome and commanding, the actor now looks vulnerable; his blue eyes are watery. He sees that I have recognised him – I feel sorry about that – and gives a sad little nod of the head before scuttling into a side room. What work does a man in his late sixties, in the business of saving his looks, have done? Must ask Candy; she knows more about fillers than Mary Berry.

3.43 pm: Turns out that the simple, painless 'lunchtime lipo' was not simple, and not strictly a lunchtime procedure either. As for being painless, tell that to a pin cushion.

I came out woozy, swaddled in bandages and equipped with a post-surgical compression garment, basically a weapons-grade Shaper Suit.

I am wobbling on the pavement outside Harvey Nichols, trying to hail a cab, when the phone rings and I answer it.

Without any preamble, and picking up where she left off, my mother says, 'The thing is Kath, love, if I do bring Dickie for Christmas he'll have to come in Peter and Cheryl's car and you know how particular Cheryl is. What if Dickie has an accident? No, I don't think I'll risk it, love. Better stay home this year. I'll be fine, I can go to our Julie's . . .'

I pretend that the signal is bad and hang up.

In the cab, I think about taking the strong painkillers the clinic gave me, but I daren't in case I fall asleep during the presentation. What was that old torture device, with the spikes on the inside? An iron maiden? Well, that is me after lunchtime lipo.

The traffic is appalling. As a result, I am late for my meeting at Brown's Hotel with Grant Hatch, known to his contacts in the retail sector as Brands. *Obviously*. Worse still, it was my firm that had requested the meeting, so to roll up late is a terrible start. Nor can I run in spouting excuses, what with Grant being a bloke – and I mean bloke, in the fullest sense of the word. Also, after my puncturing, am genuinely liable to spout. Visions of Earl Grey tea pouring out of my lipo holes in manner of Trevi Fountain. Grant wouldn't want to know about that.

As I enter the bar, he makes a point of glaring at his watch, which is the size of a snow globe and covered in multiple dials, with at least four knobs on the side. It could probably launch a nuclear strike on Pyongyang, but can it tell the time?

Grant stands up, flexing his shoulders as if to square up for a fight. He wears a black polo shirt that strains to contain what is inside it, and excessively ironed black jeans. He is hulking, and totally hairless, like a buddha who has traded contemplation for capitalism and never looked back. I can just make out the top of a tattoo behind the gold medallion at his throat. When he speaks, it is in a sarf London accent so thick you could write your fears in it.

'Kate. At last,' he rasps.

'Grant,' I say, 'please forgive me. Bit of a crisis at work. Just as I was about to leave. The markets have gone cra—'

'Hey,' he says, flashing a smile like somebody whipping out

a knife. 'I bet you're the kind of girl who has lots to keep her occupied.'

Oh, a lech. I get it. Jay-B did warn me Hatch was a Ladies' Man. Normally takes longer than ten seconds to realise what you're dealing with, but this time the creep alarm has sounded even before I sit down. To this man, I am a girl, and not just a girl: a girl who likes to have her time – and her pretty much everything else – filled up. Preferably by the likes and the lusts of him. Fine. One of those. Deal with it.

'Yup,' I say. 'Busy times.' (You have no idea, mate. When did you last lie awake worrying about the sad mental decline of your mother-in-law, your daughter's anxiety and your stomach full of lipo drainage-holes? My guess would be never.)

'So, Kate,' he says. 'What the fuck can I do for you? Or,' narrowing his eyes a touch, 'you for me?' The eyes, little beads of black, may well have been on loan from a shark.

He nods as he talks, unable to keep still. I half expect him to start running on the spot. One of those men whom you can't help imagining as little boys, forever getting themselves into scrapes; picture his mum, exhausted at the end of every day, worn out by her devotion, old before her time.

We settle down – an armchair each, thank God – facing one another over a table, rather than side by side.

'Drink,' he says, issuing instructions rather than asking a question.

I pause. 'Tea, please?'

'Nah. Get yourself a real drink.'

'What are you having?'

'Single malt. Made by posh wankers in the fucking Highlands. Liquid gold, only it costs more. Same?'

'That would be lovely, thank you.' Probably unwise, but I need something strong to numb my lipo belly.

'Good stuff,' says Grant. 'Hey, you.'

'Me?'

'No, you there.' He snaps his fingers, as if to begin a tango. Christ. *Whatever happens, Kate, you will not dance with this man.* A waitress behind me scurries to his call.

'Yes, please, how can I help you?' Smiling, anxious, polite, and possibly Baltic.

'Yeah, more of this stuff. Por dos. Me and 'er. Comprendo?'

'Yes, sir.'

Grant watches her walk away. 'Needs to lay off the Danishes, she does.'

Grant used to be a financial adviser. Now he runs a group – or, as I think of it, a hit squad – of financial advisers, which gives him access to a broad range of clients, running all the way from merely rich to so rich that their dogs have personal chefs. EM Royal plans to be one of the funds to whom those clients turn; it is my unenviable job to tell him so. How do you inform a man like this that you want his business, and that his business could really use what you have to offer, while making it perfectly clear that the wanting stops right there? Not for a long while have I encountered someone who so clearly thinks through his trousers.

'Grant, I'm here to tell you that EM Royal is really good—'

'Course you're fuckin' good!' He makes a sound midway between a bark and a laugh. 'Wouldn't be 'ere if you weren't fuckin' good, wouldya, love?'

I smile, as though savouring this witticism, before plunging on. 'Yes, well, we realise of course that you have a strong panel of investment funds on your platform. But ours is nicely diversified by asset classes: a good geographical spread; broad exposure to other currencies; good mix of defensive equities and growth companies; consistent performers all round.'

Where did I learn to speak this weird City language, which

sounds like English but is not quite the real thing? Jack used to call it Desperanto, which is perfect actually. Trust Jack to express it better than anyone else. I'm impressed at myself, but also a bit alarmed, for slipping into the lingo so smoothly, after so many years away. Feel like somebody who moves back to France and immediately, with no practice, starts chatting with the locals.

'And?' he says, gratified to be praised for his strength but keen to move on. He glances at his watch again. Maybe it is telling an Aga in Weybridge to heat up his dinner or something.

'And we would very much like to have EM Royal approved on your platform. We think it's a natural fit.' *Damn. Come on, Kate. Don't give the guy a sniff of a double entendre.*

'I bet you do. Natural fit is what I like. Nice and tight.' Too late. 'Because?'

'Because of the strength of our research team, and because, frankly, we think we're the only fund your clients will ever need.'

'Nice try.'

'We're not as cheap as a tracker fund, and we plan to keep it that way,' I reply, with a sinking sensation in my heart. 'Think of us as reassuringly expensive.'

'Yeah, good. Well, Katie,' he continues, shunting me into the diminutive. To be fair, he probably does that with everyone. If Grant had bumped into Caesar, he would have addressed him as Julie. 'I hear you. And, to be honest wiv ya, I've already done some poking abart. That's me all over.' He gives me a moment to let the beauty of this thought sink in, then goes on: 'And I reckon we might well be interested in putting you—'

'Putting EM Royal.'

'Right. Putting you on our menu.'

'That's fantastic. I can assure you . . .'

'But—' he leans into the space between us, so I can look

239

right down his polo shirt and see that the tattoo is one of a very busty mermaid, '—I think we need a private meeting to go over the details, look at the small print sortafink.'

'Of course, Grant. My colleagues will be happy to—'

'When I say we, I mean me and you, Katie. We. We need to meet. Somewhere quiet, just the two of us.'

Those shark eyes. They rove up and down. I can feel the wadding from the lipo wrapped tight around my tummy. When Richard Dreyfuss went down into the water to meet Jaws, he had a cage to protect him and a harpoon to defend himself with. All I have is a table. And, thank heaven, two tumblers of whisky, which the waitress sets down at this moment, thus creating another barrier. Bless her.

'Is all? Anything else I can help you with?' she asks.

Grant waves her away. She backs off. Again, he gazes after her.

'Bit of weight training, she'd be fine. Lose the arse. Get her on a bike. Cheers. You work out, Kate?'

I nod. 'Try to, at least a couple of times a week.'

'Yeah, thought so.' He raps his glass against mine. I sip carefully, while checking for cracks. *Come on Kate, keep it together. Keep it light.*

'So, are you a bike man, Grant?'

'Am I a bike man? Is Gandalf a homo? Course I bloody am. Hundred miles every weekend. Up to my neck in fucking Lycra. I feel like an Opal fruit.'

'You should meet my husband. Compare notes.'

Grant frowns. It's not that men like him feel challenged by other men. They just don't like the idea of other men existing in the first place. Like bulls, they want the arena to themselves.

'What's he got?' (That you haven't got, you mean?)

'Sorry?'

'What bike?'

'Gosh, I don't know. But it cost some ridiculous amount, five thousand and . . .'

Grant laughs so hard that whisky comes out of his nose. Takes a napkin and wipes it off his shirt, still laughing.

'Five thousand nuffink. Mine was ten grand before the wheels. Weighs like the same as a fucking apple. Lift it up with your pinkie.' He throws the rest of his single malt down his throat and stays like that, head back, for a few seconds. (Am I meant to applaud?) Then he puts the glass down and looks at me. 'So, Katie, how's about it? You and me. Next week, 'ow you fixed? Tuesday afternoon's a possibility. Treat you to the Dorchester, Claridge's, name your venue. We really need to thrash out some of this stuff, get to know each other better, before we move to the next stage, don't we, darlin'?'

I finish my own drink, stand up, and hold out my hand. 'Actually, Grant, I have to run now. It's been a real pleasure. And I'm so thrilled that you are considering our offer. I will of course be happy to send over a full package of information in regard to our year-on-year performance, our protocols and investment strategies. As for Tuesday, I'm afraid I won't be free, but I'm sure my colleague Troy Taylor will be happy to stand in for me and take this discussion to the next level.'

Grant considers this, ill will seeping from every pore. He is good-looking, and well-dressed, and very very rich, but at that moment he seems like ugliness made flesh. Rejection sours the man. Then he speaks, quite slowly, doling out the words: 'Yeah. Yeah, I know Troy. He's the one who told me all about you. Said you were the new kid on the block, except you was old. Fucking good at what you do, though. That's what Troy said. I suppose you've had more practice than the rest of us. Years of it. He thought we might, you know, get on.'

Ah. The lech with the bastard at his back. The plot sickens.

241

'And we *have*, Grant! So nice to meet you. See you again soon. Goodbye.'

I walk off. Behind me I hear a snapping of fingers. Last tango for Grant but, sadly, not the last I will hear of him by a long chalk.

8.39 pm: Dinner tonight is soup, healthy cottage pie with sweet potato mash, and green beans which I picked up from M&S at the station. Richard said he was going to cook, but he had a last-minute meeting with that annoying cat woman about some wellness retreat, I think. He is bent over his iPad at the table as I serve up the soup.

'Listen to this, Kate. The Government Tsar for older workers just suggested that those of us with O levels should pretend that we took GCSEs so employers can't figure out that we are, in fact, clapped-out, ancient persons of forty-three or over.'

Rich swivels the laptop round so I can see the article for myself. The Tsar says that those holding what she calls 'old-style qualifications' – sounds like something written in bulls' blood on papyrus, doesn't it? – may suffer age discrimination. While she says that she wouldn't condone telling outright lies, she says 'if you are facing this kind of unfairness then maybe one needs to play the game'.

'Play the game?' yelps Richard, letting his spoon clatter in his soup bowl. 'I know, why doesn't this woman simply announce that, unlike GCSEs, O levels were properly hard qualifications and at least us oldies with O levels can be guaranteed to be able to read, write and add up in our heads without the aid of several electronic devices.'

Oh, hell. Suddenly realise that on CV for my new job I put my O level results whilst simultaneously claiming to be forty-two. Didn't even occur to me that my new fake age means I am too young to have taken O levels, and I should have put

GCSEs instead. Such a minefield. At least no one at EM Royal seems to have noticed or asked to see any certificates. Whatever the Tsar for older workers may say, this fibbing-about-your-age lark is hard. You really need the memory of someone much younger to pull it off.

There is a sudden wail from Emily, who is hunched in her chair, knees up to her chin, dressed all in black and swathed in a scarf made from what appears to be fisherman's netting. She looks like a lobster pot going to a funeral.

'That's like so unfair, Dad,' she shouts, 'I did GCSEs and they're like really hard, OK? You and Mummy always say things were better when you were at school. It's not fair. You think I'm like totally stupid and it's like really stressy because of coursework and stuff and I only got sixty-three per cent in my English essay.'

'You *are* totally stupid,' says Ben, not looking up from his phone.

'Stop it, Ben. Get off that machine please. Richard, put your iPad away too. Can we have one dinner when the entire family's not online? What do you mean, you only got sixty-three per cent in your English, darling?' Now it's my turn to sound aggrieved. 'I helped you with your *Twelfth Night* essay. How come you got sixty-three per cent?'

Her head withdraws, tortoise-like, into the cowl of netting. 'Mr Young said it was really well written and very clever and everything, but it didn't have enough key words, Mummy. You've got to put key words in to get higher marks.'

'What *key words*?'

'Hang on,' says Richard, 'what were you doing writing Emily's essay for her?'

'Mum didn't write it, she was checking it,' Emily says quickly to protect me. 'S'not her fault I didn't get an A.'

Richard looks at her, then back at me before saying caustically, 'Don't tell your mother she didn't get an A in something, Emily. That hasn't happened since 1977.'

I see Ben's face light up in a delighted smirk; it's a look I remember from that day at junior school when, aged eight, he decided to liberate the class gerbils, 'because they wanted to be outside'.

'Exams can't be that easy if Mummy can't get an A in Emily's essay,' our resident logician points out.

'I didn't say exams are easy, Benjamin. They're just hard in a, I don't know, in a pointless, tickbox, uncreative way. That's not education in my book. Now go and start your homework, please. Emily, sweetheart?'

Too late. My daughter has fled upstairs. What now? I can hardly march up to school and complain to Mr Young. What am I going to say: 'Emily should have got a higher mark for her essay because I wrote half of it'? That'll sound really good. You know, it would be nice to have just one area of my life where I'm not a total imposter.

'Mum?'

'What is it, Ben?'

'You can do my history homework. I don't care what I get.'

9.43 pm: I was fully intending to tell Richard about the lipo. Honestly, I was, but then we got sidetracked by the *Twelfth Night* argument. And, after that meeting with Grant, I can't face any more unpleasantness. The guy made my flesh crawl, but I may have lost EM Royal several million by refusing to make myself one of our exciting incentives. As I walked out of the hotel, I thought, I'm too old to put up with this bullshit. Perfectly true. But I'm also too old to get another job and, in order to hang onto the one I've got, some bullshit tolerance, however repugnant, may be essential.

Actually, when you think about it, the cost of lunchtime lipo is an absolute bargain compared to the number of personal training sessions it would take to remove those stubborn areas now deposited in a Hoover bag off Hyde Park. Also, no need to purchase new dress for college reunion. If you look at it like that, it's a massive saving. Plus, I am now earning my own money, which is keeping the entire household afloat, and hardly ever spend anything on myself, so should not have to justify it to my husband.

Besides, am confident I could make Rich see lipo is not an example of escalating midlife crisis, as he may suspect, but prudent and essential maintenance of a declining asset. Me. (Speaking of declining assets, I paid by cheque to avoid running into trouble with the mystifying credit problem. *'Roy, did you get anywhere with working out why my credit rating is so bad?'*)

Unfortunately, after dinner, when the kids have both disappeared upstairs, Rich launches into a rant about the vast, featureless desert that is our current account. He says 'your building work' on 'your house' is to blame, although this is the man who decided to renounce capitalism and train as a £3-an-hour empathiser. So armoured is he by the righteousness of his new calling that he can't seem to see the effect it's had on me and the kids. The fact he won't even start earning money for another two years. *Two years!* By then, *I'm* the one who will need psychiatric help.

As I load the dishwasher in my best clattery, passive-aggressive manner, Rich continues to make helpful suggestions about ways we can cut back.

'The energy bills are huge, for one thing. Kate, I know you enjoy your baths, but do we have to have the hot water coming on at six am? How about just turning it on when we know we'll need it?'

I rearrange the knives, trying not to look at my husband,

just in case he has – as that last idea suggests – been replaced by the landlady of a Bexhill boarding-house in 1971. Soon he'll be putting up little placards announcing which members of the household can wash when. I am becoming, I realise, little more than a lodger in his eyes, and a slightly unreliable one at that. But there is more.

'The car. I know what you're going to say, Kate' (no you don't), 'but on both the micro and macro levels it really is more of a luxury than a necessity these days, and not a very defensible luxury at that.' The landlady has morphed into a spokesman for Greenpeace. Dear God, please don't let him say the word 'planet'.

'I know you think I'm pontificating, darling,' (you're right there, matey), 'but we do have responsibilities beyond those of our immediate family. Of course we need to get around, but I've done a breakdown.' (And I'm about to have one.) 'And if you look carefully at when we actually *need* the car these days, as opposed to when we lapse into using it just because it's there . . .'

Lapse? Did I lapse up to my mother when she was in hospital for weeks after her heart attack? Who had to lapse Ben to that jazz course in Norfolk? How on earth would Lenny get lapsed every day in the country park without a car? Richard continues to drone.

'. . . so what I'm saying is, if, if, if you felt at all able to switch to cycling, and combined that with public transport.' He is staring above my head now, as if a higher ideal were stuck to the ceiling. 'You know, it's been a real confidence booster for me, and I really feel it could do the same for you. Not to mention the health benefits. And, you know, just think of the example we'd be setting the children.'

'What example? Both of us getting knocked off by white vans on the same day, leaving the house full of orphans?'

'Don't be so dramatic, darling. Elementary road sense and a helmet will keep you perfectly safe. No, I just, I just think it would be great if Ben and Emily started to realise that they have duties not just towards us, but towards the planet—'

'Done.' I slam the door of the dishwasher shut, like a draw-bridge, and leave the kitchen.

Was he always this unsufferable? I feel like I married Jeff Bridges and ended up with a mix of Al Gore and some tree-hugging bore. It's me, I think, who has had to return to her former office in a humiliating capacity, being patronised and pimped out by male foetuses, while Mr Planet tells me how I can economise.

'You've lost weight, Mum,' says Emily, inspecting me as I enter the sitting room. She puts her arm around my waist.

Oouuch. The anaesthetic is definitely wearing off.

'Oh, do you think so, darling?' I yelp. There is no elixir sweeter than approval from that harshest of critics, one's own teenage daughter.

'Yeah, that diet's worked so fast,' she says. 'It's unbelievable.'

It is.

In this sweet moment of truce, Emily leans in close and says, 'You really OK with my party, Mum?'

Oh, God, not the party. 'Well, yes, I suppose so, love, but I don't want it getting out of hand.'

'It won't. I promise.'

'Did you say fifty people?'

Em nods, suddenly animated, eyes shining. 'It's so cool because we can like have a Christmas theme and I've got these guys who do the music.'

'As long as people don't bring alcohol.'

'Course they won't. And Lizzy's really excited. She's like, 'Wow, Em, it'll be so awesome.''

In her enthusiasm, my daughter appears lit from within, radiant. I haven't seen her look this happy since . . . The failure to come up with a moment when I last saw Em look truly happy melts any lingering resistance I might have. It's because of me – well, me and her father's midlife crisis – that she had to start a new school, has struggled to make her mark with a new group of friends. If the party helps her, how can I possibly say no?

'OK, that's fine, darling. Can you draw me up a list of food and things you'd like.'

Before I can stop her, Emily is giving me the biggest hug I've had in years, right around the tender lipo zone. My squeal of pain is drowned out by her scream of joy. 'Love you. Mum, love you so much.'

1.01 am: Can't sleep. Through the bathroom window, a new moon is lolling in its deckchair in a sky which is dark and bright at the same time. As the anaesthetic retreats, my middle hurts more and more, but it isn't pain which is keeping me awake. I know exactly what it is. Or who.

Standing in front of the mirror, I take my nightie off and brace myself to inspect the damage. I can hear Richard and his Hog Symphony through the wall, like the sound of distant gunfire. One good thing about my husband not looking at me any more is that at least he's not going to notice I've had lipo.

In the cold light of night, my naked body doesn't look too bad, not for something almost half a century old. Poor body. The stomach is blotchy with bruising from the lipo, but the good news is I have my waist back. Or I might have. The swelling after the local anaesthetic makes it hard to tell. So does the girdle of wadding that covers the incisions. *Yeuch.* Am basically a human colander. I step into the compression corset, then reach for the dress, which is hanging on the shower door, and hold it in front of me. Give me another couple of days, and it will fit perfectly. That wretched zip will purr into position.

What the hell, I decide to try it now.

The minute the dress is on, I know who I did it for. The clinic, the secrecy, the machine sucking out my stubborn areas. Not for old friends I haven't seen for thirty years, that's for sure. It's another old friend I want to look good for.

A name I never thought I'd see again. Never wanted to see again. That's what I told myself anyway, but as soon as I saw it in my Inbox I knew that was a lie. Who could believe that a name could summon so much emotion? I have missed Jack every single day since I last saw him; he is always there in my peripheral vision, teasing me, putting me on my mettle, making me want to be the best version of myself, just for him. When Grant Hatch was coming on to me this afternoon, I felt this overwhelming longing for Jack to be there, to suddenly be there right next to me, my champion and protector.

You promised you wouldn't open the email, Kate, you promised.

Downstairs in the kitchen, with Lenny lying like a rug across my bare feet, I open the laptop. I move the cursor down the Inbox, but I find it quickly, I know exactly where it is. I've looked at it so often, but never dared open it. On the other hand, I haven't pressed Delete. I'm impatient to open it now, like a child finally given permission to unwrap a present.

From: Jack Abelhammer
To: Kate Reddy
Subject: Hello again
Katharine, I seem to recall we had an agreement that we wouldn't contact each other, but I bumped into Candy Stratton's ex and he'd heard you were back in the City

working in marketing at EM Royal? I'm curious. I never had you pegged as a 'backroom boy'. It sounds a little cramped for the Kate Reddy I knew.

I was planning on being in London in the next few weeks and I wondered if I could pick your brains about something. We could maybe get a coffee depending on how you're fixed?

Jack

So much for tingling anticipation. So much for lunchtime lipo and an emerald dress. So much for a 'marvellous night for a moondance'. So much for my long-lost love. He would like to *pick my brains*. He would like to *maybe get a coffee*. Maybe. Maybe? When you've felt that much about a man and he disappears from your life, you start to think: Was it just me? Was it just some foolish illusion on my part and he never loved me? Clearly, he never felt the same. You were broken into a million pieces and the other person walked clean away.

God, I'm such an idiot. *Jack Abelhammer's an old business contact, not your lover. You're almost fifty years old, woman.* I start to cry. The disappointment is unbearable. I'm crying so hard that I almost miss the PS. It's right down the bottom, which explains why I didn't see it at first.

PS It only took me five hours to compose this short email. Not bad, huh? And not a single word in it that I want to say to you. Not one. Jx

250

14

The College Reunion

7.12 pm: How do you feel approaching a college reunion? I mean, you can have your hair highlighted to hide the grey and you can carefully apply concealer on the area under your eyes, where it settles in the fine lines like chalk. You can rummage in your jewellery box and find a 'statement necklace' to wear. (And the statement is: 'I don't like this neck and would like the old neck back, please.')

If you are particularly desperate to get into a certain dress, you may go on a crash diet or panic and spend a stupid amount of money having your 'stubborn areas' hoovered out over lunchtime. You can be waxed and plucked and purchase fishnet hold-ups on a whim, but when the day dawns you will look in the mirror, the one with the harsh fluorescent light you have been avoiding for some time, and realise this one, inescapable fact: the woman you are taking along tonight to her college reunion is more than a quarter of a century older than the one who graduated.

How did that happen? Time changes everything except

something within which is always surprised by change. I forget who said that, but they were dead right, weren't they? When I was a teenager and I used to hear friends of my mother say, 'I still feel twenty-one inside', I was puzzled and a bit embarrassed for them. Beholding those ancient shipwrecks in our lounge, I thought: how could they still feel what I felt? Surely, your mind and your emotions kept pace with your age. To grow older was to be grown-up, and grown-ups were mature. But that doesn't seem to hold true. Do we shed our younger selves like chrysalises or do they live on inside us, filed away, waiting and waiting for their time to come again?

It's spitting with rain and there's a Siberian wind threshing through the trees when I park in the temporary car park just across the road from college. With one hand protecting my blow-dry, I pick my way through the boggy grass, worrying about my fishnet hold-ups, one of which is already trying to make a run for it. Vaguely remember some warning in a magazine about not putting hold-ups on straight after a bubble bath. Why couldn't I have put on sensible, age-appropriate opaque tights?

Funny thing is, I'm not sure which Kate is going to the drinks reception in the Senior Common Room. Is it the student Kate of 1985, involved in an agonised love triangle and luxuriating in Whitney's 'Greatest Love of All' on the Sony Walkman, whilst secretly drunk on her sexual power over competing suitors? Or is it the Kate of today, mother of teenagers, libido missing, presumed dead, who will turn fifty in three months?

Who's counting.

7.27 pm: I arranged to meet Debra by the Porter's Lodge so we could go in together. We shared a set of rooms in our third year (a boyfriend in our first, Two-Time Ted) and I figure that, if I am so horribly changed as to be unrecognizable, then at least people will see the flame-haired Debra Richards and know that it's probably Kate Reddy beside her. I'm not afraid of ageing, but I know now that I'm scared of people's reaction to my ageing.

'My God, Kate, look at those children,' shrieks Deb, pointing at three strapping boat-club guys coming up the stairs from the bar. How old are they – nineteen? Can you imagine, we actually had sex with kids like that?'

'Yes, but we were nineteen too, remember.'

I can hardly hear her, the wind is blowing so hard. It carries us on its fierce breath across the court to the vast, panelled dining-hall doors, so familiar I could draw them in my sleep.

'But they're *babies*.' Deb is laughing and still pointing at the boys.

Yes, they are, and how incredibly grown-up we thought ourselves to be when we were their age. The boys glance at us, two middle-aged women in their finery, then turn away. Now, we are filed under Somebody's Mother.

7.41 pm: Drinks before dinner, and the mob of us has split into islands. Everyone stands in groups of five or six. The noisy islands consist of people who have kept in regular touch. For them this is just another get-together, albeit with posher frocks, blacker tie, and better booze. The quiet and more awkward islands are composed of crumbly men and embarrassed women staring at each other and making the very smallest of talk while they try to work out who the others are now, who they once were, and why the two versions seem not to overlap.

My island has only four inhabitants. Deb, me, Fiona Jaggard, and a man who nobody knows. He is small, neat, almost child-sized, but very correctly dressed, with oval glasses and an unwavering

253

smile, turning to listen politely to each of us as we talk. Genuinely think he may be automaton created in experimental-science lab up the road and wheeled out for his first ever social occasion.

Fiona, on the other hand, is exuberance made flesh. She always was. I remember her laughing so hard once, in the midst of a formal dinner, that port came out of her nose. People looked down the table and thought she'd been in a fight. 'That girl is one of the boys,' a boyfriend once said to me, and I couldn't tell if he was impressed or frightened. Fiona had grown up with four brothers – two older, two younger – and had spent her holidays playing cricket and building tree houses with planks. When we were all living together in a college house, the boiler packed up. The rest of us went unwashed and smelly for four days, but Fi was up at seven, cheerfully showering in cold water and singing Gilbert and Sullivan in a lusty alto.

Now she is standing here, undiminished by the years, smile undimmed, and wearing a dress of dark-red velvet. Maybe she hopes to sneeze port all over again.

'Where are you living, Fi?'

'Piddletrenthide.'

'No, where are you actually living?'

'Piddletrenthide. It's a real place. Bugger of a house, but if you get a chance to live somewhere called Piddle, you've got to take it, right?' she says, laughing at Robot Man. Is it my imagination, or did he actually bow in her direction, to acknowledge the joke? Did the graduate students who built him flick the Humour Reception switch just before they let him out for the evening?

'This bloody dress,' Fi says, shimmying in discomfort. 'Too small. Must be donkeys since I had to put on something smart. Found it second-hand in Dorchester.' She runs her finger round the high neckline. 'Too tight. I feel like a Labrador.'

'D'you remember that blue thing you wore to the ball?' Deb asks. 'The one where you—'

'Oh my GOD,' Fi says, jogging the elbow of a man coming round with a bottle of wine for top-ups. He spills some onto a thin and breakable-looking blonde in the next group, who flinches as if it were boiling water. 'I literally came out of it on the dance floor. Poor Gareth Thingummy got hit on the side of the head. Closest he ever got to me, to be honest. Not likely these days. One boob gone, three months ago. Hence the neckline.'

Deb and I both reach out to her as if she, or we, were falling, and put our hands on her arms.

'Fi, I'm so sorry, I didn't—'

'Oh, it's fine, caught it early and all that malarkey. I was lucky. GP was onto it like a shot. Felt a lump the size of a hazelnut in the shower, six weeks later they were putting in an implant. Bit of an improvement on the old tit, to be perfectly honest. Johnny was a brick. "Soon have you back in the saddle", he said.'

'Ah, men,' says Deb, then catches herself, and apologises to Robot Man, who inclines his head by exactly thirty degrees to indicate acceptance.

'No, he was bang on,' says Fi. 'No use feeling sorry for yourself. And anyway, someone's got to run the show. Won't run itself.'

'Show?'

'Riding for the Disabled. Big thing. Used to be just Piddlers, then someone got me onto county, and now, God help me, I'm Mrs Disabled Riding for the whole bloody nation. Kids from all over. Some of them never seen a horse in their lives, poor souls. Barely even been in a green field, let alone a paddock.' She finishes her drink, throwing her head back like a man knocking back pints against the clock. 'Odd thing is, they're the ones who end up loving it most. Ducks to water.'

'So your Theology degree *did* come in handy.'

'Absolutely. Whacking great halo,' she says, reaching out and physically abducting a bottle from the waiter, who stands there bereft and open-mouthed. All our glasses are refilled to the brim, except for little Robot Man's. Being half a foot taller than him, Fi tries pouring from a great height and gets sparkling wine all over his slender wrist and, I am pleased to see, his expensive-looking watch with a metal strap. 'Whoops!' she says. I wait for him to fuse and explode in a shower of sparks.

'Amazing they asked me to run anything, frankly. Was a time I couldn't even run a bath.'

'That's not true,' I say, surprising myself. Roy must be staying late for the occasion, putting in overtime to deliver memories that I'd forgotten I filed away. 'You went to Nepal to help rebuild that school, remember, and we all had to do that mini-marathon around town to raise the funds. Hundreds of us turned up on a Sunday morning. You organised the whole thing.'

Deb puts her hand to her mouth. She'd forgotten too. 'God, that marathon.'

'Mini.'

'Mini, my arse. It was a nightmare. I had a hangover before I even started. Had to stop twice to have a cup of tea with the St John's Ambulance people. Threw up outside Caius. It nearly killed me, Fi.'

'Good for you, Deb. Nearly being killed means you're getting somewhere. I should know,' she says. 'Christ, when are they going to bang a gong or something? I'm ravenous. This place is worth gazillions and they can't even give us a bowl of peanuts.'

'Ladies and gentlemen, dinner is served!' someone bellows

nearby – right behind Robot Man, in fact, who drops the handkerchief with which he is still trying to pat his hand dry. Not sure how well his evening is going. Odds on someone tipping their soup into his lap are currently, I reckon, around three to one.

'Who *was* that?' I whisper to Deb, as we join the polite stampede in the direction of the dining room.

'Who?'

'The teeny-weeny one.'

'Ah. Currently worth in the region of a teeny-weeny hundred and sixty million, if the *FT* is to be believed. That's what he sold the company for, at any rate, and it was all his baby from the start. Not bad, considering.'

'Considering what?'

'Considering what he was like before.'

'But who is he?'

'Hobbit. Tim Hobson. Don't you remember? Tiny Tim, the shaggy one on the staircase next to ours?'

'That's *Hobbit*? But he was all hairy. I mean, really hairy. You couldn't tell which way he was facing most of the time. I never knew which bit to talk to. Wasn't he a mathematician?'

'And some. Stuck around here, did his PhD, which should have been of interest to about three people. Except it turned out to be perfect for, what's it called, cryptography. Which then became his thing. So he got the research funds, started his own software business, and grew into the teeny-weeny man you see today. He still lives around here.'

Ahead of us, Hobbit is shaking his watch and holding it to his ear. I still can't square him with the Tim of old; it's like looking at a chart showing the evolution of man. I vaguely knew he was clever back then, and passionately Marxist, but I thought it was the kind of clever idealism that meant he would live in bedsits and drink own-brand coffee and go on marches and sit in the launderette doing sums on the back of betting slips. Now, the geeks have inherited the Earth. Tim probably has his own plane.

'How did you think Fi was?' says Deb. 'Same old, same old?'

'Same old, same young. She's Fi.'

'Amazing how she just seems to forge ahead, whatever gets in the way.'

'I know.'

'She may be the only really good person I know.'

'And the only really happy one, too.'

We both go quiet for a second, despite the clamour around us. I know Deb and I are asking ourselves the same question: is somebody like Fi able to do good because she's happy? Or did she become happy by doing good?

It's the sort of question that Roger Graham over there, the lanky chap with the Omar Sharif moustache, probably used to write essays about when he was here. Roger did philosophy and once asked me out to the pub 'to work through my theories of ethics'. I presumed that he simply wanted to go to bed with me; that's certainly what it sounded like at the time, and I gave serious thought to saying yes. Except when we got to the pub, he produced two half-pints of cider and a copy of Aristotle, and really *did* talk about ethics. For an hour and three quarters. I ate three packets of crisps just to keep my strength up, then left. I wonder if he remembers that night.

We are being herded now, everyone clustering around the seating plan, hoping not to be plonked next to the person they split up with three decades ago. I see my name next to someone called Marcus. Marcus? Did I know a Marcus? Was he the one I nicked an LP from? *Outlandos d'Amour*, I think, just when The Police were becoming huge. What if he wants it back?

What if that single loss has somehow triggered a lifetime of deeper vanishings? If he can't stand losing—

'Kate Reddy! I thought it might be you!'

I spin round, like someone about to be mugged. Rosamund Pilger. Roy has no hesitation in supplying the name. Typical Roz; even in my memory, she's barged to the head of the queue. Roz, the countess of careers advice and the queen of mixed metaphors, then as now.

'Roz! How lovely. How are you?'

'Terrific. As you see. And you? I heard that you had to junk that job of yours.'

'Yes, that was a while back. It was—'

'Well, *entre nous*, it wasn't much to lose, was it?' Roz always says things like '*entre nous*' or 'keep this to yourself' in the voice of a hockey coach lambasting her forwards from the touch line.

'Actually, I am now back in the office—'

'Good luck with that! My feeling is, if you take your nose *off* the grindstone, it's curtains.'

'Well, I do have some experience—'

'Water under the bridge.' Roz has, I know, made a fortune in commodities. On the other hand, she does now resemble a burst horsehair sofa, so there is some justice in the world. 'Who are you sitting with? I'm next to the Chaplain. The Rev Jocelyn Somebody. Man or woman? God knows. Probably gay, either way. They all are.' And, leaving me with that Christian thought, Rosamund Pilger is off, carving a path to her seat. I say a silent prayer for the Chaplain, whoever he or she may be.

8.19 pm: Having survived the Pilgering more or less intact, I am now sitting opposite a sweet woman at dinner. She clearly knows me, but I'm struggling to put a name to the face.

The fabulous memory that got me into this university in the

259

first place is no more. I close my eyes and make an impassioned, silent plea. ('*Please, Roy, can you get me the name of the woman sitting opposite me? Think she read Natural Sciences. Brown curly hair. Friendly eyes. Slightly too much make-up.*')

'You don't recognise me, do you, Kate?' asks the woman.

'Of course I do,' I say with more confidence than I feel. ('*Hurry up, Roy!*') 'You used to row.'

'Cox,' she smiles, 'I coxed the First boat.'

'No,' I say, 'Frances coxed the First boat.'

'*Roy, pleeaase find her name. I'll never ask you for anything ever again.*'

'Yes,' she agrees, 'and I coxed the men's boat.'

'No, you can't have. Colin coxed the men's boat.'

'I *am* Colin,' she says. 'Or I used to be till I transitioned five years ago. I'm Carole now.'

Jesus. ('*Roy, you can stop looking.*')

'Wow, that's wonderful, Colin. I mean Carole. Good for you. I'm still the same sex, but that's about the only thing I haven't changed.'

'Yes, Kate, we've all been through so much, haven't we?'

Tell me about it.

10.35 pm: Well, I got through dinner. Or dinner got through me. What I hadn't thought about were the consequences of fasting beforehand to get into the green dress. It meant that two glasses of champagne landed in a stomach which had hardly seen a carbohydrate for two months. Plus, there was the wine, which kept on coming from a never-failing source, as in a fairy tale. I should have known better, but I was strangely nervous and glugged from the glass like a toddler with a sippy cup. Then, I found out that the woman sitting opposite me at dinner, the one I couldn't quite put a name to, had changed sex.

I mean, how is that fair? Carole seemed absolutely lovely, and definitely a big improvement on snarky Colin, which is who she was when I last saw him. Her. Them. But, after thirty years, it was hard enough trying to identify people who had stayed the same gender. All those young men either ballooned into paunchy, well-lunched Hogarth squires or looked almost painfully the same, with faces slightly sunken and peering over their glasses like auctioneers. I got the instant impression that the men were dealing a lot less well with the loss of youth than the women. Don't ask me why. Boys launch themselves at life, like arrows from a bow, but they drop to the ground just as suddenly, their motive force all spent. One charged up as dinner ended, breathing gusts of port over me. A barrel of a man, who would have been bald, were it not for the last wisps of hair carefully shaped into a spun-sugar nest, like a Michelin-starred dessert, over the sweaty pink dome of his scalp.

'Kate, lovely to see you. Great dress. How's it going?'

It takes a few seconds to see it is Adrian Casey. I deduct four stone and put his hair back on, rather good thick, dark hair that used to curl under his ears and matched his brown spaniel eyes, and here he is.

'Oh, Adrian, it's been so long,' I said, kissing his cheek. Adrian fumbled in his wallet for some photos of the kids as he brought me up to date. Still married to Cathy. Nervous honk of laughter. Lives in Kent. Commutes up to London every day. Three children. Girls very bright, sailed through Eleven Plus. Boy has mild learning difficulties, Cathy organising a battalion of tutors. Hoping to get him into X or maybe Y. Pity Adrian's old school has got so frightfully competitive.

'Can't believe it, Kate, it used to be all nice thick farmers' sons.' Adrian was practically roaring to make himself heard in the packed hall. 'If one was an old boy one could get one's son into school no problem. Now it's all bloody Russians and Chinese, isn't it?'

'Is it?' I think of Vladimir Velikovsky hoping to get his son, Sergei, into Eton.

'Yes, it's the money, you know. They're all arms dealers. Head sees them coming and it's like sitting on a cash register. Ker-ching! Or Ker-Chink I suppose it is now.'

'Sorry?'

'You know, Chinese? Chink. Ha ha! We'll all have to learn bloody Mandarin next. Sticky?'

'Sorry?'

'Dessert wine? Too sweet for me, and looks like pee, but that's what the birds have instead of port, isn't it?'

Birds? Who was the last British male to refer to women as 'birds'? Probably a DJ who is now doing seven years without parole for groping underage teeny boppers during the Wilson government.

I decided I needed to go and get some air. Made my excuses and left. One of my fishnet hold-ups had gradually slunk down my leg and I kept having to hoik it back up and refasten the non-stick sticky bits to my thigh. So much for Ageless Woman of Mystery – I was more like Nora Batty.

Outside the rain had stopped and the college walls smelt of time and thyme. I breathed it in, glad to have got away from Fat Adrian. I'd come here to escape all that, to remind myself of an age before every single conversation was about schools and grades and how many UCAS points your kid got for Grade 7 Distinction on the tuba. When life stretched out before us, a prairie of infinite possibility. Last time I stood in this very spot I was twenty-one years of age, a vertiginous thought. What would that Kate make of this Kate, if she could see me now? For a moment, just one, I wish I could go back and try again.

Midnight, more or less: A group of women congregate in the college's cellar bar, on the squashy leather seats where we used to sit all those aeons ago, checking out the guys playing table football and pool. In that corner, I remember there was an early Space Invaders machine, and any conversation down here was punctuated by aggressive beeps and whooshes.

'Do you remember that Space Invaders machine?' asks Deb, reading my mind, or what is left of it tonight.

'We thought it was so amazing,' laughs Anna. 'Imagine showing it to the kids nowadays. They'd think it was a complete joke.'

'Probably a collector's item,' says Rachel.

'Aren't we all collector's items?' says Deb, waggling a bottle of red wine at my empty glass.

'Maybe we are, but a really good vintage,' I say, finding, to my surprise, that I really mean it. I think of Emily and how much harder it is for girls growing up now with social media. Their mistakes are magnified, any loneliness broadcast to the world. There was a lot to be said for living an unobserved life.

You know the best thing about the reunion? It has put the choices we make in perspective. Or are they actually choices? Sitting at that table in the bar were women who had started out with similar qualifications and ended up in wildly different places.

Rachel was probably the most ambitious of all of us. Arrived at college having already devoured her Law reading list and hungry for more. While we were reading novels, Rachel carried around a small, terse little tome called *How To Do Things With Rules*. After getting the second-best degree in the year, she joined an international consultancy firm, though not before marrying Simon in a match which was both romantic (he looked like Robert Redford) and characteristically efficient (he was her neighbour in the third year). Everything went according to plan, until Rachel had two daughters in quick succession. Eleanor, the second, nearly threw a spanner in the works, being seven weeks premature, but Rachel had it all under control, hiring an excellent nanny and moving nearer the office so she could jump in a cab and breastfeed the baby at lunchtime. Then, one morning, she forgot some papers, and went back home to see two, tear-stained, tiny girls banging at the window, faces pressed up against the glass. Inside, she went to the kitchen where she found the nanny on the phone. She had barricaded the children in the front room. After that, Rachel's confidence was shot. 'I couldn't be a great career person and I couldn't be a great mother; I was failing at both.'

Rachel resigned and the family moved to Sussex where she had two more children. Between them, the four kids do twenty-three activities a week. Eleanor has learning difficulties as a result of her very premature birth and Rachel drives her back and forth to a special school some forty miles away. It's hard, though not impossible, 'so long as you get all your ducks in a row'. The family schedule is colour-coded and runs like clock-work; the girl who chose *How To Do Things With Rules* as her school book-prize makes sure of that. Somewhere along the way, Simon deviated from the plan and ran off with a yoga teacher who Rachel calls Bendy Wendy. 'But, honestly, Simon was useless anyway. We're better off without him.' In short, my friend Rachel, who should have been a High Court judge or Prime Minister at the very least, became one of those Tiger

Mothers who reduced me to a puddle of incompetence at the school gate. Was that a choice?

Beautiful, half-Russian Anna, whose face I instantly transposed onto the heroine's when I first read *Anna Karenina*, is a foreign correspondent in a man's world. Night shifts, drinking with the boys, chasing the next story. Never a shortage of great boyfriends; ditched one and the others would form a longing queue. In her mid-thirties, a routine smear showed up something on her cervix. Mixture of radiotherapy and chemotherapy followed; eventually they took away her womb. The men deteriorated after that. Now living with a 'restaurateur called Gianni' (a violent waiter who sponges off Anna, according to Deb). Would love to adopt, but being a functioning alcoholic makes that difficult, she says, though not impossible one day. That wonderful face now marooned in puffy plumpness, Anna sports the colourful, enveloping scarf that big women wear to shield their bodies from unkind looks and thoughts. Was any of this a choice?

Anna sits next to me, cooing over pictures of Emily on my phone. 'God, she's so like you, Kate. What a knockout.'

'Emily doesn't think so. She's so self-critical.'

'Girls never think so.'

'Surely *you* did, Anna? You were the fairest of us all.'

Anna shrugs. 'No and yes. I took it for granted, s'pose. Didn't cash it in at the right time. Then it was gone. Not like you, Kate. You've done everything brilliantly. Career, great marriage, great kids.'

'It only looks like that from the outside,' I protest, thinking of lying about my age at work. Thinking of how I feel being a minion to boys almost half my age. Thinking of not having had sex since New Year's Eve. Thinking of a man I must not think of, because I'm too old for fairy tales and we don't live

265

happily ever after, we just carry on. Thinking, suddenly, that the one thing I wouldn't change from the past thirty years is my wonderful children.

1.44 am: Drunk and disorderly? Not exactly. I don't need to be drunk to be disorderly, as I once mistakenly emailed somebody. But I'm both. At least I think I am. There was a time when I would not have weaved – woven? weavered? – back across the court like this without a gentleman, or at least a boy, to prop me up. But now I am alone, unpropped. Improper but unpropositioned. It suddenly feels strange. Lonely.

'Hello!'

So much for solitude. It's Two-Time Ted, lying in a flower bed. He looks like he's fallen out of a window.

'Hello, Ted. How you doing?'

'Am pished, Kate. Quite frankry am pished. Sho shorry. You're sho beautiful, d'you know that? Why d'we break up? I mussht avbin mad.'

'You were two-timing me with Debra, Ted.'

'Wash I?

'Yes.'

'Debra Richajjjjssonson?'

'Yes.'

There is a moment when Ted could apologise for his youthful treachery. Instead, with a dreamy smile, he says, 'Lucky basssh-htard. Freesshom!'

I find this a lot funnier than I should. 'We never had a freeshom, try again – threesome – Ted. Debra's in the bar. Why don't you get out of the flower bed and say sorry to her?'

He stands up, tries to brush the earth off his trousers and misses. I turn him around and point him towards the entrance

266

to the bar. Even in his present condition, Two-Time Ted is a more solid prospect than any of Deb's online suitors.

'Hello!' I've just got rid of Ted when I'm hailed a second time.

'Roz. Where you off to?'

La Pilger is wheeling a small expensive suitcase briskly towards the Porter's Lodge. She appears to be completely sober.

'Got a car waiting. Got to get to London. Got a seven am in Canary Wharf.'

'You've got so much gotting.'

'Sorry?' She comes closer, peering at me through the gloom as if I were an exhibit in the zoo. 'Bit squiffy, are we? One over the nine?'

'Eight.'

'A word of advice, Kate. If you're serious about getting on now you're back in the City you've got to be in shape. That hamster wheel stops for no man, you know. Or woman.'

'Thank you, Roz.'

'It's true. Harsh but true. People think boozing goes with the job, but if you really want the job then the booze has to go.'

'S'great. Very wise, thanks.'

'All part of the Pilger service.' She looks around at the dark walls, the mysterious entrances to staircases, the lawn colourless in the moonlight and as smooth as a billiard table. Roz breathes in, holds it, then out. This is her allotted thirty seconds of nostalgia, I can tell.

'Funny old place. Still, hell of a stepping stone. Got to get on with life, though. Can't hang around.'

'I was just thinking—'

'Yes?' She's getting impatient now, needing to find her driver and her car.

'I was thinking how when I used to do this, and it was with a boy. You know, walking back to my room at night, that feeling of excitement of . . .' Why am I telling her this?

Roz hits that one straight back at me. 'Well, thank heavens *that's* all over.'

'What is?'

'All that malarkey. Boys and sex and all that nonsense. Fun for a bit, but what a *waste* of that time, when there are so many better things to do.'

'Like what, Roz? What's better than making love?'

'Golly, you *are* drunk. Call of the past and all that? Forget it, Kate. Personally, I couldn't be more thrilled that it's over and done with.'

'You mean . . .'

'That whole department. Bed and everything. I shut up shop years ago.'

Anyone listening would think we were discussing the retail sector.

'Blessing, as far as I'm concerned,' she goes on. 'Never quite my thing. More your area than mine. Roger Graham was saying at dinner that, between you and me and the bedpost, you were the naughtiest girl he ever slept with. Randy old bugger, that man. And indiscreet. At his age, too. Anyway,' she says, heaving a sensible sigh, 'mustn't stand here nattering. Good to see you, Kate. Got to find that bloody car of mine. Bye bye.' And off she marches, the sound of luggage wheels scrolling into the night.

I stand there a moment, listening, trying not to laugh, and teetering on the brink of tears. Roger lying to everyone about having shagged me – why the hell not? Maybe after a certain age what we wanted and what we did meld into one. Then I turn and walk straight across the lawn – forbidden territory, then as now – to the room where I've been put for the night.

Kick off shoes. Unpeel what is left of stocking and post into teeny swing-bin. Go into bathroom, switch on light, gaze into mirror, switch off light again very fast. Brush teeth in the half-dark. Drink three glasses of tap water. I get undressed, then reach over to my suitcase and unzip the compartment at the side. Laptop. I seem to be acting on automatic now, like Robot Man. Open, turn on. The false moonlight of the screen again, dazzling for an instant. Password; not too pissed to remember that, thank you Roy. Small mercies.

Inbox. *Click, click, click.* Reply. I pause, holding my breath. *Come on, Kate. Say it to yourself: I will not shut up shop. I will call up the past. I cannot live on the hamster wheel and the grindstone, however they fit together. I can be happy, can't I, whether it makes me good or not? Screw it, why not* not *be good and give happy a chance?*

From: Kate Reddy
To: Jack Abelhammer
Subject: Us
Jack. It's me.
 PS XXO

15

CALAMITY GIRL

3.03 am: Five whole days since the reunion. Wide awake, staring at cobweb on the ceiling and worrying. If I had a superpower I would be Calamity Girl, blessed with the ability to foresee disaster around every corner. Or do I mean cursed? Getting on the train every morning, the first thing I do is scan the carriage for bombers before figuring out the most direct path to the exit. How likely is it that a terrorist is on the 7.12 am from Royston to King's Cross? Doesn't stop me checking, though.

I know it's irrational. Believe me, I know. And that's just one of a hundred different worries blipping across my air-traffic controller's screen, as I'm sitting alone in the control tower, tensed to avert a collision or note any small deviation from the maternal flight plan.

Just the usual stuff. North Korea. The kids. How they're doing at school. Putting too much pressure on kids to work hard at school. The kids not working hard enough at school to get into a Russell Group university. Kids never getting a paid job, being stuck as interns till they're forty-one. Kids

270

leaving home. Kids coming back to live at home and never leaving again. Emily bringing home a drug addict with blond dreadlocks and a dog on a rope. Our finances. Richard's health. My health. My job. Not getting my temporary contract renewed. Flu jab. Death. Ben's toenails. Christmas. Emily's party. Worrying that I worry so much I will make myself ill. Doctors say stress causes cancer, don't they? Not going to the gym enough to combat stress and release endorphins. That I still haven't gone to see that Dr Libido the gynaecologist. That my periods are more like bloodbaths. Carbs. Ageing. That I'm not around enough for my mum. Did Lee Harvey Oswald really act alone? What was up with that grassy knoll? My sister resenting that I don't do my share with Mum. Did I take the wrong tone in my last phone call with Julie? (Got to be so careful.) Richard's parents. Barbara picking things up like a human magpie, becoming a danger to herself. Donald her dutiful, despairing guardian. Forgetting to order Curcumin tablets to ward off dementia. My weight. Doing well with my diet through the day, then blowing it all on a bloody KitKat at 8.33. House renovation costs. Death. Jack (*no, definitely not Jack, stop that!*).

I'm burning up here, hotter than July, nightie drenched in sweat. And still the worries keep coming. What did Jay-B mean in that email when he said 'you seem to be making your mark on the team'? (Is that good?) Not seeing my friends because work and family is all I can manage. The number of Christmas cards we get almost down to single figures, including one from a lawn-care company. Putting up cards from previous Christmases to make it look like we have more friends. (Sad.) Letting Sally down by cancelling another dog walk. That Emily seems subdued, even defeated, when she's not yelling at me. (Did she fall again? I saw a cut on her arm.) That Lenny misses

271

me now I'm back at work, waits by the door. That my Experian credit rating is inexplicably low. Would chin lipo change my life? That I keep remembering Cedric the German exchange student then promptly forgetting him again. That Mum needs to see the cardiologist for her check-up. That she tells me not to worry. That I worry. That she needs to stop wearing heels in case she falls. That I must buy Magic Skin highlighter cream for youthful appearance, as featured in *Stella* magazine. That Ben told me Emily's Facebook said she had seventy-nine accept-ances for her party. But she told me she'd only invited seventy people! That I keep getting this sinking feeling that Emily's life is like one of those Hollywood sets: all facade for the camera and nothing inside. That this is a pandemic among girls and there's absolutely nothing we can do about it. That I must remember to carry sanitary towels now in case. That the door is slamming shut on my fertile years and it grieves me, it *bereaves* me. Even though I knew I would never have another baby, to lose the *possibility* of another baby. Jack. (*I said, NO JACK*).

Constant, low-level feeling of Nameless Dread. Turning fifty. (You're as young as you feel. I don't feel young, I feel wrecked.) That I was too scared to get on the down escalator at Bank the other day. Terrified, actually. Stepped back, couldn't do it, sorry. Sorry. Don't know what's wrong with me, all of a sudden. Vertigo? *Just step on.* No worries, Conor at the gym. No worries, Kate. Need to go to sleep. Must sleep or I won't be able to cope at work. Can't sleep. Nameless Dread. ('*What's its name? ROY? Please give my dread a name.*') Must stay in control. The kids, always the kids.

Is this a normal amount of anxiety, do you think? Does every woman feel like she's by herself on duty in an air-traffic control tower? I mean, I've been anxious ever since Emily was born. That's fair enough, I reckon. What are children except parts of your heart? It's not exactly ideal to have your heart going to a party, then sleeping over at someone's house and not texting you because 'my phone died'. If you could choose someone to carry your most vital organ around, it wouldn't be a dopey teen who forgets to charge their mobile, would it?

Lately, though, I notice the worry has really stepped up a gear. Is it being back at work? Is it Perry and the Menopause siphoning all the happy hormones from my womb? Is it this chronic wakefulness at 3 am? Is it the big birthday hurtling inexorably towards me? *Uch*. I went to a lovely carol service on Saturday and, during 'Away in a Manger' I was looking around, figuring out which exit was nearest so I could get the kids out if there was a terrorist attack. The kids weren't even with me. I was in a *church*, for God's sake.

I don't want to make too much of this. It's just that, some days, the fear is almost incapacitating. I'm a teeny bit scared that I'm losing my mind.

Wednesday, 6.26 am: 'Honestly, you and your doggy due diligence, Kate!'

Sally is laughing at me or, more specifically, at my habit of scanning the path up ahead for any dogs that present a clear and present danger to Lenny and Coco. I pride myself on being able to tell from 150 metres which hounds might bite or start a fight. Generally, I admit, that's based on an assessment of the owner rather than the animal.

'Come on, I was right about those two Jack Russells, wasn't I?'

'You were,' Sally concedes. 'That man was absolutely awful. Saying, "My dogs only want to play" while the big one had poor Coco by the scruff of the neck until you went in with your wellies flying. You were so brave.'

It's very early and we have the country park to ourselves. The sky is a delicate, icing-pink, which means rain later, but, for now, it's like a preview of heaven. The gate was still locked, so we parked across the road and found an opening in the hedge. I told Sally that I keep waking in a sweat and can't get back to sleep. A fellow insomniac, she told me to text her, any time, and if she was awake she would text back. It really helps.

We are following both dogs up the glittering, icy track that runs parallel to the main road where we have found some very late blackberries growing in the hedge. We pop them straight into our mouths; smaller and tarter than the ones you find in shops, they have a light dusting of frost and taste like Nature's own bittersweet sorbet. Sally suggests we come back with a Tupperware to collect berries for a Christmas trifle. I don't even want to think about all the food I have to prepare and shop for before both sides of the family descend on us. What I really want to talk about today is not Jack Russells but another Jack entirely. Haven't heard from him since I sent that drunken email at the college reunion. Five whole days ago. Have tried hard not to run every possible reaction Jack might have had, good, bad and indifferent, on a loop-tape through my brain. In this, I have only been partially successful. Entire minutes go by when I manage to think about something else. Why hasn't he replied? I want to share all my feverish speculations with Sally. Did he get the email? Was he upset I took so long to reply to his? Is he paying me back by taking a while to get back to me (no, Jack's not childish like that). Should I have said something else? Something more thoughtful or encouraging than, 'It's me. PS XXO.' Oh, God, why did I reply at all and plunge myself into this torture of anticipation?

Truth is, I'm not sure I know Sally well enough to share this – what is it? Stupid crush? Midlife crisis? Last orders in the

Passion Saloon? We've both talked about our marriages, with Sally praising Mike's good nature and speculating on the long hours he spends alone in his shed while I gave an unfair but highly enjoyable account of Richard's cycling obsession and his constant talk of eco-friendly Svengali Joely and her hideous herby teas. We ended up crying with laughter. Only later did I wonder which was greater: the mirth or the tears.

When we get to our bench at the summit, and Sally is dusting the sparkling spilt icy sugar off with her glove before we sit down, I can't resist any longer. I mention an American client who recently got in touch again, a man I had feelings for many years ago, back when I was still working. I jabber on. How having small children made it impossibly selfish and wrong to take it any further (true), how nothing really happened between me and Jack (also true, sadly); anyway, I know the grass is never greener, it only looks that way to a person running a one-woman relay race around the cinder track of working motherhood.

Sally doesn't press me for details. She cocks her head, listens and nods, and I think I see her blush beneath her fur-trapper hat. Is her silence frosty or is it just the weather? Sal is a decade older than me, I forget that, and perhaps she takes a more old-fashioned, disapproving view than I expected. I feel so happy in her company, so held and safe somehow, that the thought she might disapprove of me causes my cheeks to redden in imitation of her own. When Lenny comes bounding up, waggily triumphant with another dog's rubber ball, it feels as if we are both grateful for the interruption. I won't bring up Jack again.

On the way back to the car, we discuss Emily's party, which is this weekend. Sally suggests removing any ornaments or pictures and covering the sofas, just in case. I say that won't be necessary; it's going to be quite a small, civilised affair, although I'm starting to have my doubts. The Carters are having a party of their own on New Year's Eve when I will get to meet Mike and Sal will meet Richard. I tell her about the thing I have christened the Nameless Dread. Mention what happened at the top of that escalator at Bank station the other day. I don't want to call it a panic attack because panic attacks are for febrile metropolitan types, not sturdy Northern workhorses like me. Why develop vertigo now?

'My mum got through the menopause fine,' I say. 'I don't understand why it's hitting me so hard.'

'I think it was different for them,' Sally says, linking her arm through mine as we come to the steepest and widest part of the path. 'Because we have careers, we start our families later, so we find ourselves going through what they used to call The Change when we still have kids at home. And our parents are old and starting to get ill or need help. I remember my mum was having chemo when Oscar was doing his GCSEs; I was torn right down the middle. And look at you, zooming up to see Richard's parents and your own mum a few days before you started the new job. Now you're throwing a party to cheer up Emily when you're dealing with those awful boys at work. It's a recognised thing, you know.'

'What is?

'The Sandwich Generation,' Sally says. 'It's in all the magazines. See, if we'd had our babies when Mother Nature intended . . .'

'At eighteen?'

'Or fifteen even . . . Well, we'd be grandmothers, even great grandmothers by the time we hit the menopause, wouldn't we? Not still trying to take care of everyone while holding down a job like you are. Honestly, it's no wonder you're anxious, Kate. You've got to find a way to be kinder to yourself.'

Lifting Lenny up and wiping his muddy paws with the towel I keep for that purpose in the boot, I say that I'd love to put less pressure on myself, but that won't be possible, not while Richard isn't working. I can definitely see the advantage of being a revered tribal elder rather than the filling in some crazy generational club-sandwich.

'What filling do you reckon I am, Sal? Tuna mayo? Egg and cress?'

Sally says she's not sure. 'But whatever it is, dear girl, you're very thinly spread. Please go and see Dr Libido, promise me?'

Once she has driven off, I check my Inbox again. Several new emails, including one from Jay-B, ominously titled: Grant Hatch. Still not the one I want so badly. Where *are you*? Please speak to me.

7.11 am: Back home, I gently suggest to Ben that maybe he could live without the three-dimensional PlayStation thingy for Christmas. After the password debacle, hopes are fading that I will find one in time. The thought of trying to rescue the situation while dealing with whatever that feral hipster Jay-B throws at me, oh, and organising bed linen and towels for twelve guests, makes me want to check into a padded cell and scream for several hours. I ask Ben casually if there's something else he would like as his main present from Father Christmas, other than the impossible-to-find, out-of-stock PlayStation.

'How about a new bike, love?'

He lets his spoon clatter into his Cheerios, splashing milk across the table, and his mouth forms that big, silent 'O' from Munch's *The Scream* – the face that always signalled he was about to unleash a Krakatoan tantrum when he was little. Unlike my daughter, my son is still emotionally transparent. He lacks the capacity for guile. I can read him like the top line of the optician's chart. This fact melts my heart.

'Noooo,' Ben cries. 'The 3D is so cool, Mum. It gives you migraines and everything.'

'Sounds healthy,' says Richard, glancing up from his phone. 'Talking of healthy, Kate, I was thinking maybe we could ring the changes this Christmas food-wise.'

Uh-oh. *Man Takes Interest in Christmas* klaxon. I stiffen, then say sweetly, 'What do you have in mind, Rich? Christmas dinner does tend to be pretty traditional.'

'Well, Joely, who has years of experience with this sort of thing, was telling me about Tofurky. It's a much lighter option.'

'Toe Furkie? Sounds like a foot fetish.'

'Tofur-key actually,' says Rich, wincing and pushing his glasses further up the bridge of his nose. 'Non-genetically engineered soya and quinoa. Very tasty and no blood sugar crashes afterwards.'

'Sounds rank, Dad,' says Emily, who is sitting on the window seat, painting her toenails black. She shoots me a conspiratorial smirk and I think: Ah, good, we're friends again because I said she could have a party and Daddy didn't.

'Emily's right, Rich. You're not seriously suggesting your parents will eat *keen-wah* on Christmas Day? Remember that time we gave Barbara sweet potato and she said it was what they used to feed to pigs during the war?'

Rich shrugs and fastens his neon-yellow belt over his windcheater: 'Christmas doesn't have to be set in stone, does it? We need to open ourselves up to the possibility of change, Kate. Actually, Joely says . . .'

Not her again. I'm starting to actively dislike this stout, wholesome, menopause-expert cat-lady without going to the trouble of meeting her first. The Gospel according to St Joely has grown tiresome. Has Rich found some kind of mother substitute or something? I change the subject and suggest brightly that Rich might like to forego his bike ride for once and get the Christmas decorations down from the loft and then accompany me to the supermarket to buy food and drink for Em's party. Rich says huffily that he is preparing for a big race in May, and he can't afford to miss a single day. 'It's not a bike ride, Kate, it's training.'

After he's gone, Ben comes over and rests his head on my arm. 'Mum, can we have little sausages in bacon and crispy roast potatoes for Christmas dinner?'

'Course we can, darling.'

'I want everything to be the same,' he blurts out in a voice too small for his body. He must have grown three inches since the summer. There are ghostly stretch marks on his back, the skin striated like a silver birch.

'Mum, where will we put the tree in our new house? I liked our old house.'

'So did I, my love, but you know we had to move so Daddy could do his course and Mummy could do her new job in London. Everything will be exactly the same, I promise. Our new house will be lovely soon. Clever Piotr will have finished our kitchen, won't you Piotr?'

'*Yrrnrsczr.*' From a crawl space under the floorboards, comes the muffled sound of Polish affirmation.

10.17 am: 'It's Beginning to Look a Lot Like Christmas' was pouring like aural hot chocolate from every shop doorway on my route into work this morning. Speak for yourself, Michael Bublé. Am struggling to understand how the kids can be breaking up from school next week. The weather is so mild and, mentally, I'm still somewhere in late October. I'd forgotten how hard it is to organise a family Christmas while holding down a full-time job. Let's face it, Christmas *is* a full-time job, and I daren't show any sign of slacking off in an office where I'm still on probation.

Word has got back that I didn't make a deal with Grant Hatch – quite the opposite, in fact. Jay-B sent me a terse email asking for a full report of the meeting with 'likely solutions re Grant going forward'. Chemical castration springs to mind. I badly need to drum up some new business to earn my keep around here. No word yet about the Russian deal. It's gone to the head of Risk, and then the Board, who will give it the final sign-off if all the checks come up OK, and if they decide that Mr Velikovsky is unlikely to be unmasked as a Bond villain hell-bent on world domination. Not for the next three years, anyway.

Troy came over and sat on my desk yesterday, legs splayed wide apart like the unselfconscious baboon that he is, and told me that the firm gets nervous about Eastern European money. 'It's not very sticky, Russian cash,' he explained. 'Tends to leave as fast as it came in, which is crap for the bottom line.'

Troy's show of helpfulness was fooling no one. I know full well he'd be cracking open the champagne if my first big success was snatched away from me. If I brought in Velikovsky it would be as if the hand grenade Troy gave me had turned into a hundred red roses.

I never had much time for this kind of office willy-waving when I was building a career here in my thirties. Not having a willy to wave helped: you can't wave a vagina, can you? I have even less time now I'm here earning money simply to pay Piotr to build my kitchen and put food on the table – well, Doritos for Emily's party, anyway. If Troy wants to patronise me, the woman who, in another lifetime, set up the fund he works on, then the Scarlet Pimpleboy can go right ahead. What matters is that I impress Jay-B, which is why I am going to make nice with some rock-star widow, Bella Baring, who my boss says is 'mad as a sack of cats'. I should really be swotting up on this bonkers woman before our meeting, but Christmas calls.

Whatever it takes, I have to get hold of a PlayStation for Ben. I promised. Decide to ring evil faceless Internet cow to challenge her in person. If righteous anger fails will throw self on her mercy, describe Ben as twenty-first-century Tiny Tim who will wither and die without gift of latest technology.

11.28 am: The office is pretty empty and there's no sign of Jay-B or Troy, so I quickly dial the Contact Us number and get a recorded message: 'If you wish to speak to a customer services adviser, please choose one of the following options: Press one for Sales, Press two for Tracking, Press three for Total Nervous Collapse, Press four if you wish to murder a member of our Help Team and display their severed head on Tower Hill. Press five to hear these options again.'

'Bugger. Why is it never possible to speak to an actual human being?'

'Are you OK, Kate?'

'Oh, sorry, Alice, did I say that out loud? Just being driven quietly loopy by the joys of Christmas shopping.'

'Tell me about it,' she sighs. 'This year, I've got to buy for my mum, my dad, my brother *and* Max. Nightmare.'

I look at Alice and try to remember what it was like when I was single and Christmas was just getting presents for four people and turning up on Christmas Eve at your parents' house expecting the festivities to commence. No point describing what is involved in creating perfect Christmas for children and husband and husband's family, especially sister-in-law, the born-again Ofsted Inspector, who brings her judgemental eye to canapés, napkins and table decorations. Put it this way, Cheryl has a Christmas Pudding Cinnamon-fragranced air freshener in each of her three toilets. I presently have one working bathroom with what Richard would call issues around sanitation and a bumper pack of Santa Claus serviettes.

I don't mention any of this to Alice. It would be like trying to explain neoclassical endogenous growth theory to Lenny. No need to frighten the poor kid. She'll find out soon enough, if that louse Max ever gets round to popping the question. Alice says she is excited about the office party, which is taking place in some club I'm clearly supposed to have heard of in Shoreditch. I arrange my features into an approximation of eager anticipation, shudder inwardly and add party to my Christmas to-do list, which is currently longer than *Finnegans Wake*. Surely attendance isn't compulsory?

'You totally have to come,' says Alice. 'You're part of the team now and all the big bosses will be there so you definitely need to show your face. Oh, and Kate, don't forget your flu jab. Lunchtime. It's on the eleventh floor remember?'

'Oh, yes, thanks.' (*'Roy, can you give me a nudge about the flu jab please?'*)

Dial the number for the PlayStation supplier again and, this time, miraculously, I get through. Am so startled to be speaking to an actual person that the whole sorry tale comes pouring out of me. How I purchased the item, but I reset the password as instructed, and, infuriatingly, that cancelled the order. Then, I bought it again, using the right password, which was great until I got an email from the company telling me that delivery would now be after 29th December.

'That is correct, yes,' says the voice.

'But, obviously, it's a Christmas present. A *Christmas* present. And *Christmas* takes place on the twenty-fifth so the twenty-nineth isn't much use to me and my son really wants this PlayStation which I paid you for weeks ago.'

'Is not possible. Out of stock.'

'Well, as I didn't cause this problem and I'm going to have a really disappointed boy on Christmas Day, I think the least you can do is . . .'

'Madam, I have the right to terminate this conversation, as I feel you are getting aggressive,' says the voice.

'What do you mean, I'M GETTING AGGRESSIVE? I'm being incredibly polite considering how utterly hopeless your company has been.' Oh, hell. Spot Jay-B coming out of the lift and quickly put the phone down.

1.10 pm: Over lunchtime, I call every possible PlayStation supplier within a twenty-mile radius of the office. Nothing. I Google Tofurky instead. Sadly, it turns out not to be an upper-class foot perversion but an actual thing: a vegan substitute for turkey. 'This holiday season, while others are sitting down to a meal of dead flesh, fill your plate (and your tummy!) with these tasty, cruelty-free meats instead.'

Sorry, despite what Saint Joely says, we are *so* not having that in my house on Christmas Day. I know just where Richard can stuff his Tofurky.

'What's that, Roy? I have to remember something. OK, can you narrow it down, please? What am I supposed to be noticing? I really have no idea what you're on about. Never met the Joely woman.'

At that moment, Jay-B comes over. He wants to brief me about Bella, the rock-star widow. He explains that Fozzy Baring's kids all have trust funds. There are three legitimate children, but as many as nine all together; since Fozzy died, more women keep coming out of the woodwork and demanding DNA tests. Bella, who was the starter wife, has three of the kids, but she prefers horses. Can't blame her. The eldest boy has been in the Priory. Depression induced by smoking too much dope. Your basic car-crash rock-sprog. Bella likes a bit of the wacky baccy herself. Hasn't got a clue about the investments.

'Your job, Kate, is to explain things without confusing her and reassure her how brilliantly it's all going. Fozzy's accountant is always trying to get Bella to move the money somewhere else so he can get a bigger slice. Greedy bastard. That mustn't happen. You're cool with that, yeah?'

'Oh, yes, absolutely, no problem. I've been reading Fozzy's autobiography.'

'*FLU JAB!*' shouts Roy, making me leap up with a start.

'What?'

'Sorry, Jay-B, just forgot, I have to nip upstairs. Back in a minute.'

'*Roy, you were supposed to be reminding me about my flu jab!*'

'*I did.*'

'*Yes, but much too late. Look at the time.*'

A nurse is sitting behind a table at the entrance to the eleventh floor. Only one person remains in the queue. Clearly, they're about to finish.

'So sorry I'm late,' I say, 'have you got time to squeeze me in?'

The nurse gives an obliging little smile and indicates a list where I'm required to fill in my name and – oh, help – Date of Birth. I scan down through all of my colleagues' birthdays. Some of them were born as recently as 1989. I could literally be their mother. Malcolm from Accounts, who is universally considered to be 'ancient', practically Mayan, in fact, was born in April 1966, a whole year after me. Luckily, and only because

I forgot my appointment, no one in the office will see that I am, in fact, the oldest person in the entire building. Only the nurse will know my guilty secret. The pen hesitates a second above the box before I decide to write down the alarming truth: 11/3/65.

6.20 pm: Am done for the day. Slink out of the office, holding my coat bundled up under my arm rather than putting it on. That way people might think I am coming back. Not that most of them bother to look up from their screens. I could trot past them on a donkey.

Make it to the main door, which opens with a sigh. Join the club. Then out into the winter air, and freedom—

'Kate.'

Well, that didn't last long.

'Alice. What are you doing out here?'

'Waiting for you.'

'But I was just in the office. And so were you. I saw you there, ten minutes ago.'

'I know, but I didn't want, I mean I couldn't really talk there.'

'Private stuff.'

'Well, sort of office stuff, actually, but private too.'

'You speak in riddles, darling. Go on, tell me, don't look so worried.'

I look at her young clear face, which, to my amazement and dismay, begins to crumple.

'My God, Alice. What's happened? What have they done to you?' A hand on her arm for support.

'Nothing to *me.*' She looks up. 'To *you.*'

'Me? Nothing's happened to me. I mean, nothing worse than usual. Your basic ghastly day, but I made it through OK.'

'I know, but . . . it's just . . .'

'Just what?'

'Troy.' So that's it. The man is a virus in a suit.

'What's he done now?'

'Well, I was in one of our meeting rooms, you know, the ones with the adjoining door. I'd gone to steal a pen from that stack of posh ones they always have at the side. And the door was open a bit, and Troy was in the other room, on the phone. I could hear every word. He obviously didn't know I was there, and . . .'

'And he was talking about me.'

'At first I wasn't sure. But he kept saying, "She". Like, "She's doing OK", and "She'll learn". But then—' Alice bites her bottom lip.

'Come on, I'm a big girl. I can take it.'

'Well, it started to get really nasty. Like, "We could totally bang her", and "She's up for it, she just doesn't know it", and then lots of horrible stuff about, I don't know, like they were having a bet on you.'

'When did you know it was me?'

'When Troy said something about how it looked like you'd pulled off the Velikovsky deal. And then of course they were joking about pulling and pulling off and God knows what. I mean, how old are they?'

'About ten and a half, mostly. Do you know who Troy was talking to?'

'I can't be sure, but at one point he went, sort of, "Hey, Mr Hatchman", or something like that.'

'Grant. I might have guessed.'

'The slimy one from a few days ago?'

'The very same. So was it just, you know, idle banter, or did . . .'

286

'Well, that's it. If they were just being silly I wouldn't have mentioned it, but it sounded as if they were actually cooking something up. Like, "OK, mate, I'll see if I can go where you couldn't. Teach her to turn you down. No one turns down the Hatchman". And Troy was using the c-word and everything. It was just so horrid.'

'Alice.' I try a smile, neither comforting nor convincing. 'It's OK, really. I've heard worse, believe me. I've been around a bit longer than you in this business, I've seen more than you have, and . . .'

'That's the other thing. Troy kept going on about how old you are. Like how you would, I don't know, benefit or something from him, from a young guy giving you one . . .'

'Forget it.'

'I mean, you're what, forty-ish? That's nothing. I was so pleased when you came to work here, Kate, because it felt like having backup, you know, girl power.'

'Especially with Troys all over the place.'

'Right. And I really didn't even think about the age thing.'

The age thing. There's me, there's my time. Nutshell.

'Honestly,' Alice goes on, in a bid to cheer me up, 'it's not as if you're—' she casts around for an extreme example, '—fifty or anything.'

I give her a big hug. 'No,' I say. 'No, it's not.'

16

HELP!

1.07 pm: Dr Libido's office is in an imposing terrace of Georgian houses on the corner of Harley and Wigmore Street. He has a six-month waiting list: all those desperate women like me who've heard a rumour he can give us our old self back. I managed to get a cancellation.

I didn't think I should put it off any longer. The time had come to seek help. Earlier today, I was sitting in the vast, chilly, marble foyer of a prospective client's building, crying my eyes out, so boiling hot that I stripped down to a camisole, exhausted because of 3 am waking, bloated and slightly stinky. Would you buy a fund off this woman? The pitch was a fiasco. Client looked at me as if I was deranged, which was fair enough after I'd called her David. To be honest, that business with Grant Hatch must have got to me more than I realised, what with him using my age as a weapon against me. Bastard. And I was really upset about Jack. Any hope he would get back to me was receding. At the college reunion, I had allowed myself to reach out to him, had set cynicism aside and decided to give happiness a shot. With everything else that was going on I longed to have one lovely thing go right and the fact it wasn't was so shitty. When I came out of the pitch, I thought, 'I will jump under a bus if I don't start to feel better soon.'

It was then that Roy, bless him, reminded me about Dr Libido. I called right there from the street and his receptionist said, 'Oh, if you're quick, you can come in now.' A miracle. Jay-B had summoned me by text for an urgent meeting, but I jumped in a cab going in the opposite direction.

Emily to Kate
Hi Mum, may be few more coming to party. lol! Lizzy invited some friends from London. Pls get lots more food and drink! Love you xx

Kate to Emily
How many EXACTLY? We don't want a riot! xxx

1.14 pm: Dr Libido's nurse looks like a young Meryl Streep, wearing crisp white tunic and trousers. She hands me a form and asks me to fill it in. I start reading and I really don't know whether to laugh or cry. The questionnaire reads like the breakfast menu from hell, only instead of scrambled eggs there are fried brains.

Have you suffered from any of the following:

Feelings of anxiety – can't stop worrying about things beyond your control? *Tick*

Disturbed sleep and waking up in the night? *Tick*

Unexplained weight gain that you just can't lose? *Tick tick*

Brain fog, trouble finding things? *Yes, that's why I have, whatsisname, Roy.*

Vaginal dryness? *Well, it's been a while since the lady garden had any gentleman callers but there's certainly discomfort and itching down there. That's one reason I don't want to cycle. Sitting on the saddle would be painful.*

Low mood? *Rock bottom, thanks.*

Irregular or heavy periods? *And how. I still have the Velikovsky hand towel to prove it.*

Emotional fragility, increased weepiness? *Surely it's perfectly normal to burst into tears at least twice a day?*

Loss of stamina in the afternoon, particularly from two to five? *Yup.*

Increased irritability and/or excessively aggressive? *WHO ARE YOU CALLING IRRITABLE, MISTER? Didn't that PlayStation supplier say I sounded aggressive? Tick bloody tick.*

Difficulty concentrating? *No. Yes. Yes. No.*

Low libido and you're not sure why? *Except when using testosterone patches sent by friend in America, no sexual feeling of any kind, until I got Jack's email.*

The best bit about this questionnaire is it has made me realise that I am not going insane. There they are, all the horrors I have been experiencing for months written down in black and white. Actual medical symptoms, not some free-floating terror that this is just the way things are now. Calamity Girl, always anticipating the worst-case scenario, is not who I really am; it's bloody biology that's all, or chemistry.

I apologise to the nurse for starting to cry when she takes some blood and she smiles that Streepish smile, serene yet steely, and says, 'Don't worry. A lot of women come crawling in here in a far worse state than you.'

In terms of interior design, in my experience, private consulting rooms aim in one of two directions: the book-lined study of a pre-war country house or the bridge of a post-human spaceship floating just off Xarquon 9. Dr Libido's haunt goes squarely for the first. The basic principle appears to be: the more you pay your doctor, the more lavishly you will be lulled into believing that the person you have come to see is not a doctor at all. I mean, look at this place. Long windows at which to stand and contemplate a world that brims with expensive illnesses. The smug gleam of walnut furniture. Wallpaper which even William Morris would have thought a bit much. Everything except a royal coat of arms. No actual medical equipment in sight, not even a stethoscope, let alone – horrors! – anything so vulgar as a syringe. There *is* an examination couch, but it is tucked away, discreetly, behind a folding marquetry screen, which was obviously designed not to conceal the desexed depressives of modern middle age but to allow French cour-tesans of 1880 to play peekaboo with their discarded garments, one by one. Pride of place goes to the desk, as broad as a billiard table, topped with a greensward of old leather rather than fuzzy baize.

And, seated behind the desk, Dr Libido himself. His real name is Farquhar, although Sally assured me that everybody, out of his hearing, refers to him as Dr Fuckyeah. It's too old and stately a name for the handsome, tanned, self-satisfied individual opposite me. You can see him as gynaecology's answer to Tony Blair, the shining hope of a political movement – the Mummy Get Your Mojo Back party. My guess is that all his patients would vote for him.

Fuckyeah loses no time in telling me that he sees several women a day who complain of anxiety, depression, mood swings, anger and panic attacks. Often their GPs have mis-diagnosed them with a mental health problem. About seventy per cent are on antidepressants. Their problems, says Dr Libido, can easily be solved by synthetic hormones, which will stabilise everything and lift the cloud under which they are living. He also thinks I have an underactive thyroid. (Just like Sally. Another bond to bind us.) Ah, yes, that might account for my being able to fall asleep standing up in a cupboard, like an ironing board. The blood test would confirm it.

'What about all the research linking HRT to increased risk of cancer?' I say, feeling that I should at least try to act respon-sibly while basically being ready to inject heroin on the spot if it will stop me feeling so bloody dreadful.

'Inaccurate information, I'm afraid, based on flawed studies.' His grin displays a daunting number of veneers, suddenly making me think of Liberace and his piano. 'A lot of women's lives are made utterly miserable when, if they are started on the right kind of HRT, all of those symptoms can be avoided.'

The truth is if Dr Libido had, at that moment, handed me a prescription for Class A drugs and the police had been waiting outside the door, truncheons and cuffs at the ready, I'd still have snatched it out of his hands. I am desperate. Sorry, I can't do this by myself any more. It's like trying to restart a laptop left out in the rain. I have to stop yelling at the kids, I need to have energy for my work, for Emily's party, for the office party. I have to make it through Christmas without murdering Richard, Cheryl, the incontinent Dickie, or all three. It would also be nice to have just a tiny drop of me left over for me.

I tell Dr Libido about Candy's testosterone patches, which I gave up for fear I might jump on poor Piotr. He says they are illegal in the UK, but if I want more bang for my buck he will give me some testosterone in a little tube. Just one dab on my inner thigh will be enough. He also prescribes nightly progesterone, which – oh joy! – will help me sleep.

Honestly, it is hard to leave that office without kissing him. Quite sure I'm not the only female patient to have had that impulse. When I pick up the prescription at the pharmacy round the corner, the holy trinity of female sexuality – progesterone, oestrogen and testosterone – I can't wait. I come outside and tear open the box of oestrogen in the same eager way that my childhood self would have unwrapped a Sherbet Fountain for that first sweet powdery hit, or my teenage self once took a new Top Ten single straight out of the bag, scarcely believing that I had this precious, prayed-for treasure in my hands. The years rattle by, and what I crave will always change, but the sheer force of that craving – the need to have, to hear, to taste, to get better – stays the same.

Rubbing some of the precious, youth-restoring gel on my arm, I say a little prayer, right there on Wigmore Street with the traffic thrumming past. 'Please give me the strength to deal with whatever life throws at me. That's all I ask. Oh, and a taxi right now would be nice. Taxi! Amen.'

So, the Christmas party. Tidings of comfort and joy! In a moment of weakness – when do I ever have a moment of strength? – I told Emily that she could have a Christmas/pre-birthday celebration. What on earth was I thinking?

It began, as everything seemed to, with the belfie. Em had been stroppier than ever since her bum went viral. Some of our fights were so furious that for days after I was still resounding like a struck gong. I shudder at what Emily makes me capable of. She sulks. Invariably, I am the one who has to broker the peace, break the silence, unless Em wants money or a lift – usually both.

Lately, I've been thinking a lot about the wise, mysterious words of my late friend, Jill Cooper-Clark. 'When you have children, Kate, the important thing is to remember that *you* are the grown-up.'

When Jill said that to me, over a decade ago now, I literally had no idea what she was talking about. I mean, *of course*, when I became a mother, I would be the grown-up and the kids would be the kids. Now, with teenagers of my own, I know exactly what Jill meant. No matter what Emily hurls at me, no matter how horrible the ingratitude or how grotesque the sense of entitlement, I cannot lash out at her childishly. For I am the grown-up. Aren't I? (A confession: there are days, or mad minutes at least, when I feel myself slipping backwards, down towards the furies of my own youth, as if to meet my daughter on her own ground. *Don't go there, Kate. Climb back up to now.*)

Meanwhile, rather than blowing over, things had got worse. I found out that Emily's misery had spread to school. Her form tutor emailed and asked me to call, which I did in a whisper from the office. (I even got Alice to stand guard nearby, in case Troy or Jay-B caught me in the act of being a mum; for a moment, again, it was me who felt like the naughty schoolgirl, having a quick smoke while someone watched out for teachers.)

Mr Baker said that Emily had seemed withdrawn and a bit isolated lately. Was I aware of any particular problems?

'What, you mean apart from being a sixteen-year-old girl in the hideously pressurised age of social media who has to jump through the stupid yet life-determining hoops of exams and thinks she can never be good enough?' It came out so angrily; I hadn't realised until that moment how worried I was. I said what I meant without meaning to say it.

'Well, um,' said Mr Baker. Presumably rocking back in his chair, holding the phone as far away as possible, and passionately wishing that he had stuck to email. There was a pause, then he gathered himself bravely and carried on. Give that man a medal. He told me that Emily wasn't unusual. Not at all. He reckoned that at least a third of the kids in her year were depressed or self-harming. (As if I was going to be reassured by that. Safety in numbers? What about danger in numbers?)

'Emily's not depressed,' I objected. Her hormones were flooding in, just as mine were receding, and we were both caught up in that perilous rip tide. But depression? No.

One of Emily's good friends in the tutor group, Izzy, who was suffering from anorexia, had recently been admitted to a psychiatric unit. Was I aware of that? Mr Baker continued.

No, I was not.

'Would you please be sure to keep an eye out and let me know?'

I would be sure.

After he rang off, I let out an involuntary wail, like a rabbit snared in a trap. Alice went 'Sshhh,' making calm-down patting signs with her hands. The shriek made Troy and another bloke at the far end of the office stop their conversation, swivel round and stare. Instinctively, I pretended to have banged my leg on the desk and hopped about in a pantomime of pain.

'*Ow, ow*, shit, *ow.*' Far better to look like a clumsy clown than a woman ambushed by maternal anguish. 'Withdrawn and a bit isolated.' My child? Emily?

Almost immediately, I felt ashamed of my reaction. This was no time for worrying what a couple of male colleagues thought of me. Fuck it. Of course I wailed after experiencing a whiff of mortal fear for my child. Because I am mortal, a mere mortal, and that's not weak. If you prick me do I not bleed? We all bleed when we're wounded, a piece of common humanity that gets overlooked in the corporate world. I glared at the two bleeding pricks, daring them to say anything. I knew in that moment I was capable of violence.

Emily was still in lessons at school. If I hurried I could be there in time to pick her up at the gate where I would hold her and tell her it'll be OK, your mother is here to protect you. With as much calm as I could muster, I told Alice what she needed to keep tabs on in my absence, after explaining that a teacher said my daughter was struggling and I had to go to her.

'Poor sweetheart, she's only eleven,' said Alice, and I didn't know what she meant. Remembered, just in time, that I was lying about Emily's age as well as my own. Grabbed my jacket and my phone. If I sprinted to Liverpool Street I might make the next train.

At the entrance to the station, outside the shoe-mending bar, a woman was sitting on the floor begging, one twig arm outstretched. She looked ancient, whether from hunger or the remorseless battering of life it was hard to say, but she couldn't be old because there was a baby at her breast, squirming in a tightly wrapped shawl. I skittered past, then stopped, turned around and took out my wallet. Didn't have time to scramble for the coins in the zip compartment so I pressed a twenty-pound note into the woman's bony hand before leaping down the steps towards the platform. Boarded the train just as the guard's whistle blew and fell, breathless, into a seat in an empty carriage. No one else heading home at this time of day. As the grey circuitry of London gradually gave way to browns and greens, I thought about Emily and about the baby in the beggar's arms – the two becoming a single thought. That baby couldn't know his or her mother was pleading for money on the streets of some foreign city, commuters swerving past her crumpled form, her dirty clothes. To the baby, the poor, wretched woman was a place of safety and comfort; it wanted no other mother, and it never would. It killed me, that thought. It just killed me.

Back home, I put Lenny in the car and drove straight to the school. Parked opposite and waited till the kids came out. Spotted Emily and her gang. Was I imagining it or was she tagging onto the back of Lizzy Knowles's group as a drowning person clings to a life raft, or did she just happen to be a few feet behind them?

Emily was bewildered when I called her name and, for a moment, I wasn't even sure that she would cross the street and come over. She seemed to be weighing up whether or not to ignore me and walk on by, but Lenny recognised her and barked his delight through the rear window. She might avoid me, but she would never disappoint Lenny. Without thinking, once Em was in the car, I drove straight to the country park. My daughter thinks walks are for losers, the old or the criminally insane, but that afternoon she allowed me to link arms with her and we followed the path Sally and I always take up the side of the hill. I made Em wear my dog-walking fleece while I shivered a little in my office clothes.

'Why did you pick me up from school, Mum? I'm not seven,'

she said. We were sitting right at the summit on mine and Sally's bench.

'I wanted to see you, darling. Mr Baker called and he was just a little worried that you weren't, you know, your usual self.'

'I'm fine,' she said flatly.

'We never had a proper talk about that belfie business, love.'

'Mu-um, how many times? It's no biggie, OK. You literally don't understand. Basically, that stuff happens the whole time.'

'Still, it can't be nice having people see your . . .'

'Didn't get that many Likes anyway.'

'What didn't?'

'#FlagBum. Didn't get that many Likes.'

I didn't know what to say. It took a few seconds to process. Emily's main concern about the belfie was not the fact that her naked bottom was seen by thousands of people, but that it wasn't a big enough hit. Or didn't get enough hits or Likes or whatever they are. Not for the first time, I felt like I'd woken up in a parallel universe where all the values I was brought up to believe in, such as modesty and decency, are inverted, no, perverted, that's it, perverted.

'It's cold, sweetie, are you warm enough?' I said this so I had an excuse to pull her close to me. She leant in, resting her head on my shoulder, and I willed all the warmth and strength I had in my body to pass to hers.

'Do you think you might like to see a counsellor, sweetheart?'

Silence. 'What do you think, eh?' I pushed.

'Maybe, yes.'

'Good. OK, so we can fix that. Sometimes, it's good to talk to someone.'

'Not a counsellor like Daddy,' she said quickly. 'He only cares about his bikes.'

298

'That's not true, Em, you know Daddy loves you very much. He's just . . .' He's just what? I struggled to find a word for what Richard is at this moment, apart from absent. 'Right, so I will find a really good person you can talk things through with.' Someone who understands this stuff better than I do because I am completely at a loss for the first time since you were born, I thought but did not say.

On the walk back to the car park, with Lenny leading the way, Emily said, 'Lizzy's going to have a New Year's party, Mum, she's like really popular.'

Lizzy again. How long before Emily would be able to see her 'best friend' for what she is?

So, full disclosure: that was why I went along with the party. I thought it would be a chance for Emily to not be withdrawn and isolated, to get some friends round, or, if she didn't have any friends, to get some. To shore up her position in the year group. To be more than just that sad loser tricked by Lizzy Knowles into showing her naked arse. To enter the charmed circle of the Popular, the Holy Grail of every teenager. I wanted what, in fact, I have wanted every single hour since that magic day when my first baby entered the world. I wanted her to be happy. How desperately we want them to be happy.

Richard wasn't so sure. 'I still can't believe you said Emily could have a party, Kate,' said Richard, examining his new bike lock (what, another one?). 'I don't want a house full of drunken teenagers doing drugs and trying to have sex with each other. A party, in fact, is what I want less than anything in the world.'

This was strange. Rich always used to be the easygoing parent while I was the reluctant disciplinarian. When did we change sides?

'They're not going to be drunk,' I beamed encouragingly.

'We'll be serving alcohol-free mulled wine, and no one is going to do drugs or have sex. Emily has nice friends. They're not like those kids you read about who crash a party they've seen on Facebook and trash people's houses. Seriously, you need to have a little faith in the younger generation, Rich.'

I wanted to tell him the real reason for the party, I really did. But the lies, or the not being honest, had got too complicated by then. Truth is, I didn't really tell him anything much any more. Richard had gone off into the forest on his own journey of self-discovery, as people do at our age, but he forgot to drop a trail of crumbs for me to follow him. I had no clue where he was and I'd stopped trying to find out, mainly because he didn't seem to notice or care that I wasn't looking any more. Too much of the time, I felt like a single parent.

Another admission. I thought that a party might be good, not just for Emily. Anything that would offer some distraction from the hourly torment of wondering why there was still no reply from Jack.

Anyway, what with Em being so disorganised, and so many calls on everyone's time, there was no guarantee that the party would even go ahead.

The party went ahead.

Saturday, 7.17 pm: The Night of Doom begins with a ring on the doorbell. I open the door and two burly boys in black T-shirts and low-slung jeans barge in, bearing armfuls of boxes and cable.

'Where d'you wan' the speakers?' grunts one.

'You Emily's mum?' grunts the other.

Not waiting for a reply they barrel through to the kitchen, with me fussing around in their wake.

There is a dish of cooked mini-sausages sitting on the kitchen table. The burly boys pick up the dish and plonk it next to the sink, each taking the opportunity to claw a handful of sausages and munch as they work. I hear my mother's voice in my head, loud and brisk, exclaiming, 'D'you know, they didn't even say please! Whatever happened to manners?' More of me than I would care to admit to agrees with her, even if it makes me feel like a late Edwardian, but I wouldn't dream of telling them off out loud. Instead, my disapproval comes out as a single harsh tut. More than a tut: a cluck. If I'm turning into a mother hen by half past seven, ruffling her feathers with disapproval, what the hell will I be like by midnight? The burly boys glance up at the sound of the cluck, then at each other, and give a leering grin. Delightful.

7.49 pm: Doorbell. The first guests. Three elves. Correction: three elvesses, vaguely recognizable as Emily's classmates, though not, as far as I am aware, her friends.

'Hiya!' they chorus, cutting past me, each in forest-green micro shorts, a Rudolph-red crop top, and a dangly hat with a flashing bell on it. Can't help thinking that the gift-wrapping up at the North Pole must be slowed down considerably if the wrappers all insist, as these three do, on wearing four-inch wedge heels. As they move towards the sitting room, already shrieking with collective mirth, I note that the back of the crop tops, when they stand in line, forms a seasonal message. 'Santa's.' 'Little.' 'Humpers.'

8.13 pm: Give up answering doorbell. Leave door open. What's that parable in the Bible, the one I learned in Sunday school, about the host who issues a general invitation to all guests? 'Go ye out into the highways and the hedges and bid them come . . .' Something like that. A lovely idea, and undoubtedly as Christian as you can get, but I always thought, on the quiet,

301

that it was asking for trouble. I mean, what happened when he ran out of napkins? Had he forewarned his party planners about the sudden spike in numbers? Well, now I'm him. But without the charity.

9.14 pm: Finbar and Zig or possibly Zag have set up in the kitchen. Or, to be accurate, the kitchen has made way for them. On the table is a pair of what I still, I'm sorry to say, call record players. A vast, sullen boy stands over them, wearing headphones like halved grapefruit, nodding intently to the music's thump. Some sort of amplifier is sitting where the microwave normally lives, which raises the question of where the microwave has gone. Presumably it has taken the place of the loo cistern, which has moved to where the fish tank used to be, meaning that the fish tank is now the new hi-fi. Wires snake out of the door toward the sitting room, where speakers the size of the Cenotaph are planted against each wall. In truth, the entire house has been transformed into one large speaker. Doors rattle to the beat, and a large crack, like a lightning bolt, has appeared in the window halfway up the stairs. That'll be the eighteenth-century antique glass that we had mended by a gnarled old glazier, who took it away to reforge it in the fires of Mount Doom, or wherever, and returned it miraculously healed for a mere four hundred quid. He won't like the crack.

Richard is suddenly beside me, listening appreciatively to the music, which just at the moment sounds like a squad of navvies demolishing an acre of tarmac.

'Just like you said, darling. Christmas carols round the fire. Oh, and look. They're thoroughly enjoying your mulled wine.'

'That's quite enough sarcasm, thank you!'

In one corner of the sofa, a boy is holding out a plastic cup one-quarter full of wine. A girl with bleached plaits, like Heidi's evil twin, has reached into her bag, brought forth a half-bottle of supermarket vodka, and is topping him up. His cup runneth over, with a sort of pale pink poison. In fact it runneth over over my sofa, which until two hours ago was a subtle creamy beige, and now will never be cream again.

'Why is it always vodka?' I ask. 'Vodka's horrible. Doesn't taste of anything at all. And why is it always girls who bring it these days? Shouldn't the boys pull their weight? I used to think it was daring to have a Bacardi and Coke when I was seventeen.'

'Oh, the girls bring it because they want to be one of the boys,' Richard says, strangely knowledgeable. 'And they don't want to pull their weight, they just want to pull. And they like vodka precisely *because* it tastes of nothing. Right now, Kate, their sole purpose in life, their only reason for being, is to get drunk, and vodka gets you there quickest, with no taste or flavour to get in the way. Drowning their sorrows and all that.'

I look around at Emily's guests. They're sixteen, most of them. Seventeen tops. They really shouldn't have collected enough sorrows yet to need drowning, but they are turning out to be the unhappiest generation. I wonder. By giving them a vocabulary of sadness and hurt feelings have we relieved their suffering or encouraged them to think suffering is the norm? They're so suggestible at that age.

Richard gazes around, surveying his domain. Then he gestures towards the staircase, up which various couples are swarming remorselessly, like extras in a zombie film. 'There they go!' he says cheerfully. 'Off to play a nice quiet game of Trivial Pursuit, just like you said they would.'

My husband, I can see, is genuinely torn. On the one hand, he holds the entire situation in a kind of despairing contempt; at this instant, our house, and all who sail in it, is about as far from his ideal life as it is possible to get. Not enough chakras.

On the other hand, he is grimly relishing the delectable satisfaction of being proved right in his predictions of disaster. Neither emotion is very becoming. Any notion that these kids, stupid and reckless as they are, might actually be enjoying themselves for once – or merely being kids, for heaven's sake – is lost on him. He is, in the truest sense, a killjoy. Certainly, he has done a fine job of killing my joy of late. No sooner does the thought blaze up than I damp it down, but it was there.

9.33 pm: Letting poor, bewildered Lenny out into the back garden, I find, of all things, a copy of *Sense and Sensibility*. It normally lives in the little bookshelf in the downstairs loo. For a stirring moment, I wonder if someone has retreated there for a dose of peace and quiet, and started to read; I remember doing that myself decades ago, whenever a social event of any kind was all too much. On the other hand, if someone was reading the book in the loo, what is it doing out here?

I pick it up. Pages are missing. Whole chapters are missing, ripped out in what looks like a rush. Marianne may still be there somewhere, but Elinor's a goner. Then a waft of something sick-sweet passes me by. I inhale. A gust of weed. I follow the waft, and find three earnest-looking boys and one girl, sitting on the cold grass, rolling joints. And yes, they are using Jane Austen for paper. Should I applaud their literary taste or yell at such wanton destruction? 'Well, gentlemen, how nice a sense of decency is shewn on this occasion! To be conducting yourselves thus, in the company of a lady!' That's what I should say. But I don't. I just ask them to stop, and they laugh.

10.10 pm: Richard is now standing guard by the front door, determined to confiscate alcohol and only admit those who have invitations. Since no one has an invitation, this is a testing experience. Also, everyone is in Christmas fancy dress, which is unlikely to speed the identification process. He is soon involved in a heated dispute with a snowman.

10.43 pm: Look out of kitchen window to see several Santas haring down the side of the house and entering via the back garden, hotly pursed by a team of reindeer in fake-fur onesies. Donner appears to be trying to mount Blitzen, thus forming what I'm afraid is a festive twosie.

10.51 pm: My daughter wanders past. What with the heaving sea of strangers, I had forgotten she was here at all.

'Hi Mum, d'you like the music?'

'Quite. Actually, Em, I didn't know you were having a disco.'

'It's not a *disco*, Mum,' says Emily, rolling her eyes. 'No one's had a disco in like forever.'

My daughter has changed into a diaphanous, flesh-coloured body with glitter over her nipples. Plus a pair of silver hot pants with the words 'Happy New Twerk' picked out in red on the back. She is wearing flesh-coloured fishnets, but I can still see some scabs on her thighs from that time she fell off the bike.

'Darling, what on earth are you wearing?'

'Just chill, Mum, I'm the Miley Cyrus Christmas Special.' Her arm is linked in the arm of – well, I never – her frenemy, Lizzy Knowles, the belfie-boomer in person. Oh, well, if you can't beat 'em, invite 'em to your party. Lizzy is sporting red knee socks and a T-shirt that reads, 'O, Come On Me, Faithful.'

Control yourself, Kate. Remember, you are doing all this so that Emily doesn't feel so left out. Mind you, is it really any easier being left in?

'Hi, Kate,' says Lizzy, 'this is awesome. Like, so Christmassy.'

No, you horrid little witch, Christmassy is Andy Williams in a reindeer-patterned sweater. Christmassy is making very careful patterns on a chocolate yule log, with a fork, to make the icing look like a tree. Christmassy is angels and archangels. That's what I think to myself, but I keep my mouth shut, which is more than can be said for the guests. Their mouths are all wide open: shouting, glugging from cans, or glueing themselves, seemingly at random, to other mouths. My house is roughly as quiet as a Grand Prix.

Midnight: Richard is standing by himself, in the utility room, guarding his cycling stuff and thoughtfully munching a carrot. I raise an eyebrow.

'Snowman's nose,' he explains. 'He was being a pain. So I reached out and wrenched the bugger off. Now he can't breathe.'

I am slightly concerned as to how the night will end.

12.20 am: Someone shouts that there's a problem with the downstairs loo. I charge in to find vomit spewed over a wide area and the snowman snorting snow through a straw. Being noseless has clearly not undermined his drug habit. He *could* be sniffing the pack of royal icing I bought for the Christmas cake, but I fear not. I tell the snowman to get out or I'll call the police. He stares at me with his little coal eyes. I back away.

1.11 am: A beleaguered Richard is rationing access to the afflicted toilet. It's like Custer's Last Stand. Only those in direst need are allowed to use the loo.

'Number Ones or Number Twos?' booms my husband at any kid who tries to enter. 'If it's just Number Ones, then do it in the garden!'

A hysterical Emily finds me collecting discarded Bacardi Breezers under the coffee table. 'Mum, it's sooo embarrassing, Daddy is like literally asking people if they need a poo or a wee. If it's a wee they can't use the loo and have to go in the garden. Please make him stop.'

1.30 am: I go upstairs to our own bedroom, the one with the small, unfinished en-suite bathroom and the large printed and laminated sign reading 'Do Not Enter' stuck to the door. To my surprise and relief, there is no one inside. Amazingly, the kids have obeyed the instruction. I find that oddly moving; after all the chaos and the raising of hell, at least they have some respect for boundaries left. At least they know parents, too, require their own zone. At least they—

'Oh.'

Two kids are having sex in the en-suite. They have ignored the sign on the bedroom door; they are not not entering, in a big way. The girl is sitting next to the sink, on what will henceforth be known, in tribute to this memorable night, as the depravity unit. Given her current location, I estimate that her fanny is right on top of my toothpaste. Her legs are wrapped around someone, her eyes are closed, and I don't recognise her. The boy I don't recognise either, mainly because his bottom is the only part of him that's really visible. He doesn't miss a stroke; probably hasn't heard me walk in.

For maybe four seconds, I stand and watch. Not because I am a sad voyeur, or because I am too indignant to speak (though I am), but because what they are doing, and the zest with which they are doing it, seems like a vision of long ago. It's like turning on the TV and finding a Western. Has it really been that long? When was my last Wild West?

The girl opens her eyes and sees me. Recognises her hostess. Gives me the most polite and well-bred smile I have seen all evening, and whispers, 'Nearly finished.'

I turn and creep away, out of my own safe space and right into my danger zone. In Ben's room, mercifully empty because he has a sleepover with Sam tonight, I turn on my computer and scroll through cyberspace for any sign of Mr Forbidden Fruit. Nothing from Jack. Still nothing. You know how the sight of other people being happy, kissing, making love, can make you long so badly for those things yourself? That.

2.25 am: In what, by his standards, counts as a remarkable initiative, my husband has found a way to get rid of the guests. There was a time when it seemed that all of them – Sixty? Eighty? Threescore and ten? – would be stuck in the house until morning. The whole place was still reverberating, until Richard went into the larder, reached behind the dog food and flicked the fuse reading 'kitchen sockets'. The turntables ground to a halt. The speakers spat and died. Richard came out of the larder ostentatiously bearing a jar of coffee. 'Got it,' he said.

That was a good start, but there is still a mob, swilling and milling restlessly, and craving further mayhem.

'How can we herd them away?' I ask.

Richard looks at me and then, to my astonishment, kisses me on the cheek.

'Brilliant,' he says.

'Brilliant what?'

'Brilliant you. The verb. You're right, we don't kick them out. We herd them. For God's sake, half of them are dressed as reindeer anyway. They deserve to be herded.'

So what does Rich do? He only gets in the car and rounds

them up, doesn't he? Sometimes he can use his killjoy, party-pooper powers for good and not for evil. He actually sits there in first gear, headlamps on full beam, and as I usher them out of the house onto the street outside, he revs and growls the car and slowly inches towards them, so that, grudgingly but steadily, they mooch and moo away down the road, some locking antlers as they go. Where they go, God knows, but right now it isn't our problem.

Last out of the house is a young man in corduroys and cashmere sweater, plainly sober, who shakes my hand, and then Richard's, and says, 'Thank you so much for an absolutely delightful party. I feel terrible about leaving you with all this mess. I would love to come and help clear up in the morning, but sadly I have to be in work by eight. But thank you again, and, if I don't see you, have a lovely Christmas.' Then he gets onto a bike and pedals off.

Richard and I watch in awe as he rides away.

'Who on earth was that?' Richard asks.

'I'm not sure, but I *think* it was the baby Jesus.'

3.07 am: At last. Richard and I are in bed. The party is over. Nobody died. To that extent, and that extent only, it was a triumph. Emily and the nine comatose Santas who have crashed on the living-room floor can damn well clear up in the morning. Emily seemed transformed tonight, contented and glowing in her own skin. She actually came up, pulled me onto the dancefloor, and we sang 'Jingle Bell Rock' together at the top of our voices. As I turn onto my side and drift off this thought makes me very happy.

3.26 am: I ask Rich to please stop snoring.

'I'm not snoring,' he says. We both sit bolt upright and listen. The porcine snufflings are coming from the wardrobe. Richard stumbles out of bed and flings open the door. A reindeer, missing the bottom half of his costume, is slumped next to an angel, who is missing the top half of hers. They are lying on my beloved Joseph sheepskin coat. The reindeer opens its eyes. 'Oh, hi,' he says, 'you must be Emily's parents. Great party. Awesome.'

Aftermath of Emily's Party:

Number of calls by neighbours to the police: 4

Number of letters received from neighbours saying, 'You're an absolute disgrace to the neighbourhood': 1

Estimated clearing-up time: 13 hours

Number of empty bottles actually collected: 87

Number of half-empty bottles found on shelves, in wardrobes, under kitchen sink, behind loo, etc: 59

Number of Carlsberg lager cans discovered so far in flower beds: 124

Date at which garden can reasonably be expected to be a Carlsberg-free zone: between 2089 and early twenty-second century

Number of years Richard will be able to crow, 'I told you so': 35 or until death us do part

Estimate for redecorating hall and living room, replacement of window pane and toilet cistern: £713.97

Despite all of the above, I still think it was a good idea. I would willingly spend every last penny, and allow my house to be trashed, if it stopped my daughter being withdrawn and lonely.

'Everyone says it was like the coolest party ever, Mum,' a buoyant Emily reported over breakfast a couple of days later. 'I know Daddy thinks it was like really bad, but they're usually much worse. At Jess's party, they gave the chickens alcopops and they all died.'

17

THE ROCK WIDOW

Monday, 1.46 pm: Barbara has been arrested for buying a chainsaw with a stolen credit card. Sorry, *what?* It takes me a moment to process what Donald is telling me down the phone. The train enters yet another tunnel and he breaks up. My body and my briefcase are on the way to West Sussex to meet the Rock Widow, but my mind is up in Yorkshire with my poor father-in-law.

I call him back and he continues the story. 'You know Barbara started tidying everything away because of the dementia, Kate?'

'Yes, yes, I do.'

'Well, Margaret—'

'The carer?'

'Yes, well Margaret generally leaves her handbag on the side and Barbara found Margaret's purse and took it. Not stole it, she was tidying up. She didn't know she shouldn't. Then, this morning, I left her on her own for ten minutes while I went to the shop to get the paper and some milk and she escaped through the conservatory door and wandered off. Got on that Hopper bus at the end of our road and ended up at B&Q, you know the one by Asda?'

'Yes, go on.'

'Well, Barbara was in B&Q and she had a few bits in her trolley, but the girl at the till got suspicious because of the chainsaw.'

'I can see that.'

'Quite a large 58cc petrol chainsaw, which did excite some comment. Barbara tried to pay with Margaret's credit card, but she didn't know the PIN, of course, and the girl called the manager who then called the police. Luckily, they found our address on Barbara's library card, which was in her pocket.'

'Oh, Donald, I'm so sorry. Is Barbara distressed?'

'No, love, she's happy as Larry. Took quite a shine to the police sergeant who brought her home. Ryan, Sergeant Protheroe he is.'

'Oh, that's nice.'

'Not really, Kate, love. I'm afraid Barbara thought because Sergeant Protheroe was in uniform that he was me. Well, me about seventy years ago, any road. And she did try to have a bit of a kiss and a cuddle with him, you know. Quite embarrassing it was.'

I shudder to imagine my eighty-five-year-old mother-in-law grabbing the copper's goodness-knows-what because she was under the impression it was her lusty young RAF navigator. This is a thought simultaneously funny and impossibly sad. Barbara, thirty-five years my senior, whose mind is as unmoored as my body feels, is still capable of believing herself to be that gorgeous young seductress who jumped on Donald, a Justin Trudeau lookalike, just back from a bombing mission to Germany. The thought of Barbara's untethered animal hunger as she chased the Ghost of Sexcapades Past is mortifying.

I experience a momentary twinge of fellow feeling. Hadn't I been humiliated when I was looking longingly at Roger Federer's twin on the Tube and he offered me his seat? Our bodies continue to make fools of us as we age. Lust doesn't die to spare the sensitivities of the grossed-out young who prefer not to think of wrinky couplings, and – this is really cruel – carnal feelings are among the very last to check out.

'I don't understand, Donald, so did the police arrest Barbara?'

'At first, yes, but that was a young constable did that. Sergeant Protheroe, well, when he turned up he could see Barbara was very confused, so they're not pressing charges. Quite the drama we've had here, Kate. I hope you don't mind me calling. Cheryl and Peter, they're in Italy, you see.'

I can hear the strenuous attempt to make light of it in his voice. He must have been terrified when Barbara went missing and mortified by her trying to get off with Sergeant Protheroe.

'Donald, I think we should come up. We could start looking—'

He stops me before I can go any further. 'Barbara doesn't want to leave her garden, Kate, love. Well, neither of us does. The magnolia tree, well, we always know it's spring once that's out.'

'I know, I know, but . . . OK, look, we'll discuss it when we're all together at Christmas. Not long now. Will you be all right till then?'

'Oh, aye, don't you worry about us, Kate, love. Look after yourself.'

In the minicab on the way to the Rock Widow's country pile, I Google care homes in the Leeds area. Finding the one that looks least grim and institutionalised, and which allows pets, I dial the number. 'Hello, yes, I'm calling on behalf of my in-laws, Donald and Barbara Shattock. I wonder if we could make an appointment to look round Hillside View.'

2.30pm: 'Laylah. Belshazzar. And Mikk.'

'And, sorry, they are how old now?'

'Um, Belly just turned twenty-one. I remember having to give his date of birth to the police the day after the party, and one of them said, "Happy Birthday for yesterday", which I thought was not very nice.'

'No, quite. And, forgive me, I just need to get this clear: your late husband had, I believe, other children, besides these three? There were, um, other . . .'

'By the cartload.' Bella Baring takes a drag on her BO Vape – the kids were smoking them at Emily's party – and releases a delicate plume of smoke circles. 'We know of nine for sure, including my three. It was six until Fozzy died, and then three more came out of the woodwork. There's a coincidence for you. Once it was clear how much money he'd left, they suddenly thought, oh, he might just be their dad. Honey?'

I look around, but nobody has entered the room. Is she addressing me?

'I'm sorry?'

'Honey in your tea? Makes the medicine go down and all that.'

'Oh, no, thanks, I'm fine as it is. Delicious.'

My tea is not delicious. It is pale and bitter, with what appear to be cuttings of hedgerow floating on top. At the bottom is a sluggish dust, possibly shaken from an upturned Wellington boot. But it is what I was offered by Bella upon my arrival, and the rule is that you must, as the briefing document puts it, 'accede whenever possible to the demands of the client'. So I am acceding, sip by sour sip, and trying not to make a face to match.

314

'People always think I have pots of the stuff. They think I'm a real Baring. As if poor old Fozzy would have lasted a day in a bank.'

Only five minutes in, and this already feels like one of the strangest client meetings ever. Jay-B was absolutely insistent that I needed to get down here to 'hold the hand' of the famous Rock Widow. After the fuck-up with Grant Hatch, I must redeem myself. This has to go well. Jay-B heard rumours that Bella might be thinking of taking her loot elsewhere, which would be a disaster. Consulting the file on the train, before Donald broke the news about Barbara and the chainsaw, I have discovered the following: Philip Rodney Baring, born Stockton-on-Tees 1947, died 2013, was known to millions of adoring, if permanently deafened, fans as Fozzy. His ashes were scattered at Glastonbury and promptly trampled into the mud. Bella, his widow, presides over both his financial estate, much of which is invested with EM Royal, and his geographical estate, which stretches for many green acres in every direction.

'Actually, Bella, one of the things I'm here to tell you today on behalf of EM Royal is that you really needn't worry about your assets.'

'That's what Fozzy said to me in nineteen eighty-three, when he saw me in a bikini.' And with that, the veteran blonde explodes into a combination of cackle and coughing fit, gasping for breath and waving a hand at me to indicate that she is not, despite appearances, about to follow her husband to the grave. When the laugh has subsided, I press on.

'As a sterling investor, you will naturally be concerned, above all, with your global asset allocation. I can assure you that the spread of your portfolio, which we set up at your request and whose fluctuations we monitor on a daily basis, is designed to ensure a minimisation of risk, so that if, for instance . . .'

Bella stops me, palm raised, like a traffic cop.

'Yes, Tereza?'

A maid has appeared, possibly from a trapdoor in the rug.

'Miss Bella, the llama he is in the hi-hi.'

'Oh, God, not again.' She turns to me. 'It's Phil. They're very loyal, you know, and when Don died in the spring it was simply awful. Off his feed for weeks. We were told they were brothers when Fozzy got them, but now we think they may have been gay. Have you heard of same-sex llama love before?'

'Well, not recently—'

'And now he's taken to wandering into the ha-ha and staying there all day. Either he's moping or he wants to escape. See the great wide world. Sorry, back in a minute. Lead on, Tereza.'

She levers herself out of the faded Kilim armchair, stretches, says 'Old bones' out loud, lights a cheroot, and follows her maid out of the door.

I gaze out of the window at the sopping parkland. Rain has not spared Dullerton Hall today, or, from the look of it, any day this year. It's more like staring at a watercolour than being in a real place. A large grey patch, some way beyond the terrace, marks the spot where the helipad used to be. Weeds have festered in the cracks. Why does Bella linger on here? Why not sell up, bank the cash with us, and move somewhere warm and dry?

'I should move, I know,' she says, barging back through the door to answer my unspoken question. Yikes. Don't tell me she's a mind-reader as well as a wealthy widow. Maybe decades of smoking weed has lent her psychic powers.

'But Mikk hasn't quite finished school. He's on his fourth, poor boy. Even Bedales had enough of him in the end, which is saying something. Anyway, the new place in Devon suits him down to the ground, though you can't find it in the league tables. I think they're so unfair, don't you?'

'I do.'

'And I would hate it if he had nowhere to come with his friends in the holidays. They're such interesting young people. Very fluid.'

'Bella, as far as the children go, your children that is, again, I can put your mind at rest. The yield from the trust funds Fozzy set up is amply sufficient to—'

'It's Chuckup that really bothers me.'

'I'm sorry, Chuck—'

'The Ukrainian. Can't remember her full name, sounds like a bad hand in Scrabble, but Chuck's in there somewhere, so we just call her that. Boobs like hot air balloons. Face like a knife. The one Fozzy fell in love with towards the end. Or thought he did. He was on so many drugs in the last months – you know, medical drugs rather than play drugs – that he could have fallen for the bedside table. Or the dog bowl.'

'From what I understand, though, Miss Chuck— has no legal entitlement to any—'

'Course not. But she has all these ghastly texts he sent, saying, my love, my only Chuckup, you mean the world to me, everything I have is yours, rhubarb rhubarb. And the papers can't get enough of that sort of stuff.'

'Honestly, Bella, it sounds dreadful, and I know how upsetting it must be for all of you, but I can't really see that this, er, this young Ukrainian lady—'

'Young is right. Twenty-two. Not a lady, fuck no.'

'—that she represents any substantial threat to the integrity of your holdings. Of course, on my return to London, I will ask our legal department to double check the status of—'

'Two things.' Bella sits upright. Suddenly, without warning, she looks like someone who means business, rather than a very weary witch, running out of potions. A gleam of purpose shines in her kohl-rimmed eyes.

'Can I be frank with you, Kate?'

'Of course.'

'It's Belly. He's a bright boy, ever so charming when he wants to be, but he lacks motivation. No drive, not like Fozzy. Mooches around all day. And I feel that, if he could just get a foot on the ladder, in something solid, you know . . . I'm not sure, at the moment, he even knows there *is* a ladder.'

Ah, so that's it. The cry that goes up all over England, as the parents of the privileged run headlong into the brick wall of ordinary life. Money has eased their kids through school and college, and bought them tutors for each subject with A*s to match, and now the easing stops. And it turns out that the kids, after all that cosseting, are not very special, or not very able to get up in the mornings and go to work and do as they're told, or just not very good at being anything other than kids. At which point, the parents panic, and start to call in the favours. Not that I would say as much to Bella, even though we both know the deal.

'Bella, let me be honest with you. Internships are extremely hard to come by these days, and even though they're unpaid they're just as competitive as proper jobs; but, of course, I'll see what I can do. I'm sure that Belshazzar,' (*don't laugh, Kate*), 'has lots to contribute and, well, if EM Royal can help him find his mojo then it would be our privilege to assist a client we value very highly.'

This is a flat lie. From what I have heard of Belly, he can't be relied upon to find his own trousers. Not long ago, the *Mail* ran a grainy photograph of him and a friend trying to feed Big Macs to one of the lions in Trafalgar Square at three o'clock in the morning, 'because it was hungry'. The thought of having that dopey druggie in the office as my assistant . . . Still, I may have to babysit Belly to keep the client onside.

'Thank you, you're a darling.' Bella is beaming with relief.

I think of Calamity Girl, of the problems I have with Emily and Ben, keeping them out of harm's way, teaching them that there's no such thing as a free lunch and, funnily enough, that lesson seems even harder here in the Land of Plenty. I think of Sally's Will and Oscar, still drifting in their late twenties, and of lovely Antonia, moving from one internship to the next, pursuing the Holy Grail of a permanent job. People are not so very different really.

'Do you have kids, Kate?' Bella wants to know.

I hesitate a fraction before deciding to tell her the truth. 'I sure do. Emily will be seventeen next birthday. Had a bit of a rough ride this year to be honest. Pressure of exams, pressure of having to photograph yourself every five minutes to show several hundred so-called friends what a brilliant life you've got, plus having a party-pooper mum who won't let you use a fake ID card to get into clubs. She has so much more than I had at her age, Bella, but it doesn't seem to make her happy.'

'You're telling me,' she sighs. 'I grew up in a council house in Catford. And you have a boy too?'

'Yup. Ben, typical teenager. Occasionally looks up from a screen to ask for a lift or some cash.'

She laughs, that crackly smoker's laugh.

'You said there was something else, Bella?'

'Yes. Fancy a ride?'

For a second, I think I'm being invited to my first ever orgy. Blimey, a proper rock debauch, in a country house, with tiger-skin rugs, dripping wax, and lines of coke on the eighteenth-century sideboard. Mind you, I'm amazed she would even bother these days, with Fozzy not around.

'Ride?'

'On Samson. You'll love him. He's ever so gentle.'

'Well . . .'

'Don't worry, I was a bit freaked out the first time, too. He's enormous.' (Save me.) 'Come on, I'll lend you all the kit.'

And so it comes to pass that, twenty minutes later, I am very slowly being led around a paddock on the back of the largest horse I have ever encountered in the flesh. Gazing ahead to the prow of his noble head, and turning round to survey his distant rump, I am left with the clear impression that Samson goes on forever. It's like sitting on the deck of a furry aircraft carrier. And his motion, likewise, is stately and dignified, without a jolt or a jerk. I couldn't fall off if I tried.

Bella walks next to me, holding his bridle. Around us, the rain has lightened to a drizzle. Just as I am reflecting that this, of all things, was not in the job description, Bella says to me: 'Kate.'

'Still here, amazingly.'

'You've passed.'

I look down at her, far away. Samson must be eighteen-hands high, I reckon; I might as well be hiding in a tree house.

'Passed what? Is there a test?'

'I wasn't going to tell you this, but I've been thinking of moving the Fozzy funds elsewhere.'

Ah, so here it comes. Without meaning to, purely by way of a reflex, I pull the reins. Samson stops dead.

'Where to?'

'Gonzago Pierce.'

'What? Why them?'

Cool it, Kate. You're stuck on an animal, but you're still at work.

'Forgive me, Bella, I mean, of course we'll respect any decision

320

that a client chooses to take, but in this instance I should strongly advise you, in your own best interests, against re-investing funds that we have rendered secure on your behalf for many—'

'What's wrong with Thingummy Pierce?'

'Cowboys.'

'Says she, sitting on a horse.'

I laugh, and Samson picks up the slight shake in my hands and sets off again.

'Anyway,' says Bella. 'It's all off.'

'What is?'

'The cowboys. One of them came down last week, just like you, except he was a smoothie in a suit, a bit wet behind the ears, and we got along fine until I mentioned a ride on Samson, then he started making all these excuses. So, I dragged him out here, and he took one long at this gorgeous creature and did a bunk. Literally ran back to his Merc and drove away. And I thought, if that's how he handles himself when faced with a horse, what on earth would he do in a crisis? All those bears and bulls you read about in the *FT*, I ask you.'

Can't be entirely sure, but I think Bella believes that bear and bull markets feature actual animals. Best not to say anything.

'How could he panic,' I say. 'Samson is heaven. I feel calmer up here than I've done in weeks. I don't want to get off. Or down, or whatever you say.'

'Exactly. That's the right answer. So, thanks to you, I'm sticking with EM Royal. All right with you?'

'Very very all right. Thank you, Bella. We will repay your trust, I can promise you that.'

'Don't push it, sister. You're a bloody bank, you don't repay anything. Hup!'

And with that, at a single encouragement from his mistress, Samson starts to trot, and I begin to bounce.

'Help!'

'Hah. Wait till we try a canter.'

Half an hour later, I find myself standing in the stable yard, tingling in all sorts of interesting ways and parts. Maybe once your sex life is over, big black stallions are the way forward? Bella is back at the house. Samson, safe in his stall, munches and gently steams. He has already received a carrot from my hand, with thanks. He may be the best new friend I've made in years. Sorry, Sally.

6.27 pm: Got back to the office flushed with triumph, both from my ride on Samson and from knowing that I'd just saved EMR from losing a client. Checked my email, as I'd been doing pretty much on the hour every hour since I emailed Jack. Can't decide who I'm more furious with: him for being such a bastard and not even acknowledging my message or me for being a bloody fool and caring so much. Emboldened by my success with Bella, I couldn't bear to wait any longer. Started a new email to him. 'Hi Jack, Just wondering if you got my . . .' No, too fake-casual. 'Hi, I know email can be slow but . . .' Too sarcastic. 'Hey, are you still alive?' Too desperate. I decided not to send any of them. What if he didn't reply again? I'd feel even worse. *Have some self-respect, woman!*

Quick glance around the office. No sign of Jay-B, so I quickly email him a report on Bella, copying in Troy, making sure to point out my heroic role in saving the day. Can't afford to be modest, not after I pissed off Grant Hatch. Not if I want to keep some sort of job after Arabella gets back from maternity leave. The time will be up before I know it.

Looking around at my thirty-something colleagues, heads bowed over their workstations, I have to suppress a bitter laugh. A woman my age, who has taken seven years out of her career, is not welcome here, but it's knowledge of family and kids that helped me win Bella Baring over today. I believe that. Sure, I know how to handle a financial crisis, but I also understand what it's like for a client to get married, to lose a parent, to have miscarriages, to divorce, for kids to struggle and for parents to be scared for them. Even the rich are scared for their kids, and they have plenty to be scared about. Clients like Bella are concerned about our fund's performance, of course they are, but once they know their money's safe what they really want is to talk about the problems in their lives and to be heard. It would take me a thousand years to teach Troy to do that. Is London Business School running a course in empathy and feminine intuition? Not a chance.

The Rock Widow's problems are cushioned, soothed and stroked by money, but never solved. I think ruefully of my own, like finding a decent care home 160 miles away and a non-existent PlayStation and getting myself ready for an office party tomorrow night, which I would actually pay to get out of because the only face I want to see won't be there, oh, and attending Ben's carol concert in the afternoon and drumming up some new business and . . . what did Sally call it again? Before I leave for home, I go to my System Preferences, then prepare to change the password from Imposter42. Type in the new one, twice. Sandwichwoman50.

18

THE OFFICE PARTY

7.08 am: Funny, isn't it? You spend the first five years of a child's life praying they will go to sleep and stay asleep. When they become a teenager, you spend every morning trying to wake them up. Today begins, as most days begin, with a battle to get Ben out of bed.

'Donwunna. Goway!'

'Ben, please. I'm not doing this for my benefit. Remember, you've got your Christmas concert this afternoon.' I draw the curtains, which only prompts further groans.

'Goway.'

'I've hung a clean shirt on your wardrobe door, darling, and there's a nice clean jumper here. Need to look smart, OK? Wear your black shoes, not your trainers. You'll be on stage.'

With great reluctance, he hauls himself from the horizontal. 'Don't have to come, Mum.'

'Of course I'm coming, darling. I wouldn't miss your concert.'

'You're in London. S'nothing special. Not worth coming all the way home for.'

'It's special to me, Ben. Omigod, look at those toenails. Where are my scissors?'

'Get off! Mummy, get offffffffff me.'

Having cut at least an inch off Ben's gross camel hooves and deposited the shards in the bathroom bin, I pop my head around Emily's door. The room is in chaos. The window blind is broken and has been left to dangle, half-closed. Discarded clothes, bags and shoes shipwrecked across the floor. The bedside lamp has been knocked over by the accumulated wall of Diet Coke cans. I can see some of her school books, coated with dust, under the bed. If a space gives you a clue to a person's state of mind, then my daughter is in trouble. It upsets me to see it, it really does, but any attempt to tidy is seen as criticism not help.

At least, since the party, things have been better between us. Still feel like I'm walking on eggshells, scared that with my throat-choking worry about her emotional state she'll just shut me out again if I do or say the wrong thing. Debra says Ruby's exactly the same, so I try not to take it personally. Emily stirs in the bed, pulls her chrysalis tighter about her, but does not wake. For a while, her features were too big in her face and I thought she had lost her beauty, but lately she has grown and the face has realigned and is in proportion again. When she complained that her nose was too big – she wanted a nose like Lizzy's – I told her that the girls with the teeny neat features now often look bland and characterless when they're older. She didn't believe me, but it's true.

My secret pleasure is to come in and look at my daughter when she's asleep; I can see the five-year-old in her face so clearly.

7.27 am: Piotr has lifted all the floorboards in the kitchen. It's even worse than I feared. The copper pipes are so old they have turned to turquoise dust.

'Oh, great. Another bloody expenditure in your marvellous period bargain, Kate. How much is that going to cost?'

Richard is addressing both Piotr and myself with what feels uncomfortably like dislike.

'Is possible not expensive,' says Piotr cautiously. 'I have boiler friend . . .'

'I'm sure you do,' says Richard rudely. 'I'll be late tonight, Kate.'

'Darling, I told you. Remember, I have the office party tonight and it's Ben's concert this afternoon. I'll see you there. And can you try and be back for the kids tonight because I may be late? Please?'

Fastening his helmet, Rich says, 'Why are you going to the party? Bunch of City wide boys getting off their heads on Bollinger. Can't think of anything worse.'

How about not being able to pay our mortgage or our bills, which will happen if I lose my job – isn't that worse, Richard? This I think but do not say. Instead, I deploy my best client smile. 'You know, I'd really rather not go, darling, but it's important I show my face. The chairman will be there and the whole boss class basically. I need to network.' As I say this, I realise that it's actually true. Over the years, I've seen so many women do a brilliant job, often outshining and outperforming their colleagues, but then, when it's redundancy time, they're always first out the door because they didn't bother to build alliances with men they disliked. That was my attitude in the past, but I can't afford to be choosy now.

'Well, OK,' Richard concedes, as though he's doing me a huge favour, 'but Emily and Ben can get their own dinner. I'll try to be back by nine.'

'But I'll see you at the concert anyway?'

'Yes, oh yes.'

Piotr and I watch him mount his bike and cycle off through the gate, already picking up speed.

'Richard, he is wasp, I think,' says Piotr.

'No, not wasp, Piotr. Bee. In English, we say busy as a bee.'

'No, Kate,' Piotr says, narrowing his eyes. 'Is correct. Richard is wasp, I think.'

11.07 am: If Monica Bellucci can become a Bond Girl at the age of fifty, then I have no reason to fear going to the office party tonight at the age of forty-nine and three quarters, do I? It's all over the news. Amidst the general astonishment that a female so ancient could be cast opposite 007, I notice no one points out that the actress is entirely age-appropriate for Daniel Craig, who is forty-seven. I guess that, according to Debra's principles of Internet dating, a forty-seven-year-old male movie star can never fall for anyone over thirty-five. Monica Bellucci should presumably consider herself lucky to play Bond's arthritic mother-in-law.

Spend morning at my desk doing 'research for clients' whilst obsessively studying website pictures and comparing Monica today with the young Monica in her first modelling shots. Thirty-two years ago, her astounding eighteen-year-old beauty struggled to make itself known through layers of make-up and a hairstyle that was part poodle, part Jennifer Beals in *Flashdance*. Somehow, it's really comforting to know that even Monica Bellucci had an awful Eighties perm. Most girls in my year at college obediently got one, following fashion like the style sheep we were. Major error. The Eighties perm looked like pubic hair on steroids.

Bitter Irony of Being a Woman No. 569: when you are young and beautiful – because, let's face it, youth *is* beauty – you seldom know how to make the best of yourself. (Look at Emily, a size six hiding in a sludge-grey, baggy 'boyfriend' jumper and never ever showing her legs unless you count those terrible ripped jeans. Sorry, 'vintage distressed' jeans.) By the time you've figured out what works, youth has got its coat on and is hurrying out the door, and you spend your time and money finding lotions and potions and procedures that will strive to recreate the effect that Mother Nature bestowed for free. The one that you took totally for granted. For instance, my bathroom cabinet at home is a shrine to the Goddess of Anti-Ageing. Let's call her Dewy. Pots and vials of serums and moisturisers, all promising to put the clock back to the year when my 'beauty regime' consisted of Anne French deep cleansing milk in the white bottle with the nubby blue top, which I used to wipe the oil off my skin. The self-same oil that I must now jealously guard to stop me becoming a dried-up old prune.

'What the fuck? Can't believe they chose a granny to be a Bond girl.'

I swivel my chair and my nose almost ends up in the pinstriped crotch of Jay-B. He is standing very close, looking over my shoulder at the screen and giving the divine Monica a crude, appraising stare.

'Not bad for an old bird, though,' he admits with some reluctance.

'I would,' sniggers Troy.

By the way, since when did British City boys all have to have names like American basketball players? We know they're really public schoolboys, married to Henriettas and Clemmies, who catch the 6.44 from Sevenoaks.

'You would what?' I ask innocently, taunting the young ape to go further.

Troy's face contorts into a leery grin, he leans back in his chair with his hands behind his head and his shiny shoes up on the desk. 'I would, you know. Give her one.'

There is that moment, you may know it, when men are loudly weighing up a woman like a piece of meat, and another woman, who is present, has to decide whether to collude with them or to keep a complicit silence and give only a mildly pained smile. In my experience, pretending to be one of the boys on such occasions is the safest strategy. Otherwise you risk being labelled humourless or feminist – probably both. But I'm not in the mood. Not today, when my Christmas to-do list is longer than the Treaty of Versailles, Ben's carol concert is this afternoon and a woman almost exactly the same age as Monica Bellucci is in this very room pretending to be forty-two to a pair of ignorant boys.

'How gallant of you, Troy,' I say. 'I'm sure Monica Bellucci, arguably the most beautiful actress in the world, would be thrilled to know that you'd be prepared to do her a huge favour and have sex with her.'

Troy is uncertain how to take this. A blush spreads up his pale face till the skin around his ginger sideburns glows red and pimply. He looks at Jay-B to see what his reaction should be. There is a moment, no more than a few seconds, when it could go either way. I could be out on my ear. Then, Jay-B says, not unpleasantly: 'Few years to go till you face the big Five–O, eh Kate? Glad to see you've got time to surf celebrity websites.'

Think, Kate, think.

'It's research,' I say quickly. 'Anti-ageing. It could be a really big area for us. Did you know that the desire of American women to mask the signs of advancing age with creams and other beauty products is expected to grow the market to one hundred and fourteen billion dollars next year? That's up from eighty billion three years ago. Astonishing, actually. Even in the recession, the prestige beauty products – those are the high-end creams you get in department stores – have increased by eleven per cent, according to Nasdaq. So, oil is going down, Sony Pictures is down, but moisturiser is the new gold.'

'Wow,' says Jay-B, letting out a low whistle. 'A hundred billion on snake oil? Why do women waste their money?'

'Because guys like you believe that thirty-five is the age when women check out. Because women my age have outlived our hotness, our ability to be pleasing to you, and, therefore, by some crude reckoning, our relevance and status in society are diminished, so we fake youth for as long as we possibly can. Even if it means we end up looking pickled or paralysed. Because that's why I am rubbing oestrogen into my arm every morning, and taking a progesterone tablet every night, and occasionally putting a pea of testosterone on my inner thigh, which is called HRT, but is nothing less than youth retrieval therapy. Oh, and some of us are so desperate and crazy we even pretend we are seven years younger so we can re-enter a jobs market that treats us as a clapped-out liability.'

Did I have the guts to say that out loud? Sadly, not.

'Well done on Fozzy's widow, by the way, Kate. Talk about horse power. See you later at the party?' says Jay-B with what I hope is not a wink. 'Dress to Impress.'

I always do.

To: Kate Reddy
From: Candy Stratton
Subject: Party Panic!
Katie, do not, repeat DO NOT, get Botox for the first time on the day of the office party. You can't risk it. You could end up with one eye closed. Not a good look unless

you're going as a pirate. The cheek stuff I told you about is more than $1,000 per shot. It's meant to lift and restore fullness that we lose as we become wizened old hags. The goal is the apple-cheek look, not constipated chipmunk.

Also there's this cool new sculpting thing where you freeze the shit out of fat lumps and they vanish. Not sure how.

Just get your hair done for the party, invest in the finest corsetry from Agent Provocateur and don't stand in direct light. You look pretty damn amazing for 42!!

XXO C

From: Debra Richards
To: Kate Reddy
Subject: Shoot me!
Hi hon, how's your festive season going? With office parties, you can either conduct yourself with a dignity becoming to your professional status or end up drunk and shagging in the loos with some junior administrator from Canvey Island. With spots on his back. *Eeuw.* No prizes for guessing which option your very old and desperate friend went for.

In other news, Felix got suspended. School says he was caught sharing Fat German Hookers porn! More worryingly, he has run up £1,800 charges because phone company collects my monthly payment for his phone, but they now claim they don't have to inform me of any other payments made on that card. I'm a lawyer and even I don't know if that's legal. Don't have time to spend all day on phone yelling at them.

Felix is fucked. His mother is fucked. By spotty Kyle

331

from Canvey Island. Kids are going to spend Christmas in Hong Kong with their father and perfect Wifey No. 2. Hate hate.

BTW what are we doing for our 50ths? Am finding that whole concept very scary as am well on the way to whiskery hagdom with no man in sight. Did you say the divine Abelhammer was back on the scene? Tell me all your guilty secrets. I need cheering up.

Am sending you virtual Christmas card and we need a big catch-up soonest.

Love love Deb xx

From: Kate Reddy
To: Debra Richards
Subject: Shoot me!

Please please come for Christmas, darling. I can offer you an exciting selection of demented elderly relatives, a practically vegan husband who is more hairless than either of us, two non-speaking teenagers and a total bitch of a sister-in-law. You would be doing me a huge favour if you came and jollied everyone along. Please say Yes. Spotty Kyle would be most welcome too if he doesn't have a better offer.

Sorry to hear about Felix. Aren't all boys watching that stuff? After Emily's belfie nothing surprises me any more.

Am DEFINITELY not doing anything for my 50th. Don't wish to advertise my cronedom, thanks very much. EM Royal thinks that I'm 42 and they can't find out my real age or I'll lose my job. Got to keep it hush hush.

Nothing to report about Abelhammer. Stupidly, I replied to his email and haven't heard a thing back. He's

probably trolling all the women from his past. Hate, hate!

Please let's do something fun for YOUR 50th? I'll book the stripping fireman.

Huge hug,

K xx

PS Fat German Hookers – is that really a thing?

4.23 pm: Ben's concert just ended, and it was a triumph. To think I was actually resenting the time it would take me to get the train back home for the school concert, then turn around and head straight back to London for the office party. Nine days till Christmas and I reckon I have approximately fifteen days' worth of tasks to do. Would it really hurt to miss the Christmas concert just this once? Richard would be there for Ben, wouldn't he?

Come on, who was I kidding? Emily still remembers the single ballet recital I missed in the summer of 2004 when she played the part of a dancing vegetable. It is inscribed in indelible ink in the Ledger of Maternal Neglect and will, no doubt, be raised on the Day of Judgement.

Just as well I went to the concert because it was Richard who wasn't there. He texted me to say that he'd forgotten he had an important mindfulness meeting. How about being mindful about his own bloody child? Rich's college is literally ten minutes from Ben's school, as opposed to my workplace, which is at least an hour and twenty minutes away but, somehow, I made it and he didn't.

One change for the better since I was last in full-time employment is that parents are allowed, almost encouraged, to leave the office to attend children's special events. At least firms try to appear flexible and family friendly now because, if you're tagged as a Neanderthal outfit, you won't attract the brightest graduates. The free market, as Milton Friedman said, does work, even in favour of decency and compassion on occasion. Though, I notice no one at EM Royal dares to work part-time.

When I told Jay-B that I was popping to my son's Christmas concert, I thought about all those times I lied to Rod Task if I needed to be at a school meeting or a Nativity play. Always coming up with a 'male excuse' about the traffic or something. Being a working mother back then was to be a double agent: you lied for a living. A male colleague who announced he was off to his son's rugby match was a hero; a woman who did exactly the same was Lacking in Commitment. At any moment, she could be diverted onto the Mummy Track, that career path to paperclips and irrelevance. I fought that relegation with every fibre of my being. I would not have it that being a mum made me less good at my job. I was great at my job, really I was. In the end, what made me quit EMF was the thought that my kids were suffering from the punishingly long – unnecessarily long, stupidly, inhumanely long – hours I spent away from them. They needed me, yes, but it turned out I needed them too. And our family was running on empty and the only person who could fill that emptiness was me.

Such a vivid memory, suddenly. (*'Cheers, Roy!'*). I was standing in the playground at St Bede's; it was the evening of the parent–teacher meetings, and I was waiting for Richard. Winter. It must have been because all the commuting fathers, who had come straight from the station, were hurrying in with their thick dark coats and their briefcases. Each man stopped to ask me where they might find their child's classroom. They knew the name of their kid – hey, credit where it's due! – but, generally, that was the limit of their knowledge. They didn't know who the child's teacher was, sometimes didn't even know what year group they were in. They had no clue where the little coats and bags were hung up, or what was in those bags. And I stood there in that cold, dark playground thinking, how could this ever possibly be fair? How could a woman compete when men were allowed to be so *oblivious*? One parent not knowing who the teacher was, not knowing what went in the lunchbox, not knowing which child in the class had the nut allergy, not knowing where the PE bag was, or which stinky little socks needed washing. OK, one parent could be oblivious. But not two. One parent has to carry the puzzle of family life in their head, and mostly, let's face it, it's still the mum. Professionally, back then I was competing with men whose minds were clear of all the stuff that small children bring. I used to envy them once; now I feel only pity.

Anyway, it was definitely the right call to go to the concert, and Richard really missed out. In the middle of 'Jingle Bells', our boy did an amazing solo on percussion which, in typical Ben fashion, he had forgotten to mention. You know those moments when you see your child in a whole new light? Well, this was one of them. That sulky, hoodied creature who grumps and slumps around the house was transformed into a glorious young musician moving deftly from drums to cymbal, while clearly enjoying himself. His syncopated sleigh bells nearly brought the house down.

Now, we are having tea and mince pies in the hall.

'You look pretty, Mum,' says Ben, separating himself from friends in the jazz ensemble and coming over to say hello.

'New hair.'

I even get a hug, well, an awkward sideways clasp, more like a collision than a hug, but I'm not complaining.

'Oh, hello, Kate.' I turn to see the oppressively elegant figure of Cynthia Knowles, who is holding a box of mince pies. 'It's

335

fine to donate these mince pies, Kate,' Cynthia says with a tinkling laugh. 'No one cares that you haven't made your own any more. Do you remember that loony woman we read about who distressed supermarket mince pies, took them to a school carol concert and pretended she made them herself?' Oh, yes, think I vaguely remember her. (*Roy?*)

9.29 pm: The office party is in Shoreditch. Of course it is. Any district of London that I took care to avoid when I first came to London aged twenty-two is now, by definition, the place to be. How does a wasteland become a hotspot? Property prices, for a start, as people retreat further from the hub until they find a zone they can just about afford. Then they make a hub of their own, and wait for the service industries to follow. Easier these days, of course, since you don't take a wreck of an old warehouse and tart it up. You barely tart at all. You sweep it and rewire it and throw out all the junk but keep the bare brick walls and the naked piping. Ventilators are very à la mode. First you install wifi and a coffee machine the size of a fairground booth. Then you buy a job lot of Formica tables and rutted wooden benches and clanky metal chairs from a school that just closed down. Lastly, you hire a brace of blokes called Thaddeus and Job with beards that hint, incorrectly, at a long and distinguished career in the merchant navy. Voila. You have a café.

The party is in a place called The Place. Or, to be precise, '#thepl@ce'. That's what it said on the email. It was going to be at somewhere even more brutal by the name of Number Forty7, which is, needless to say, located at number 103 on some grotty side street, until one of the company directors looked it up and saw the words 'Grime crews'. Which, again, sounds like something to do with the merchant navy, but apparently refers to the kind of music that makes your brain rattle around your skull like a pea in a whistle. So that was out.

I enter #thepl@ce trying not to feel like a total #pr@t. The lighting is of that wintry dimness which would have my mother fussing around the room, switching on every lamp and muttering, 'You'd think somebody had died.' Personally, I blame it on all those Nordic thrillers on TV. None of the detectives would dream of using anything brighter than a torch to inspect the latest corpse. And where else is any self-respecting serial killer meant to lurk, if not in a swathe of shadow? I feel I should be wearing a homely knitted sweater, with my hair scraped back, and maybe a pair of rubber gloves to pick up crucial clues. Rather than what I *am* wearing, which is my lovely, black satin Dolce & Gabbana dress, ten years old and still going strong. It hikes the right bits up and holds the wrong bits in: job done. Completely wasted here, of course, given the neo-Finnish gloom. From more than two yards away I might as well be dressed in a bin liner. Monica Bellucci could walk by, in nothing but her smallest pair of knickers, and hardly anyone would notice. She would be little more than a fragrant blur.

I really really don't want to be here – all this pretending to be someone I'm not just to make myself acceptable to these people. Beyond a certain age, you don't want to stand on the edge of a party, plucking up courage to dive in. I need a drink. A waiter stalks past, with no hair on his head, his chin, his upper lip, his eyebrows, or, I shudder to imagine, anywhere else at all. But he does have a tray in his hand.

'Erm.'

'Yes?' he says, swivelling round and looking cross.

'Sorry, excuse me, but would it be possible to have one of

those?' A very modern encounter, this: the anxious, old-school middle class apologising to the robotic new age for having done nothing wrong. He frowns, still peeved by the interruption. A waiter who does not want to wait. His tray is triangular.

'Castro. Or Gangnam,' he says.

I have nothing to say. No words will meet the case. *Come on, Kate, at least try.*

'Oh! What's in the Gangnam?'

'Glencarraghieclaghanbrae. Garam masala. Stout.'

'I think I'll try a Castro, please.'

The man-machine hands me my drink and marches off, barely able to restrain his wrath. My cocktail is in a jam jar, obviously. Much more cutting-edge than a cocktail glass, though it's hard for your mouth to get any purchase on the screw-top rim, and the probability that it will have an actual cutting edge is ominously high. Holding it, I sense an overwhelming urge to run off and collect tadpoles with a net. Or a dotted cloud of frogspawn, so that you can watch them hatch.

'Kate.'

Now it is my turn to swivel.

'Jay-B! Hello.'

'Kate, can I introduce our chairman, Harvey Boothby-Moore. Harvey, this is our new recruit, Kate Reddy, from Marketing.'

The chairman looms up, coming close, then closer still. Either he's trying to get the measure of me, in the deep twilight, or I've caught him in the middle of a game of hide and seek. I can see him thinking, 'Warmer. Warmer . . .'

At last he stops. His gaze rakes me up and down, as if I were in the paddock at Ascot. Long time since I had my fetlocks inspected. At least my flanks are pretty good after doing nine thousand squats with Conor.

'Good to have you on board, young lady,' he says. 'Heard great things about you. Keep it up!'

Young lady, eh? OK, it's dark here, but I'll take that.

'I shall, thank you.' I take a sip of my Castro. If someone could distil those blue sanitising blocks that you hang under the rim of the toilet, this is what they would taste like.

Harvey backs away, ready to move on, then pauses. 'Well done with the Russkies,' he says. 'Buggers are rolling in the stuff, but it's not always easy to make them cough up. Trouble is they know their own bank balance, but not their own minds. If they have any, *hrump-a-hrump*.' I can't swear, but I think that was the Boothby-Moore idea of a laugh. Like a bullfrog trying and failing to suppress a burp.

'Well, actually, I found them surprisingly amenable to our ideas,' I say, lapsing with ease into fluent corporate blah. Another slug of loo cleaner, to get my courage up. *Ouch*. Bloody jam jar. 'Especially if one tries to engage them at the personal level.'

Harvey smiles.

'I bet one does. *Hrump*. Isn't that right, Roy?'

'Troy, sir.'

'Toy? As in boy?'

'Troy.'

I hadn't noticed that Troy had joined our group, sidling out of the murk and hovering expectantly just behind my left shoulder.

'Like the war,' says Harvey. '*Hrumpa*. Don't you agree, young Troy? Kate here did a good job with our Russian friends?'

'Of course. That's what I said at the time,' Troy replies. He said nothing of the sort, the creep. Did everything he could to mess it up. Is he still bent on revenge?

'Anyway,' says Harvey, summing up, as dominant males like

to do, with a single, sonorous clap of the hands. 'Well done, you lot. Happy Christmas and all that. Don't get too plastered if you can help it. Need to hit the New Year running. *Hrump-a-hrump.*' He moves on, with Jay-B as his wingman, steadily working his way around the party and bringing one conversation after another to an awkward halt.

'Champagne?' Troy is offering me a glass.

'God, an actual drink in a proper glass. Thank you. Is there anywhere I can put this, um . . .'

He takes my jam jar and puts it on the lid of a closed grand piano. That will not end well.

'What have you got there?' I ask. He is nursing something brown and sticky, in a chemical flask.

'Gangnam. My fourth. Does the business.'

'I'm sure it does.' There is a pause.

'Cheers, Kate. Happy Christmas!'

'Cheers.'

We sip in silence, while the music hums around us, overlaid with the horn section of human laughter. 'Love that dress,' Troy says.

'My trusty old Dolce & Gabbana.'

'Those Italians, they know how to make the most of a woman's figure. Not that you need much help in that department, Kate.'

Christ. The bastard just flicked the flirting switch. Watch out. Operation Screw the Old Lady, the one he plotted with Lech Hatch, is clearly under way. Thank you, dear Alice, for tipping me off.

'Be perfectly honest with you, I noticed it the first time you walked into the office.'

'That's kind of you, Troy. Bit nerve-racking coming back to work after time out. Glad you thought I looked OK.'

Troy moves closer. Close enough to feel his curry breath on my neck. He squeezes his eyes and licks his lips.

What he does next I still can't quite believe. Puts down his drink, lowers his head towards me, as if to impart a confidential secret, and murmurs: 'You know what time it is?'

'Sorry, no.'

'It's the time that, ten years ago, you'd know you'd pulled.'

It takes me a couple of seconds to understand. Oh, I *see*. This acned urchin would be taking me home to bed around now, if I were a decade younger and still worthy of being fancied. The calculating swipe at my age is clearly designed to wound, and, dammit, it does. That's what I mind most: not the insult itself but the fact that, as the c-word himself would say, it does the business. A knife slipped in between the ribs and given a twist. Not that I'll give him the satisfaction of seeing how mortifying it is.

'In your dreams, Toy,' I say, trying to stay as cool and as level as I can. 'Or is it Boy?'

With that, I carefully pour the rest of my champagne into his Gangnam, missing not a drop. He stands there, numb and dumb, a rich mahogany froth rising in the flask and spilling over the edge. Then, I carefully position one heel on top of his shoe, followed by the whole of my body weight. Troy lets out an extremely satisfying yelp.

'Give my love to Grant,' I say. The yelp stops. Then I turn, not too fast, and walk away. Time to get out of here.

'Kate?' I stop. There is no escape. There is never any escape.

'Alice, hi,' I say. She is wearing a Santa-red dress, of a length that was insanely fashionable around Christmas 1922. It looks astounding on her.

'Wow. You. In that. Wow!' My powers of speech have yet to recover from Troy's cruel jibe.

'I was a bit worried I looked like a prezzie under the tree.'
Her cheekbones glitter as she catches what little light there is.

'What's wrong with that? Who doesn't want a prezzie?'

'Max for one. Not tonight.'

'What?'

'He said he would come with me, come here, meet you and
everyone else. Then he cried off at the last minute. Sent me a
text saying he had some work thing of his own. But he doesn't
have a job. There's a waitress he likes at the tennis club.' She
tips her head back. 'I feel like such a flapper.' Tears are gath-
ering, and she doesn't want them to brim over and ruin her
make-up.

I can't think of much to tell her, so I take her hand. 'Men,'
I say at last.

'I know.' She sniffs and laughs at the same time, and it comes
out in a small explosion: a snarf? I dig into my bag for a tissue.
Help. The last packet got used up in a single wodge, when
Lenny came back from the bottom of the garden having rolled
in something unspeakable. Fox poo, probably. Ah. One left,
strangely unused.

'Thanks,' she says. 'Kate, can you stay here a minute or two?
I just need the loo, back as soon as I can, promise. Don't go
anywhere. I only want to talk to you. Not guys. If you see any
more champagne or anything, grab it for both of us, OK?'

'OK.' All I want to do is go home, take this stupid dress off,
raid the fridge, make a hot drink, give Lenny a cuddle and
watch some property porn on TV. 'I'll be right here.'

I look around. Harvey the Hrump is in a distant corner,
clapping his hands, Jay-B bobbing at his side. Troy, though
limping, is dancing with the only black woman in the firm,
leaning in to talk to her, in intimate roars, against the thump
of the music. What can he possibly be saying to her that is

not altogether embarrassing? I wouldn't put it past him to congratulate her on her natural rhythm, in which case she will take a step backwards and slap him in the chops. You go, girl.

I feel very lost, suddenly, in this dark place, thronged with people younger than me, their bodies uneroded by the years, their energies consistent, their memories sharp, their hopes so ridiculously high. Come on, Alice, where are you? How long does it take to have a pee and dry your crying eyes?

'Kate?' Oh God, not another one. Can I please be left alone? Just this once?

'Kate.' A touch on my arm. Wearily, I turn.

You?

And, with that, dear reader, I do something rather impressive. Something I don't recall doing ever since I was waiting for a vaccination, at school, aged nine, and Karen Milburn did it first, and then my best friend Susan next to her, then the girl after Susan, then me, then Carol Dunster, and so on, like a row of dominoes.

I faint. That's right, a true, honest-to-God, swirling-mist, Disney-princess swoon. Only this time I don't wake up on the floor of the gym, with Mr Plender the PE teacher leaning over me in a tracksuit, looking annoyed. I wake up still upright, or almost upright, gently held in the crook of one arm by a man I thought I would never see again in this world or the next. And the first thing I say, God help me, is: 'How long was I gone?'

Jack Abelhammer considers. 'About seven years, I make it. Give or take a week.'

'No, silly, now. How long did I black out for?'

'Seconds. Don't worry, silly, I caught you. Nobody noticed. You're fine. Are you fine?'

'You sound as if this sort of thing happens to you all the time. Women fainting in your arms.'

'It's true. They keel over as I walk down the street.'

'I hate you.'

'It's great to see you too.'

For a moment, I stay there, not wanting to move.

'Please release me.'

'That's what Elvis said. Can you stand?'

'I think so.' Slowly, bracing against his grasp, I manoeuvre myself back to the perpendicular. The room still swims a little.

'Drink this.' He offers me a tumbler. I sniff. Proper alcohol, not a cocktail. Down it goes in one.

'Aaah.'

'Better now?'

I stand back, wavering a touch, and look at him. Damn the man, why did time have to leave *him* alone and trash the rest of us?

'Much better, thank you.' I try to sound prim. It doesn't work. 'Jack, I'm terribly sorry, I don't mean to be nosy, but what precisely the fuck are you doing here? At my Christmas party?'

'Oh, it's your party, is it? Do you want me to leave?'

'No,' I say, looking down, 'I want you to stay.'

'So, I went to your office, and—'

'You what?'

'Your office. The place you work. Come on, even you must go there *some*times.'

'But nobody told—'

'You weren't there. You were out with a client. So I made enquiries, and the very nice lady on reception said—'

'Dolores. Downstairs.'

'Dolores. A treasure.'

344

'A battle-axe. How did you get anything out of her?'

'I have my methods, Watson. So I said I was your date for the Christmas party, and I'd forgotten—'

'How did you know about the Christmas party?'

'Dolores told me.'

'My date? After seven years, you just show up and you're my *date*? Come to that, why didn't you reply to my bloody email?'

'I thought what I needed to tell you should be said in person.'

'Kate.' Another voice. Oh dear God.

'Alice. How was the, the—'

'The ladies' loo? It was fine, thanks. Like a loo. For ladies. Hello,' she says, turning to Jack and holding out a scarlet-nailed hand. 'I'm Alice.'

'Alice. I'm Jack.' He takes her one hand in both of his. I merely swooned, but she melts, as if next to a naked flame.

'So, how do you two know each other?' she asks. What she means is not 'how' but 'how well'.

I try breeziness. 'Oh, you know, we ran into each other a few times, a few years ago, I mean, a few times.' For heaven's sake, Jack, help me here. Take the distress out of the damsel.

'I was a prospective client of a bank where Kate used to work,' he explains. 'She was very persuasive.'

'I know,' says Alice. 'Kate can talk anyone into anything.'

'Then we kept in touch, on and off,' (no, we didn't), 'and I happened to be in town, and thought I'd swing by to say hello. See how the new job is going.'

'Riiiight.' Alice looks at Jack, then at me, then back again at Jack. 'And you both lived happily ever after.'

I bury my nose in my empty glass, breathe in the lingering fumes as if they were an ocean breeze. Beside me, Jack is a calm sea. I very badly want to hold onto him. Or float away on him – either would be fine.

'Yes, pretty much,' he says at last.

'Starting when?' Alice asks.

Jack nods his head, weighing things up, looks at me, looks at her, then replies: 'Starting now.' He takes her hand again. What about *my* hand? 'Lovely to meet you, Alice. Beautiful dress. Excellent party. Will you excuse us? Kate, are you coming? Kate.'

I gaze at Alice, who raises her eyebrows.

'Alice, I, I—'

'Kate, go now. Before you don't.'

'But.'

'But nothing.' She glances over my shoulder. 'Jay-B is coming back with Hrump. Second helpings. Go *now*.'

In the end, I grab Jack's hand, not the other way round, and we scarper, like twelve-year-olds caught smoking behind the bike shed. I turn round to Alice as we go.

'See you at work!'

'Hope not.' And the young woman, who fears she is unloved and may stay that way, watches an older woman, who fears the same thing, make a grab at happiness.

Alice thinks: I don't know how she does it. But I know why.

19

COITUS INTERRUPTUS

11.59 pm: Sex. Don't worry, Kate, it'll come back to you. It's not terribly complicated. Like riding a bike. No, I don't want to think about bikes, or Richard's bike gear in the utility room. As we are going up in the lift, to the tenth floor of the hotel, a line from a book floats into my head. 'It was getting to be known that was embarrassing: all that self-conscious verbalization over too many drinks, and then the bodies revealed with the hidden marks and sags like disappointing presents at Christmastime.' (*'Roy, who wrote that?'*)

The only person, apart from Roy, who I can pretty much guarantee will be able to tell me where that line comes from is standing in the lift with me, his face pressed into my neck, his arms holding me tight. I can't ask Jack if he recognises the quote because then he will know I am nervous. Nervous that undressing me will be an anti-climax, that I will be a disappointing Christmas present, that we've waited so long for this moment and it turns out we're just two middle-aged people. The lovers I pictured us to be, smooth-skinned and firm of flesh, hungrily lunging at each other with joy and confidence, feels impossible to conjure in these anxious seconds as the elevator ascends.

The first time I saw Jack, I looked at him across the desk in New York and I thought, I wonder what it would feel like to have all that energy inside me. Out of nowhere. It made me blush just thinking it. He saw me blushing and he laughed. He knew, I bet he knew. I'd never experienced anything like that before. I'd barely known the man for forty minutes and my body was already over-riding my conscience or any other qualms. I think it's the only time in my life I was ever felled by desire – I mean brought to my knees by it. I like to think I'm a level-headed creature, but Jack spoke directly to my body, which gave its permission without consulting the rational centre in the brain, the one generally charged with captaining the ship. 'O Captain! My Captain!'

We are at the door to his room now and Jack is swiping the key card, trying to get the little light to turn green and let us in. Not working. He tries again. Rubs the card on his coat sleeve. Again. No green light. Amiably, while holding onto me, Jack kicks the door, then, with some ferocity now, he kicks it again.

He kisses the top of my head and takes my face in his hands. 'Here's the thing. If I go downstairs to the front desk to get another damn key card, you won't be here when I get back, will you?'

'I will. Of course I will.'

'No, you won't. I know you, Katharine, you'll think it's a sign.'

'Maybe it *is* a sign, Jack.'

'It's not a goddamn sign. I'm telling you. The card doesn't work. The forces of the Universe are not arranged against us.

348

It's a dumb piece of plastic, not an Old Testament God trying to tell us not to make love.'

After another kiss, he leaves me, sprints the length of the corridor to the lift, turning back impishly for half a second to wink at me, and goes to get a replacement key. I turn and walk the other way.

It is a sign.

Jack to Kate

'Had we but world enough and time, this coyness, Lady, were no crime.' I was left in the hotel room with two champagne glasses and a huge anti-climax. Where did you go? Let me guess. Urgent meeting with the part of you which thinks you have to keep doing everything for everyone and not one damn thing for yourself? Climb down off that burning stake, Joan, and give a guy a break. J XXO

For the first time since we met, Jack sounded angry or at least highly pissed off. I didn't blame him. When he turned up at the office party, I could not have been more excited. Wild again, a child again. As we walked towards Old Street looking for a cab, our combined breath making speech balloons in the frozen air, I was drunk on happiness. But once we were at the hotel, all the doubts started elbowing their way to the front of the queue. I was too old, too encumbered, too beholden, too otherwise engaged. I had responsibilities, promises to keep, a dog to walk. Morality aside, I didn't feel I could subject this handsome apparition to my bikini-unready body. I needed a few weeks' lead time for tummy, legs and deforestation down below; I knew enough about recent trends in pubic hair to guess that Jack hadn't seen a retro Eighties bush since, well, the Eighties. The front I was putting on, supported by corsetry

and the D&G dress, was just that, a lovely facade. I wasn't
ready to let Jack backstage.

Kate to Jack
I'm so sorry. Please don't be angry. I'm all over the place. I've
got so much stuff going on with the family at the moment.
And I don't know who I am. Please know that I wanted you
then, wanted you from the first moment we met, and can't
imagine ever not wanting you. K xxx

20

MERRY CHRISTMAS

10 am: 'Glory to God in the highest, and on earth peace, good-will toward men.' So sings the heavenly host, which means a company of angels, by the way, not a chiselled chap in a velvet jacket clasping a bottle of fizz. Although I could do with a heavenly host right now in this kitchen, not a grumpy husband in Lycra. Notice that there is no mention of goodwill toward women. Funny, that. I guess we are far too busy dealing with those bracing gusts of ill will caused by every single family member nicking our personal stash of Sellotape, so there is none to be found when we sit down to wrap the presents. Then there are the multiple calls – oh joy! – on our limited time. Such as carrying Nigella's turkey in brine, slopping around in a large bucket, into the back garden. At this time of year it's 'fine' to leave the soaking turkey in a cold place, according to the recipe. Check! If you put it in the garden, though, make sure the turkey is securely covered to protect it from 'foxy foraging'. Double check! I'm not taking any chances with twelve people for lunch.

With more swaddling than the baby Jesus and a baking tray and cast-iron casserole dish to weigh it down, Nigella's turkey sits in its bucket on the garden table, so I can observe through the kitchen window. It gives me immense satisfaction, feeling I have not only got ahead of the game, but that I will be serving to my in-laws a bird far superior to anything yet produced by my sister-in-law. Ah, Cheryl, who combines the culinary expertise of Escoffier with the social skills of Tyrannosaurus Rex.

Cheryl is married to Peter, Richard's accountant brother, and they have three perfect sons. Somewhere along the way, I have lost track of my nephews' accomplishments and awards, but, luckily, Cheryl always keeps us up to date via her helpful summary in the family's hand-printed Christmas card. The first two boys all got ten A*s apiece in their GCSEs, plus Grade 8 Suzuki sodding harp or lyre or something – I think that was Edwin. Barnaby soon joined him in the National Youth Orchestra, the youngest non-Asian child to be admitted, which is simply amazing, really, as Cheryl will be sure to mention while she flicks through Ben's Grade 3 piano book with rapturous condescension.

'Oh, *look*, Barney! Ben's doing that adorable little Scottish jig you played when you were in kindergarten.' You get the general idea.

Edwin is now at Harvard – 'Oxford's not what it used to be, is it?' – and is sure to find a cure for cancer if only they can give him time off from the Olympic rowing squad. He won't be joining us for Christmas. Probably on a space mission. All of that I can just about take without hospitalisation, but Cheryl's kids – wait for it – put on a coat to go outside. *Without being asked*. I mean, how is it possible to train a boy to do that? I've never managed. Ben's idea of wrapping up warm is, with extreme bad grace and muttered obscenities, to pull on one hoodie over another hoodie. Privately, I think our children are better looking than Cheryl's – hideously shallow of me, I know, but I need something to cling on to.

11.15 am: 'Kate, are you sure about that turkey in brine business?' asks Richard.

My mum and her dog, the doubly incontinent Dickie, have already arrived; Debra is in front of the telly with a tumbler of Baileys watching *Love, Actually*; the rest of them are about to turn up, and I'm making sure there are enough clean napkins and cutlery to go around.

'Obviously, I'm sure about it, Rich,' I reply. OK, I don't reply. I snap. Apart from the revolting Tofurky suggestion, this is the first interest he has expressed in the food provision for his entire family (three meals a day over the next four days!), and it sounds like a criticism, when, quite frankly, abject gratitude on bended knee with a rose between his teeth is what's called for.

'Nigella's turkey,' I say stiffly, 'is marinading in the bucket in the garden with oranges and cinnamon sticks, which will make it incredibly tender and easy to carve. Emily, will you put that phone down and help me, please? I need you to iron the napkins.'

'*Iron the napkins?*' repeats Emily. She sounds like Lady Bracknell pronouncing '*Hannnddbag*'. 'Literally no one irons napkins, Mum. It's not like *Downton Abbey*. It's a family Christmas. Just chill, OK?'

'It's easy for you to tell me to chill, young lady, when you have done absolutely nothing towards Christmas. Will we be getting dressed today at all?'

'Let me iron the napkins, Kath, love,' says my mum, who is

always quick to deflect my wrath from her beloved grand-daughter. She'd have told me to get off my backside and be quick about it if I'd been as idle as Emily is at the age of sixteen, but Mum has mellowed over the years and is now all fond indulgence. For some reason, I find this maddening to the point of homicide. Oh, and you're not allowed to say a kid is lazy or idle any more, even when they *are* idle and lazy; they are 'lacking in motivation'.

'Mum, can you let Dickie out, please? He's done a wee over by the fridge.'

'Oh, I don't think that was Dickie, love. Probably Lenny. He never does that at home, do you, Dickie? Let's go in the garden, there's a good boy.'

As my mother and her peeing pooch go out, Rich looks up from the kitchen floor, where he is in patient negotiations with the primeval Aga. 'Why can't we use paper napkins?' he asks.

Oof! Why do men do that? I mean, surely they know they're treading on thin ice – they can hear the groans as the frozen water stirs and cracks beneath their feet – yet still they plough on, taking no heed of the 'Beware, Back Off!' neon sign flashing above their spouse's head.

I give it to him straight. 'We can't use *paper* napkins, darling, because, since we were married, your mother has regarded me as the kind of slattern who grew up in a home so common we probably used the word serviette. Which we did, as it happens. And Cheryl makes her own stollen and wreath and probably offers oral sex to Santa Claus to bring her Monica Vinader earrings. So that is why we will be using linen napkins at Christmas dinner. Standards will be maintained. Next question.'

Stressed? No, I'm fine, really. Much better since Dr Libido gave me the HRT. It's as if I was a churning sea and the hormones have calmed me. I even think my memory may be a little better. (*Roy, do you think we're remembering better?*)

Since the kids are both in the kitchen scarfing the sausage rolls I was saving for Boxing Day, I pick the moment to tell them that we will be having a technology break (sounds better than ban) over the next couple of days. No texting, no Facebook, no Internet access. If I'd informed them I was going to chop off a limb each and boil them with the ham and cloves, it could not have gone down worse.

'You must be kidding,' says Ben, in the middle of unplugging one set of headphones from his ears and replacing them with a second set, hanging round his neck.

'Mum, you're like such a hypocrite,' says a scowling Emily. 'You check your phone the whole time.'

'I do not!' She's right. I do. I'm addicted to Jack's texts, feel frantic if there's too big a gap before another one lands. Scared after what happened – or what didn't happen – that he'll give up on me for good.

'Look, you two, I'm perfectly serious. I think it will be really nice if we can all focus on our family for a few days. The people you are physically with deserve priority over those you are not with. I don't want phones at the table. You don't get to see your grandparents very often. And if we can please watch the same thing on TV together rather than us all living in these parallel worlds when we're in the same room?'

Ding! Without thinking I check my phone and the kids burst out laughing. Text from Jack. Stab the button to make his beloved name vanish. I can't cope with two worlds colliding, not today.

Jack is spending Christmas with friends in the South of France. Even though I deserted him at the hotel, he turned up at the office two days later, just as I was leaving for the holiday, carrying a large present. 'It's not for you,' he said when I protested. I opened it and it was a PlayStation 4. Clearly, in my intoxicated (by man not alcohol) state I'd mentioned I couldn't get one for Ben, and Jack had called in a favour. 'I thought you'd probably like this for Christmas more than anything else I could get you.'

You'd swear the man was trying to make me love him or something.

'Emily, where are you going, darling?'

'Out.'

'I can see you're going out, but Grandma and Grandpa and Auntie Cheryl and Uncle Peter will be here soon. When will you be back?'

'Late,' she says, pulling on my sheepskin coat.

'You can't be out late, darling.'

'Everyone's out late. S'Christmas.'

'Surely people are spending time with their families?' I say carefully. Trying to avoid a major explosion here. Still tiptoeing through a minefield with my daughter. Need to present scene of harmony and festive good cheer when the Northern contingent arrives, rather than Emily screaming and swearing.

'I've still got some bits to wrap for the cousins. Can you help me, love, please? You're our best wrapper.'

'Donwanna.' She's standing by the back door, her arms folded as though she were hugging herself tight. Looks oddly vulnerable for someone who wants to go and do some intense Christmas socialising.

'You don't want to? OK, so if I give you a list can you pick up a couple of bits in town for me and buy something for Grandma Barbara? You know she's very forgetful at the moment, so maybe some perfume or talc that she might recognise. She loves flowery scents. Or sweets. Turkish delight, something soft that's not too hard to chew?'

''Kay,' says Emily, visibly relaxing now that I've said she can escape.

'I'll just get my purse, darling.'

As I turn to fetch the money, Em opens the back door and standing outside is a woman I don't recognise. I say woman, but she's more like a large child. Maybe one of Santa's elves fallen off the sled. Wavy, shoulder-length auburn hair, pointy nose, and freckles. She's wearing pixie boots, a brown beret and a brown-needlecord pinafore dress over a floral T-shirt. Presumably the winner of our local Pippi Longstocking looka-like competition. May well live in the sky.

'Hello, I'm really sorry to bother you on Christmas Eve. Is Richard in?' the elf asks in a squeaky voice. Mellifluous Scottish accent. Although she is standing perfectly still, I get the distinct impression that her favourite form of movement is skipping.

'Um, he was here, but he's just popped out to get some logs, I think. Can I help?'

'It's Joely,' the elf says. 'I work with Richard.'

Double-take. *This* is Joely, stout purveyor of disgusting teas and menopausal advice?

'Oh yes, of course! Joely. Joely. Yes, hello. From the coun-selling centre. Rich has talked a lot about you. Come in, please do come in and wait.'

Joely looks as reluctant to come through the door as Emily is eager to get out. Both the same build and height, they stand there blocking the threshold, neither able to move on account of the other.

'Emily, this is Joely, Daddy's colleague at, um work.' I'm struggling to reconcile this sprite with the woman Richard has mentioned. Judging by the look on my daughter's face, Emily isn't that impressed either. I try again. 'So, Joely does yoga and meditation, and lots of healthy things. Joely, this is Emily, our daughter, and I'm Kate. Please, won't you come in. It's cold. Rich should be back any minute.'

'S'okay,' she says, walking backwards away from the house. As if she suddenly got cold feet. Don't know why, I was perfectly nice. I can see her red bike leaning against the fence. 'Don't worry. It can wait. Sorry to bother you,' she says.

'Not at all. I'll tell Richard. It's very nice to . . .' But she disappears as suddenly as she appeared. Emily, too, has gone.

'Who's that girl?' my mother asks dubiously. 'She's not dressed for the weather.'

'Oh, she's a colleague of Richard's. Mum, please can you look in that cupboard next to the Aga for the big glass trifle-bowl?'

How long would it take for me to see? Not to look (I'd been looking all along), but how long would it take me to *see*. To see what the fabled Joely was doing turning up at our door unannounced on Christmas Eve; to see what lurked behind that sweet, billowy, brown-needlecord pinafore? Amazing what we don't notice if we don't care to notice or, let's be honest, if we simply don't care.

Too busy and preocuppied, I suppose. A lot on my plate right now, or, rather, a lot to get onto plates, starting with smoked salmon and blinis.

'*Did I remember sour cream, Roy? Where did I put it?*' Normally I pride myself on being quick, but it's Christmas, and Roy seems to have gone off duty. I try him again.

'Roy, is there something I should know about Rich's pixie colleague Joely, who sleeps in a buttercup? Roy? ROY?' No answer.

Eventually, Roy comes back from the stacks at the back of my mind, just as I'm stirring the double-cream custard for the trifle and waiting for it to thicken (if it boils you've had it, six egg yolks basically thrown away). I am concentrating hard.

'*I am experiencing a high volume of calls,*' says Roy. '*Your patience would be appreciated at this busy time.*'

'*Excuse me, Roy, you're what passes for my memory since my brain became a sieve. Don't do this to me. Roy, get back here please. You can't have Christmas off just because I've had two glasses of mulled wine and my mind is a mess because all I can think about is Jack.*'

'*Abelhammer is filed under Joyful/Painful Life Experiences. Do not open file till 2029.*'

'*I'm well aware of that, Roy. It's just that he's turned up again and I don't know what to do . . . And now someone else has turned up, not merely in my life but at my bloody back door, if you please, and I can barely place her. And what does she do, anyway, little Joely, apart from sit on her toadstool and practise bending her right toe until it touches her left ear? You know what, Roy? Forget it. Forget I asked. Drop the whole thing. Right now, I just need to get through the next forty-eight hours without an act of domestic homicide. And I need Richard to help me bring in the logs and get the mistletoe up.*'

'Kath, where will I find the potato peeler?'

Sometimes my mother's helpfulness is more than I can bear. 'Mum, please sit down, will you? The potatoes don't need doing till later. Not now.'

'But what about the parsnips? Why not get ahead. Stitch in time saves nine, you know.'

My mum will be the last person in Britain who truly believes in all the ancient sayings and saws, and runs her life accordingly. She eats an apple a day, for one thing. I have never seen her suck eggs since she became a grandmother, but I bet she could manage it. If we were having a goose for Christmas, she would insist on making sauce for the gander, too. Enough, naturally, is as good as a feast, although not at Christmas in our house it isn't; it feels like feeding the five thousand. I always buy far too much veg, and find it in the garage in March, rotted to primeval soup. What's so touching is that Mum is genuinely happier for keeping the faith with former times, and with all the old wives who have come before her and told the tales. Happier than the rest of us, certainly, whose idea of collective wisdom is a thread of peevish comments on TripAdvisor.

So, I know exactly how to feed her the next line, like a stooge in a Vaudeville act.

'Fine words, Mum.'

'Fine words butter no parsnips, Kath.' And she actually winks, bless her. 'But I do want to make myself useful.'

'Well, if you *really* want to cut little crosses in the bottom of every Brussels sprout . . .'

It's like a starting pistol. She almost breaks into a doddery run to reach the vegetable drawer and get cracking. Poor innocent sprouts. No mercy will be shown.

Every year, my mother makes us a Christmas cake. I don't like any Christmas cake except hers. It has just the right balance of fruit and crumb and brandy. It's occurred to me that, one day, maybe not so many years from now, I will have to make the cake myself because Mum will no longer be here to do it. I bury that thought like Lenny buries his bone in the garden, but my mind keeps going back to it, as if to prepare myself. Once you've lost one parent, you know what's coming. Losing Dad was different, though; mostly he was a gaping hole where a parent should be. My mother is the earth beneath my feet.

'Christmas wouldn't be Christmas without your cake, Mum.' I say it aloud when she's over by the sink starting the sprouts.

She gives a little shake of the head. 'Not sure it's quite up to the usual standard this year, love.'

I don't think I've told her enough what the cake means, what she means. She's never been one for saying 'love you', my mum, as her grandchildren and their friends do every five minutes. A different generation, my mum lets the cake say 'love you' for her.

'Please will you teach Emily to make your cake, Mum?'

4.27: pm. Carols from King's on the radio, making a matchless Christmas mood, both holy and hopeful. Peter and Cheryl have driven Donald and Barbara down to us, so everyone is here safely. Well, just about. Barbara is making anxious circuits of the kitchen and I see her put two smoked salmon blinis and a lemon squeezer in her pocket.

To be fair to Cheryl, she waits as long as eight minutes before confiding to us that poor Barnaby is having terrible trouble deciding between offers from Princeton and Cambridge. Rich nods sympathetically at his nephew's predicament. I disembowel a pomegranate. Debra, who is making coleslaw for me, and who has already, to my knowledge, drunk a bottle of Baileys, says, 'Oh, poor you. It must be terribly difficult deciding between two such great universities. Looks like my son, Felix, will be choosing between shelf-stacking at St Tesco and Pentonville prison.' My sister-in-law ignores this; she walks around, cooing, 'Oh, Kate, this house has *so* much potential.'

I don't care. Piotr has built us a wonderful kitchen. Praise be to Piotr. I gave him a Christmas bonus tucked inside a card, and he said he might not see us for a while because his father was dying back in Poland. 'Only age he's fifty-nine, Kate. That's not correct, isn't it, lose your father like that?'

No, that is most certainly not correct. I kissed Piotr on the cheek and hugged him. He has been such a comfort to me since we moved here that my eyes filled with tears when we said goodbye – but then tears seem to have been my personal weather system these past few months. There's been more flooding than over the Somerset levels.

Mum has finished the sprouts. Now she's asleep in the chair by the Aga. Miraculously, there is no sign of a present from Dickie on the newly hoovered carpet. Ben and his boy cousins are playing Monopoly at the table – no electronic devices in sight. Yay! Even Emily has condescended to get out of the foul leggings to which she is surgically attached, and put on something pretty for her grandparents; true, what she is wearing resembles honeymoon lingerie more than an actual dress, but nonetheless, an effort has been made. Donald took Barbara to the hairdresser to get her hair permed before the drive down South, and she's wearing a smart red Jaeger dress with gold buttons that I recall from previous festivities. It hangs on her, these days, rather than fitting; you can sense the fragile frame beneath. The sharpness of old bones. We all know, though, that Barbara would be pleased to know she had made an effort.

I used to wince, every Christmas, when Barbara told Richard, as she always did, that he shouldn't have gone to so much trouble, when all he had ever done was to buy a single present, at four o'clock on Christmas Eve (for me), plus one very smelly Camembert and some red wine. How I miss that Barbara now. She says next to nothing. Does she think next to nothing, too, or is her mind trembling with thoughts that she cannot voice?

So, this Christmas Eve she sits there, with half a smile, near the fire, clutching Emily's hand. They look like a Victorian watercolour of a parlour at peace, although few Victorian young ladies wore glittery pedal-pushers under their party dress. Or, for that matter, disclosed to their fond mamas that portraits of their rear ends had been passed around the general population, like a keepsake. Thank God that hateful belfie business is over and done with.

'Here, Grandma, I got you some soap. Sort of an early Christmas present. You can use it tonight if you like. It's lily of the valley. I tried them all out in Boots and this one smelled the nicest. Like you. I mean, like you like. Whatevs.'

And on that elegant note, Emily hands Barbara a present. Three soaps in a box, badly wrapped, but still. In this case, it truly is the thought that counts. (I glance across at Cheryl, who is sitting on the sofa next to her husband. As she sees the box, she nudges him in the ribs – just a quick jab of the elbow, but enough to indicate her satisfaction at the lowliness of the gift. Precisely what she would expect of this household. Cow.)

To our surprise, Barbara lifts the box to her face and inhales deeply. A puzzled look, which very slowly clears, like the lifting of a fog. Then, to our even greater surprise, she speaks.

'I used this the other day, love.'

'Don't worry, Grandma, I'm sure I can swap it for another one.'

'In France.'

'France?'

'We were in this lovely place in the countryside.' She turns to Donald. 'You drove all the way, love!'

Donald looks at her, then down at his hands.

'There was a bathroom, we had to share, it was down a corridor, but ever so clean. And I had a bath, with lily of the valley. You said I smelled nice afterwards. Only last week. What a coincidence! And now I have this. Thank you, Kate.'

'Emily.'

There is a long silence, during which Richard puts a log on the fire and kicks it into place with the toe of his shoe. Barbara's eyes slowly close.

'Our first holiday abroad,' Donald says, almost whispering. 'June nineteen fifty-nine. Barbara's right, we did drive all the way. In our Austin Cambridge. Broke down just outside Calais. "Welcome to Europe", she said, and we sat there laughing.' His eyes are rheumy and moist. 'And there was this little place, middle of nowhere, we were just tired by all the driving. With those sausages they have instead of pillows?'

'Bolsters.'

'Bolsters. And the bidet, that was different, she couldn't so much as look at the thing without laughing. And all the things on the menu we couldn't understand.' He smiles, and looks at Emily. 'Sometimes, you know, it's funny, sometimes I envy her. Your gran. Thinking it all happened last week like that.' He clenches his fists tight, like a small child making a wish. 'If only, eh?'

Peace and goodwill. Laying down memories for the children, passing on recipes for cake, so that they, in their turn, will lay down memories for their children. And maybe one Christmas forty years from now, Emily will remember the lily of the valley soap which, for a few precious minutes, brought the grandmother who loved her so dearly back by her side.

The only sounds are those of the fire's crackle, the soaring harmonies of the carols, and a delicate descant of snores. The King's choristers are bang in the middle of 'Angels from the Realms of Glory' – one of those endless Glo-o-o-ooo-rias – when Cheryl lets out a shriek.

'Good grief, Kate, is that a dog out there in your garden with a huge great bird in its mouth?'

364

From: Candy Stratton
To: Kate Reddy
Subject: The Dog Ate My Turkey
Honey, you're kidding, right? That has got to be the best Christmas disaster story EVER. Please tell me you got devil-dog Dickie euthanised? And how about getting the bitch sis-in-law euthanised too?

What did you give them all to eat – Heinz beans? Trust me, you're gonna see the funny side one day.

What's the score with Abelhammer btw?

XXO C

From: Kate Reddy
To: Candy Stratton
Subject: The Dog Really Did Eat My Turkey
When will I see the funny side? In about 30 years, if I'm lucky. Rich chased Dickie down the garden and managed to wrestle the turkey out of his mouth. Seems that Rich had been inspecting the turkey in brine and didn't put the lid back on properly. Typical of him: interfering, 'trying to be helpful', and causing chaos. I cut the turkey leg off and thought I could salvage the rest.

Then I looked in the bucket and smelt the brine. It stank. I have a horrible feeling that a corpse would smell this way, left on a battlefield. Cheryl said that it was 'unseasonably warm' for December and that it was all my fault because the brine needed to be kept cold. I should have put it in the fridge. Thanks a lot, bitch. Pardon me for not having a fridge the size of an airline terminal, like you and Peter do. Sorry about that.

And I couldn't blame Dickie because my mum loves him more than her children so I said it would be great to have a change and eat ham and roasted vegetables for Christmas dinner.

Does this ever happen to Nigella?

Don't bother to answer that.

Kxxx

PS Abelhammer showed up at the office party and I am helplessly hopelessly in love with him and we almost did it, hallefuckinlulia, but the hotel room key didn't work. And the whole thing is impossible because my Sandwich can't take another layer. And now he probably hates me. I'm so confused.

*11.59 pm: *Six hours late, Roy shows up. I am still wrapping stocking fillers, even though no one believes in Father Christmas and everyone else has gone to bed. Roy says, 'Disguise, I see thou art a wickedness, Wherein the pregnant enemy does much.' What on earth is he on about? 'That was Emily's Twelfth Night essay, Roy. Wrong memory! You really need to get a grip.'*

NEW YEAR'S EVE

Drinks with Sally and her family. Drinks beginning at a civilised time, thank God, not a late-night binge starting at 10 pm and going on till four in the morning. There was a time when I would have been content to sing 'Auld Lang Syne' around the piano, and get pawed by complete strangers on the grounds that all concerned had made it through another year on Earth, but, frankly, I'm too bloody auld for that. Fine if you're standing by the Thames and watching the Mayor blow half his annual budget – quite rightly, in my view – on an eye-scorching fire-work display, but not when you're stuck in the countryside with the roads turned to skating rinks by midnight.

So, at half past seven sharp, or as sharp as you can get when herding teenagers, we pile into the car, with varying degrees of reluctance (prize for most remorseless moaner: my son), and arrive at Sally's place. My first visit to what she calls her HQ; until now, Sal and I have always met on neutral ground – the best and only spot, oddly enough, for the sharing of confidences, and the gradual unveiling of hidden truths. Home, for some reason, bites the tongue.

'You must be Kate. We meet at last. Come on in!'

'And you must be Mike?' A fully fledged Mike, by any standard. Bearish, beaming, and a bit cumbersome, garbed in a formless russet cardigan that was, I trust, knitted by canny crofters in the Hebrides.

'Richard, hi. Mike. Ben, hello. Brilliant. Emily, gosh, just like your mum.' Flames dart from Emily's eyes, but Mike rolls ever onward. 'I mean, lovely, God, come in, all of you, coats there, drinks in here, Sally somewhere around, excellent. Welcome all.'

Handshakes that sprain your wrist before you've even made it through the door. If this was Dickens, there would be a punchbowl. Enter the living room, buzzing with chatter. Oh, look. There's a punchbowl.

Is it a sign of middle age, or has it just got worse – that sudden lurching wish, upon entering a room and seeing wave upon wave of unknowns or unremembered knowns, to back off and try your luck elsewhere, or, failing that, to hide behind the sofa until somebody blows the all-clear? Never mind. It's not a habit to hand down to the children, certainly, so on we go, into the throng, searching in rising desperation for a friendly face.

'Kate, you came!'

'Sally.' We embrace.

'Late Happy Christmas. Early Happy New Year. Happy something, anyway. How was it?'

'A dog ate my turkey. No, it was really good, I'll explain later. Sally, this is Richard. And Ben. And Em— hang on, Emily *was* here; she seems to have disappeared.'

Full disclosure. We had a last-minute Emily crisis. Complete meltdown. She wasn't supposed to be coming with us tonight, being officially too old and too cool to spend New Year's Eve with her boring family. Then, this afternoon, I found her curled up tight as a shell in bed. After a bit of coaxing, she admitted that Lizzy Knowles was having this huge New Year's Eve party, and only two girls from the whole year weren't invited. Emily and Bea. Emily was devastated. She had arranged to stay over at Ellie's house. 'Ellie was invited to the party, so Ellie texted Lizzy to say, "Can Emily come because she's staying at mine?", but Lizzy still said no.'

I was spitting with anger, but not a bit surprised. Em said Lizzy had started being weird to her after Emily's own party was a big success.

'Seriously, what kind of kid does something that malicious?' asked Richard when Em was upstairs taking a shower.

'Oh, a Queen Bee who doesn't like one of her drones taking the spotlight away,' I said. My daughter was frozen out by her alleged best friend. This was revenge served icy cold. It was too late to make another plan so, between us, Rich and I managed to persuade Em to come to the Carters'. I told her I was sure there'd be loads of kids there – I wasn't sure, but I had a bad feeling about leaving Em alone in the house.

So, thank God, now we're here and it transpires that Em just glimpsed someone called Jess on the far side of the room whom she is friends with on Facebook, and has never actually met, but who is really great and probably like her favouritest person ever. So that's a relief. Any port in a storm of adult sociability. Shrieks of uncontainable delight as Em and the girl greet one another like long-lost sisters, and I pray it's some small salve to her pride after Lizzy's cruel snub.

Sally, meanwhile, is desperate to introduce me to her lot. I am presented to Will, then Oscar, then Antonia, all of whom are then required to meet Richard, then Ben, and at some point Emily, if she can be unpeeled from the company of Jess. That's the downside of bringing one clan into contact with another: by the time that everyone has been introduced, it's practically time to go home. Ben wanders off, parks himself at a side table, and crunches his way glumly through a bowl of Twiglets. (Later he will be found playing video games, quite cheerfully, with a group of boys in another room. Asked who they were, in the car on the way home, he says he didn't get their names. They knew their way around a games console, and that was enough. Such are the callings cards of twenty-first-century youth.)

It's strange to meet Will and Oscar at last, for real, having seen them only in photographs; and especially strange to meet them in winter. Something about their hale blondness suggests that they should only be approached in summer, in cricket whites, lightly smudged with grass stains.

'Will, you did remember to take the sausages out of the oven, didn't you?' Sally asks.

'Oh Christ, bugger, sorry Mum, I was just about to—'

'I only asked you three times. I even stuck a Post-It note on Oscar's forehead an hour ago.'

'Yup, right, on my way.'

A thin, high, electric wail comes from the kitchen.

'Smoke alarm,' says Sally. 'Too late.' She doesn't even seem that bothered. This sort of thing has obviously happened so often that it's become a ritual. In the end, you despair of despair. I know I do.

'Mum,' says Oscar, appearing at her side, 'I couldn't just borrow your card, could I?'

'What for now?'

'These tickets. They're for February, which is miles off, but right now you can get them online on special—'

'To do what?'

'Just a band. You won't have heard of them or anything.'

'Oscar, the tickets won't go in the next two hours. Ask me later.'

'But that's the whole point. They might . . .'

'How are we all doing?' Mike to the rescue, brushing his son aside in his effusiveness, and, from his frown, urgently troubled by something. 'Bloody hell, Richard, that's an empty glass. Not something we put up with in this house. Mea bloody culpa. Quick, someone, all hands to the pump, give this man a drink! Here, better idea, come with me.' And my husband, half protesting, is hauled away through the crowd as if he were a troublemaker instead of a guest.

'So that's Richard,' says Sally.

'So that's Mike,' I say.

Sally puts an arm around me and squeezes, then leans in close. 'Thank God for us, that's what I say.'

'Thank God.' And I mean it.

Antonia strolls by, a doting, dopey boy in tow.

'Boyfriend?'

'He wishes,' Sally says. 'I wish, I suppose. She's still being bicurious or biconfusing; I can't keep up. She agreed to go to the cinema with Jake just before Christmas, and he more or less wet himself.'

'I can see why. She's gorgeous.'

'If only she were a little less gorgeous and a bit more confident, poor darling. That old cliché about beauty being a burden
turns out to be true. Who knew?'

'It's true. The most beautiful girl in my year at college never
married, ended up an alcoholic, as if she couldn't bear it. Seems
so wrong. All you ever want, *ever*, is for the children to be
happy. I can't believe I'm saying this, but it matters even more
than an A* in GCSE Geography.'

Sally gasps. 'I can't believe you're saying that either. I'm truly
shocked. I mean, without the A* in Geography, where are you,
Kate? How can you possibly hope to succeed in life, at anything?
What would Churchill have done without his A* in bloody
Geography? Or Gandhi?'

We drink together, glasses raised.

'*Penélope Cruz.*' I've been meaning to tell Sally that Roy
found the name of the actress her daughter reminds me of.

'Sorry, no, I'm Sally.'

'No, Antonia. That's who she reminds me of. I knew it was
someone famously lovely. Penélope Cruz. Lucky her.' I drain
my glass. 'Must be a Spanish granny or something, tucked away
in the family tree. Castanets and all.'

The smile fades from Sally's face like breath off a mirror.
Without more ado, she reaches out past me, and pulls another
couple into the frame.

'Phyllida, Guy, have you met Kate? Kate, this is Phyllida and
Guy, from all of three houses away. I *so* wanted you to meet them.
Kate's my friend from Women Returners, our dogs are best mates.
Will you excuse me, I just have to pop into the kitchen and see
if that boy has left us anything edible.' And, with that, she's gone.

Four minutes to midnight: As the room quells and settles,
seeming to take in a communal breath before the chimes of

Big Ben, it's a piercing reminder of what the past twelve months have been like for me and Richard. We've now rounded the lap of a full sex-free year. Oh, God, how did that happen? Are we really that old? I know that, since Perry, my body has felt like the scene of a pitched battle, and I haven't much wanted anyone else invading it, but I wonder if Rich is having his own manopause. Who knows, he may have been feeling as bad as I have. Welcoming in the New Year has never felt more freighted with uncertainty, or more lonely. As everyone fills their glasses, or grabs a half-drunk one, instinctively I look around for my husband.

'Dad's on his phone in the kitchen,' Emily says, suddenly by my side. 'He's so weird.'

'Probably talking to Grandpa,' I say.

'Don't think so judging by the soppy look on his face.'

I am, it has to be faced, almost fifty years of age and, until Jack showed up at the office party, the most exciting, sensual thing in my life was the discovery of a new hyper-absorbent kitchen towel on Special Offer in the Co-op. Two for £3. You think I'm joking? I've got to do something about this. What 'this' is I don't quite know, but something must be done.

Emily puts her arms around me and I rest my head on her shoulder. I forget she's taller than me, my baby, particularly in those heels. 'You OK, darling?'

She smiles, but her bottom lip is wobbling and I hold her tight. 'This is going to be a great year for you, I promise. We're going to get everything sorted, OK? Say, "Yes, I believe you."'

'Yes, I believe you, Mum.'

'Good. Do you know how proud I am of you? Well, you should. I've got the best girl in the world. Lucky me. Now, where's your brother? Do you think we could disconnect him from *Mortal Kombat* to say hi to the New Year?'

At midnight precisely, as the room bursts into full-throated song, a *ding* announces a text on my phone:

Jack to Kate
The other night, you told me this was going to be Kate's Year of Invisibility. But I will always see You. See only you. J XXO

NEW YEAR'S RESOLUTIONS
1. Prepare self emotionally and physically for fiftieth birthday. Apply oestrogen daily to avoid decrepitude and anxiety. Take Glucosamine for joints, Vitamin D3 for mood, Curcumin to ward off dementia and help Roy with forgetfulness.
2. Make effort to spend more time with Mum and stop my sister hating me.
3. Settle Barbara and Donald in nursing home.
4. Enrol for 'It's Tough Parenting Teens' course. Wean kids off technology and encourage them to spend more time IRL.
5. Pluck up courage to tell work you are not really forty-two (maybe AFTER they've extended my contract).
6. JACK???

21

THE MERE IDEA OF YOU

JANUARY

3.12 pm: So, here I am, lying in bed with my lover. Which is not something I ever expected to say again. Not in this lifetime, anyway. It's a typical London afternoon for early in the year – rain in the air, people bumping into each other on the pavement, commuters getting cross, trains running late, lives going nowhere, dark on the way in – and the best thing about it is, I don't care. I get fired for bunking off early from work? No sweat. Ben and Emily have nothing to eat and end up going to McDonald's? Fine by me. Christ descends once more in glory, with flaming cherubim and all the heavenly host? Put them on hold. I'm lying in bed with my lover. That's what matters.

We even have the trimmings. The ice bucket containing an empty bottle of wine. The artless strewing of clothes about the room, on which no set-decorator could improve. The sign hung outside saying 'Do Not Disturb', to which I had to be forcibly dissuaded from adding, in felt-tip pen, 'Until Next Xmas. And the Xmas after that. Thanx', as if I were twenty years old or something. As if the past eight years, since I met Jack, have simply been folded up and put aside. Think of all the time we wasted not doing this, all the hours and minutes and seconds we could have been doing this. Everything, as ever, comes back to time.

'When did you last eat?' Jack asks, as we sprawl and laze. When sprawling becomes an Olympic sport, I'll be ready.

'About twenty minutes ago. You mean you didn't notice?'

'Now, who would have thought a nice girl like you could have a mind like that? Is it a British thing? I say again: when did you last eat? Think before you answer.'

'Sorry, no thinking allowed. Not today. I'm having a think-down Thursday. No thoughts. No lists. Feelings and doings only.'

'OK, could you feel your way into room service?'

'But that would mean getting *up* and going *all* the way to the bathroom and going through the *whole* palaver of putting on a towelling robe. And then,' I say, turning over to make my point, and looking at him, at that wonderful face, 'there's all that business of holding a fork and bringing the food to my mouth. I simply haven't got the energy. Or I *have* got it, but I want to conserve it. I can eat food anytime.'

'So that's a no.'

'So that's a whatever. Or whatevs, as my children would say. You see, they haven't got the energy for three whole consonants. They must get it from me.'

'How are they?'

'Look, Jack. Kind of you to ask, and, if you really want an answer to that question, I will give it to you. But it's now January, and I have a meeting I really have to get to in mid-March. And I would need at least from now until July to talk about Emily. That's before I even start on Ben. And . . . look, I do want to talk to you about them, I really do, just not at this precise moment, OK?'

'Fine,' he says, and I feel his hand on me. Hands. 'And your marriage?'

The sound I make is not to be found in any dictionary. You would need a word that combines sigh, snort, laugh, and groan, with a hint of withering chuckle. 'Oh, that's much easier. We could order room service right now, and I'd have given you my marital woes before Gianfranco turned up with my luke-warm cheeseburger and limp fries.'

'This is a five-star hotel, I'll have you know.'

'Sorry, but any fries served in any hotel, anywhere in the world, by the time they get brought up to the room, are sad and cold and limp. Unlike,' I say, using my own hands in return, 'the people in the rooms.'

'The not being limp, it's a tribute to you.'

He stretches out. All the better to enjoy me with. So much unwinding to be done, for the both of us, since life wound us up and pulled us apart. I'm not making any excuses for being here. Jack was waiting for me outside the office; he said we were going to lunch, but, when we got to Claridge's, he walked me straight up the main staircase and, when we got to the room, this time the key card worked. 'It's a sign,' he said. I didn't argue. I was fed up of fighting myself.

Now, he says, as if mentioning yesterday's weather: 'I got married.'

I stop right there. Hands, arms, mouth, me: everything comes to a halt. I sit up.

'I didn't know. Thanks for telling me.'

'If I'd told you before, would we be here now?' he asks.

'I—' Pause. *Careful now.* 'That's not the point.'

'So what is?'

'The point is you're married.'

'Was. Was married. As in not any more.'

'As in divorced or just separated?' I'm finding it hard to take this in. Jack got married since I last saw him?

'Divorced, don't worry.'

'Since when?'

'Since about a year and two months after I married her. Which was five years ago, more or less. I think we can safely set the whole thing down as a mistake.'

'Would she say that?'

'She would. Even more than me. No hard feelings.'

'All feelings are hard, you know that.'

'Mmm, talking of which . . .'

'No, Jack, come on.' I sit there on the bed, sheet drawn up over my breasts, knees pulled up to my chin. 'So what happened?'

'Didn't work out.'

'That's it?'

'That's it.'

'Cross your heart?'

'Hope to die.'

'Please don't. Where is she now?'

'I have no idea.'

'And –' this needs to be done '– what was she like?'

'Is, not was. I hope. Well, she's in her forties, British, married but not happily, two great kids, works in finance, smart as a whip, funny as hell, too hard on herself, very polite and well-behaved in that British way until you get her into room 286, at which point you realise she's basically a jungle cat. My type.'

'Jack.'

377

'C'mon, it's not an interrogation. She reminded me strongly of a woman I was in love with. I thought it was a good start. She was twenty-nine when we met.'

'Why are you telling me her age? Why is her age what matters? Why is it always age? Stone age, bronze age, right age, wrong age, twenty-nine, forty-nine . . .'

'Her age was a problem.'

'Why?'

'Because she'd never seen *Bewitched*.'

Even I can't help smiling. 'Oh, well, in *that* case . . .'

'Right. If you're too young to have seen Samantha making Darrin do exactly what she wants, even though she loves him and looks like the perfect American wife—'

'Which Darrin?'

'Right again. You see, that is the correct response. Which Dick? York or Sargent?'

'York, obviously.'

'Of course. But Sargent was a good guy. Gay, you know.'

'Interesting.'

'Isn't it? He was a Grand Marshal in a Gay Pride parade in LA. And you know who else was there with him? Samantha.'

'No! Seriously?'

'In person. The divine Miss M. If you want to pick a parade, that's the one to go for.'

'Excuse me, but aren't we straying from the issue here?'

'Excuse me back, but no.' Jack looks at me. 'That *is* the issue. What matters is not who you go to bed with, but who you can talk to – I mean, really talk to – when you're lying around afterwards.'

'Like now.'

'Well, now's OK—'

'Hey, thanks.'

'But the afterwards has to go on for a bit longer if you want to be really sure.'

'How much longer?'

He takes a damp tendril of hair on my face and curls it behind my ear. 'Oh, you know, forever and ever, world without end. No more than that. Let's not get carried away here.'

There is a moment of reflection. I put my hand to his cheek.

'Do you still miss her? Do you call her? Straight answer, please.'

'No, and no. Damn straight.'

'Did you love her?'

'Kate, I married her.'

'Not the same thing.'

'What there was . . . what I felt for Morgan was . . .'

'*Morgan?* You married a woman called *Morgan?* Hang on, are you sure she *was* a woman? Could that be the problem here? Are you sure she wasn't a Welsh rugby player? Or an open-top sports car?'

'Or a library.'

'Well, that would be fine, but honestly: Morgan?'

'I know. Anyway, how can I put it? I felt as much as you can feel for someone who didn't know who McEnroe's doubles partner was. Or even care.'

'Peter Fleming. How many Grand Slams?' I mean it.

'Seven. Marry me.'

'You cannot be SERIOUS. The ball was OUT.'

'Marry me. Kate. Please. I'm serious.'

'I can't. I'm already married.'

'People can get unmarried. Or demarried.'

'Because the person they married doesn't know the name of McEnroe's doubles partner?'

'Well, that mainly,' Jack says, with a shrug. 'But then there are all the minor reasons. Like, you know, the thought of being happy for the rest of your life because you're making the other person happy. Giving them a chance to prove that they can do the same for you. Peace on earth. Justice for all. The little things.'

'How do you know you can make me happy?'

'I don't. But I should tell you now, I have a lot of money riding on this. At extremely favourable odds.'

'Oh, I'm just a wager for you?'

'Sure. Just playing the markets. Like any other day.' He swings round, and over, and on top of me.

'Oh, I get it. Spread betting.'

And that makes him laugh, and the laugh makes him shake, and I tell him to stop. He seems surprised.

'Are you done?' he says.

'Nope, sorry, I'm just getting started. Watch me.'

'No, are you done with the interrogation? For now?'

I reach out and bring him close, whisper into his ear. 'No further questions, Your Honour.'

4.44 pm: I had to get back to the office, but he insisted we had afternoon tea first, downstairs under a chandelier so big it looked like the world's pushiest stalactite. There was a pianist noodling on the baby grand in the corner, playing standards from *The Great American Songbook*. I said I didn't want anything to eat, just Earl Grey would be fine, but now I am polishing off all the teeny crustless sandwiches the waiter had brought. Egg and cress stacked on honey-roast ham stacked on cucumber stacked on smoked salmon and cream cheese. Sandwich Woman cannot live on passion alone.

Jack sits there, watching the ravenous woman opposite him with obvious amusement, while asking me questions about work. I want to tell him everything because there is no one I can rely on more to reflect me back at me, no one whose honest advice I would rather have. But if I tell Jack that I lied about my age to get a job he will know that I feel vulnerable about my age and then he will know that I'm older, maybe even older than he thinks, and then I will be diminished in his eyes too, which will be unbearable.

'I lied about my age.'

'You did what?'

'To get a job. A headhunter wouldn't put me forward for a non-exec directorship because he said that I was "outside the cohort parameter". Which is code for being almost . . .' *Say it, Kate.* 'Basically, I will be fifty in March and, apparently, that makes me unemployable, well, in the City anyway.'

Jack passes me the scones. 'You're kidding me, right? You can do a better job than five guys put together.'

'Thank you. But the fact is I took time out to look after my mum and my kids while doing bits and pieces of financial advice, and that doesn't look great on a CV. So, I knocked seven years off my age, because I thought I could pass for younger, and I managed to get this job on my old fund.'

'The one you came to sell to me?'

'Yes, that one. And it's not such a great job, but it pays the bills, which is what I need right now because my husband is retraining and I am the breadwinner. And the guy running the fund, Jay-B, he's thirty.'

Jack hands me the clotted cream. 'Let me guess. Asshole who doesn't know who McEnroe's doubles partner was?'

'You may laugh, Jack, but I need the job, I really need it. And it's hard pretending that I have kids who are eleven and eight or ten and seven or whatever they are because I keep almost making mistakes, and one day I really will make a mistake, and the Boy who is my boss will find out and I'll be fired and . . .'

'Listen.' He puts a finger to his lips, indicating that I should shush.

'What?'

'Listen, Kate.' Jack gestures towards the piano.

Did he plan this? I recognise it at once and very softly start to sing along. 'The very thought of you and I forget to do, the little or-di-na-ry things that everyone ought to do.'

For one perfect afternoon, they were playing our song.

It couldn't last.

22

MADONNA AND MUM

10.35 am: Until you start trying to conceal your age you have no idea how many ways there are to give it away. Teen idols, pop stars, fashionable restaurants, famous football matches, Olympics, moon landings, children's TV programmes, historical knowledge, having seen any movie made before *Pulp Fiction*, being able to spell. Each and every one of them is a potential trap for a woman pretending to be seven years younger.

Since I've been back at work, I've done really well avoiding the question of how old I am. For example, I've learned not to call the GP's surgery from my desk to make an appointment because they always ask for your date of birth, and that is the one thing I must never speak aloud. When my young colleagues were raving about Kate Bush's live concert comeback, I was careful not to reveal how much I loved 'Wuthering Heights', Bush's debut single, when it came out in the prehistoric mists of 1978. There was one close shave, though, when Alice spotted *Parenting Teens in the Digital Age* in my bag.

'But your kids aren't teenagers for ages, Kate,' she said.

'Be prepared is my motto,' I said, ducking under the desk to put something in the bin and hide my consternation. I feel particularly bad deceiving Alice who, I suspect, sees me as something of a role model. If only she knew.

At this morning's meeting, however, the topic of age was unavoidable. Madonna fell backwards down some stairs last night, cracking her head and her back with a sickening thump. Most people would have lain there in a crumpled heap, crying with pain and shame; I know I would have. But Madonna got to her feet and resumed a staggeringly athletic dance routine. Instead of receiving the universal awe and plaudits that were her due, jokes about old ladies were soon trending on social media. Sure enough, in our first meeting of the day, Jay-B told me to look into companies manufacturing stairlifts.

'Madonna's gonna need one now, so it figures the share price's gonna go up,' he said with hand-rubbing glee. Like most posh boys of his generation, Jay-B talks like a drug dealer from Baltimore, rather than a nicely brought-up boy from Bushey, Herts. (Real name: Jonathan Baxter, if you please.) This makes me want to (a) smack him on his Rolexed wrist and (b) tell him to lose the glottal stop and pronounce the endings of his words properly, but as his junior (in status if not in years) that's not possible.

'Madonna's not an old lady just because she fell,' objected Alice, eyes flicking my way for moral support. 'It was some stupid backing dancer who pulled her over. It was really mean of Radio 1 to say they wouldn't play Madonna's new song because she's too old. How old's Mick Jagger, for heaven's sake? No one says the Rolling Stones are sad leathery old gits, and they're absolutely ancient.'

'Madonna *is* bloody old,' said Jay-B, swivelling on one of

his ridiculous, pointy shoes towards me. 'What is she, Kate? Must be sixty or something?'

Careful, Kate.

'Oh, she must be somewhere in her mid-fifties,' I said vaguely, as if being in one's fifties was as remote from me personally as Nova Scotia or the Falkland Islands. 'Though you'd never be able to tell how old she is,' I added, suddenly ashamed of my unsisterly cowardice. 'After all, Madonna is the Queen of Reinvention.'

'Queen of Reincarnation, more like,' cackled Troy. 'Old trout. Give me Taylor Swift any day. She's hot.'

'Anyone got the inside track on HSBC?' asked Jay-B, moving on.

I know her age. Of *course*, I know her age. Fifty-six. I've always been grateful to Madonna. Not just for getting me through my college finals with 'Into the Groove' – the works of Jane Austen will forever be confused, in one mind at least, with *Desperately Seeking Lady Susan* – but for being older than me. No matter how old I am, Madonna will always be six years older. There is a certain comfort in that. If she can walk down the red carpet in a crazy, black-lace matador's outfit with her pert white bum showing, like a little girl who came out of the lavatory with her dress tucked in her knickers, then I can't be that ancient, can I? That's one reason I still miss the Princess of Wales. We will never know how Diana would have navigated middle age, and how fascinating that would have been to watch. We rely on older women to walk through the minefield ahead of us, so we know where it's safe to step, and not to step. I like the fact Madonna refuses to watch where she puts her foot. If, sometimes, she takes a tumble, so what?

When I was a kid, fifty was considered old. Nanny Nelson, my mother's mum who'd been in an iron lung as a girl and walked for the rest of her life with a limp, had her old-lady uniform picked out by the time she was my age. A floral-print dress worn over a full-length, flesh-coloured slip, comfy M&S cardie in a pastel shade, tan stockings so thick they looked like cake batter, zip-up sheepskin ankle booties that she wore as house slippers as well as for going outside to bring in the coal they stored in a brick outhouse. And she never dyed her grey hair; dyeing your hair was for frivolous, wanton women, Jezebels who stole husbands and touched themselves Down There.

No one expected a fifty-year-old to be having wild, imaginative sex or getting 'bikini ready' or holding down a demanding full-time job or mastering Snapchat or getting her midriff bulge sucked out by a Hoover in her lunch hour. You bought a Playtex girdle for special occasions, slapped on some Pond's Cold Cream, a spot of lipstick, a spritz of Elizabeth Arden's Blue Grass, and that was that. Nanny Nelson got through the menopause sitting in a high-backed chair next to an open window, drinking pint-glasses of Lemon Barley Water and watching *Crown Court* on the telly. But that was an eternity ago, when Nan was still an elderly person, not an Indian bread.

I won't lie. There are days when menopause makes me want to curl up and die, but the HRT Dr Libido prescribed is definitely starting to make a difference. Joints not aching, skin no longer dry, juices flowing, feeling that I can manage stuff again, the skies over air-traffic control that much clearer. My afternoon with Abelhammer suggests that my libido is in reasonable working order, and I can't wait to try again, just to make sure. Dr L also gave me some thyroxine, which means I don't have to fight falling asleep every afternoon. Curling up isn't an option, and neither is dying. Nor is being fifty, or letting my hair be its natural colour, whatever that is. I won't let it take me over. I can't.

Still, I was mighty relieved we got through the Madonna conversation with my own cover story intact. As far as Jay-B was concerned, Kate was only forty-two, and a viable employee, not an old trout like the Queen of Pop. It was then that the door to the meeting room swung open and in came a trolley followed by Rosita.

'Oh, hullo, Kate!' The woman bringing our coffee was beaming, clearly delighted to see me.

My blood ran cold. Rosita worked in the canteen when I was here in 2008. We bonded when they insisted on taking photographs of Rosita sitting behind a desk because they wanted to feature some non-white employees in the corporate brochure to prove how committed EMF was to 'diversity' (untrue, insulting and quite possibly illegal, but they did it anyway). There's been such a turnover of staff in the interim that I haven't seen a single soul I knew back then since I started here in October. Not one. I didn't think there was anyone left who could recognise me and give the game away.

'So happy to see you, Katie,' said Rosita. 'What you doing here?'

'Oh, hi. Uhmmmhhmm.'

'Kate works here,' said Jay-B irritably. 'You two know each other?'

Do you believe in divine intervention? I'm not sure I do, but at that exact moment Claire from Human Resources appeared at the door, behind Rosita. 'I'm so sorry to interrupt, Jay-B,' she said. 'Kate, I'm afraid it's your mother. She's had a fall. Your sister called the switchboard.'

Kate to Richard

Mum's had a fall. Suspected broken hip. Julie's with her at the hospital. I've jumped on a train. Please don't say anything to the kids till I know what's happening. Lasagne and green beans for dinner in the fridge. Lenny's food is in the utility. Give him wet and dry and fill up his water bowl. Expecting a delivery of tiles tomorrow for our shower. Please sign for them. Emily needs to get on with her revision. Can you remind her gently? K xx

4.43 pm, Beesley Cottage Hospital: Last time I was up here visiting my mum, I confiscated her high heels and hid them at the back of the wardrobe. Most women in their mid-seventies don't need to be told that flat shoes are the sensible option. They slide unprotesting into slip-ons; with good grace, they accept that tottering along in stilettos is no longer wise. Not my mother. When she came down for Christmas, I took her to a small shoe-shop on the edge of town, and when the girl brought back a selection of robust, age-appropriate footwear, Mum held up one pair and said loudly, 'They look like rubber Cornish pasties, do these.'

'We find our older ladies like the grip and the stability that this particular shoe provides,' soothed the sales assistant.

'I'm not elderly,' objected my mother.

Now, here she is lying on a bed in a side-ward, much whiter than the sheets, having fallen down some steps whilst wearing what she calls 'my good day-shoes'. She found the ones I'd hidden. Black patent with a gold buckle. One shoe, its two-inch heel bent back to one side, sits forlornly on a chair with Mum's clothes beside it.

She's asleep. I kiss her cheek and hold her hand, her crêpey hand, gnarled now with arthritis, probably from all those vegetables she peeled, the dishes she washed. Even at Christmas she was busy doing, always asking, 'What can I do next?' Never happy sitting down. I can feel the sparrow bones beneath the loose skin. The first hand that held mine.

'You didn't need to come all that way, love.' Her eyes are open now, a milky film across the left one.

'I heard you'd been out dancing again.'

She smiles. 'Is it Tuesday?'

'No, Mum, it's Thursday.'

'*Is it?*' She's still confused after her fall, the nurse said.

'Emily and Ben?'

'They're good. Really good.'

'Beautiful children. Such beautiful children. The nurse says I fell over.'

'Yes, you cracked your hip. But you're all right now, thank goodness. Julie and I'll look after you.'

'Is it Tuesday?' Agitated now. Upset.

'Yes. Yes. It's Tuesday, Mum. Don't worry.'

'Are you stopping, love?'

'Of course I am. I'll be right here. Where else am I going to be, silly?'

That seems to calm her. She shuts her eyes and allows sleep to carry her off. My mother looks so small and shrunken in her hospital gown. Julie's gone home to pick up a nightie and some toiletries for her. As I knew she would, my sister is already using the accident to redouble her campaign for me 'making a bigger contribution' and generally getting at me. We quarrelled. In the car park, just after I'd got to the hospital. Ancient rancours rankled. Julie drove off, her parting shot hanging in the air like gunsmoke: 'If Mum goes home it's not you who'll be taking care of her, is it, Kate?'

I am sitting here, by the bedside, willing my mother to get better, to be her old self again, and that is because I want her to be well, more than anything I do, but also because Julie's right. I can't stay with her, not for much longer. I play the voicemail left for me by Jay-B. This is the second time I've listened to it. Says he's 'extremely sympathetic to your situation, Kate, but do keep us posted'.

Translation: you have two days more out of the office tops before we start looking for someone else. It would be slightly different if I had a proper job, but I'm just maternity cover. The last thing EM Royal wants is to find cover for the person who's covering. My position there is as precarious as my mother in her patent heels.

I pull the chair closer to the bed and switch my phone off. About time I started following the advice from *Parenting Teens in the Digital Age*. I don't want any messages from work, or from anybody else. I want to give my mother my full attention. I listen to her breathe in and out, watch the hospital gown gently rise and fall.

Despite her tumble, Mum's face still bears signs of being carefully made up: foundation, powder, her hair freshly washed and curled this morning before she went out to her 'do'. 'Make the best of yourself', she always said to Julie and me. It was her mantra. How she hated it when I came home from college that time in a pair of washed-out green dungarees. ('What in the name of heaven do you think you're wearing, young lady?') My mother's generation, their role was domestic, maternal, ornamental. Femininity, womanly self-image was vital, a matter of survival because, if you couldn't attract a mate and hang onto him, society had precious little use for you. No wonder she always judged my appearance harshly. I see it clearly now. Mum wasn't putting me down, she was arming me for battle the only way she knew how. No wonder my life – a life not lived by, through and for a man – seems so mystifying to her.

Aren't I guilty of something similar with Emily? I am careful not to comment on her weight, of course I am, but I hate pretty much all of her clothes except the ones I bought; is there some hardwired thing that makes you scold your daughter if she doesn't look presentable enough to attract the opposite sex? Are all mothers secretly Mrs Bennet in *Pride and Prejudice*, fretting about their girls' marriageability? Times change, but not the imperative to pass on your genes.

'Jooo.' Mum is talking in her sleep. 'Jooo.' For a moment, I think she's calling my dad. I lean over and put my hand on her cheek. 'It's OK, you're all right, nothing to worry about.'

She loved him, despite everything – she could never stop herself. For Julie and me, Dad was an open wound, an embarrassment who only featured in our lives when he needed a loan. ('Can you sub me till Saturday, love?') He even turned up at my office in the City once asking for investment in one of his crazy schemes. Security thought he was a tramp. I've never felt the gap between where I came from and the place I'd got to so acutely. At least my kids have got a loving father they can rely on, even if Rich has been a bit elusive lately.

I remember the evening my first boyfriend, David Kerney, put two and two together and worked out that he and my father belonged to the same table-tennis club. 'Oh, your old man's a right ladies' man,' he said. 'He's got Elaine and Christine both on the go.'

I must have been fourteen – Ben's age – and it was a shock to realise that the world would have a view on my parents, and not necessarily a favourable one. That tingle of shame stayed with me; I can feel it now.

For Mum it was different; Dad was her first and, I'm guessing, her only lover. We can hardly comprehend what that would mean to a person now, those of us who can count our sexual partners on two hands or more, and may even have forgotten some altogether. As for Emily's generation having virtual sex

391

on a phone with people they've never even met; what does that spell for human intimacy and commitment?

Mum stirs again and I find myself thinking: what would she make of Jack? Well, she'd recognise the irresistible charm, that's for sure. But, no. I give my head a shake to dislodge the idea. Jack doesn't belong IRL. Impossible to imagine him meeting my mum, Julie, seeing my home town. I'm not ashamed of it – I was when I was young and insecure – but, still, it would be like taking Cary Grant to KFC. With that incongruous image in mind, I lay my head down on the bed, next to my mother's hand, and drift away.

When I switch the phone back on two hours later, there is an email from Debra. (Subject: Shoot Me!) Don't even bother to open that one, not another Tinder pervert cock-up. There's a text from Emily, which, mercifully, is not acid at all. Says she's meeting friends IRL instead of online. And one from Abelhammer – the sight of his name, as always, causing a feeling of deep delight, desire, bordering on helplessness, stronger than ever since our cream tea. I ask myself what it was in me that I set about hanging my heart around Jack's neck with such abandon. I've never had a reckless moment in my life and yet now, with this man . . .

Jack to Kate
When will I see you again? When will we share precious moments? Can we at least get Afternoon Tea? In London tomorrow. I remain your devoted servant, J x

Kate to Jack
Are you really reduced to quoting the Three Degrees at me? It used to be Shakespeare. My mum had a fall and I'm at the

hospital with her. Won't be back down South for a few days. Maybe tomorrow. Miss you. K xx

Jack to Kate
Really sorry about your mum. Can I help? Just say the word and I will leap tall buildings in a single bound. I knew you'd be familiar with the next line of the song, that's all. (*'Roy, Three Degrees lyrics, please.'*) XXO

Mum seems a lot brighter after her sleep. She asks me to look in her handbag for her reading glasses. I notice her building society book has got a wad of notes in it. That's odd. Must be at least two hundred pounds. Not like my mother to carry lots of cash. I let the book fall open in the place where the notes are and spot a dark cluster of recent withdrawals on the right-hand page. £1,700, £2,600, £3,300, £950. £2,100. Good grief.

'Have you been on a bit of a spree, Mum?'

'What's that, love?'

'I know you wanted a new carpet, but I didn't know it was going to be woven from gold.'

'Oh, it's not for the carpet, love,' she smiles, taking her glasses from my hand. 'Our Julie says you need to pass money on to your children while you're young enough or the government'll take it off you later on. That's right, isn't it?' A sudden note of doubt in her voice.

Steady, Kate, steady. 'Yes, yes, that's right. You're allowed to give so much as a gift, Mum, every year. It's very kind of you.'

'Julie says you and the children can have some as well.'

'We're fine, Mum, don't you worry. You hang onto your nest egg.' At that moment, I notice my sister standing perfectly still in the doorway. I've seen that look on her face before.

Forty years before. When the coins I was soaking overnight in vinegar to clean for Brownies went missing, and Julie swore she hadn't seen them.

We don't exchange a single word on the drive back to Julie's house. My sister lives behind the school where Mum used to work as a dinner lady, ten minutes' walk from our mother's house. I haven't been here for a while and there have been definite moves to smarten up the estate. New windows on some of the houses, potholes filled in. One place that had been boarded up, after a problem family was moved, is being rebuilt. The year is still young, and the wind unkind, but the sun has come out for the occasion.

Julie says nothing as she fishes the front-door keys from her bag, lets us in, takes me through to the kitchen, and puts the kettle on. Then she stands with her back to the counter, still in her coat, and faces me.

'Go on, say it,' she says.

'What? Say that you've been helping yourself to Mum's savings account, telling her she needs to give her money to you or it'll be taken off her?'

'You're the financial whizz kid.'

'Julie.'

'OK, OK, our Steven got himself in a bit of trouble online. Kept trying to tell you about it, but you're always busy.'

'What kind of trouble?' Steven is in his twenties now, still living at home, still looking for a job, though never looking too far from the sofa, as far as I can tell. His father left years ago and there have been a couple of live-in boyfriends since, neither of them good enough for my sister.

'Something to do with betting,' Julie says, snatching the tea towel from the ring by the sink and squeezing it tight in her fist. 'All I know is he thought he was on a winning streak and it got out of hand.'

'How much?'

'Twenty-four grand.'

'Christ.'

'Yeah, but what I didn't know is he thought he could borrow to pay it off. One of them day things.'

'Payday loans.'

'That's the one. Well, they came to the door and he was shitting himself . . .'

'Have you got the contract?'

'You what?'

'Steven must have signed something for the loan.'

'I don't know, I'll have to ask. He's probably lost it. He loses everything, that lad.'

'Sounds like Ben. Can't find his own socks when they're on his feet.' Trying to reach out here, soothe the moment, find some common ground. It doesn't work. My sister flies back at me.

'If that lad of yours can't find a bloody sock it's because you've spoiled him rotten and fetched and carried and—'

'Julie, please—'

'Please nothing, you take them on fancy holidays, where was it this year? And oh, Mummy, can I have a new PlayStation, please Mum, the old one's out of date. And Mummy, I'm worried about how many A bloody stars I'm going to get in my exams, please can I have a special tutor to help, like all the other rich tossers' kids? And meanwhile poor Auntie Julie, *proper* poor, who lives up North in a house the size of your kitchen, oh, she's fine, she can take care of Grandma, right? I mean, it's not like she's got anything better to do.'

'That's not—'

'And oh, Mummy would love to help Auntie Julie out, but

she's ever so busy helping people with too much fucking money make some more money, you know, just in case they run out of helicopters, 'cos you never know, do you? Like you want to get to Abi bloody Dabi in a rush, and money can buy you everything, right, especially with Mummy on your case. I mean, money really can buy you love, can't it, Kath?'

'No, it can't.' I'm staring down at the floor.

'Well, let's find out, eh? Let's hope that some of that lovely cash comes out of the fucking skies, what do they call it, the trickle-down? Trickle all the way into Steven's pocket, so's the men won't come knocking at the door at half past six in the morning. Next time they said they'd bring a dog. Well, I love that lad, he's a fucking idiot but I love him, he's mine, and he's got no A levels, none, and no bloody tutors, thank you, and no father to speak of, he's got debts up to his ears and he's scared shitless, and if I have to borrow money from Mum, our mum, to stop that, then yes I bloody well will. 'Cos money can't buy you love, can it, but it can stop someone from going up to your kid and breaking his fucking arm, and that'll do me. That's love where I come from. Where *you* come from, in case you've forgotten.'

My sister stops for breath, chest heaving, like a long-distance runner. I make no reply, but get the jar of coffee out of the cupboard and the milk from the fridge. Make two large mugs, set them on the table, and sit down. Julie stays where she is. Then she fetches a tin of biscuits and puts them between us.

'Not your fancy kind,' she says.

'Thank God. I hate fancy biscuits.'

'You're just saying that.'

'No, I'm not. Like I hate posh chocolates.'

'Never had them.'

'You haven't missed much. Client gave me a box he brought

396

from Switzerland, made a big fuss about how special they were. Told me to keep them in the fridge because they had fresh cream in them.'

'That's disgusting.'

'Too right. I had one and it was all oily. Like conditioner. So I rearranged the rest and did the bow up and gave them to someone else as a birthday present at work. Then I got the biggest bar of Fruit & Nut I could find and ate the whole thing.'

Julie puts her hands around her mug, for warmth. 'So we haven't lost you completely then?' she asks.

'Lost me?'

'To all the tossers.'

'Never will do, love. Don't worry.' I reach out and take a custard cream. As I take a first bite, I see Richard's face wincing. Unrefined carbs! He'd probably make biscuits illegal.

'Julie?'

'Still here.'

'So, if we borrow some of it from Mum now and I give some – sorry, I haven't got that kind of money going spare with Richard not working – will Steven be all right? Or is there some rolling clause that keeps him in debt forever?'

'I, I don't know. I just have this bad feeling he'll get sucked back in.'

'That's not going to happen. But look, one thing about the tossers. I mean the tossers I work with. They know about loans. It's what they do.'

'Yeah, but those are for millions and millions. Steven's unemployed.'

'Same principle. I give you a fiver, or five hundred million, doesn't matter. We agree the terms and then you pay me back. That's why, if there *is* a piece of paper about Steven's loan, or even an email, it would be a big help. Then I can show it to a friend at the office and we'll work this out. Honestly, it'll be fine.'

'You think?'

'I think. The only bit that really worries me about all this is Mum.'

'I know. I'm sorry.'

'I mean, you know what she's like. She'd give us the clothes off her back if we asked her for them—'

'Or even if we didn't.'

'Exactly. But that's all the more reason not to take advantage of her on the quiet.'

'But if I told her the real reason why I needed the money, can you imagine, it would kill her. Steven got the flu last year and she was calling every ten minutes, said she couldn't sleep with the worry. Imagine if I said there were these big blokes at the door wanting to beat him up. She'd bloody die.'

'I know, you're right.' I sigh and sip my coffee. 'It's not the white lies, Christ, look at me. Not telling the truth is like my basic diet.'

'Thought that were Fruit & Nut.'

'Chocolates and lies. Sounds like a film.'

'What lies do you tell, then?'

'Well, everyone at work thinks I'm forty-two for a start.' At which my sister laughs – the first happy sound she's made all day. *Go with the happiness, Kate, while it lasts.*

'How come?'

'I couldn't get a job if I told them I was going on fifty.'

'You're fucking joking,' my sister objects, suddenly on my side again. 'What's up with fifty? Do they think your brain dries up with your womb or what?'

'That's about it.'

'Rubbish. You were always the brightest. Not like me. You

got things before anyone else saw there was anything to get. Our Steven, he's like you with arithmetic. Barely has to see a column of figures before he's got the answer. Daft bugger thought he could beat the odds, though, and no one does that, do they?'

'Julie, I want to make a contribution to Mum's care. You do so much, you're on call twenty-four seven.'

'I'm not taking your money. I don't need paying to look after our mother.'

Here's the nub of it. Money may not be the root of all evil, but scrape back the earth a little and it's the seed of most family resentments. 'Look, if you weren't here Mum'd be on her own and we'd have to be paying someone to go in, wouldn't we? Remember my friend Debra? Well, her mum's got dementia and they're paying one thousand two hundred quid a week for some place on the South coast. Daylight robbery. You'll do a much better job than any care worker and Mum'll need a lot of help when she comes out. Because we've got you nearby we're saving all that money. It makes financial sense if I give you something every month.'

I can see that mentioning financial sense has been helpful for Julie's pride. It mustn't look like charity.

'Well,' she says cautiously, 'if you think I'm worth it. Not going to lie, it'll be a big help way things have been here.' My sister reaches across the table and takes my hands.

'Kath, I'm sorry about what I said . . .'

'No, you're right. My life's a mess. It's a mess with money and a nice house, but it's still a mess.'

'Try a mess without money some time.'

'Could happen, Julie. I may have to sell the helicopter. Well, the backup one, anyway. The standby chopper at the bottom of the garden. I mean, what a bloody disaster.'

'How would little Ben get to school on time?'

'Poor lamb.'

'With one sock.'

'Now you'll make me cry.' For a minute, we are twelve and fourteen again, giggling on our beds about boys. Some things never change. Not many, just a handful, but enough.

Friday, 7.21 am, Beesley Cottage Hospital car park: As if to prove his Auntie Julie right, my pampered princeling woke up this morning, noticed that his personal maid was absent and was not impressed.

Ben to Kate
Wheres football shorts

Kate to Ben
Did you check the bottom drawer in your chest of drawers where the summer sports kit is kept? Xx

Ben to Kate
not there

Kate to Ben
You can do better than that, sweetheart. Check the chest of drawers again and then ask Daddy to help you. Did Sam borrow them after the sleepover? I just have to talk to Grandma's nurse, but I will get back to you in 10 minutes.

Ben to Kate
not my responsability. When u back

Kate to Ben
Responsibility has three 'i's, mister! And it sort of is your

responsibility as you're a big boy now. Grandma is a lot better and I'll be home tonight. Remember to eat breakfast and take two Omega fruit softies – in orange bottle next to the bread bin. Remember to wear your bike helmet, OK? And make sure your phone is charged not like last time! Miss you. Xx

Kate to Richard
Please can you stop meditating or whatever it is you're doing and help Ben find his football stuff? My mum's fine in case you were wondering. Kx

Correcting Ben's spelling of 'responsibility' could be seen as 'unsupportive' and 'hypercritical', which are specifically forbidden by *Parenting Teens in the Digital Age*. Book says I need to 'tweak' my parenting skills 'to keep up with the developing young adult'. Apparently, this means 'strengthening child compliance through positive reinforcement'.

Bugger that. Julie's right. I need to stop babying Benjamin and help him to grow up.

Richard to Kate
Calm down please. I am picking up a lot of negative energy which is very destructive. Everything is absolutely fine here. Please give Jean my love.

9.44 am: The senior nurse has invited me to take a seat in her office, a pleasant room with French windows looking onto a green space – you couldn't call it a garden exactly – with newly planted young trees: birch, I think. Mum would know, so would Sally. On the wall behind Nurse Clark is one of those year planners; it bristles with coloured stickers and reminders for medication to be given.

She has just handed me a clutch of forms about 'continuing care needs' when a call from Jay-B jangles my mobile into life. Ben's latest prank is to give his technophobic parent the ringtone of a phone circa 1973, when my mother still used to go into the ice-cold hall, pick up the receiver and say, 'Batley Four-Two-Nine'. That world of telephone exchanges and operators who spoke with the clipped consonants of Celia Johnson feels impossibly distant.

Since her fall, past and present have blurred for my mother. One minute, she is here with me in the present day, the next she is holding my hand and taking us, Julie and me in our matching pinafore dresses, to Sunday school. Mum made those dresses herself from a Simplicity pattern; I remember her kneeling on the floor, holding pins in her teeth, as she carefully laid the paper on the material. No matter how little money we had, she always wanted her children to look smart. I inherited that from her.

'They're dead complicated, them forms,' says the nurse.

I don't like her. I made up my mind about that the minute we met. I don't like her harshness disguised as jollity. She is cruel, I think. I don't like the way she talks about my mother as if she weren't there, or adopts the sing-song voice you use to a small child when addressing her. But, please observe, how strenuously nice I am to the nurse! My face aches from using every reserve of charm I possess. I treat her like my most important and most difficult client. I need her to like me because I am about to leave my mother in her hands, and I fear that, if I annoy her for some reason, or she thinks I'm some posh Southern cow, then she could take it out on Mum.

'Yes,' I say, glancing down at the mobile, 'but I want to get the best support for Mum that I can.' A second voicemail from

Jay-B – oh, hell. I can practically hear his manicured fingernails drumming on his desk. Need to get back.

'Not bad news, I hope?' says the nurse eagerly. 'Now, please don't worry about your mum, Kate. She's our responsibility and we'll make sure she's fine until she's right enough to go home.'

'Thank you so much, you're very kind. My sister, Julie, she'll be in this afternoon. Can you give Mum my love when she wakes up?'

'Of course we will. Your cab's here.'

On the way out, I look in on my mother who is in a deep sleep. The tube in her left hand has created a throbbing, inky blue vein which looks painful. Every time I leave her, since the heart attack, every time, the same unspoken thought: is this the last time I'll see you? Wish I could stay. Can't stay. Duty calls. But duty also says this is where you should be. After all these years, I'm still serving two masters: love and work.

*Roy confirms the next lines in the Three Degrees song Jack quoted: 'Are we in love, or just friends?/Is this my beginning/ Or is it the end?' Good question. 'What's the right answer, Roy? All suggestions gratefully received.'

23

NEVER CAN SAY GOODBYE

Monday, 2.30 pm: Through the candle flame, across the snowy linen of the tablecloth, glass of deep red Burgundy in hand, Jack Abelhammer trains his gaze upon me. Waiters glide soundlessly past. The double string of pearls around my neck, his latest gift, loops downwards, into the shadow between my breasts. He reaches out towards me. Fingers graze.

That, at any rate, was how I had pictured the scene. Which only proves that picturing, which is what women spend half their lives doing (well, I do), is a total waste of headspace. For here we are – face to face, it is true – in Gino's, an all-day café located in the groin of Aldgate East. Gino's is a lot like Michael's, (Candy's and my old haunt), although the teaspoons are plastic not metal. Wedged into the adjacent table are three builders, churning through their mountainous breakfasts at half past two in the afternoon. ('Why d'you have bubble instead of chips?' 'Got cabbage in it. Roughage. Keeps you regular.' 'Fuck off. If you're so regular, mate, why'd you turn up at half past eight this fucking morning, rather than quarter to like the big man says?') I have a cold coming. You cannot see the shadow between my breasts, but you *can* see the sore patch underneath my nose from all the blowing and sneezing, so that's the Ingrid Bergman impersonation buggered.

'I'm sorry about lunch today, Jack. And dinner the night before last. And that thing later in the week, that we talked about, I don't think I'll be able to do that either. Not with Mum the way she is. I need to go back up when they let her out to settle her at home. And things are a bit of a mess with my sister too.'

'Oh, what kind of mess?'

'You don't want to know.'

'Actually, I want to know everything about you if that's OK?'

'It's just horribly complicated.'

'Try me. I did a minor at college in Applied Chaos and Complexity Theory.'

'Perfect. Sounds like my life.' The truth is I'm reluctant to share the sordid hinterland of the Reddy clan with Jack. I don't know if my glamorous, funny beau can bear too much reality. Our relationship has never been stress-tested in the real world of tricky teenagers, ailing parents and gambling-addict nephews, and it never will be.

Jack must have read my mind because he says, 'C'mon, Kate, you really think you can shock me?'

'No. It's just, well, when I was at the hospital, I saw that money had been taken out of my mum's building society book.'

'Her checking account?'

'Sort of. Savings. I mean, quite small sums to . . . well, cab money to you, Jack, but large for my mother. And it turns out my sister had got Mum to give her the money because Julie's son, that's my nephew, Steven, he'd been online gambling. Got

405

totally out of control, then the stupid kid thought he'd found a way to pay it back.'

'Let me guess. Shark name of Duane prepared to lend at a very reasonable one thousand two hundred and ninety one per cent APR?'

Despite everything, he makes me laugh. 'Oh, I see you're already acquainted with Mr Duane, the Robin Hood of Redcar.'

'Sure am. Good Credit Record not needed. Cash will be in your hand in ten minutes, you gullible, terrified poor person.'

'How do you know so much? You've never been gullible or poor.'

'Let's just say I gained some valuable insight after my mom got into an abusive relationship with a casino.'

'She was a gambler?'

'A happy drunk. She thought the roulette wheel was her new best friend. Got in too deep, was scared my dad would find out, tried to hide her losses. We had some pretty interesting gentleman callers at the house when I was in eighth grade.'

'That's terrible. What did you do?'

'I came up with a smart strategy to amortise the loans.'

'But, you were only a kid.'

'Technically, yes, but you can become an adult pretty quickly if you have to. Now, Katharine, can you please explain the relationship between squeak and bubble?'

'Jack, I'm sorry, we really don't have long.'

'Don't worry, Kate. We have plenty of time.'

'Until you fly back to New York next week.'

'Yes, and there's this amazing thing you can do nowadays. Friend of mine was telling me about it. Apparently, you can fly back in the other direction, too. Turns out I don't have to stay in the United States for the rest of my life. I can come back again. To see you.'

'And then what?'

'Then we come back here. To Gino's. I'm going to come here, again and again, until somebody tells me what bubble is. Whatever it takes.'

'What about your job?'

'I run the company, Kate. Nobody owns me. I own me. And my job is a good excuse for coming here to see you. Until, you know.'

'Until what? Till you've had enough?'

'Till you own me,' Jack says.

'Hostile takeover bid.'

'Exactly. Aggressive merger. Remember I have shares in you.'

I look down at my cup. I ordered a latte, but what arrived is more like a rock pool on a polluted shoreline. Stir it once with the plastic spoon, twice, ten times, stirring my thoughts. I have to tell him.

'I can't be with you, Jack. Please don't be angry. I'm really sorry. I've tried before. But I tried and failed. Remember. Years ago, when we met, and I thought, like a Disney princess, that all my dreams had come true. My Prince had come.'

'My lady—'

'Please. Listen to me. And you *were* my prince. I checked. You still are. In an ideal world, we would run a terrific kingdom, the best, and I would love to live there with you, I really would. But . . .'

'I knew there'd be a but. There's always a but.'

'But the world is not ideal. Never was, never will be. Ideals are for people who are free, for people who can act for themselves. I can't, I have to think of other people. I have so many people who depend on me. The thing with ideals is they don't inspire. They screw you up, make you sad, always dangling there out of reach.'

407

'I should warn you, Katharine, that you're talking to an American. We have ideals like you British have rain. It's what makes us raise our eyes to the skies every day.'

'You said it. We have rain. And I'm almost fifty, Jack, and I feel so fucking rained on. I worry all the time about my children, my daughter especially; I worry about my mum, my sister, my husband's parents, my best friend who's basically a functioning alcoholic, my dog, my work, my health – which frankly is a bit of a landslide. And I know it sounds pathetic, but it's all too much. I can't break free, I just can't. You're wonderful, but you're, you're . . . being with you is like watching the skies. Heavenly, but it doesn't *get* me anywhere. I'm still here.'

Jack's turn to stir. 'Well, I hate to raise it,' he says. 'But how about the L word?'

'The what word?'

'L. Don't you have that over here?'

'We do. It stands for Labrador. The one guarantee of emotional support that everyone in this country can rely on. The Beatles said it best. All you need is Labrador. Da-da-da-da-dah.'

'Well, there you go. People will think we're in Labrador. And they'd be right. We are. And when people are in Labrador, it's generally agreed that just being there gives them the strength to do something about it. Make it work.'

'But don't you see, strength is the one thing I don't—'

'Please,' he says, smiling. That smile. Never fails. 'Your turn to listen now, OK? I completely understand about the rain. You can't switch it off; it's not coming out of a tap. Those things, all those worries, are real. But so is us. Look at us. We're as real as, I don't know . . .'

'As the human hair currently floating in your cappuccino.'

'Exactly. The special of the day. You are *such* a romantic, Kate darling, you know that?'

First time he's called me that. Sounds great. I can bear a lot of darling from Jack.

'So am I, probably more of a romantic than you. What I say is, Christ, why not try walking through the rain? It's not the getting wet that's killing you, Kate, it's the standing there and getting wet and never making a move. Once we start to move, nothing else will feel as bad and impossible as it does right now. Move.'

I reach across the white tablecloth, past the candles and the cut-glass crystal, and the red bottle of Sarson's vinegar, and take his hand.

'Oh, Jack, why are you so bloody hopeful all the time?'

'American, Ma'am. Guilty as charged.'

'I just, if I'm honest I just can't see a way that things are ever going to change.'

He leans across the table and kisses me. 'OK, so I'm having some time in France before flying back to the States and you have all my contact details. And you can email or text me or call me any time and Jackson 5 third album. Kate? Go!'

Give me a second. 'I'll be there?'

'You got it. Now, what can I get you for your birthday?'

'Nothing, honestly, there's nothing to celebrate.'

We stand up and we kiss again. He must have my cold by now, but such is love. Jack puts a twenty-pound note under his coffee cup, to commemorate the occasion.

'Oh, God, now we'll have to come back,' I say. 'Gino will be waiting for us, like Tristan.'

'Any time,' says Jack. One more kiss, and I think, this could be the last kiss, the very last. As we leave, the voice of a builder, like a carolling angel, rings in our ears.

'Give her one for me, mate.'

We'll always have Gino's.

Outside, it's raining and I watch him walk away from me. *Again. You sent him away again.*

3.39 pm: Feel totally numb on the way back to the office, but there is good news. Alice greets me with a hug. Gareth has brought half-bottles of white wine and plastic glasses from the canteen. Troy is nowhere to be seen, and I soon discover why. The Board has approved Vladimir Velikovsky as a suitable client.

'They had certain caveats about "potential future outflow", etc,' Jay-B says as Gareth is pouring for all four of us. 'It would be bloody awful for the bottom line if he walked out the door in twelve months as Russians tend to when they're not getting thirty per cent returns.'

'Well, that's *my* job, isn't it? Making sure the client is happy. I'm confident we can do that. Can't we, Alice?'

'Anyway, good job, Kate. Cheers!'

'Cheers, everyone! We must start looking for a boarding school in need of a new science block that will be happy to have Sergei Velikovsky as a pupil.'

'You're kidding,' says Jay-B.

'She's not. Kate is EM Royal's expert on bespoke tutoring services,' says Gareth, actually winking at me.

'All part of the service. Alice, will you take a look at the league tables? Spot any struggling old schools that could do with some Russian dosh.'

'Will do.' She's been a bit subdued since getting back after Christmas. Max spent the festive season in Barbados with Mummy and Daddy. After five days, when she hadn't heard anything, Alice cracked and texted him, 'Do you miss me?' and Max replied, 'Course.'

She showed me his text. No kiss, no 'of' before the course, not even a full stop for heaven's sake. The guy's a jerk. An ungrammatical jerk.

'It's not great, is it, Kate?' she said.

'Well, I must admit I've seen more enthusiastic declarations of devotion. Look, Alice, you deserve better than this, sweetheart. You know what they say, "Don't put all your eggs in one bastard."'

She grins despite herself. 'Who says that?'

'Well, I do. And so should every sane woman in her late twenties. You know my views on that subject.'

She nods. 'I know. I've tried to move on, honestly I have. But I love him. Can't help it. While we're on the subject of love, I like your Jack.'

'Jack, he's not mine,' I say, choosing my words with care. I know now that he's mine; I just can't be his, that's all.

'Course he's yours,' says Alice decisively. 'Never seen anyone who was more anyone's in my entire life.'

The team – I realise I'm starting to think of Gareth and Alice as *my* team – return to their desks and I just sit there to savour what is truly a bittersweet moment: the Velikovsky triumph balanced against the aching defeat of saying goodbye to Jack. Can't imagine life without him, like a world without music or sunlight. At least the VV deal means EMR will probably extend my contract when Arabella gets back from maternity leave. If so, I can start to plan for the future. Not stress quite so much. Maybe Calamity Girl can take it easier, get out of the air-traffic control tower once in a while, see the house finished, steady the ship. It's all perfectly manageable. Pick up my phone and there's an email from someone at Emily's school. Oh, no. Please, no.

411

From: Jane Ebert
To: Kate Reddy
Subject: Emily
Dear Mrs Reddy,
I've tried to contact you several times by phone without success. I'm afraid we may have the wrong number for you? I head up the Child Protection staff here at the school. It was brought to our attention recently that a pornographic image of your daughter, Emily, was shared both within her year group and then more widely. A male and a female student have been suspended as a result.

We treat cases of this kind with the utmost seriousness. I would like to invite you to come into the school to discuss Emily's situation and work through any issues arising from it.

Jane Ebert
Acting Head of Sixth Form

I snatch up my bag and coat and head for the lift, issuing instructions over my shoulder. 'Alice, sorry, got to run. Something cropped up at home. Can you cover with Jay-B for me?'

'Sure. Kate?'

I turn to see her eager young face. 'Yes?'

'Honestly, it's been such a brilliant day. Well done, you.'

24

For Whom the Belfie Tolls

Monday, 7.03 pm: Just back from school. Mrs Ebert filled me in on what had been happening about Emily and the belfie. I thought it was safely in the past after Josh Reynolds zapped any future social media circulation of Em's bum, but it turns out the image had been saved on certain kids' phones. Lizzy Knowles and her boyfriend, one Joe Clay, basically made sure the entire sixth form had seen it, and Joe, egged on by Lizzy Macbeth, had since been torturing Emily with threats to send it to family members via Facebook. All of this only came to light, Mrs Ebert explained, because, a few days ago, a member of staff confiscated Joe's phone when he caught the boy looking at porn during a lesson. As the mobile was unlocked, the teacher was not only able to look at Joe's photos, some of which were pretty hardcore, but also spotted #FlagBum with Emily's name next to it and many lewd comments underneath. The school suspended Joe and Lizzy immediately although, when Emily was called in, she begged them not to.

'Emily said she didn't want any more trouble,' Mrs Ebert sighed. 'It's incredibly difficult to know how to respond. We know there's a huge amount of sharing sexual images among teenagers, Mrs Reddy, and we do want to clamp down on it. But we're in uncharted territory, and I'm afraid to say many parents are still in denial. Lizzy Knowles's mother actually argued that we had breached her daughter's human right to privacy by asking to look at her phone, and threatened to take legal action against the school.'

Cynthia? I bet she did. Never rattle the gilded cage of the Tiger Mother. I looked at Mrs Ebert as she rubbed her forehead vigorously with her knuckle. Probably the same age as me, but more lined and careworn. Imagine trying to deal with parents like Cynthia Knowles, who always take their ghastly child's side, not the poor teacher's. That's another huge change since I was a kid. Whatever happened to backing up authority? Parents can't be bothered to discipline their offspring any more – either too busy or too timid – and then they get irate when someone else has to do the job for them. It must make Mrs Ebert's life hell.

'What I don't understand,' I said, 'is why this is surfacing now when the belfie incident happened at the start of last term. Emily made an innocent mistake sending a picture of her summer tan lines to Lizzy. She wasn't sharing sexual imagery, Mrs Ebert, I assure you. I had no idea that this would . . .'

'Come back to bite her?'

'On the bum, unfortunately.'

We both laughed, that poor harassed woman and I – the acrid, despairing laughter of two adults dealing with something no one in human history has ever had to face before. 'Look, Mrs Reddy.'

'Kate, please call me Kate.'

'Look, Kate, I'm not going to lie to you. We didn't get on to Emily's belfie fast enough because we simply don't have the resources. I'm a teacher not a porn-squad detective. If I spent

414

all the hours online that this problem deserves, well, I'd never be in the classroom. We do, however, have the option of involving the police.'

I told Mrs Ebert that, if Emily didn't want Lizzy and Joe Clay expelled, then Emily's father and I would support her. We didn't wish to make an official complaint. Tempting though the prospect was of screwing up any future Oxbridge application by Lizzy.

'What they did was absolutely revolting,' I said, 'but two kids can't be held responsible for a global epidemic. Emily's not underage, so I think involving the police is too extreme. These are young people with their whole lives ahead of them. Hopefully, this will have given them a nasty scare.'

I thought of Debra's Felix, that lost, insecure boy kicked out of school for looking at Fat German Hookers online. I thought of Ben and what he might be getting up to on one of his many electronic devices. While the temptation was there, no child was safe. You were kidding yourself if you thought it couldn't be your son or daughter next.

Mrs Ebert said Emily had been seeing the school counsellor, the one I'd arranged after her form tutor called me. Details were strictly confidential, of course, but her teachers thought she was doing much better and she did seem to have detached herself from Lady Macbeth and found a new friendship group.

'Emily's such a lovely girl,' Mrs Ebert said, and I could only nod vigorously while shaking her hand. I was too upset to reply.

Kate to Emily
Sweetheart, we need to speak. Where ARE you? Xx

Emily to Kate
Am at Jess's house doing our History. I'm fine. Pls don't worry bout me! Xx

Kate to Emily
Love you xx

Emily to Kate
♥ u too xx

8.23 pm: House is quiet. Ben at Sam's, Emily still at Jess's. I called her and she said they were having a great time, please could she stay a while longer. I'll talk to her about what Mrs Ebert said later. I can't stand the thought of her carrying all that hateful stuff alone. Am mincing Lenny's claggy, hypo-allergenic food with a fork when he starts growling. It means that Richard's coming. This is new, this growling at Richard – protective of me, I suppose. I've been psyching myself up to tell Rich about Emily and the belfie, and now is the time. I should never have tried to hide it even though Em made me promise not to tell him. Like Mrs Ebert said, the belfie was always going to come back to bite us one way or another.

So, am feeling both guilty and nervous when Rich comes in and puts his helmet on the counter. But I notice he looks even worse than I feel, positively queasy in fact. He seems terrified, like we've been burgled or something. And I see the scared way he looks at me and I think: oh my God, my mum has died. Or his mum has died. Or something's happened to Ben.

'What's wrong? Is everything OK?'

'I've got to tell you something,' he says.

'I've got to tell *you* something,' I say.

'No, Kate, I *really* have to tell you something. I feel, well I've been feeling for some time that I'm very stuck and I need to direct my energy where it wants to be.'

'Your energy is mainly directed towards your bike, Rich. I agree it might be better if it was directed at your children for instance. Look, I need to tell you, Emily's had problems at school. I've just been up to see the head of sixth form. Em took a picture of her bottom to compare tan lines with other girls after the summer holidays and one hideous girl, Lizzy Knowles, you know the one, well, she posted Emily's belfie, that's a photo of your bum, on social media and it went viral.'

Richard winces, the same pained look he gives when he catches me watching *Downton*. 'Why would Emily do something so idiotic?'

'Er, because she's an adolescent living in a Big Brother culture that encourages them to display themselves on social media. And they get addicted to the adulation and the Likes and they swipe right, or left, and they become objects to each other, not soulmates, and no one has any concept of privacy and the whole thing is fantastically fucked up quite frankly. Sorry, I was going to tell you before,' I say.

'Sorry, I was going to tell you before,' Rich says.

'What?'

'What? I've been trying to find a good moment to mention the pregnancy.'

'EMILY'S PREGNANT?'

'Joely.'

'*What?*'

'Joely's pregnant.'

'That girl who came round here at Christmas? Tofurky Joely?'

'Yes. She thought she might be losing the babies.'

'Babies. Plural? Twins? Yours?'

He won't look at me. My God, he's serious.

'Is this part of your spiritual development, Richard? Tofurking Joely while I'm working my arse off to keep the show on the road?'

'Kate, look I hope and believe we can sit down and discuss this in a constructive and civilised manner.'

'Really? Civilised? You think so, do you? What happened to, "Sorry, we can't have baby number three because we can't afford it, Kate. Because we've moved into a new phase of our lives, Kate. Because we don't want to go back to broken nights, Kate." The baby you decided I couldn't have?'

'I know how this looks,' he says, 'and I am incredibly sorry, really I am. It got complicated and you and I, we'd stopped talking and I should have, I didn't . . .'

'Use contraception? Or does Joely prefer to calculate her fertility by the cycles of the sodding moon?'

Richard doesn't answer immediately. Instead, he studies his cycling shoes and asks politely if he should pack a bag, as though he were going away for a long weekend, not leaving a relationship more than a quarter of a century old. I look around the kitchen, this room I have been doing up, along with the rest of the house, to make a wonderful home, a family fortress against the worst that life could throw at us.

And that's when it comes pouring out of me. All the rage and resentment which has been accruing interest in the Bank of Righteous Indignation. Richard's selfishness in putting his desire to do something meaningful and retrain as a counsellor before our financial security. 'How many men could have the luxury of doing that? No wonder all the other people on your bloody counselling course are women. Women with rich husbands who can indulge them as they take two years' unpaid leave to get a qualification while paying for extortionate therapy as well.'

A low blow, I admit it, but I was high on my sense of injustice, deeply upset about Emily, torn in half by sending Jack away so I could stick with the family Richard was now ditching for a pregnant pixie.

'How old is Joely anyway – twelve?'

'Actually, she's twenty-six.'

'God, she's half your age. What a cliché.' On I scorched. How many women would go along with the choice Richard had made? How many wives would get a stressful, full-time job when they were in the middle of the bloody menopause and feeling like death so their husband could 'enjoy living in the here and now' and perch his bony arse on a meditation mat? And how about Richard's increasingly long absences? Missing Ben's concert because he had to do mindfulness with Joely. Leaving me to worry about his parents, my mother, our children. Spending all our money – *my money* – on gear for that bloody bike of his.

'What exactly have you contributed, Richard?'

'That's not fair, Kate,' he says, literally reeling backwards from the verbal assault and falling into the chair by the Aga. 'I sold my other bike to pay for my therapy.'

'You sold your bike? When did you sell it?'

'I sold it over the summer to Andy from the club. He gave me four grand for it.'

Richard sold his other bike?

'Roy, there's something very wrong here. What am I supposed to remember about Richard's bike? Something happened with Richard's bike. Please find it, Roy. I don't know what it is, but I know it's really important.'

Lenny starts barking furiously and even bares his fangs at Richard. I get down on the floor and put my arms around his neck.

'We should never have got that bloody dog,' says Richard.

If anything sealed our marriage's demise, it was that remark. I don't bother to reply. Instead, I kneel there stroking my beloved friend, allowing him to administer urgent licks to my face.

You know, the strangest thing is how remarkably little I felt. About Joely. About the twins. (Twins? I told Alice men who

419

leave always go off and have twins. I didn't ever think that would be me.) I was shocked, yes, and distraught about the marriage we once had, Rich and I, but even in that first blast of hurt and outrage I knew I wasn't destroyed. The truth is I'd been living alone for a long time. Isn't that why I failed to put two and two together about what was going on with Joely? God knows Richard mentioned her enough, maybe he was even willing me to notice and challenge him, but I'd already tuned him out. I felt so desperately alone I started calling to Jack, willing him to be back in touch with me. And now I'd sent him away again, for good.

'Yes, Roy, what is it?' A memory surfacing. Something important, vitally important. Something I've been struggling to piece together, to put into words. Something about Richard's bike. My faithful old librarian is bringing it to me, I can hear the flipflap of his carpet slippers as he approaches, footfalls in the memory; he's almost here now. 'Come on, Roy, you can do it. Something about the bike.'

'Oh, God, I've been so blind.'

'You weren't to know about Joely,' Richard says. And then I start crying, really crying, and it isn't for us. 'I don't give a damn about Joely. Can't you see? It's Emily. Emily said she fell off your bike.'

'Did she?'

'She said she did. But she couldn't have because there wasn't a bike for her to fall off, was there? You sold it. Emily lied to me. Her legs. The cuts on her legs.' Closing my eyes, I see them now; they are regular, almost like thatching – one cut after the next in an even show of force and penetration. Stupid, stupid. *Of course she didn't fall off a fucking bike. What's wrong with me?*

'Kate?'

'She didn't have cuts because she fell off a bike, did she? Mr Baker said a third of the girls in Emily's year are depressed or self-harming. He *told* me, but I wasn't *listening*. I never thought Em would cut herself, not in a million years.'

'I don't understand.' Richard comes towards me, extending his arm, clearly distraught about Emily, but he is afraid to touch me, as if I'm on fire.

Tears are streaming down my face. I'm not weeping for myself and my menopausal woes, not for keeping it together at work pretending to be forty-two when I felt like I was ninety-six, not for my mum who fell off her high heels, not for Barbara who can remember the Latin words for shrubs but not the names of her own sons, not for Julie worried sick about Steven's gambling debt and too ashamed to tell me, not for telling Jack I can't violate the sanctity of my marriage and be with him when, all along, it turns out Richard has been seeing someone else. No, I'm weeping for my daughter who was so horribly sad and desperate that she could do that to herself. And I looked, but I was blind, heard her crying, but I was deaf.

And now a bell is ringing distantly. Don't ask for whom the belfie tolls, it tolls for thee.

'What's that noise?'

'Someone at the door,' says Richard.

'What?'

'The doorbell.'

On autopilot, I walk across the kitchen and turn the handle. A boy Ben's age is standing on the doorstep holding a small suitcase and a large box of Mozart marzipan chocolates. 'Good evening,' the boy says, 'I am Cedric from Hamburg. Very happy to meet you.'

25

CUT TO THE QUICK

11.20 am: You know if some big bad misogynist bastard set out to design something that would make girls feel totally crap about themselves, which would prey on every insecurity and diminish their sense of agency in the world, then he couldn't come up with anything better than social media, could he?

I mean, it's almost diabolically fit for purpose. Inviting a young female to photograph and scrutinise herself over and over before offering an image up to the world for comment. Oh, and you can Photoshop the picture so your waist looks teenier and your boobs look bigger, and your lips look poutier, and then you'll never dare be seen IRL because your online self is so perfect that the normal one is doomed to disappoint. That'll really help with all those teenage feelings of self-loathing and worthlessness.

Just one of the confused, angry, helpless thoughts I have had in the hours I've sat right here, on the orange plastic benches at the SHo Clinic – that's the Self-Harm Outpatients Unit of our local hospital. I'd never noticed the green, single-storey building before, tucked right behind the maternity unit. In a somewhat macabre way, the clinic turned out to be quite the social scene. The first time Emily and I came here, we were told to take a seat in the waiting room where we found three other girls from her year at school, also accompanied by their shellshocked parents. The girls half-smiled at each other, but then looked away; no one was sure about the etiquette in this strange new club they belonged to. Richard was supposed to be with us, but he had to accompany Joely to a scan that same afternoon. I was worried that Em would see this as another betrayal, but she just sighed and said, 'Honestly, Mum, Dad's such a plonker.'

One of the surprises I got after we broke the news that Richard and I were splitting up was that, while both children love their father deeply, they didn't have an especially high opinion of him. On hearing that Dad had a girlfriend, who was pregnant, Ben said, '*Eww*. Gross.' Emily was more outwardly emotional but, from the start, I was determined to make something positive out of this seismic event in our family life. If I overdid the Julie Andrews 'raindrops on roses and whiskers on kittens' routine, well, staying cheerful for the sake of the children helped keep me going as well. Once Richard had moved out, Ben grew three inches overnight and announced he was going to set me up a Tinder account 'to find you a boyfriend, Mum. So long as me and Em get to vet any weirdos, OK?'

I didn't mention Jack. What was there to say? I had sent him away and he had only texted me once since – a coolly noncommittal message about Provence being lovely at this time of year. After the way I'd treated him, I didn't feel I had the right to crawl back and plead for a second chance. Besides, the last thing the kids needed was another stranger entering their lives while their dad was shacked up down the road with Pippi Longstocking.

I just about managed to keep work going through this period, although it was a struggle. I didn't want to let Emily out of my sight. I was tormented by the fact she had been cutting herself without me noticing. When he called me that time at the office, Mr Baker told me a huge number of kids in her year were self-harming, but for some reason I was obscenely, irrationally confident that my own daughter would never do such a thing. Not Emily. How could I be so oblivious? What darkness had crept into my child's tender soul that she would cut into her own flesh with something sharp, repeatedly, on purpose? The marks on Emily's thighs were like angry cross-hatching, as if she had scraped against dozens of brambles, over and over. I couldn't see them without a sick lurch in my stomach.

When Emily was a few weeks old I cut her baby fingernails with rounded scissors and accidentally nicked her skin. Her cry, that first astonished accusation of treachery, came back to me a thousandfold when I saw the slashes on her legs. All those mistakes you make as a mother accumulate – is there a total-iser, do you suppose? – so you are doubly pained when they are injured as they get older. Maybe because you can do less about fixing things for them.

The counsellor here at the clinic said that Emily was no longer cutting herself: Lizzy's betrayal at New Year had shocked her into leaving the poisonous group to which she had clung so desper-ately. It was a really good sign, he said, that Emily was now comfortable enough to walk around the house with bare legs. It was when they were still hiding it that you had to be worried.

I blamed myself, of course I did. Had I not nurtured my daughter's self-confidence well enough? Did all our stupid bickering about clothes and juice diets and messy bedrooms make her feel she couldn't confide in me? Was I too anxious that she did as well as her A* peers in exams, and did I fail to protect her from that anxiety? In short, did I expect her to be the crazy, high-achieving workaholic I'd been for most of my life? Guilty as charged.

When Emily got home from Jess's house, the same night Richard told me about Joely and Cedric the German exchange student showed up at our door, she looked at my face and, instantly, she knew that I knew. Arm in arm, we went upstairs, sat on my bed and cried. 'I'm sorry. I'm sorry. I'm sorry,' we both said at the same time.

'I'm sorry I didn't know, my love.'

'Sorry I didn't tell you, Mum.'

It was agony for her to show me, and agony for me to look, but Emily's anguish was the greater. I might have guessed that the poison began with Lizzy Knowles. After some stupid kid left a boyband, it was Lizzy's idea that her group should join the #Cut4 cult to prove the depth of their devotion and grief. Emily told me it trended on Twitter; there were actual diagrams of how to do the cutting, and girls around the world shared images of harming themselves. *Uch.* The counsellor said Emily was particularly vulnerable because the belfie going viral made her ashamed and anxious that her friends didn't like her. For someone of my generation, all this was hard to get your head around, let alone the fact that it had become commonplace. Look at them all, sitting around me in this waiting room – lovely young women who seek to control emotional pain by inflicting it on their blameless bodies.

'Hello, Kate.'

I look up. Cynthia Knowles. (*'Thank you, Roy, I do recognise her. In a pink Chanel suit it could hardly be anyone else.'*)

'Funny place to meet,' Cynthia says. 'I mean, what strange

times we live in.' Nervous laughter. 'Lizzy, she's had a bit of a blip. And Emily too, I suppose . . . Such bad timing.'

'Sorry?'

'Their AS's are coming up in a few weeks. Hopefully, we can put all this behind us by then. It's just the marks in the AS will affect the A level grades, you know. I've looked into getting extra time for Lizzy in the exams, but self-harm doesn't count as a disability yet, I checked. We don't want this business –' with a heavily ringed hand Cynthia gestures around the room full of deeply unhappy girls '– to get in the way of their goals.'

There is that moment, you may know it, when all the pent-up anger inside you finds its perfect object. Cynthia is that object. 'My only goal for Emily,' I say, 'is for her to feel happy and loved and for her to realise that nothing else matters very much in the great scheme of things. I don't need to look to my child's exam results for my own self-worth because I have a job. Oh, here she comes now.'

Emily gives me a shy little wave as she emerges from a door opposite.

'Hi, Mum.'

'Hello, my love, shall we go?' Emily holds my hand and, as we turn towards the door, I say, 'Oh, Cynthia, just one more thing.'

'Yes, Kate.'

'Per se you can fuck right off.'

'Mummy, you swore at Lizzy's mum,' says Emily on the walk to the car.

'Did I, darling? That was very bad of me. Now, who wants to share a Five Guys vanilla milkshake?'

Julie to Kate

Hi there, just to say Mum's doing great, settled well at home. Don't worry about that Steven business. Got it all sorted.

426

Feeling much happier. Let me know if you need any moral support with the divorce. I'm a world expert! J xxx

From: Kate Reddy
To: Candy Stratton
Subject: 50th
Hi hon,

No, there's absolutely nothing I want for my Big Hideous Birthday. You know I've almost forgotten about it in all the chaos here and I definitely don't want a party. Planning on spending it quietly with the kids and the dog.

I don't know how to tell you this, but found out Emily was self-harming. Her lovely teacher told me it's extremely common. They're all doing it apparently, boys as well as girls. I Googled some websites and it's horrifying.

It's just so alien to me. I knew that I had to look out for anorexia, but THIS. I didn't know anyone who cut themselves when I was 16, did you?

Anyway, Em is doing much better, thank God. She's seeing a counsellor she really likes and he prescribed some medication, just to get the anxiety under control. We have done some family therapy sessions at a self-harm clinic and I have to admit Richard has been really great and supportive. Finally, all that counselling training pays off. Result!

It's still a work in progress, and it will take time, but Em stopped cutting a while ago and she isn't hiding her scars any more, which everyone says is a really good sign. She's been sleeping in my bed, just like when she was little, and I feel this primal urge to hold her close and give her comfort. Tbh, I much prefer sleeping with Emily to her dad!

Kind of you to say that Richard deserves to live unhappily ever after with the wellness elf. I sort of agree, but when I stop feeling angry I think that Rich was just really unhappy and our time of life can be brutal and shit happens. Particularly when a 26-year-old nymph is offering to get mindful with you.

Trying to keep everything as pleasant as possible. Being really positive with the kids and saying that 'Change is Good', as Madam Jekyll said to Mrs Hyde. We need to find a way to make this work for all our sakes. I'm coming to the end of my contract at EMR in a couple of weeks. Really need them to renew it or I don't know how we'll manage, particularly as I'm probably going to end up supporting twins. Pray for me!

In answer to your question, Jack was back in the picture and, briefly, my lover. Hammer every bit as able as we'd hoped. Plus, the guy bought me a clotted-cream tea so pretty near perfect. But I sent him away. Life is too complicated already. Plus, plus, I'm a big girl now, nearly that great unmentionable age, and I can manage by myself. For all the reasons above, I'm not exactly top of my own To Do List at the moment.

I'm Still Standing. Love you. K xx

26

REDEMPTION

12.20 pm: Just coming out of a meeting with a potential client on Threadneedle Street when I see Jay-B's been trying to contact me. Three voicemails, two texts, one email. Blimey, must be important.

From: Jay-B
To: Kate Reddy
Subject: Fucking Disaster!
Kate, major redemption threat from Geoffrey Palfreyman, our biggest private-client investor. Says they're unhappy with mediocre performance. Thinking of switching funds or increasing other asset classes at our expense. £25m down the toilet. Spoke to him. Doesn't want to see any more sales people, fed up with sales talk, wants to see fund manager. Not sure it should be me. Palfreyman's your aggressive, self-made Northern patriarch basically. Get in here as soon as you can. We need strategy or we're fucked.

I scan the street for a yellow light. Forget it. Cab will be too slow at this time of day. Run for Bank station. Shit. How many times have I told Jay-B that when the fund has a less-than-stellar performance that's the time you need to get out and hold the client's hand? Even if performance is dreadful over many years they will often stick with you if they feel loyal to their adviser. Who's been looking after Palfreyman, then? Some jerk with a First from LSE and zero bloody clue about human nature.

I get through the barrier when, suddenly, I remember. Oh, God. Bank. The escalator. *It's OK, Kate. If you move towards it in this group of people, all you have to do is step on. No need to look down. No need to see the terrifying Escher drawing of moving stairs with steely teeth beneath your feet.* Such a long way down. Heart pounding. Nearly my turn to step on. No, I can't. Sorry, I need to step back. Sorry. The man behind me is furious. 'Make up your bloody mind!'

He shoves me out of the way. I see a guy in uniform watching me. 'Excuse me,' I say, 'are there any stairs I can use?'

'One hundred and twenty-eight steps down, Miss,' he grins apologetically. 'Come along, young lady, I'll get you on.' Grabs my elbow and steers me back towards the escalator. 'Don't look down, just keep looking at me, yeah?' What a lovely face he has, a kind face. 'There you go.'

He releases my elbow, and I'm on! The escalator jolts my bones, but I steady myself. Heart rate slowing. No worries. Think of Conor: 'Yer doin' grite, Kite.' Think of the kids, keeping the job for the kids now I am a single parent. Strange that Palfreyman would withdraw now. More likely to pull out after three years of crap performance, not one, which suggests he's fallen out with the guy looking after him. Years ago, Rod Task would give me all the clients that were complaining or about to leave. I used to challenge myself to not just turn them around, but to make them even more profitable and to stay with us even longer. More often than not it was about listening, empathising and finding mutual interests. Once I had got their trust back I could then recommend someone new to take on the relationship. Almost always, I would recommend a woman.

1.01 pm: The whole team is gathered in Jay-B's office. There is an uneasy silence when I walk in and take a seat next to Alice. Our boss is parchment pale, his cocky Tintin quiff drooping over his forehead. No time for styling products this morning, eh? Things must be bad.

'So,' Jay-B begins, 'now that Kate's joined us, we need to work out what's happened with Palfreyman.'

'Gone to bloody buggery,' murmurs Gareth on my other side. On the pad of paper in front of us, Gareth is busy drawing a hangman scaffold.

'What we have to work out, guys, is whether this is a process failure or a human failure. Troy, you were handling the client. What's your explanation for this fucking mess?'

Oh, joy. Troy is in the firing line. It couldn't happen to a nicer guy. Alice nudges me and we turn to look at the office stud whose face is puce to the pointy tips of his ginger sideburns.

'It was all good,' says Troy, 'last time I spoke with him. No problems that I could see.'

'Did you go up to Yorkshire to explain to Palfreyman when the quarterly results came in?' That's me speaking now.

Troy squirms. 'Didn't see the need. I explained on the phone that things were good.'

'Good?' says Gareth incredulously. I see he has added a noose to his scaffold. 'In what way can a return of only two per cent seem good in these markets?'

431

'He, Palfreyman, well, he was a bit bummed we'd sold Rolls-Royce, said he wouldn't have done anything that stupid or unpatriotic . . .' Troy trails off.

'Did he say anything else?' I ask.

'Well, he was screaming at us by email about performance compared to three of our competitors,' Troy admits miserably.

Ah, we're getting to the nub of it now.

'And did you go back to him and say that our performance is as good as the others, but it only looks weaker because of the layer of fees taken by the controlling company? Plus, he needs to look at like-for-like time scales – even being off by a month or a quarter can make a big difference. Our performance is not great right now, but it's actually better than those competitors'. It's a question of making him trust that we know what we're doing. We've been in a bad place before – nineteen ninety-eight was much much worse, two thousand and two was dire – and the fund has always bounced back brilliantly. That's a matter of historical record.'

Christ, I feel like leaning forward and banging my head on the table. The stupidity of these, these *children*.

'Kate, how do you know what happened here in nineteen ninety-eight?' Jay-B is standing over by the window, hands clasped protectively over his crotch. In the dazzling sunlight, it looks like the distant Shard is coming directly out of the top of our baby boss's head.

'I—'

Think for a minute, Kate. Think about your birthday coming up. Think about what it will mean to lose this job and have to go back to Women Returners and start all over. Think about Richard leaving you. Think about how much we need the money. Think about the fact that you will be owning up to your true age if you tell him the truth now.

432

'Well, Jay-B, the fact is I was running this fund in nineteen ninety-eight and, I have to say, I was doing a much better job of it than you are, young man.'

Alice grabs my wrist as if we are on a giant rollercoaster cresting a hill and she's about to scream. Gareth clamps his mouth shut in an attempt to cut off a guffaw, and ends up making a squeaky fart sound like a whoopee cushion.

'You were running this fund?' Jay-B repeats robotically.

'I certainly was. In fact, I should probably say that I set it up, and it did surprisingly well in what were pretty hostile conditions back then. And, yes, everyone, that makes me scarily ancient; forty-nine, almost fifty, I should say.'

I think of going to pitch the fund to Jack in New York that first time (did I really have nits?). He loved it. No, he loved me. And I loved him. Don't we know within a few minutes of meeting someone if we have to adjust the frequency? I knew instantly with him, we had our own wavelength (do not adjust your set) and I remember that burst of pure happiness. Only very rarely do you get that sense, once or twice in a lifetime, if you're lucky. We were lucky, Jack and I. Several billion people on the planet and we found each other. How great is that?

It was a gift and I gave it back. And now, here I am, at half-time. At best, fifty is half-time, isn't it? And the need to feel alive, to be reminded one is still alive, not merely chauffeuring one's kids to their own lives, is suddenly intense.

'This is fucking incredible. I don't know what to say,' Jay-B says.

'Doesn't matter, we haven't got time for a chat anyway. We need to get someone up to Palfreyman asap. Alice, see if you can get us a helicopter from City airport. Quick as possible, please, and dig up as much as you can on Palfreyman: wives, kids, background, hobbies. Gareth, I need you to pull up everything we have on the client's assets, returns and our relative performance with competitors over the past twenty years.'

'Helicopter?' Troy's mouth is agape like an oriental carp.

'Yes, Sir Geoffrey needs to be made to feel important. We need to show him how very important he is to EM Royal. And if we land a helicopter on his lawn and crawl across it on bended knee before he can pull a very large amount of cash out of our fund then maybe he'll get the right idea. Oh, and Troy?'

'Yes.'

'Tuck your shirt in, boy.'

3.10 pm: Never been in a helicopter before. Not a major fantasy of mine, to be honest, and now, having done it, I think I was spot-on. True, there is a passing kick of liberation, as you take off – going not along and up, like an airline passenger, but just *up*, as in a lift – and ascend into the heavens, gazing down at London as it shrinks. After that, however, it's just noise. Clatter and wobble, with a side order of mortal fear. Some people may have Tomb Raider ideas of jumping out of their dream chopper into a jungle, on a classified mission, but, believe me, not for a second did I feel like Lara Croft. I felt like a mug in a dishwasher. Also, I wasn't entering a combat zone. I was landing in Yorkshire, to the surly annoyance of some sheep.

Still, we got to duck down as we disembarked, as custom requires. (Who has ever been tall enough to get beheaded by a helicopter? Apart from basketball players?) And it worked. Not for us – Alice and Gareth and me, the crack squad dispatched by EM Royal, or at least the only trio that was up for mission impossible – but for our target. Geoffrey Palfreyman. I could see him, standing at his French windows, legs planted firmly apart, hands on hips. The assessment began before we even hit the ground.

'So, you've joined the Rotory Club', he says, as we take our seats in his drawing room. I can just about make out the far wall, although binoculars would help. ''Ow was it?'

'Fabulous,' says Alice.

'Smooth as anything,' I say.

Gareth says nothing, because Gareth is not here. He is still in Sir Geoffrey's bathroom, throwing up helplessly into Sir Geoffrey's loo.

'Thanks for coomin',' says our host in a Yorkshire accent so dense you could cut it like fruit cake. 'Sorry about the wasted trip.'

'Well, that's what we're here—'

'Bloody waste of time. I've seen the figures, I've 'ad a look round, and frankly I could do better elsewhere. So I'm movin' it all, the whole fookin' lot, to one of your competitors. With whom you can't compete, so don't pretend otherwise. Should 'ave kept the chopper running, love.'

Hence the lack of hospitality: no tea, coffee, biscuits, water, or, in Gareth's case, a St Bernard with a small cask of brandy under its neck. Sir Geoffrey was not one for niceties, and small talk would only impede the process. Talk is meant to be big.

Alice pipes up. 'Actually, Mr Palf—'

'Well, Sir Geoffrey,' I say, shooting a ray-gun glance at Alice. If there is one man in England who will want to use his title on every occasion, at any time of day or night, it is the solid citizen who stands before us, athwart his hearthrug, toasting his arse at the five-foot fire. Him and a couple of actors, who want to feel as if they were personal friends of Falstaff. It *could* be that Lady Palfreyman murmurs 'Geoff' into his hairy ears, during the rutting season, but I wouldn't put money on it.

435

'I have laid out the figures for you here, Sir Geoffrey,' I say, pressing on regardless, and taking a sheaf of papers from my briefcase, 'and I hope you'll see that they do not necessarily tally with the figures that your team arrived at. I won't bother you now with every last detail, but the digest is all there on the opening page. Once the fees are taken into account, I think you'll see that our performance, contrary to what you are proposing—'

'Are you saying I'm wrong, love?' he asks. His jaw juts out towards me, further than seems anatomically possible. This is what Sigourney Weaver must have felt like at the climax of those *Alien* films.

'No, I'm saying that your advisers have not taken the full picture into account.' Hit it back over the net, as the teachers used to say when getting us ready for school debates. The harder the shot coming towards you, the more power in your return.

'My advisers, I'll have you know . . .'

'We at EM Royal *have* definitely been at fault, I admit,' I say, keeping the rally going, 'but the fault is not a statistical one.'

That stops him. Now he has to show curiosity.

'So what is it, then? 'Ow 'ave you fooked up, love?'

'By not making it quite clear, across the company, that you are the single most substantial private investor who has ever engaged our services.' Not true, not quite, but he won't know that. And he wouldn't want to know. 'And that that is a great responsibility. And a privilege.'

'Who for?'

'For us.'

'Why should I care about you?'

'A good question.'

'So answer it.'

'Because we are able to offer you returns on those invest-

436

ments, year on year, that will rival anything tendered by the competition. We are also the most reliable custodians of your wealth, not just for now, but for future generations. For your children, for your clients' children and their children. As these documents demonstrate. And also –' he opens his mouth to respond, but I don't let him '– that we are alive to your particular needs and concerns.'

'What bloody needs? Look around you, love. Do you see anything I need?'

I look around. Apart from a very large Gainsborough, the only object of interest is Gareth, loitering on the fringes of the action. His face is eau de Nil. Maybe he died in the bathroom and has come back to haunt us.

'Well, it struck me, going through your file in recent days,' (in fact, leafing through it in a cab on the way to City Airport), 'that in comparison to some of our other major clients your involvement in the philanthropic sector has not received adequate attention.'

'Calling me a mean bastard?'

'On the contrary. It's on record that you purchased a new MRI scanner for North Yorkshire Hospital trust, after your youngest daughter, Katherine . . .'

'Kate. Like you.' So he has bothered to learn my name. Good.

'After Kate was, as I understand, taken extremely ill in her teens. She made a full recovery, thank God, and you were admirably keen to show your gratitude, but you chose to keep your donation private.'

'That's my business.'

'Precisely. It's your business. And we want to make every effort to help you run that business. Your records indicate, further, that you made a really very generous donation to several musical societies in the county and beyond, and to Opera North—'

'That's Jeannie. Loves her singing. Always did.'

'Wonderful. But the names of yourself and Lady Palfreyman appeared only in small print at the back of the programme, for instance, for the recent production of *The Magic Flute*.' Alice found that out, in a five-minute phone call.

'And your point?'

'My point is that, were you in the US, say, your involvement in these kinds of charitable works would not be a sideline to your investment activity. They would be part and parcel of it. Your giving would not be some secret. It would be a way of signalling, not just to the financial community but far beyond, that you are a major player. Britain punches well above its weight in many respects, but it has consistently punched below its weight in philanthropic terms. We pride ourselves on a wealth of good deeds and voluntary work at the micro level, I'm sure you see that in every village round here, but we've never been good at the larger picture. The tradition is there, but it's been patchy; you have to look back to the great industrialists of the eighteenth and nineteenth centuries to see it in action. The wonderful libraries, museums, the concert halls. Many of the visionary philanthropists were from this part of the world, too, not from those softies down South. Now, they really *are* mean bastards.'

A small intake of breath from Alice. A chunky grin from Palfreyman.

'So, what you're saying is . . .'

'What I'm saying is, restart the damn thing. The tradition. Make a splash. Set a trend. Make other wealthy families think, "bloody hell, those Palfreymans are doing all right. Brand new concert hall (named for Kathleen Ferrier perhaps), just went up in Leeds with the Palfreyman name on the foundation stone. Why aren't I doing something like that?"'

'Kathleen Ferrier? Me mum's favourite,' says Sir Geoffrey.

'Mine too. I grew up on "Blow the Wind Southerly". Mum heard her perform in Leeds.'

'My mother too! Could have been at the same concert, couldn't they? Still live round this way, does she?'

'She does. Twenty miles thataway.' I gesture out across the lake. 'So putting something back into the cultural life of the area that made you. And all the while you can be sure, completely sure, that your investments, the funds that will power that kind of enterprise, are performing as strongly and as securely as possible in our hands.'

'Down among the softies.'

''Fraid so.'

'Why not come back this way if you're so keen on the place?'

I look at him. *Tell the truth for once.*

'I've got to get the kids through school and university. Pay for that lot first. Husband just left me, so need to get things back on track. Houses are definitely a lot better value up here. I'll take the train next time, mind. That helicopter was not my cup of tea, to tell you the truth.'

'Bit rough, was it? First time?'

'Yup.'

'So why take it?'

'Urgent case. Needed to see you very badly.'

'Don't let Jeannie hear you saying that.' He pauses, then walks over to a cabinet. 'Let's have a fookin' drink. Settle your stomach. Bit late for Mr Petal over there, he's a lost cause, but you girls could do with one.'

And so we stand, two minutes later, all four of us, each with a glass of whisky in our hand. Nothing else was on offer. Beside me, Gareth wavers like a reed in the wind.

'Cheers.'

'Cheers. A toast. Here's to EM Royal,' Sir Geoffrey says, 'and, while we're on the subject, Her Majesty the Queen.'

'The Queen,' I say loudly and fervently, and drain the contents of my glass. It's like being bitten awake. 'Um, forgive me, Sir Geoffrey, do I take that to mean . . .'

'It means that you've changed my fookin' mind, lass, something that last happened to me on a racecourse around twenty-five years ago. Pal of mine told me to back a different horse to the one I fancied.'

'And did his choice win?'

'As a matter of fact, it did. Maid of Honour, 11 to 4. I made two hundred quid that day.'

'I like to think we can offer you better returns than that.'

'I bloody well hope so. Anyway, I've said I'll stay now, and I'll stay. Man of my word. Cheers. But I want you on the case, mind, not that daft ginger apeth.'

'Of course,' Alice and I say together. Gareth slips from the room, presumably to call London and give them the good news. Or else to regurgitate his Scotch.

Sir Geoffrey is back in front of his fire now. He looks me in the eye, unmoving, his own eye as hard as flint, and says: 'I'm a soppy old bugger, you know. I can't say no to a Kate.'

Too fookin' right.

6.01 pm: On the flight back with an excited Alice – Gareth decided to stay over in York and get the train in the morning – when a text arrives from Emily. 'Mum, is it OK if Luke comes for dinner? Don't get your hopes up he's not like a real boyfriend just someone I'm seeing. Please don't be embarrassing, OK? Love you xxx'

Kate to Emily

How could I possibly embarrass you, darling? Love you too xx

I dozed off for a few minutes. Utterly sapped after giving everything I'd got to win Sir Geoffrey round. When I wake, I see Alice has used her pashmina as a pillow for my head.

'No wonder you're tired,' she says.

'Good tired, though,' I say. 'The best kind of tired.'

We're about to land when my phone rings. A number I don't recognise. 'Alice, can you call our driver, I'd better get this.'

'Hello, Mrs Reddy?'

'Speaking.'

'Hello, this is just a courtesy call to alert you to a high level of spending on your Viva card and five missed payments. We're sure you are aware of this, but we wanted to bring it to your attention.'

'Sorry?'

'We take five missed payments very seriously.'

'I haven't missed any payments.'

'The spending is on Play Again. Multiple repeat purchases.'

'What?'

'We have notified you by post.'

'I haven't opened my post.' Who has time to open their post?

'The outstanding amount is six hundred and ninety-eight pounds. We ask you to settle this immediately as there is no direct debit set up.'

If you rack your brain too much, does it actually seize up? I'm trying to think, but my head feels like an abandoned building. (*'Roy? Roy, help me here!'*)

'Mrs Reddy?'

'Yes, sorry, still here. Yes, obviously, this is unacceptable, shouldn't be happening, and I will make steps, sorry, take steps to ensure that it, it . . . it stops happening.'

Lucky I'm not giving a presentation to Sir Geoffrey. I sound like I'm translating from Martian.

'We wanted to alert you, in case there is any suspicion of fraud, in which case we would advise you to put an immediate stop to these payments.'

'Ben. Roy thinks it could be Ben.'

'Excuse me, Roy who?'

'Sorry, Roy is my . . . my assistant.'

Funny look from Alice.

'Sorry, I think I may have tracked down the problem. Let me deal with it right away. Goodbye.'

Benjamin! Bloody hell. No wonder my credit rating is so crap. Looks like Ben has used my card and registered it to his bloody Play Again game. Roy did try to warn me. Which is greater, shock of unpleasant revelation or sheer amazement at the maths? Probably the latter. The equation, by my calculation, goes as follows: If X spends Y hours playing *Zombie Road Rage* or whatever on his phone, then the number of undead being splattered across the tarmac, multiplied by pi, will equal the number of man hours, or woman hours, that X's mum – call her K – will need to work, in addition to her regular employment, in order to pay for X's fun.

The joke being that Ben would find all of this perfectly reasonable. I should be calling him, right now, to sort out this mess and shout him into some kind of shame, only 1) I haven't got the strength at the end of today of all days, 2) By comparison with the belfie this is quite a modest abuse by my family of technology, and 3) Ben never answers his phone. Because, of course, actually speaking to another human is the one thing that teenagers refuse to do, despite having a phone practically grafted onto their palms. Also, because he's much too busy playing *Zombie Road Rage* or *FIFA* or *Bubonic Babies* to talk.

Kate to Ben
'Ben, we need to have a serious talk about the bill for all those extras for your games that you didn't tell me about. I don't have direct debit on that card and you nearly got me arrested!'

Ben to Kate
Soz lol xx

Talk about Helicopter Parenting.

27

GUILTY SECRET

3 am: When did I decide? About what I had to do? It took me a while but it was no coincidence, I feel, that a female friend showed me the path. Emily was sleeping soundly in the bed beside me, in what I still thought of as Richard's place, although dear Joely was welcome to the Hog Symphony. Em had taken all of the duvet, naturally, when I found my eyes open at 3 am, the hour when mothers wake and wonder if their children are happy. For once, it wasn't Perry and the bloody menopause. Thanks to Dr Libido and daily hormones, the night sweats had ceased and the vast mental weariness had lifted. If I was not quite my old self, then at least the new one no longer feared the future. My phone lit up in the dark and there was an email, so I read it.

> **From: Sally Carter**
> **To: Kate Reddy**
> **Subject: Guilty Secret**
> **Dear Kate, I've been wanting to write to you for some**

time, since we had that talk before Christmas, in fact, when you tried to tell me about your feelings for that American guy. I know you were looking for some response, even support, from me, and I know I disappointed you, let you down badly, when I didn't say anything. I wanted to, very much so, but I found it impossible for reasons I couldn't bring myself to explain to you then. But I would like to try now as, clearly, after separating from Richard, you are wrestling with some big choices about your own future. You said that it's the kids that matter now, they are your priority, but it matters that their mother is happy too.

Do you remember I showed you those photos of me in Lebanon? You said I looked like an insanely happy Audrey Hepburn? Well, you were right. I WAS insanely happy. The man behind the camera was called Antonio Fernandez; he was my colleague but, more than that, he was my lover. The bank assigned him to me as a sort of colleague/chaperone when they sent me to the Middle East and we were both annoyed at first – me because I didn't need looking after by some haughty Spaniard and him because he thought trailing around after some Englishwoman was beneath him. Looking back, I suppose we were like those couples who get thrown together in a screwball comedy and come to love each other, despite everything. That was us.

We were both married. I had Mike and the two boys, who were three and one then. Antonio had a relatively new wife and no children. Neither of us was looking for anyone else and I was horrified to find myself becoming hugely drawn to this wonderful, magnetic man. Both on a professional and a personal level, the whole thing was impossible. I loved my family and I would never have done anything to hurt them. But Antonio knocked all that certainty away. Morality, loyalty, none of it meant anything compared to the overwhelming desire I felt for him.

Even thinking about Antonio now – his eyes, his body, his playfulness, the way he said my name – sends an electrical current through me.

We were together for almost five years, blissfully happy, enchanted times before we had to return permanently to our respective homes. In 1991, the bank gave Antonio a very senior job in Madrid and summoned me back to London. We talked about making a life together. He said he would give everything up and move to England permanently so I could take care of Will and Oscar and we would be a family. He made it sound so plausible but, whenever I was away from him, I would lose confidence. All I could think of was the mayhem that separating from Mike would unleash – my mother would never have forgiven me – and how I couldn't be that selfish. I was brought up a Catholic and divorce was shameful, an abomination.

I knew what it would cost me to give Antonio up – well, I thought I did – but I felt it was better for me to bear that sorrow alone than to inflict it on my innocent children and the good man I had married.

A couple of months after I saw Antonio for the last time, in Beirut, I noticed that my periods had stopped, but I put it down to the shock of losing him. I was a zombie, just moving through my tasks, feeding the boys, putting them to bed, but secretly terribly depressed. By the time I realised what had happened I was already five months pregnant. Too late to have an abortion, even if I'd wanted one, which I didn't.

I told myself that maybe the baby was Mike's, but really I think I knew. When she was born, she had this skullcap of dark hair and amazing coal-black eyes. There was no doubt whose she was. I joked a lot about having gypsies in the family – true, on my dad's side, way back – and it was good she was a girl so the fact she looked nothing like the two boys wasn't as stark.

I called her Antonia for him. It was the one thing I allowed myself. He would never know about her because I convinced myself that was unfair; it might damage Antonio's life with his wife, and any children they had, so it was better I didn't tell him. Mike would love her as his own, and so she would have a fantastic father, which he absolutely has been in every possible way.

Does Mike suspect? I think he both knows and doesn't know. Antonia is so different from the boys, brilliant at languages and she was instinctively drawn to Spanish, which was wonderful but also made me very sad. Perhaps it's possible to not know what it suits us not to know?

You're the first person I've told my secret to, although I wanted to tell my dad when he was dying, but I didn't dare.

I'm telling you now because I'd like to say that it's OK if you stay put with what you've got so you don't upset the apple cart and you ignore the call of the great love and the passion. You tell yourself those things are passing illusions and other things are more important. But that would be a lie. For me at any rate. I have had a good and blessed life, Kate, but I have missed Antonio every single day for twenty-four years and to see him in the face and being of my beautiful daughter is both my greatest pleasure and the purest agony.

I sometimes wonder if Antonia's panic attacks and depression are linked to my deception. Whether she has a sense of something missing. If I should tell her the truth or not. Another thing I torture myself with!

I saw that you noticed something on New Year's Eve, when you met her and said she was like Penélope Cruz. You are so acute, Kate, just one of the reasons I feel grateful to call you my friend.

It's much too late for me but, as your friend, I want to tell you that I chose wrong all those years ago. Which poet was it who wrote about choosing wrong? If I had my time over, I would make the leap and choose life and love, not duty and convention. Only you can decide what's right for you, of course, but I want you to know that you will have my full support if you do make a life with Jack. It is Jack, isn't it?

I do hope this isn't too shocking and it doesn't upset you. I've been crying as I type so it may be a bit confused! It felt important that I should tell you.

Sending you all my love.

Sally x

28

11TH MARCH

The Day of Invisibility

Time. It all comes down to time in the end. The young they want to get older, the old they want to get younger. Somewhere in the middle, at the halfway mark, here I am, Janus-like, facing forwards while looking back. Janus, the god of gateways and goodbyes, transitions and new beginnings.

Funny thing is I never worried about getting older. Not really. Youth had not been so kind to me that I minded the loss of it. I thought women who lied about their age were shallow and deluded, but then I went and bloody well joined them, didn't I? It had to be done if I wanted a job. No alternative. Women my age are past it, don't you know that? It's a sad fact but women, women like me, that is, we're starting to get the diseases of men; the coronaries, the strokes, the stomach cancer. But men aren't getting the diseases of women. We turned ourselves into men to succeed in a world designed by them for them, but they never learned to be us, and maybe they never will.

This is strength, not weakness. I know that now. You know a lot when you've lived for as long as I have.

Was there a round of applause when I got back to the office, having saved the day with Geoffrey Palfreyman? There was. And so there bloody well should have been, frankly. I didn't succeed despite being almost fifty; I succeeded because I had five decades of living under my belt, of bitter experience, of hard graft, of riding the rapids of family life, in sickness and in health. You can't fake that.

By one extra stroke of good fortune, the chairman happened to be in that day and was told of my remarkable feats up North. 'Kate can stay until she's a hundred as far as I'm concerned, if she goes on pulling off deals like that. Look at me,' Harvey hrumped, 'I own this bloody outfit and I get up to pee four times a night.'

What happened next? Oh, yes, my birthday. I almost forgot. Sally and I had agreed that we would walk the dogs on the day itself. Spend it quietly. No fuss. I wanted it to pass as painlessly as possible. Just our usual, then dinner later with the kids. Emily had drawn up a menu of all my favourite dishes and shopped for the ingredients. Ben said he would buy After Eight mints, part of the heavy-duty repayment plan for his gaming debts. After my helicopter ride, I sat him down and explained that the phone company didn't tell me if he didn't stay within his phone contract monthly amount. The bastards don't care if reckless teenagers spend crazy amounts of money they don't have. Ben admitted he'd become so obsessed with the game that he had no idea how much the stuff was costing. I was angry with him, but mainly I was cross with myself for not teaching my kids about financial management. Oh, and don't get me started on the Silicon Valley geniuses who deliberately designed software so children get addicted. I hope I live long enough to see them in court on charges of enslaving the minds of an entire generation.

11.35 am: The view from the top of our hill is particularly glorious today. Spring is quickening – I love that the first tremor you get of a baby in the womb is called quickening – and it feels as if all the plants and creatures know their time has come again. The hawthorn is in blossom and, everywhere you look, the hedgerows are Nature's bridal bouquets. 'No, they're blackthorn,' Sally says, bending to peel a sticky bud off Coco's nose. 'Blackthorn's always first, then hawthorn comes after.'

'What would I do without you, David Attenborough?'

'I do have my uses, you know.' She takes my arm as, for the first time, we select the wide, mown path down the centre of the hill. I have only known her for six months or so, but already Sal has become one of those invaluable people who pick up the baton when our mother's nurturing powers are waning, and create a new kind of family. I thank Sally for her email. Tell her I have never received a better one in my life, but that I can't follow my heart as she suggested. 'With everything that's happened, Sal, I just can't. And Jack's not even around any more.'

'We'll see,' she says. 'Oh, stand still, Kate, stand very still. Quiet. Very quiet.'

About twenty feet away from us, a small bird has emerged from the short, clumped grass, and is rising vertically into the sky. It can't be, but it looks like the bird is propelled upwards by the force of its own song, which has a sweetness and intensity like nothing I've ever heard before. If the loveliest perfume in the world could sing it would make that sound.

'Do you know what that is, Kate?' Sally says softly.

Funnily enough, I think I might. 'It's not a lark ascending, is it?'

We watch, enraptured, as the bird whirls and twirls, soaring on its own private thermal in an ecstasy of liquid notes.

'It's a sign,' Sally says. 'I've only seen a skylark once before, on the day my dad died. He's singing for you, Kate.'

'It's not a sign,' I say, and my heart sort of pleats.

'*It's not a goddam sign. I'm telling you,*' Roy throws in my face.

'*Hey, who asked you to stick your oar in, silly old archivist? Be quiet, please.*'

'*The forces of the Universe are not arranged against us. It's a dumb piece of plastic, not an Old Testament God trying to tell us not to make love.*'

'*Yes, Roy, I do remember what Jack said, thank you.*'

Lenny and Coco race towards the gate to the car park, but Sally suddenly says she feels a bit wobbly and needs something to eat, so we turn right and drop in at the café. I push open the door and see Emily first. (Emily!) Then Debra. (Deb!) Then Julie. (Julie!) Then Ben, who is filming me on his phone, obviously. Then – oh, I can't believe it – Candy Stratton, with a smile wider than the Brooklyn Bridge.

I find myself mobbed like a pop star. Arms around me, kisses on my face. 'Happy birthday, Mum.'

'Thank you, darling, oh, look who's here. Look who's here! Oh my God, what a wonderful surprise. Everyone's taken time off to be with me!'

Candy stands back a little, awaiting her turn until, finally, we stand there, face to beaming face. 'What the hell are you doing here, Stratton?' I say.

'I wouldn't miss you getting older than me for the world, Reddy. Hey, what is that foxy garment you're wearing?'

'It's called a fleece.'

'Honey, you know I love you, but you're not gonna get laid wearing a sheep.'

The owners have made a cake and there is pink champagne, all arranged by Sally. I blow out the candles – five of them, very tactful, thank you very much – and everyone sings 'Happy Birthday'. Then Emily and Ben give a joint speech in which they point out that, although their mother is from the past, and always will be, she is actually pretty cool.

'Mum is a great mum,' Ben says, his voice cracking, and I feel he is thinking, at that moment, of Richard too. We had been a unit to them for so long – Mum 'n' Dad – and learning to love us separately would be hard. We will get there, but it will take time.

Back at the house, while the kids are showing Candy and Julie around, Sally hands me a large brown envelope.

'What's this? Not another surprise.'

'If you open the card,' she says, 'I believe it will explain.'

It has a painting on the front. A mountain in France, Mont Sainte-Victoire, painted in these vivid blues and purples and soft greens. Cézanne, although it makes me think of the Matisse I saw at Vladimir Velikovsky's palace. Same sumptuous colours. The card's inscription is in a familiar hand.

WHEN YOU ARE OLD AND GREY AND FULL OF SLEEP,
AND NODDING BY THE FIRE, TAKE DOWN THIS BOOK,
AND SLOWLY READ, AND DREAM OF THE SOFT LOOK
YOUR EYES HAD ONCE, AND OF THEIR SHADOWS DEEP;

HOW MANY LOVED YOUR MOMENTS OF GLAD GRACE,
AND LOVED YOUR BEAUTY WITH LOVE FALSE OR TRUE,
BUT ONE MAN LOVED THE PILGRIM SOUL IN YOU,
AND LOVED THE SORROWS OF YOUR CHANGING FACE.

Underneath, Jack has written, 'While we're waiting for you to get old and grey, here's a plane ticket. Totally transferable, front of the bus. Sally gave me your passport details. Lovely woman, by the way. Enjoy the rest of the day with the kids. See you in Provence. Come any time. I'll be waiting. Hurry. J XXO'

'I can't go to him. It's impossible. The kids and the dog.'

'That can be taken care of,' Sally says briskly. 'I met your Jack. He seems like a very fine person. Pity he's so poor.'

'Now is not a good time.'

'If not now, when? Right, where will I find the cutlery?'

After dinner, while Emily, Ben and Candy are watching *Game of Thrones*, Julie and I Skype our mother, who seems in high spirits. 'Can't believe it's half a century since I had you, love.'

'Don't remind me, Mum.'

'You'll always be my baby.'

Then, Julie and I take our drinks out into the garden, wrapped up in coats, so Jules can smoke.

'So happy you're here,' I say.

''Course I'm bloody here. Where do the years go, Kath? Not that long since we were leaving our teeth under the pillow for the tooth fairy. Now it's only a few years till we put our teeth in a glass on the bedside table.'

'That's a cheerful thought. By the way, how's Steven doing?'

She grins. 'Oh, he's brilliant, no trouble at all since your American friend got him sorted.'

'What American friend?'

'Jack. He said to our Steven that the City of London is full of gamblers, you just have to learn how to play the odds. And he was the man to teach him. He could open a few doors if Steven was willing to smarten up his act. Well, Steven's that good at figures just like his Auntie Kath, so Jack got him a position as a junior trader. Since Jack came we haven't had any more bastard loan sharks at the door, any road.'

I'm speechless.

'I'll get a rocket for telling you. He said not to mention it. Sworn to secrecy we were. He's bloody lovely, isn't he? Mum thought he was great.'

'Mum met Jack?'

'Yes. He said he'd pay back what Steven owes in the form of a loan, but Steven's got to give Jack something every month from his wages. Thank God he's sorted it.'

'How did he find you?'

'Rang round all the Reddys in town. Said he'd always wanted to visit Yorkshire. Interested to see "the place that made her", that's what he said. "The place that made her." Lovely way of speaking, doesn't he? Is he your boyfriend, then?'

'God, no.'

'Well, I'd get in there quick if I was you, love,' says Julie with a filthy cackle. 'You're fifty now, you know. Not many drop-dead-gorgeous rich guys going to be forming a queue, are they?'

'Thanks, sis. I'll bear that in mind. More wine?'

After they've all gone up to bed, I let Lenny out in the garden for a final wee. The full moon casts a lake of light on the garden and the dog's inky shadow bounds across it. I breathe deeply. So, that was my fiftieth, I think. Nothing to be feared, plenty to be happy about, not the unbridgeable Rubicon that Calamity Girl was so scared of. I am still amazed by what Julie told me. So kind of Jack to go all that way and help Steven and not take any credit for it either. Julie said he'd sworn them to secrecy. Still, my heart did whisper that he'd done it for me.

A few weeks after my birthday, when both kids had sleepovers with friends and Lenny was in doggy holiday heaven with Coco and Sally, I took my plane ticket out of its brown envelope and booked the flight to Marseille. I texted to say I was coming for the weekend.

Jack to Kate
What kept you?

On the flight, I have the luxury of time to think. For once, it's just me and my thoughts and Roy, of course, to help me review the twists and turns my life has taken in the months since the belfie.

My marriage has crumbled but, miraculously, my spirit has not. I think back to my surprise party at the café, nearly all my lovelies gathered together in one place, the joy of seeing Candy IRL instead of online. Food for my soul. Emily and Ben at my birthday dinner (lasagne, chips, salad, ice cream, After Eights) so grown up, so pleased that they were cooking for *me* for a change. Looking at Emily, enchanting in a red-silk dress (*my* dress, Madam!) I thought: 'I will probably take years to recover from what she did to herself. We mothers are forever entangled with the people we created.' I feel Emily's pain in the body she sprang from, always will till the day that body is no more, but kids are more resilient than us. Already Em is putting it behind her, starting to look at universities, thinking of her future. Luke is helping. After he came on the scene, the selfies stopped almost overnight. Nothing like seeing your image reflected in the eyes of a besotted boy to remind you that you're desirable and worthy of love. When someone loves you, really loves you, the opinion of the world doesn't mean a damn.

Emily and Ben are seeing Richard regularly now and gradually overcoming their instinctive aversion to Joely. After all, she is carrying their baby brother and sister. I was a good wife to Rich, I hope, but I was sleepwalking through life, lulled into

456

that state of spousal somnambulance, not unusual among married couples. You just keep on doing what it is that you do, trying to take up as little space as possible in your own life to make room for everyone else.

Not unhappy is not the same thing as happy. (*'Thank you for the reminder, Roy. Was it Sally who said that?'*)

Candy actually. Oh, of course it was. Typical Cand, always insisting, in that American way, on giving yourself permission to be happy or something. For crying out loud, I'm British. I apologise if someone bumps into me. I really thought that, at my time of life, Not Unhappy would do.

I pushed Jack away because I thought he was a threat to my life when, all along, he was my best shot at a happy life. I think of him that afternoon at the hotel, every single thing I have ever wanted in a man plus cucumber sandwiches without the crusts. And work. Going really well at last. Meeting with the chairman the other day, he said that Troy was sacked for bloody screwing things up with Palfreyman, Jay-B was being moved across, and might I consider assuming temporary leadership of the fund while they assessed the situation? I said I would be absolutely delighted to take on my old job, but not on a temporary basis. (That is the kind of thing a desperate woman looking down the barrel of irrelevance would agree to, but not this she-phoenix, not this revenant revived.) Chairman said he'd get back to me. You know, I thought there was no way back to that person I used to be. I thought it was all over for me.

'Not for you, Kate. It's not over for you.'

'Oh, Roy, that was Sally, wasn't it?'

The first time we spoke. Imagine if I hadn't gone to Women Returners and met Sal. So indispensible to me now. And Sally's letter about Antonio, the great love she forfeited: one of the reasons, perhaps the main one, I'm on this plane today. Maybe the Jack thing isn't so impossible after all? Him in the US mostly, me getting the kids through the last bit of school and university; meeting up, getting the kids used to the idea of him gradually. As the plane begins its descent, the thought still isn't quite formed. Something like, if I have to save everyone else, I need to start by saving myself first. How hard can it be?

I was expecting Jack to meet me at the airport, but instead there's a driver holding up a placard with my name on it. We drive north towards Aix then veer east where the land rears up from the bushy green earth. The massive limestone ridge – I recognise the mountain from my birthday card – is our constant companion. It's so warm here compared to home – like an English summer. *'Yes, what is it, Roy?'*

'A place in Provence with its own micro-climate where you can sit outside in just a T-shirt in winter. Jack told you about it the first night you had dinner.' So he did.

We pull up outside some old, peeling iron gates beyond which is a house with a tumbledown tiled roof. A *mas*, is that what you call it? Still no sign of Jack. A walled garden. My God, look at that. How old is this place? And who does it belong to? Ivy on weathered stone. Dusty skeletons of lavender past. An actual peach tree. (For the first thirteen years of my life, I didn't know peaches grew on trees. They grew in tins.) My only slight concern is that, much against my will, an image flickers into my mind: of watching *Beauty and the Beast*, the Disney version, with three-year-old Emily, no more than, oh, fourteen times on successive days when she had chickenpox. Primed by this, I have a genuine fear that I may be welcomed not by a dashing American gent with a large portfolio and kind eyes, but by something angry with a pelt and hooves, and tusks

458

sticking up from his lips. Oh well, you can't have everything. Cracks in the windows, crumbling edges of bricks: this place needs work. Someone should buy it and love it back to life. Not exactly what I had in mind for a romantic weekend.

A doorway, open, into the cool of a kitchen. I take my shoes off and feel the worn, uneven floor under my feet. On the table is an envelope propped up against a jam jar, containing stalks of lavender. Inhale. Addressed to Kate Reddy. Inside, a card, which says: 'Belated Happy Fiftieth, Period Gem in Need of Restoration'. Oh, very bloody funny.

'Hello.'

I run at him, absolutely confident as I kiss the face off him that, this time, I know what I want. Never wanted anything or anyone more. Never will.

I can tell he's surprised by this new certainty in me, but he doesn't put up any resistance. 'Hey, Happy Birthday for six weeks, two days ago.'

'Thanks.' Long pause, long gaze around me. 'Nice place, bit of a wreck, though.'

'Yes, I thought so.'

'I was expecting a talking teapot.'

'Be my guest.'

'So you *do* watch children's cartoons. I knew it.'

'My guilty secret.'

'I can handle it. You should see mine.'

'Can't wait.'

'Julie told me. What you did for Steven.'

'I didn't do it for Steven. Purely selfish. One big worry off your back, more time for you to give to me.'

'If you say so, but it was a wonderful thing to do. I'm really grateful. Can't thank you enough.' I go over to the sink under the window, well, the place the window would be if there was glass in the panes. Jack follows, wraps his arms around me from behind, and I lean back, enjoying the feeling of being held.

'That mountain, it's the one on my birthday card.'

'*Vraiment.*'

I turn the tap, which judders and jolts. Eventually, water of some description comes out coughing, rusty. I run my hands and wrists under the flow. *Take it easy, Kate.* Heart is pounding.

'Don't drink it,' Jack says, 'there's bottled in the fridge. I also have wine. Quite a bit of it: enough for a couple of hundred years.'

'Sounds good. How long will we be here, or are we going to stay somewhere with a ceiling? You do realise I packed for the Four Seasons – heels, silk dress. Wish you'd told me we were camping, I'd have brought my fleece.'

'*Mais non, Madame*, we have zee four seasons right 'ere. There's spring outside, *voila!*, summer in zee aircon-less conservatory, autumn leaves clogging up every single drain and it's winter all year in zee freezing bedrooms.'

'Genius. Who owns this place, anyway?'

'Oh, it kind of belongs to this couple I know.'

'They must be mad.'

'Yeah, they kind of are. She's nuts about doing up old houses. Or maybe she's just nuts all over. Yeah, maybe that's it. Completely crazy. I hear she goes and rides horses with the widows of dead rockers. And she lies about her age and cheats at mince pies.'

I shake the water from my hand and turn round.

'Jack, no.'

'No what?'

'Please tell me you haven't done what I think you've done.'

'I haven't done anything. Yet. I was going to get you a scarf,

460

but then I saw this over Christmas, when I was driving by, and I thought that we, you and I, *us*, we could maybe take it on. Work on it together. Beautiful older broad with terrific bones, just needs some care and attention to bring her back to life. A project. Something for us to invest in. I'm not a great fixer-upper, but I can take instructions from a woman who is.'

'You cannot be serious. When am I going to find the time to live in a bloody French ruin and do it up?'

'Hey, if you don't like the idea I can call the agent, say we're not interested and get the scarf instead.'

I can feel my eyes roaming around, seeing what could be done here. If you opened up the back of the house and put in big windows, the view of the mountain would be spectacular. Piotr could come and help. Paint the shutters that perfect blue-grey that I love. Suddenly, Roy is back from the stacks, bringing something he wants me to remember. *'Not now, Roy. Can't you see I'm busy?'* But he hands me the memory anyway – a piece of piercing wisdom from my dear friend Sally: 'If I had my time over, I would make the leap and choose life and love, not duty and convention. Only you can decide what's right for you, of course, but I want you to know that you will have my full support if you do make a life with Jack.'

'Jack?'

'Yes, Ma'am?'

'You're not paying for this, you know. It's going to be fifty-fifty, right down the middle. But only if I get my promotion. Only if they give me my fund back.'

'That's a yes.'

'No, it's not a yes. It's just not a no.'

'Not a no is British for yes. I can work with that. Kate darling, for your birthday I wanted there to be a kind of joint present, for the two of us.'

'Very thoughtful, Mr Abelhammer. Let me guess, a tandem? A see-saw? A tennis court? A game of snap?'

'Well, snap comes into it. Quite a lot of snap. Matching cards, over and over again.'

'So, what is it, this surprise gift for both of us? Jack?'

He takes my damp hands in his, leans close, then closer, then closer still, and says to me:

'Time.'

29

AFTER ALL

Sixteen months later.

Barbara died towards the end of summer. We were celebrating Emily's exam results in a pizza place when Donald rang to tell me that the children's grandmother was gone. The last time I'd visited them up in Yorkshire he got upset because Barbara was taking part in a musical afternoon at the care home.

'It's nice they do activities here,' I soothed.

'But Barbara wouldn't want to play a tambourine,' Donald said, gesturing helplessly at his wife as she raised and lowered her instrument without giving any sign she knew what she was doing or taking any pleasure in it. 'You know she would have hated it, Kate, love.'

He was right. Barbara would have absolutely loathed that stupid tambourine. She would have considered it to be beneath her dignity – that lofty, lifelong elegance of which Alzheimer's had so cruelly robbed her.

I was desperately sad as I watched Emily and Ben absorb

the news – their first everlasting loss – but I was also glad my mother-in-law had gone to a place beyond humiliation, perfectly safe now from people who were simply not up to it.

This morning, before the funeral, the kids climbed over the back fence of the old family house to cut some of Barbara's flowers. There's a 'Sold' sign out front, but the new owners haven't moved in yet. What could be better, really, to lay beside the grave, as she is laid to rest, than the Bishop of Llandaff: vivid scarlet heads on black stems, picked by her beloved Emily and Ben?

'*No smoking by the Bishop of Llandaff.*' Roy reminded me and, despite everything, I smiled. Barbara had high standards, even for dahlias.

Poor Em is in tears, gripping my hand, as the last words of the burial service are intoned. On my other side is Ben, so much taller now, comically so, as if every day were spring and he was sprouting; at this moment, though, he bears the lost and bewildered air of a much smaller boy.

Relieved it's still the holidays and we don't have to rush back. I am on compassionate leave from EM Royal, and Alice has strict instructions that no calls or texts should be sent to me today. I fully expect them to start again at midnight.

Over the other side of the grave are Richard and Joely, with Alder and Ash. (I know. I tried. 'It's our favourite tree, Kate. It has such resonance in mythology, too.' 'Richard, it's what falls off the end of a cigarette. Or the leftover bits of a bonfire.' No use.) Richard, to my immense satisfaction, appears not to have brushed his hair for six months and his eyes have almost disappeared into dark troughs. He has a small but definite pot belly. In short, he is the father of twins. Put that in your pipe and smoke it. On the other hand, after a series of tortured telephone conversations, and setting aside all sore feelings, he asked if I would please accompany the kids to his mother's funeral. 'Look, I know how unbelievably crap I was to you,' he said. 'Don't think I don't know and I'm really sorry. You don't know how sorry I am. Since Mum died, I realise that you're still my family, Kate, and Dad, he really loves you. Can't stop saying what a bloody fool I was to run off with that little hussy.'

We both laughed and I offered my ex-husband the olive branch I could sense he craved. 'Donald will come round to Joely, you'll see, Rich. He's potty about the twins. They're so lovely.'

Credit where credit is due, Joely defied the low expectations we all had of her. Putting her New Age gifts to good use, she became a blessed support to Barbara, giving the bewildered old lady a herbal brew to support memory, and aromatherapy massages, one of the few things she seemed to find calming in the last few months of her life. (Who knows, maybe the scent in the oils could bypass the desiccated brain cells and travel to a place where some essential part of Barbara lived on? I hope so.) Joely is still breastfeeding the twins, who sleep in the bed with her, and she's announced her intention to continue until they start school. I reckon Richard has four years until he has sex again.

Next to Richard's fledgling second family stands a bevy of Barbara's friends. All are immaculate in their mourning garb and, being of the last great Sunday School generation, word-perfect in the liturgy. All dab their eyes with lace handkerchiefs politely stored up their sleeves. All were told not to bring anything for the post-funeral tea, which is being held at Cheryl and Peter's, and for which Cheryl has created a spreadsheet. All, I am quite certain, will have disobeyed the order. And all will follow my mother-in-law on her final journey, over the next ten years, fifteen at most. What on earth will this land be like when these good, amazingly strong women of the wartime generation are all gone? Well, my lot will have to take our seats in the front row, that's all, and our daughters will be there right behind us, and their girls behind them before we know it. Granddaughters and – dizzying thought – great-granddaughters. The Sandwich Women go on, holding it together for generations to come. That's what really matters, isn't it? Love never dies; it just takes different human forms.

Earth to earth. Handfuls are lightly tossed into the grave. Emily can't bear it and buries her face in my shoulder. One last blessing and then, as a cloud passes mournfully overhead, we turn and walk back along the gravel path, among much older graves, towards the church. My heart is too crammed for any words, and my legs feel a little unsteady on the bumpy ground; knowing me as he does, however, and preserving his own wise silence, Jack offers me his arm, and then his whole self to lean on, before turning to offer Emily his other hand.

I think an ending is out of the question. The loose ends in a story get tied up only for another strand to unwind. After Barbara left us, I felt sure that Donald would follow soon after. Instead, having finally sold the house, he moved into a care home himself. A small, surprisingly magical place, it allowed residents to garden and keep pets. Donald formed a bond with a nervous refuge Collie called Alf who filled the vacancy left by Jem and grew unafraid in the old man's hands. Every week, pupils from a nearby primary school came in to do reading and art with the residents. Donald told the children stories about being in the Royal Air Force during the war while they made a squadron of Airfix Lancaster bombers from kits he bought them; the ancient navigator issuing the instructions while nimble young hands stuck pieces together with glue. The planes would eventually go on display in the town library, with Donald's memories of youthful peril alongside. He was a big hit on the local TV news when he ignored a patronizing old-git question and seized the chance to criticise cutbacks in the armed forces. 'The price of peace is eternal vigilance, and let's not forget it,' he said. Donald fully intends to live to see his hundredth birthday, when he promises that he will come down to London and take me to the Savoy Grill for roast beef and – what else? – Yorkshire pudding.

Donald wasn't alone in getting a new lease of life. With her hip replacement, my mum was not only back on her feet, she started dancing again. Against my specific instructions, she purchased a new pair of black patent heels.

'You'll never change her now,' Julie laughed. 'I think Mum might have a boyfriend and all. How come she gets one not me?' My sister was so much happier after Steven started work as a junior trader in the City and moved in with me and the kids until he had money for his own place. That immensely stressful job can shred the nerves of a brilliant university graduate, but not my nephew, who shrugged and said the cut-throat environment was just like school. 'It's only placing bets on whether a product is going up or down, Auntie Kath.'

'If you don't mind, Steven, in the City we like to call that "taking a position", not "betting".'

'Whatever. Fifty K a year plus bonus. Bloody brilliant, eh?'

Yup, bloody brilliant. When Steven took Julie to Florida for her birthday at Easter, Emily volunteered to go up and stay in her aunt's house. 'I can do my revision in peace and keep an eye on Grandma, help her with the shopping, can't I?' This was a first. My child relieving me of a worry. I could hardly believe Emily was old enough to do such a thing, but she was.

As for her brother, my shambolic boy recently came home with a red-haired goddess who answers to the name of Isabella. Ben – a girlfriend? How the hell did that happen? When Isabella sits at our kitchen table, with her charming conversation and her lovely manners, I think: does she actually know I still cut her boyfriend's toenails? You should see the way Ben looks at her. Exactly the way he looked at me when he heaved himself up in his cot after a nap. (The mother of a one-year-old boy is a movie star in a world without critics.) I'm not jealous, at least I hope I'm not, but this other female in my boy's life brings with her a premonition of loss. Not ready to lose him just yet.

Work went on getting better. After I outed myself as a senior citizen, in financial-service years at any rate, all the energy I'd spent lying about my age could be channelled more productively. Confirmed in a permanent senior position, I had a lot to prove. I swore to my team – *my team!* – that we would grow the fund back to where it was when I'd left my job all those years ago. I managed to talk Sir Geoffrey Palfreyman into starting a community bank in our mutual home county which made loans to families in difficulties at very low interest rates. Sir Geoffrey was delighted with his new role as celebrated philanthropist, but not nearly as a pleased as I was to put the bastard payday loan sharks who had almost destroyed Steven out of business.

My dear Alice stayed by my side, growing in confidence and finally dumping the chronically uncommitted Max shortly before her birthday.

'Catch-32,' she said one morning.

'What?'

'Kate, you said it's the age by which you really should have signed up the prospective father of your children. So, I've given myself a year to find him. Hope it's enough.'

Soon after, Belshazzar Baring came in for work experience and promptly fell head over heels for Alice, offering her a life of stupendous ease as the wife of a rock-sprog. Luckily, Alice was too smart to fall for that and, as I write, her hoping goes on.

As for my darling Jack, after the children had been through so much change, I wanted to introduce the concept of Mummy's boyfriend very slowly. Jack flew back and forth to the States for a while and we met up on the occasional weekend at the house in Provence where we ate bread and pâté on old tin plates in the kitchen and made famished love in a four-poster bed festooned with cobwebs. There I was fretting about how to introduce him to the kids when, one Saturday, on the way to the supermarket, Emily casually said, 'Your American guy sounds awesome.'

I practically did an emergency stop, before pulling into a lay-by. 'How do you know about him?' I said, thus giving the game away.

'Steven. He told me and Ben like how Jack helped him get out of big trouble and found a job for him. Steven said he's so cool.'

'Well, yes, I suppose he is . . .' How could I begin to explain to this person I loved what the other person I loved meant to me? I was nervous so I settled for plain facts. 'Sweetheart, I got to know Jack through work when I sent him this embarrassing cheeky email that was meant for Candy.'

'Could have been worse, Mum,' said Emily, placing her hand on mine. 'Could have sent him a photo of your bum by mistake.' And we laughed, my daughter and I. Then I started the car and drove on.

ACKNOWLEDGEMENTS

I'm never sure about sequels. In *I Don't Know How She Does It*, I thought I'd said everything I wanted to say about combining work and motherhood. Then I got older. My family moved into a new phase of life, as did my body, and I found myself wondering, 'How on earth is Kate coping with this?' I thought she might help me laugh at all the craziness of mid-life, so I wrote it down.

It wouldn't have happened without Sharon Dizenhuz, hilarious sage of Scarsdale and wise-cracking Candy to my doubting Kate. Nor without the most incredible moral support from Louise Swarbrick. Thanks also to my top team of financial advisors, Miranda Richards, Penny Lovell and Sasha Speed, who made sure the work stuff was spot on, especially the black stallion.

I am incredibly blessed in my agent, Caroline Michel, who has enough optimism for both of us, even if she will keep insisting that I write novels. Thank you to my brilliant editor, Hope Dellon, of St Martin's Press, who presided with fierce, kindly vigilance. I can't thank her enough, nor Kate Elton and Charlotte Cray at HarperCollins UK who made such invaluable suggestions. And Sara Kinsella, most eagle-eyed copy-editor and my publicist extraordinarie, Ann Bissell.

Not many novels feature the menopause, although half the human race will go through it. With the help of Dr Louise Newson, I tried to tell the bloody truth. An expert in hormone replacement therapy, Dr Newson believes that no woman should have to suffer Kate's debilitating symptoms. I agree. Let's break that taboo for good.

My gratitude to my first readers, Ysenda Maxtone Graham, Sally Richardson, Amanda Craig, Awen Lobbett, Kathryn Lloyd, Hilary Rosen, Sophie Hannah, Amanda de Lisle, Gillian Stern, Karen Merrit, Anne Garvey, Claire Vane, Angela Young and Janelle Andrew. Their encouragement and good advice kept me on track. Thank you to Emma Robarts for suggesting Women Returners and for years of wise counsel and lovely dog-walks (Biggles RIP). Special thanks to Michael Maxtone-Smith, the first male guinea pig to be exposed to this book and claim to love it. He should be fine again in a couple of years.

Early episodes of 'Sandwich Woman' were published in the *Daily Telegraph* where Fiona Hardcastle was the best midwife a girl could wish for. Thank you to my marvellous editors, Jane Bruton, Victoria Harper and Paul Clements. Your support means the world to me.

A book which is so much about mothers and daughters owes a great deal to Ruchi Sinnatamby and Jane McCann, who lost their mums while it was being written. Remembering always Selvi Sinnatamby and Janet Marsh, both wonderful mothers and grandmothers. Their lovely granddaughters, Charlotte Petter and Chloe McCann, are the next layer of the Sandwich. And, in that way, the love will never die.

Most of all, I thank my family. Evie Rose Lane and Tom Lane are remarkably patient with their mother and her stupid questions about which button you press and, 'What is a dick pic?' Yes, my loves, I am 'from the Past', but the future is yours. I'm so lucky to have you.

Without Anthony Lane, there would be no book and no me either. I thank him for his peerless literary criticism, for the meals on a tray and the intravenous jelly babies as I staggered towards the finishing line. If you go to bed every night with a man reading P.G. Wodehouse, eventually those blissful comic rhythms will get into your head. For some reason, he often likes to read aloud the bit about the lady novelist. 'The Adams woman told us for an hour how she came to write her beastly book, when a simple apology was all that was required.'

Sorry, darling.

Allison Pearson
June 2017